A LAND WITHOUT HEROES

by

JOHN MARTIN

ANGLIAN
PUBLISHING

First published in the United Kingdom
in hardback form by
Anglian Publishing,
Sackville Place, 44–48 Magdalen Street,
Norwich, NR3 1JU

First Edition: October, 2002

A CIP catalogue record for this book is available from the British Library.

ISBN: 0-9543172-0-3

Printed and bound in the United Kingdom by Short Run Press, Exeter, Devon.

DEDICATION

This book is dedicated to Jan and Ena Czogala and their families, without whom it could not have been written, and to all the victims of Hitler's war regardless of their nationality, race or religion.

Acknowledgements

I am indebted to numerous people and institutions in the preparation of this novel.

Principally, I am grateful to Jan and Ena Czogala and their families to whom this book is dedicated. Many hours of unselfish conversation in Britain and Poland were indispensable to the research effort required by the subject.

I am grateful also to the Norfolk Library Service in assisting me. It remains true that one can obtain the use of any book stored in a British library in a short period of time and at a trivial cost. The Wiener Library in London was helpful to me in identifying the fate of the Jewish citizens of P.

A number of my friends and business colleagues encouraged me to persist at times when I needed it and made helpful suggestions.

Lastly, my wife Larisa was steadfastly patient and helpful throughout the writing of the book. I shall be eternally grateful to her for putting up with me, for her assistance in word processing and her numerous helpful hints and suggestions.

John Martin
Norwich   October 2002.

A PARADISE OF BLOOD
AND SOIL

"Time is fulfilled, and the Greater German Reich is about to be realised. The bloodstreams, the protuberances of dissipating national powers come together into a new, greater ethnic body. There is no more outside and inside. All German consciousness and *Germanic existence in this world is one unified organism given life by one heart, given spirit by one son, disciplined by one power, led by one will – educated and led by its maker Adolph Hitler* ... which is for them (the returnees to German occupied territory in Poland) a promise and the host of infinite happiness."

Heinrich Himmler, greeting ethnic German returnees from Soviet occupied Polish territory at Przemysl, January, 1940.

THE COMMANDMENTS

"Love the Lord your God with all your heart, with all your soul and with all your mind."

"This is the first and greatest commandment, and the second is like it."

"Love your neighbour as yourself."

Gospel according to Matthew: 22: 37–39

THE GOOD DEED

"The light we see is burning in my hall:
How far that little candle throws his beams!
So shines a good deed in a naughty world."

**Portia, Act V Scene 1, 'The Merchant of Venice',
Shakespeare**

FICTIONAL STATUS

CHAPTER 1

HE SAT DOWN on the kerb and placed his head in his hands. An overwhelming nausea seized him, black and pulsating, such as he had not known for many years. He cried out in Polish: "Nie znowu, nigdy."* He was short of breath and panting and tears coursed between his fingers.

It was an early September morning in 1947. The skies above this neat terraced Victorian street were clearing: grey clouds reluctantly gave way to blue, as gusting winds stirred the first falls of autumn leaves. The slanting rays of pale golden sunshine illumined the top-half of the terraced houses opposite him contrasting with their sooty darkened exteriors. Overnight rain gleamed on the pavement. It was almost beautiful.

The silence of the night was passing and in the distance the high street would soon be noisy with early morning traffic.

He did not know how long he had sat there before a neighbour going to work stopped. "Adam, my dear old mate, what's up? Are you all right?" Then he saw what Adam had seen, a broken shop window and in crude black paint on the shop door the words: 'GO HOME. ENGLAND FOR THE ENGLISH' and a Nazi swastika. "Good God, Adam, the bastards. Don't worry. We can deal with this." His neighbour ran back to his house and returned with some paint stripper and a cloth. Vigorous rubbing removed some paint: but it was not a quick job.

"George you mustn't, you will be late." Adam protested, pulling himself together and getting off the pavement.

"No trouble mate, it's coming."

* "Not again, never again".

Together they got rid of the worst of it, although the door remained smeared black as a reminder of the visitation until Adam could get round to painting it again. "It could have been worse," said George, "you haven't lost anything. They don't amount to anything, Adam. Call the coppers. They will sort it out."

But Adam did not think that they amounted to nothing; or that it was a good idea to call the police to sort it out. He had heard it all before in another place and at another time. It hadn't been all right. So far from sorting it out the police had sided with the perpetrators – and had joined in. They were all in it together. Of course, this was England – but that was the sort of thing they said in Poland. "After all," they said, "we are Polish...."

At this time Adam was twenty-four years of age. He did not look English, which was, perhaps, to his advantage, because a little above average height, he was well-built, fair haired and handsome. He was a country lad, bright-eyed and glossy-cheeked, with a clear white complexion which rarely darkened. His demeanour was challenging: "Here I am," it said. "Make of me what you will, I am confident it is enough." He looked at you straight in the eye, which could be disconcerting. "I will tell you what I think without hesitation and in plain words and I think you must do the same," he seemed to say. The straight-speaking inhabitants of Clerkenwell liked his qualities and accepted him as one of their own.

Adam started to unload his van as he did on six days of the week: King Edward potatoes, tender young carrots, large cabbages replete with dew; and fresh fruit, which today were strawberries and raspberries; the very best from Covent Garden market. He was one of the very first there every morning, and knew what to buy and from whom. As with many immigrants, he worked hard: he wanted to be excellent and to succeed. It made him well-liked in the market and the traders looked out for him. They knew he was a farm-boy: that he knew his produce and what could be expected at any time of the year, and what was fresh and juicy.

By the time of his first customer, he had filled his shelves and piled them high with the best of everything available at this time of year and carefully arranged and priced. He stood back and admired his bright and shining shop: newly-painted in green and yellow with chequered red and white linoleum; and with a modern check out and cash register.

The shop front was tastefully painted in dark green. Written in bold white letters over the shop window were the words: 'Corner Shop', and in smaller print, 'Convenience Store' and in small gold letters over the door, 'Proprietor Adam Chwistek.' He knew it was good. "Too bloody good," he said to himself.

It was a good trading day. His shop served a number of neat and well-maintained terraced streets and while not prosperous the local people had money: there were City clerks earning regular wages and traders busy with the postwar tasks of reconstruction. Full employment and the war had created jobs for women and, while they were poorly paid, it meant that there was more than one wage-earner in the family – and steady money. As his reputation grew, he attracted high street trade and passing traffic. The shop was open at all hours. He ignored the regulations on shop hours and anyone who tried to enforce them. His shelves had to be cleared that day and he stayed until his last chance of doing so had gone.

At the end of the day his customers knew that there were bargains to be had as Adam would be clearing his stock: the poor and needy and temporarily impecunious were regulars. Sometimes he put things aside and charged nothing: and sometimes he brought things in for which he charged very little – trout he had caught himself, and sausages and pies which Eva made and cooked. He used to say to his customers: "No, it's no trouble. When you have money you can pay me something." Or: "Take something you need. I know you will pay me when you can. No, really, think nothing of it." He said to himself: "It's common sense. They will come back – and they will speak well of me."

He did his best for most of the day, although his heart was not in it; but in the mid-afternoon quietness he gave up, locked up and went home, leaving a boarded-up window as a reminder of the day.

He parked his van by the side of his shop and walked. The streets were very similar but his was a little meaner than most. In his street the houses were smaller and less well-maintained: and there were gaps where bomb damage had been cleared but nothing rebuilt. His house was freshly-painted. When Eva and he had married some six months ago he had bought the house for a song and, with the assistance of his father-in-law, he had repaired and decorated it, and with the rest of his savings he had bought the shop.

He let himself into an immaculately clean hall and then to a tiny kitchen: distempered white-walls, sparsely furnished but with bright and cheerful colours. He was pleased to be home. The room had a woman's touch. Freshly hung curtains, which matched the tablecloth, and the last of the summer roses in a vase on the white-painted window-sill, proclaimed this kitchen to be a place of love and hope.

Eva was at home. She started work early and was usually back by late afternoon. She worked as a sempstress in a makeshift building within walking distance of the house turning cuffs and collars and stitching on sleeves, sometimes on a machine and sometimes by hand. The factory was badly lit and poorly heated but none of the twenty girls crowded into it minded in the slightest. They performed their tasks to the sounds of radio music through a tannoy: 'Music While You Work', it proclaimed itself.

They gathered like a flock of small birds in the morning and whistled and sang all the day long. Eva was quick and dextrous and loved her work. The wages were poor but there were productivity payments for which she always qualified. At the appointed closing time a hooter sounded, and the whole of this chirpy flock swooped for the entrance and scattered over Clerkenwell. Eva flew with the flock, excited to be going back to her new home, to Adam and to their evening.

Eva was small, slight and lively. At twenty she was four years younger than her husband. It could not be said that she was beautiful for her face was too thin and her features too angular to achieve popular acclaim. Without being fat, she had a full figure, which at the time was considered a womanly asset. She had the glow of youth and the desire to be attractive. Her light fair hair was fashionably long and wavy. She made-up. She had, for Adam, several overwhelming virtues: she had opinions and spoke her mind; she stood for no nonsense; and she was loyal to all who were close to her and a staunch friend.

This evening, as on many others, Adam poured out his heart to Eva: about his day and about the incident; about not understanding it, about his fears of it, and of what might happen. Eva put her arms around him. She comforted him as best she could, sensing those things which she did not understand and which she would never comprehend about this man: a man who had overwhelmed her with his needs and boldness, and whom she loved so fiercely and completely.

She was thoughtful but forthright: "Adam, dearest, there is nothing to worry about. Stupid, ignorant children, I expect. It's not likely to happen again. Leave it alone, dear. Promise me you will. You have had too much rough stuff in your life. Don't go after trouble. Promise me."

And although he wanted to go after those who had done it – and not without argument – he did promise her.

She had lit the copper boiler for hot water and he went and had a bath. Afterwards he felt his tiredness and got into bed, between clean white sheets and plumped-up goose-feather pillows. "This must be the best bed in the whole of England," he thought, "perhaps the whole of Europe."

As he lay there he heard the sound of a horse and cart in the street below and the cry of the vendor: "Any old clothes, any old clothes." He thought: "Where there are horses there is manure."

The idea was so immediate that he believed he could smell the droppings. His garden, where he grew as many vegetables as he could, needed it; and if he did not collect it quickly someone else would. He knew he should get up: but his tiredness was too much. Later Eva found him asleep. She kissed him. "Goodness knows what I've let myself in for," she thought.

For her this poky two-bedroom terraced house in working-class Clerkenwell was a social step downwards. Her family had moved out long since to the leafier more respectable outer London Boroughs. The more stuck-up of her relatives would look down their noses at them. They wouldn't visit and she could imagine the gossip. "Good riddance," she murmured quietly to herself, "we shall be all right. I'm sure we will." She closed the bedroom door gently behind her so as not to wake him and went quietly down the stairs.

Although she had been reassuring to Adam, Eva was distressed by the day's incident. She paced around her small house as if marking out her territory. Except it was not all her own: for it seemed to her that what was recognisably simple and comforting was because of her – the neatly-made muslin curtains and pretty flowered cushion covers – and what was richly coloured, exuberant and ornate was down to him. Outside in the garden *her* wallflowers, irises and lobelias in their narrow beds blazed against the sooty walls while most of the garden was full of *his* vegetables – and if she opened the window – the smell of *his* manure!

She smiled to herself at the incongruity of it: two strong life forces, touching, mingling but not as yet merged. But it saddened her. Why was it not conjoined? By now there might have been a oneness. It was what she wanted. Given all that had gone before, it might now be impossible for him. She hoped not.

CHAPTER 2

IN AUGUST 1939 the Polish Silesian town of P. stood twenty kilometres from the River Oder and the German frontier. It was a market town of some ten thousand people. Within its catchment area lived a remarkable diversity of peoples. Most people spoke two languages; Polish, Russian, Czech and German – and, one in six, Hebrew.

On market-days the babel of all these languages was heard. Despite this diversity, historically there was very little racial tension in the town and every reason to believe that its citizens enjoyed the choice of customs, costumes and trade. In the market one could eat kielbasa and wurst,* and soup and fresh bread: a variety of foodstuffs from a diversity of stalls and traditions.

On one side of the modest square stood an imposing building built in brick but rendered white in a Palladian style with pillared columns and numerous steps. Dating from the 13th century, and once owned by a powerful Prussian Duke, it had served as the administrative centre of an entire region under the control of an alien power. Now it was empty and dilapidated, the fabric visibly decaying and the steps occupied by peddlers. It gazed out like Ozymandias in mute appeal to the past and as a threat to the future.

Further up the hill stood the Grand Duke's castle. Built in the style of a French chateau it commanded views for many kilometres around and all it surveyed was it's own: great pastures, lakes and forest as far as the eye could see. This domain was a hunter's paradise and bison, wild boar and deer roamed freely. In the lakes and rivers fish multiplied. And in these green and pleasant lands the Duke, his family and

* Polish and German sausage.

his friends – with the help of gardeners, foresters and gamekeepers – held unchallenged sway.

In these territories the word of the Duke was law: but not quite *all* the law for even under the Partitions, when there was no Poland, the town of P. was a free town and governed itself. All over Europe throughout the nineteenth century the crowned heads and aristocracy of Europe maintained their privileges with care, for the memory of the French Revolution was a powerful reminder of the fragility of their social position. Successive Dukes knew that they had great power but that they might wake one morning to discover that they had none.

In P. the Duke and his family were benefactors. The castle was a major source of employment in the town and part of the Duke's vast wealth went into charitable and religious causes, including a hospital for the poor. This beneficence was combined with caution. The Duke was careful to maintain the hidden escape tunnels of the castle which reached far out into his grounds. When one of his sons was found guilty of minor indiscretions in the town, the Duke was insistent that he serve his seven-day gaol sentence. And in the post-first-world-war period, when tensions were high between Poland and Germany, the Duke had one of his sons join the German army and another the Polish: in this way he reasoned he had a two-way bet and the chance to maintain his Polish possessions.

P. was prosperous. Being a free town encouraged the self-confidence and impudence on which entrepreneurial activity can thrive. Apart from their own well-managed small farms and businesses serving a domestic market, the proximity of the German frontier stimulated a variety of legal and illegal trading to the benefit of everyone, and sometimes to the tax collector. The inhabitants of P. felt that they could make money and possess property: indeed they had always felt it and it had always been true.

Yet it should not be imagined that life in this pleasant and prosperous town was best characterised as one of Illyrian peace and beauty nor that it was a hive of modern technological progress. Most people lived a life of struggle and difficulty, of quiet desperation, the pattern of which was marked by births and deaths, the seasons and the weather.

Despite the obvious changes which industrialisation brought and the daily movement of thousands into the coal mines and steel mills, everything changed and moved slowly: bad roads were traversed more often by horse and cart, bicycle and on foot than by car or bus; and most things and people hardly moved at all.

P. and its surrounding villages remained a place in which its in-habitants stayed a lifetime; where one's family and neighbours were more important than community; and a world in which honour and fair dealing were respected more than power and position. In such a world men made their way slowly and the recognition of their virtues and vices rarely spread far; but reputation, once established, was not easily changed for the better or worse.

In this world news spread slowly and the means of it were more likely to be the weekly market and the visiting doctor or vet than the telephone or letter: the telephone being limited in supply, and letter writing constrained by the literacy of the possible writers.

For most people this was not a society of banks and money and the blessings that were most commonly recognised were good health and character, which the prudent did their very best to preserve.

It was a life with few safeguards other than a large family. A man struck down by an accident or illness not of his own making, without remedy of fortune or state welfare, would be rescued or sustained only by family or friends.

At these times of misfortune large family networks acted as 'Wellington squares': as each family member fell another rose to fill his place – and then another and yet another until the battle was either won or lost. When a parent died an untimely death or a child was left an orphan others came forward to bring up and care for the child; grand-parents sustained adult children and their families; and children happily supported ancient relatives.

The predominant religion was Roman Catholicism. At each and every family happening the church was there; and at each and every moment its counsel was sought and given. The precepts of the church supported the survival of its adherents: the sanctity of marriage and the difficulty of its dissolution, lasting unions; the absence of birth control, a ready supply of children; the forgiveness of sins, the preservation of family; and the importance of charitable acts done publicly, a non-State welfare system. And over all these jealously guarded precepts hung the ultimate sanction of eternal damnation and hell-fire.

The worship of the one true God was not an activity that came cheaply. In good times and bad the church enacted its tithe from both the rich and poor, the good and the dissolute. When the congregation gathered for worship on the Sabbath it did not do so in a poor stable but in a substantial building gilded in real gold to the glory of God in the highest.

So in the absence of a caring State, the great strength and shelter of the Polish citizen came from his family life whether he was Jew, Catholic or Lutheran. But that great strength was paradoxically his weakness. Both family and church were sustained by the conviction – or rather the need to accept – that the sins and shortcomings of its members were to be forgiven, so long as they were subsequently and sincerely repented. And as times changed for the worse there were many more sins to forgive.

It always seemed that the threat lay without. When threatened, these communities drew closer together in order to survive, forgiving their members but not the stranger: the time when Jew and Christian, Catholic and Lutheran, German and Pole could cohabit happily came under strain and each community looked to itself.

During the 1930s, as the menace of Poland's mighty neighbour across the waters of the River Oder grew, tensions had risen: there were more German refugees, many of them illegal and some, Jews, unceremoniously dumped across the border. Upon the death of the country's benevolent dictator, Pilsudski, who had a Jewish wife, the extreme right grew in influence and anti-semitism became rife. The German minority, nowhere more vocal than in Silesia, grew more vociferous and aggressive. Poland's multitude of minority national and cultural groups grew increasingly anxious and active in their need to protect themselves.

All these groups gained some victories: the anti-semites succeeded in closing doors to Jewish educational and professional aspirations; and the requirement for all Jewish businesses to display their ownership enabled local fascists, very often with the active connivance of the police, to raid and rob them; while the Polish nationalists succeeded in banning the teaching of German in Polish state schools.

As the Polish reaction to German threats intensified, many prominent Germans in the town fled to Germany where they formed with others an alternative Silesian administration in waiting, while their colleagues left behind, and organised through German clubs liberally financed from the mother country, continued with their pro-German agitation.

To Adam these matters were not theoretical but daily realities. At his local school he sat among his polyglot school-friends of many national backgrounds and tongues. The majority of these were Polish, as was the classroom language spoken, but in the playground other tongues could be heard and the lines of friendship were along distinct national and racial groupings.

He did not learn much at school. It was a poor rural area and times were hard. At harvest times, and on other occasions when they were needed, up to half the class absented itself to bring in the harvest or to fill in for a missing or sick relative. The teaching staff did their best to arrest this flow, and on several occasions Adam hid out of sight at home while an embarrassed parent sought to explain his absence to an indignant school teacher. He got into the habit of not going to school when it suited him: to go fishing, shoot rabbits in the woods, or drift off on his own or with a friend.

While work was hard and unremitting, it was not without fun. At fruit-picking – and with the excuse of getting rid of the fruit stains – men and women, boys and girls, dipped into the cool river. As swimming costumes were unknown, the men and boys splashed naked in the water and the girls, covered only by loose-fitting pinafores, joined in. At these moments the precepts of a governing church were forgotten as beer-fogged minds and basic instincts prevailed.

The only school subject that he really enjoyed was history. This was because of Miss Zbucki with whom he had fallen in love. Miss Zbucki was not like the other teachers: she was young and shapely with soft brown eyes and a smile that lit up her entire face. She loved her subject, the children in her class, and her country. She would sit on her desk in front of the whole class and swing her long slim brown legs up and down – not at all like the legs of his mother and sisters.

When she was standing in front of the window, and the light was right, you could see through her long skirt. In her class the boys vied with each other to sit in the front row so as to get the best view. Miss Zbucki believed that this pushing denoted enthusiasm for her subject: which in a way was true, for in loving Miss Zbucki, Adam and the other children came to love history and their country.

Miss Zbucki told her children the most incredible things. She said that when the Great War of 1914 broke out the thirty million people who considered themselves to be Poles had no State of their own. They were governed by Germany, Russia, and Austria, and some people would say, of which she was one, by Latvia and Lithuania. In 1914 there had been no Poland for one hundred and twenty three years so at that time there was not a single person who had lived in an independent Poland which was recognised by other countries and which could be found on a map.

She told them about the glories of the old Polish state, which she said had been so successful, enlightened and progressive that it had led the reform of the Europe of its time. This liberal Poland was so advanced that its programme of reform had aroused dreadful feelings of jealousy and fear among its despotic neighbours. These States decided that they dare not risk liberal changes in Poland for fear that they would start revolutions in their own countries and bring to an end their despotic regimes. So they joined together to commit a great crime: they invaded Poland and divided it up between themselves.

Miss Zbucki said that she would tell them a secret. She told them what Polish people had done to survive under these occupying powers, and how ordinary people kept alive their Polishness and *their vision of Poland* while subject to another country; and she explained what they did to keep *their personal identity and their freedom* while serving a foreign master.

Miss Zbucki gave the children a warning. These foreign powers did not truly accept an independent Poland; they remained jealous. At the slightest pretext and opportunity they would fall on Poland again; and the more successful and enlightened the new Poland turned out to be, the greater would be their resentment and anger. It was their historic task as the new generation to save Poland – the children did not understand how they could be expected to do this – and if it could not be done they too would have to learn the lessons of *how to survive under a foreign power*, as Poles had done throughout the ages.

Miss Zbucki said that if they were going to be able to save Poland they had first to learn *to respect and love their Polish neighbours, whoever they were, and however strange they might seem*, and that in loving them, they would come to love their country. Tears came into her eyes and to those of many of the children.

Adam looked around at his classmates. Could he love and respect them? There was no problem about Miss Zbucki or Emilia, with her fair hair in bundles and her special way of walking, which waved her hips from side to side; but could he love Joseph with his acne, greasy ringlets and black cap; or fat greedy Pavel who was always elbowing him, and making jibes about his father? With the greatest of respect to Miss Zbucki he did not think he could live up to her expectations.

Miss Zbucki was a proud and passionate woman. She knew that the children were puzzled: they wanted to understand, to believe her, but they hesitated. She tried to find the right words. She said: "In your religious studies children you are told that Christ asks us to love our enemies. That's right isn't it?"

The children nodded indicating assent.

"It seems impossible to us doesn't it? Impractical, even sentimental."

More heads nodded.

"What *you* must understand is that you are not asked by Christ to *like* your neighbour or your enemy. *All you are asked to do is to love him: that is to tolerate your neighbour, respect him and, if you can, honour him.* Get to know him a little and be friendly and helpful. Do you understand the difference?"

They nodded and murmured that they did: but really they remained as puzzled as before. It was difficult to get started with this idea. The boys thought that this business of turning the other cheek was unmanly and would lead to very bad things being done to you.

Miss Zbucki said that Poland was the heart of Europe. Not only was it at the centre but in a very real sense it was the heart: when the heart was healthy the whole of the European body politic thrived; and when it weakened, poisonous toxins were at work elsewhere which at some time would reduce Poland. At this heart the arts and sciences flourished; medicine and philosophy advanced hand in hand; and indeed the whole of the human condition improved.

Adam thought long and hard about these propositions for they puzzled him. He did not think them right. It seemed to him that Poland was more like a sandcastle. Great care might be taken in the building of this castle, and when finished it looked very fine; but then you had to wait anxiously as the tide turned to see whether it would be swamped. You knew, as you watched the relentless advance of the sea, that your sandcastle would be demolished, but you hoped that you were wrong.

Sometimes it seemed that you were wrong: the waves hesitated and the line of surf in the sand fell back. You knew that if the waves faltered, the waters would abate and your sandcastle would be safe. But in your heart you knew it could not survive: that the sea was remorseless. The waves would continue to advance, the water would lap around your castle and slowly reduce it to nothing; or worse, a mighty wave would smash down and destroy it in an instant. All those hopes and all that effort – and for nothing.

Adam lived with his family of three sisters on the southern fringes of the town in a brick-built farmhouse with ten acres of land. Elsewhere in P. his family owned other property and friends and enemies alike – including the tax authorities – wondered just how they had acquired the resources to purchase these assets.

Grandfather had been caught smuggling goods across the frontier and had lost seven houses sequestered as a fine: but this setback, which was disastrous at the time and had slowed his social progress, had not stopped him. Shrewd marriages had added a little but not much. And then there were backhanders to his father. But even when all these things were added up and allowed for the acquisitions could not be fully explained.

It was late August and Adam slept among the rafters of the barn. It was water-tight and warm straw covered the floor. On one side, where a gate and pulley had been fixed, the wall was slatted and through its openings sunlight slanted across the rafters gathering strength and depth as the sun rose, creating a dancing symphony of tiny grains, mites and flies which rose and fell and drifted in and out of the light.

Below him the cattle stirred as their time came. Pungent smells and steam reached him through the floorboards enveloping his wakening. Knowing him to be there, the cattle summoned him to perform his milking duties and the mucking-out.

As he woke the disagreeable thought of going to school was in his mind: but then he realised that his school days had ended. Schooling had been extended for two years in the hope that he could follow his fathers example and enter an army staff college but as the threat of war grew, and the reality of soldiering dawned on all the family, his mother grew anxious for him and he was withdrawn from school. Adam had lost a career but he was not sorry. For some time now he had been making his way as an embryonic entrepreneur: he was in business and making money, and you couldn't make money by lying in bed in the morning.

He had slept in the barn for over six years. It had started because he could not bear any more the late night arguments between a drunken father and a questioning and insistent mother: and not just arguments, things got thrown, plates were smashed, and usually his mother came out of this the worse.

He thought of these encounters as being about 'dad and his women'. His father was a handsome man and in his way influential and in a position to have women. He was very tall and big. His face was rounded and his skin shone like a freshly-washed and ripe apple. He had a large military moustache which he waxed on important occasions. As the years had passed, and at times of good living, he had become fat. His upright military bearing, and attention to detail in his clothing, for his suits were always tailor-made, enabled him to carry his fatness well. The gravity of his official bearing was spoilt a little by his walk.

For a man of his size his steps were short and his toes pointed out in each stride: so much so that his enemies dubbed him 'the goose'.

Unlike most of the inhabitants of P., Ludvig was well-educated and well-read. The son of a university professor, he had been privately schooled and was fluent in several languages including German and Russian and in his own Polish tongue. He had inherited his father's intelligence but not his good sense or judgement. In his desire to be influential and important he had sacrificed his sense of fairness and decency: and in so doing he achieved place but lost the respect and unqualified allegiance of those around him.

With the exercise of a little family influence, Ludvig was appointed a minor customs official; and, by being in the right place at the right time, he was given special duties as a policeman in P. It was his job to trace German refugees, especially Jews, who were dumped across the border by train, and to track down the cross-border smugglers of contraband and people. Although small, P. had some significance as a route of entry for opponents and victims of Nazi persecution, the more desperate of whom crossed the River Oder by night in small boats.

Silesia was an attractive destination for German refugees: large German towns were close to the border, and Silesia was easy to hide in; German families had settled in Silesia over many generations under Austrian, Prussian and Polish administrations. Many refugees had relatives in Silesia, and with German as likely to be spoken as any other as a first language, it was easy for Germans to escape detection.

His father, Ludvig, hunted down these illegal immigrants regardless of how they had arrived and wherever they hid: Austrians, Germans, Czechs; communist or social democrat; Jew or gentile; it was all the same to him.

The distinction that really mattered to the refugee-hunter was between those who had money and influence and those who did not. If a refugee had money he might be spared: but wealth did not guarantee that you would be ignored, for it was necessary for an official to show that he was doing his job, that refugees were being detained and deported, and to demonstrate his honesty by the occasional declaration of attempts to bribe him. Sometimes his father received favours from women, and Adam had heard him boast about his conquests.

Of course, anything his father did was small beer. Many Germans who were not refugees from the Nazi regime, but whose nationality was not documented to so-called definitive standards, found themselves liable to deportation. Many old scores were settled: farms, houses, and businesses could be seized and their owners deported. In theory the law courts could be used to protect these people and on occasions they did. But judges could be bribed by both persecutor or victim and outcomes were unpredictable and slow: often there was no time available to the victim for judicial process and by the time of a court hearing both he and his assets had been disposed of.

The methods of disposal used by the police could be unpleasant. Fearful of German officialdom on the German side of the River Oder, who after all had been complicit in deporting many of the victims in the first place, the police were known to take deportees by boat to the middle of the Oder and then to force them overboard. If you could swim, and cope with the strong currents, you might make it to the other side. Of course, not everyone came into this category and the bodies of mostly old people and children were washed up regularly on both banks of the river.

It used to be Adam's habit on a Sunday morning to take the early morning bus from the town centre to the Oder with his friends. It was easy to reach the German side. The bolder and stronger could swim there while the others took a ferry. There were no passport requirements. On the boat you had to sign a form giving your name and address and confirming that you would return the same day. No one checked that you did.

One day they found a dead body, swollen and deformed, wedged into the bank on the Polish side. In trepidation they had reported it, first to the ferry police and then at the police station itself. No official seemed shocked or concerned enough to do anything about it and the body was left to decompose in the river.

After that Adam could never go swimming there. He thought of all the bodies that might be left in the river; bodies that might float onto the banks or, if you were swimming, might collide with you. He dreamt about bodies in the river; in his dreams they called to him for help; he bumped into them; and sometimes he became entangled with them, their arms clasped around him, their dead weight dragging him down, so that he knew he would drown too. Sometimes there were bodies that disintegrated as you touched them. Some bodies had recognisable faces but they drifted out of reach as he tried to recover them. He often woke violently after these dreams and gasping for air.

In the course of his work, his father acquired a bad reputation in the town and surrounding villages. At school the Chwistek children were given a hard time of it and once Adam had been beaten up badly on his way home. If Adam had loved his father he might have drawn closer to him in these days: he could have excused him, and assumed the attitudes of greed and bigotry, so common at the time, as something to be taken for granted, even emulated; but he did not love him because of his mother's tears.

As he grew older he knew that dislike had turned to hate. Adam despised his father because he spent the family income on maintaining a lavish style of life for himself; and because, as a consequence, he had been forced to be the man of the house before his time, earning and protecting the income they all needed, and hiding the hard-earned cash.

Ludvig was often short of money and would come looking for the hidden cash, and Adam had to be increasingly inventive in secreting it. His father had an old bridal-strap which he kept on a hook in the kitchen: it was two inches wide and of thick leather. If denied money his father would come after him with the strap. While he did not succeed in landing many blows on the yelling, struggling boy, those blows that did hit their mark caused considerable damage: the weals and bruises were extremely painful and lasted many days.

Adam's mother and sisters tried to help him. Mary, his elder sister, used to hide the strap, and when and if they heard his defiant yells, his family would drag him away or stand in front of him to prevent his father reaching him. Sometimes Ludvig hit his daughters by mistake. When sober and in funds his father would regret these fights, but at the time he did not care: the money was his and should not be stolen. "A man has to be the master in his own home," he said, though he knew that they all thought less of him for what he did.

Adam was a schoolboy when he assumed the responsibility for ensuring that the family had enough cash for their everyday needs. Their money came from three sources: the sale of farm produce at the farm gate; the renting out of rooms in the farmhouse; and in winter the delivery of coal using the farm-carts.

Adam took these activities in hand: the right produce at the right time beautifully clean and presented appeared at the farm-gate, a marked improvement on the haphazard methods of the past; the bedrooms were freshly distempered and new bedlinen was bought in the market; and efficient delivery schedules increased the sales of coal.

While remaining simply furnished, the rooms became attractive and appealing and new house rules for the lodgers were devised. Farm prices were raised and his mother and sisters were given instructions on handling and cleaning the produce. Adam advertised room vacancies and product prices outside the farm and by placing cards in local shop-windows: and room occupancies and farm sales increased.

All these efforts increased their income, and money could be put aside: but it was not enough. His father's earnings did not reach the family except in an indirect way. In Ludvig's mind he had made his contribution already: it was his wisdom and cash that had secured this pleasant farm and its livestock. He brought home what he could; game in season, large meat joints, cheeses and wines. What more could a man do?

Adam thought that the key to commercial success and more money was to trade. That was how the Jews in the town became rich: they traded. Why not him? Adam did his research and reached his conclusion. He decided to enter into business on his own account as a producer and retailer of ice-cream; and in this, and fortuitously, his father helped him.

His father's position in the town gave him many advantages. All business activities had to be licensed and his father, for a small remuneration, could ensure that an applicant obtained one. Ludvig often came into confiscated goods. One day, quite out of the blue, Ludvig brought home an ice-cream production machine. It was a thing of beauty: a sort of cart, exquisitely crafted in mahogany and consisting of a wonderful brass drum surrounded by compartments for ice to keep the ice-cream cold. It was split into sections, so enabling up to twenty-two different flavours to be provided; and it had a brass handle for churning the cream.

The younger children fell upon it as a kind of toy with the first thought that they might make ice-cream for themselves; but Adam saw it differently. If the practical problems could be solved the Chwisteks could go into business as ice-cream manufacturers and distributors: and that is what they did.

The machine came with a handbook which explained how you produced ice-cream. The constituents presented no problem for them with milk, cream and various fats coming from the farm and flavours from the town. The major difficulty was finding a regular supply of ice. In the winter ice could be taken from the river. Adam was able to devise a technique for cutting blocks of ice and storing the resulting small ice-mountain, protected by sawdust, in the barn. This ice could be used up to May after which the higher temperatures made it impractical.

Adam discovered a small Jewish manufacturer of artificial ice in a market town twenty kilometres to the south. The ice could not be collected before mid-night, and it was some 4.00 a.m. before the horses and cart returned to the farm. It was this routine which decided Adam that he should come into permanent occupation of the barn, for in using it he disturbed no one. He could settle the horses and slip into his warm straw bed at any hour. In the barn he felt in charge of his business as the guardian of his own ice-mountain: not a mountain of gold as yet but anyway a mountain of some sort.

On this particular August morning, when he woke, he thought of his ice-cream. He needed to be through his morning tasks as fast as he could as he was off to the Fete in R. and, if the weather was fine, he could expect to make bumper ice-cream sales.

In the kitchen his mother was already at work preparing breakfasts for the lodgers. At this time, Sophie Chwistek was a woman of thirty-eight years of age. Of mixed Polish–German parentage she remained a woman of striking good looks. She was dark haired and remained slender despite the thickening of age and the bodily effects of hard physical labour. Her bone-structure was very fine which made her photogenic and surprising. In some lights she would appear plain, while in others she was strikingly attractive; but whatever the light, she always appeared kindly and strong; the lines around her eyes and mouth were witness to the fact of her constant good-humour and pleasantness, while the firmness of her lips to her resolution.

At this time, like many women of her age and background, she lacked the schooling that her obvious intelligence and energy merited; and she found herself committed to a daily routine of struggle which she would not have chosen had other opportunities presented themselves.

Sophie blamed no one for her situation nor did she have any self-pity. She thought herself lucky: she had four children that she loved to desperation and a handsome husband, that contrary to the gossip of family and friends, she continued to love and admire. She loved him for his good looks, his eloquence and his courage.

As for his womanising, she had decided to tolerate it so long as it did not threaten her marriage or too openly humiliate her. In return for this she was loved by him; and the family, despite a whirligig of emotions, confusions and despair, maintained a constant course under her firm tutelage.

But this morning she was anxious: "Joseph's here. Be nice to him." Adam groaned. He had tried to warn him off the night before. Contact with his former classmate was unavoidable as Joseph's father owned the small factory that produced Adam's ice and Joseph was sometimes to be seen at collection times. Yesterday Joseph had enquired whether he was going to R. and when it was confirmed he said: "Can I come. I won't be a nuisance. I can stand in for you when you want a break. I can bring my violin. You know I always attract people when I play." And as Adam hesitated he made an offer: "I'll split my takings with you." Adam sort of mumbled. He hadn't said 'Yes,' but on the other hand he hadn't said 'No.'

The truth was that he didn't want to be seen with this Jewish boy with his black cap and ringlets. It wouldn't help him to sell ice-cream. But it was true that he was amazingly good on his violin: which is how his mother had met him, playing his violin at weddings and parties. His mother liked Joseph because he talked to her about things that no one else could; about literature, music and the ballet. He made her laugh: and he laughed a lot too, which Adam could not remember him doing at school.

Adam thought that he had put him off. But apparently not. "Adam," continued his mother, "you know that I don't really want you to go but, if you do, I want you to go with Joseph."

She thought it safer for him not to be alone. Two days before when she had been in the market-place the talk was of an imminent German invasion. German radio broadcasts were increasingly menacing. Radios were being played in the market and the traders had picked up that Britain and France had renewed their guarantee to come to Poland's assistance if Germany attacked. No one believed that they would. Why would they? If they hadn't helped Czechoslovakia, why would they help Poland? And how could they anyway, with Britain thousands of kilometres away from Poland and without an army.

However, the repeat of this guarantee had seemed to slow things down and the invasion had not happened. But these German troops remained massed on the frontier and Sophie could remember the first world war: once armies were assembled it was difficult to stop them fighting.

War might happen at any time and, when it started, they would have to flee. They had already made preparations by loading a wagon in the barn. Sophie believed that Ludvig was on a German hit list and that the Germans would arrest him. It was not only his police activities, which must have been well known to the German administration in waiting, but his past record which would work against him.

In 1916 Ludvig had served in the German army and had been captured by the British. When the war was drawing to a close he had volunteered to return to Silesia to join a partisan movement operating behind German lines. Technically, he was a German army deserter. These partisan veterans paraded every year in the Silesian town of Opole where no doubt they had been photographed by German-speaking zealots. Sophie thought that the Germans were a very thorough people and would have records of all this anti-German activity.

As Adam got up and moved to leave the kitchen his mother said: "Promise me you will not be late. If something happens and you hear about it you must come back right away. And before you go, say goodbye to Mary."

His sister was in the basement-kitchen cooking animal feed in three large vats on three ancient cookers. The smell of cooking pig-swill was dreadful. Mary was cheerful and pleased to see him as ever. She was dark haired and animated like her mother, but not so beautiful: she was smaller and plumper, but to his eye very pleasing. Her face was rounded and more Polish than German and her expressions and speech were quick and perceptive. She had a way of anticipating you, interrupting you in mid-sentence and completing your thought. Very often this completion was far more successful than anything you might have achieved on your own, and so you did not mind the interruption.

Mary left you with the impression that you were a very clever fellow, and you were glad that she had noticed it. It might be imagined that there was artifice in this, in her ability to flatter you and put you at your ease. It was certainly feminine and disarming, but unconsciously so. However, Mary was an intelligent girl and had done well at school until the needs of the farm had cut her schooling short.

As Adam looked across the kitchen at his sister he felt very proud. It was a moment of change, he knew that, and no one knew what these changes would ask of them. There would be all sorts of difficulties, he was sure of that; but with Mary their chances would be better. She had helped him and it was his turn now to help her. Impulsively he kissed her and ran from the room leaving her blushing but pleased.

So much against his will he set out with Joseph to go to R. He with his ice-cream cart and its heavy load, and Joseph on his sister's black bike with chain-guard and high handlebars; both mightily slow on any hill and, given poor brakes, frighteningly quick on any slope; scared and exhilarated in equal proportions.

CHAPTER 3

THEY WERE AN unlikely pair, this gawky orthodox Jewish boy and the sturdy fair haired farm-boy, but they made it to R. and to the unpretentious field where this fete was being held.

It was the major show event of the year for R., and agricultural machinery stands vied with produce and livestock for attention. There was a display ring for horse-jumping and livestock judging and on the fringes, where they pitched their ice-cream cart and assembled their small ice-cream kiosk, there were beer tents and hot food stands.

Soon these tents were busy with people determined to enjoy themselves despite the gathering crisis: local farm-workers, and townsfolk who worked in R.'s burgeoning factories – and their children – all enjoying a day out. While across a small river which skirted one side of the field, and where anglers quietly bid their time, and over gentle green fields and rolling hills purple on the horizon, other men with murderous intent waited impatiently to fall upon them.

They did good business and despite himself Adam had to admit that Joseph was good for trade. Joseph had laid a large red handkerchief on the ground to one side of the cart and he played his violin, and how he played; Polish folk songs, Hungarian gypsy music, ballads and gigs. Then in his own words, to indulge himself, extracts from Beethoven, Mendlesohn and Brahms. "Guess Adam," he shouted, "how many of these composers are Jewish?" Adam didn't know.

The handkerchief filled up with small coins as Joseph and the music were appreciated. It was hot and crowded and by mid-afternoon they ran out of ice-cream and retired to the beer tent, where Adam drank beer and Joseph lemonade.

The tent was fairly crude. At one end on trestle tables covered by blue and white checked tablecloths was the bar and along the length of the tent there were uncovered trestles and benches in rows. It was crowded, noisy and smoky: children and dogs played in the gangways, but the games-players pursued their sports oblivious to all.

"Where did you learn to play the violin like that?" asked the admiring and envious Adam.

"From my Uncle. He's very good. He used to play in an orchestra. It sort of runs in the family. We all play some type of instrument."

Adam realised that he knew nothing about Jews like Joseph. Hardly anything about Joseph at all really. He knew that his father ran several small businesses in P., and that he had a very pretty sister, but nothing else. Nothing about his religion or why he dressed in the silly way he did, making himself so obvious and inviting ridicule and envy. In a way he did not want to know. It was dangerous to get involved with Jews. You could get beaten up by the members of the German clubs and you wouldn't find a policeman to help you.

But Joseph was all right. He quite liked him and wanted to know more about him.

"Where did you get your name?" he said.

"What, Joseph? That's biblical."

"No, Trout. Your surname. I've never come across anyone with a name like that."

"Well, there is a family story, but I don't know whether it's true. Anyway, it is probably something like this. At the end of the eighteenth century with the Third Partition everyone under the occupying authorities had to register themselves as citizens. Your family would have done this. The difference for Jews is that we lost our communal rights and Jewish names and the local registrars had to come up with new names.

Some of these registrars must have had a sense of humour or they had become desperate – there were rather a lot of us – so the names they chose became very peculiar. My grandfather believes that the registrar who named us had been fishing and so on the next day used all the fish names he could think of." Joseph laughed: "It might have been a lucky escape. Who knows what he was up to the day before that?"

"And why do you come to our school and not the Jewish school at the synagogue," Adam persisted.

"It's my father's wish. He thinks that we Jews should do more to be part of the community, so he sends us to the state school. The others laugh at him. They say that the more you gentiles know about us the more you will dislike us, and the greater the opportunity for you all to do us down," and he laughed again.

Joseph wanted to ask him something. He shuffled his feet and twisted his body awkwardly. "Adam," he began hesitating after every few words, "I'm sure you know that the next few days will be dreadful – the invasion I mean. Even if the Army resists for a while we can't win. In Silesia we will be overrun in no time."

Adam protested about this at first. The Polish army had been very active in Silesia building fortifications and gun emplacements. The soldiers who were being billeted in the villages were confident and cheerful. But Joseph was adamant and made his case very carefully. Adam realised that Joseph knew far more about these matters than he did. In the end he said weakly that he supposed Joseph to be right.

"We Jews will have no chance. Adam, you may not know that in Germany dreadful things have been happening to Jews." He told Adam about the camps, the death camps he called them, the beatings and deportations – and not only of Jews, but anyone who opposed the Nazis were treated in the same way, but especially the Jews. Adam said that he knew about that although actually he was shaken by some of the things Joseph had told him.

Joseph said awkwardly: "*Will you help us?*"

"*Help you! How can I help anyone*? My family will need help and my dad will be a target. We shall have to hide and leave P."

Adam found himself shouting and Joseph, who was not surprised, quietened him down.

"What I have in mind is that *you* have Polish friends and relatives in other parts of the country who might be willing to hide us. The family is willing to split up."

Adam looked at this Jewish boy with his ringlets and cap and his Jewish features and mannerisms. How could anyone hide him? It was absurd and dangerous. *It was everyone for himself.*

Joseph went on: "Think about it, Adam. We have money you know and we are willing to pay. Money might help you and your family."

Adam did want to think about it, but not then. It was time for cards. In these tents it was usually possible to get yourself into a card game. Of course, they were usually fixed in some way; but if you observed them closely you could work out if they were and, with practice, how. Adam looked 'fair game' to the players and with a nod and a wink he was usually let in.

Adam was good at cards. He had discovered that the secret of success was observation. In these games it was usually true that the other players simply gave far too much away. Drinking did not help them: they were careless in the handling of their cards; their expressions revealed their true state of play; and if they were combining against an outsider, their signalling systems were too obvious. And they under-estimated Adam. *"After all, he is only a boy,"* they said to themselves.

Adam chose his group carefully and played steadily while he worked it all out.

He was willing to lose and while losing to limit his stakes. So when he began to win no one begrudged him, and they did not notice that the stakes had risen. Adam always had a clear strategy and careful limits: in this game the objective was to cover all the costs of the day so that the ice-cream sales were all profit. Once he had achieved this objective he stopped. No one had lost too much money. No one was aggrieved. *"A nice boy,"* they thought, *"and smarter than he seems."*

So when Joseph had offered him half of his takings, as they had agreed, he refused. Joseph had been helpful and he had achieved his objectives for the day. They set out for P. in the evening light, content and well-fed, and rode back into the eye of the storm.

Cycling busily ahead of Joseph, Adam thought about his proposition: and the more he did the more absurd it seemed. What could he do, a boy of sixteen whose father was likely to get arrested, and who had a family of his own to look after? *"The Jews will be all right, they always are,"* he said to himself.

The approach to P. was on a high ridge that curved through a conifer forest which gradually thinned out as they descended. The first glimpse of the farm showed that something was happening, but visibility was quickly lost. As they got nearer he could see the farm cart in the yard being packed and secured and reaching it he was overwhelmed by his sisters relieved at his return.

His father had received a tip off that the invasion would come in the early hours of the morning. It was hardly needed as the radio was reporting rumours of troops mobilising on the borders. Their radio was one of few in their neighbourhood and people had gathered on and around the courtyard wall to listen to the news played loudly through the kitchen window.

Rosa, his younger sister, had jumped on him and was refusing to be removed until he promised to sit next to her and hold her hand; and the farm dogs jumped up at him, and then ran around the yard in circles, adding to the general state of nervous excitement and confusion.

Rosa's mop of curly fair hair, with her sturdy frame and energetic activity, gave an immediate impression of security and sureness. But Adam knew this was misleading, that the threat and talk of war had greatly disturbed her and that she needed him. Adam was her hero and she attached herself to him as tightly as she could. Adam hugged and cuddled her as she demanded, finding in her closeness as much comfort as she obtained from him.

Uncle Janek, his father's brother, and his wife Hanika, were to stay at the farm and look after it. As Ludvig did not know where to go or with whom to stay, his brother could not reveal his whereabouts under questioning no matter how hard he was pressed. As darkness fell they left with cheers, tears and handshakes from neighbours.

Before leaving his mother had taken Joseph aside and had spoken to him kindly. She had given him a basket with some of her food store: a cured ham, some cheese, sausage meat and fresh eggs. He heard her say, as he protested: "I want you to take it. You are a good boy and your mother will appreciate this." He saw his mother kiss Joseph very tenderly and that she had watched him ride away until he was out of sight.

They rode to the south east making steady progress in light traffic. To begin with they were in high spirits with the children chattering away as if going on a holiday adventure, but as the enormity of what they were doing sank in they became quiet and thoughtful.

Sophie sat upright beside her husband waiting to take over when he tired. It had never crossed her mind not to undertake this journey into the unknown although she might have stayed and left her husband to find his own hiding place. At this time, she told herself, her husband and the children needed her. The important and unstated verity for her was to keep the family together and to keep her husband safe.

She did not blame Ludvig for their plight. To her mind he had always done what he had thought right. Perhaps, he was not always correct, and maybe the mistakes were bad; but everyone made mistakes, and she was sure that he had done his best.

Ludvig was deeply anxious. He had enough sense and experience to know that his chances of evading German punishment were slim. He could hide but eventually he would be found. It was a journey without any prospect of success, and in taking it he knew he was endangering them all.

Ludvig's tip off was accurate and with the dawn they knew that German forces had crossed the frontier. In the distance they could hear the crump of bombs and the noise of heavy guns, and they could see the rising grey plumes from direct hits. The traffic became heavier and, as they left main roads to avoid aircraft and armoured vehicles, everything slowed down. They all travelled at the speed of the slowest vehicle and, when there was a breakdown, they all came to a halt.

They stayed overnight at farmhouses, where the local farmers, despite their own problems, were usually able to feed them, with supplements from Sophie's storehouse. Through listening to the radio, they kept track of the progress of the war. Adam had a map on which he plotted the positions of the Polish and German armies. It was clear to him that the war was going badly and then, after a very short time, that Poland had no hope. Joseph had been right.

The family bunkered-down together, sometimes in the wagon or on farmhouse floors. If there was a bedroom to spare the women shared it, and Adam and his father slept together on a floor. Adam did not find this easy: he had never spent so much time with his father, and there was a tension between them. Ludvig was restless and had taken to wandering off on his own. He was prone to outbursts attacking the ineptness of the authorities and complacent elites letting down the Polish people: the lies of politicians, the deficiencies of the army and the stupidities of generals.

One night his father woke him. "Listen," he said slowly and deliberately, keeping his voice down although nobody could overhear them. "I want you to promise me something. I know we don't get on at the moment and I'm sorry about it. When you are older you will understand. It's too late to do anything about it now. I have had a job to do. Unpleasant, I know, but it had to be done and I did it well." Adam said nothing. His father continued: "I like my job and I'm not going to apologise about it, and especially not to you."

Adam remembered the body in the water and his nightmares. He thought his father looked different. His cheeks were hollowed and his face looked as if it had fallen in. Adam had always thought of his father as vigorous and young for his age, but at this moment he saw that he was older. He saw that his father's thinning hair was greyer and that the skin around his eyes had turned red with dark patches under them. He was frightened by him and tried to get away, but his father grabbed him by the arm.

"Let me go. There is nothing I can do for you."

"Yes there is, listen. Something very bad is going to happen to me. I know that now. And you must look after your mother and sisters. Promise me."

Adam wriggled free and made for the kitchen door.

"You stupid man …," the words hardly came out, "that's what I do, that's what I do now."

Adam ran out of the door into the darkness and found an outhouse to spend the night in, sobbing uncontrollably into old sacks, which served both as his mattress and blanket.

In the morning his father said nothing to him. There had been some bad news which had quietened the adults and changed everything. The radio reported that Soviet troops were massing on the eastern frontier and that an invasion was imminent. They were now a few miles south of Lvov and in the path of any Russian invasion.

The choice was between the devil and the deep blue sea; and they chose the latter – to go back home to the farm. At least under German occupation they would be able to speak the language, and with German grandfathers on both sides of the family they should be all right; that is except Ludvig, who was to be dropped off on the way back at the home of Sophie's elder sister Paula in Katowice, where hopefully he could be hidden.

They joined the flow of, what was to become all too quickly, human misery: and this time the flow was westward.

On the journey back there was no joking. Rosa held on as fast as she could to Adam and cried steadily and they all prayed a little, in their own ways, that they would not be attacked or stopped. At least, Sophie thought, a German soldier would understand the imperative of fleeing from a Russian invasion.

The roads were crowded with a variety of horse-drawn vehicles, fleeing in all directions. Occasionally Polish army units and foot soldiers joined the columns some moving up to the front and some in retreat. For safety, and in fear of air attack, and whenever possible, they kept to minor roads becoming enveloped in the dust-clouds of very hot days.

In the air Adam watched silver-coloured German planes diving and swooping like exotic birds and they heard the unmistakable noise of screaming Stukas as they dive-bombed columns of traffic.

Occasionally they saw German infantry filing across fields in orderly and disciplined procession. Adam thought them very fine and better than the Polish soldiers they saw on the roads.

Closer to their destination they were stopped by an advance party of a German column. A German captain, a regular soldier, asked them some questions in a civil manner. They answered him in German, and when he concluded that Mary was the most fluent, he asked to borrow her. "Do not worry madam," he said to Sophie, seeing her fear, "we only need her for a few minutes as we are short of an interpreter. Pull up by the side of the road and we shall bring her back." And two hours later they returned her, with a thank you and a smile. These Germans are perfect gentlemen, they all agreed.

They reached Katowice without any mishap. At this time Katowice was a large, bustling industrial town of over three hundred thousand people. The town was built on huge reservoirs of coal. While care had been taken not to mine too close to the town, an increase in its population and a spread of its habitation took place year by year. Cracks in the buildings indicated that part of the town was sinking slowly: coal dust begrimed the buildings and deposited a fine layer of black on its roads: everywhere you could smell coal.

Katowice was big enough to hide in; but Ludvig had his doubts about staying there. Sophie's sister, Paula, was married to an Austrian butcher, whose shop and slaughterhouse was in a quiet part of the town's outskirts. His brother-in-law, Herman, had lived in Poland for the last ten years but Ludvig thought of him as pro-German. He knew that Herman had been enthusiastic about the *anschluss*, the incorporation of Austria into Germany. Herman had joined the German club in Katowice, and educated his daughter, who was the same age as his own youngest daughter Lucie, at a German school. Would Herman be willing to hide him, and even if he would do so, could he be trusted?

"Nonsense," exclaimed Sophie, when he raised the issue, "family comes first."

Ludvig was not so sure.

But they were greeted with great joy and relief for their safety, and Ludvig was reassured. They stayed overnight. For safety Herman put the horses and the cart in his outbuildings and they talked long into the small hours about how they could manage in these uncertain and dangerous times.

Paula persuaded them both to bring the Chwistek's youngest daughter Lucie to her as soon as it was possible to do so. She and Herman could look after her. Lucie would be good company for her daughter, and it would take the strain off Sophie. When Sophie protested that it would be expensive for her sister, it was agreed that she would bring some food from the farm from time to time as in war, no doubt, there would be shortages. The two sisters made arrangements for a visit in two weeks time when hopefully things would have settled down a little.

Early next morning a tearful family left their father in the doorway of this modest house and with Adam taking the reins they made their way back sadly over forty kilometres to the farm.

CHAPTER 4

SOPHIE SAT IN her kitchen taking her usual morning break. It was her first meal of the day: vegetable soup from a cup and eaten with rye bread. At least that had not changed in the period of four weeks in which her world had crashed around her. She was surprised to be sitting in this familiar place as if, at least for her, life was continuing as normal.

On their return to the farmhouse, her sister Hanika had fallen upon her shrieking, tears streaming down her cheeks, stricken and ashen faced.

"It's my fault, it wouldn't have happened but for me – going back to the house."

"What wouldn't have happened? For God's sake Hanika. What wouldn't have happened? What are you talking about?"

"Janek, he's been shot. He's dead. The Germans shot him."

And the story tumbled out.

The speed and ferocity of the German attack had taken them by surprise. Polish radio had broadcast hopeful accounts of the Germans being beaten back and it was some time before they realised how bad the situation had become.

Hanika believed that she had time to go back to their cottage in a village one kilometre from the farm to recover some valuables and things of sentimental value, for she feared that their home would be looted. While she was there, German troops entered the village and experiencing some isolated resistance had started to machine-gun the houses. Hearing the guns, Hanika had dragged a mattress into the backroom and wedged it with the kitchen-table into a corner as her protection. German troops had entered the house and fired their weapons throughout the ground-floor before, thinking it empty, they had left. Bullets had lodged in the mattress and had splintered the table but miraculously she had survived.

Janek, worried about her absence, had gone to find her, taking his shotgun with him. This was a useless weapon fit only for shooting rabbits, but it was all he possessed. Down the road he met some neighbours fleeing from his village and they told him that his wife was dead. "She could not have survived," they said. They had actually seen her enter the house and then, in horror, it being machine-gunned.

Janek should have returned to the farm but consumed by anxiety and rage he pressed on. Hearing gun shots his neighbours had looked back. It seemed to them that Janek had opened fire on a German motor cyclist, without effect, who had returned it with his mounted machine-gun, killing Janek outright.

Later in the evening, when the troops had passed through the village, Hanika returning to the farmhouse found her husband's body by the side of the road. Hanika was inconsolable. No amount of assertion that she had not caused his death, and that it was a German soldier who had killed her husband, could assuage her grief and sense of guilt.

Hanika had not been able to bury her husband until ten days later, and then not properly. Eventually, with the help of friends, they had ignored the German-imposed curfew to bury him in the village churchyard, without ceremony or a tombstone and the time to grieve.

Adam took this news very badly. It wasn't that he felt close to Janek, but he was *his* uncle. He had been shot like a dog. Many others had been killed. The Polish radio, before it had been silenced, had told them of a whole nation dying.

Adam thought of Miss Zbucki and her saying that it was up to them, the young people, to save Poland. He lay on the straw in the barn angry and confused. He must do something brave and defiant. What could he do? He came up with a plan. His mother, preoccupied with other things, saw the execution of this plan too late to prevent it. Adam had painted the farmhouse fence, a stretch of fifty metres fronting the main road, in the red and white colours of the Polish flag.

It must have been noticed almost immediately for in quick succession she was visited first by a Polish official warning her that Adam's gesture was unwise and dangerous to her family, and then by a German staff car with three occupants one of whom they saw by his uniform to be a member of the SS.

In between these visits Sophie had attempted desperately, to Adam's protests, to paint over the fence in white distemper: but she hadn't completed her task by the time of the second German visit and even those parts of the fence that she had painted remained wet.

The soldiers were very correct. The elder, she thought a sergeant, and an obviously decent and respectable sort of person, took their personal details: their names, ages, their occupation and whether they had German parentage. He asked whether they owned the fence and who had painted it. Sophie said that she was the owner and that she had painted it. She said: "I had been meaning to do it for some time but was short of paint. The fence needed an undercoat so I used all the spare paint I could find before painting it white. The fence has always been white."

The nice sergeant smiled: "Madam," he said, politely but coldly: "where is your husband?"

Sophie had thought about the answer to this question, and had rehearsed her reply.

She said: "Before the invasion started we went to see my husband's relatives in Lvov which, as you know, is occupied by the Russians. My husband decided to stay but the rest of the family wanted to return."

The sergeant smiled again. He asked for the names of these relatives and their address and then gave them a warning and some advice. He told them that Polish Silesia was now part of Germany and subject to both German law and the law of the governing authorities. The new regulations were posted in the town square and in other places and they must read and obey them. These regulations were tough but fair. If they obeyed them they would be all right but if they were flouted in any way they would be punished and without mercy. He asked about the livestock and took down every detail. The Germans clicked their heels politely and went away.

When nothing had happened over the next few days Sophie thought that they had escaped punishment. When a further week had elapsed, and at the arranged time, and accompanied by Lucie, she thought it safe to go to Katowice. She packed the largest food-basket she could carry and hiding it carefully beneath a shawl caught a train in P. to Katowice.

The train journey of forty minutes was perfectly normal. Lucie who was an intense and self-absorbed little girl, pretty and finely featured like her mother, was excited by the unexpected journey and the prospect of seeing her cousin. She ran up and down the three-carriage train and her mother had to recover her on more than one occasion before at last she settled down.

Apart from Lucie's high jinks the journey was uneventful. Sophie did not notice anything or anyone different; and she was not alarmed or frightened in any way. The walk to her sister's house from the station took her some twenty minutes. It was straightforward; she saw no strangers and she wasn't stopped. So she arrived at her sister's house in good spirits to be greeted enthusiastically.

A bottle of good German wine was opened to celebrate: but before any could be taken, there was a knock on the door. Two plain-clothes policemen announced and identified themselves. They arrested Ludvig and asked them both to come with them to the central police station in Katowice. Here their names were registered and the time of the arrest was recorded before they were both taken back by car to the police station in P., where they spent the night in the cells.

Ludvig was familiar with the police station but he saw no one he recognised. He learnt later, that on the coat-tails of the advancing army came a platoon of alternative officials and enforcers, and that his former colleagues had experienced a fate similar to his own: that seemlessly and effortlessly the new apparatus of control had already been put into place.

In the morning he was given a cup of coffee and led into an interviewing room where two uniformed Germans confronted him. He recognised from his own police practice that these two Germans played 'good guy' and 'bad guy', and he knew what to expect. The 'good guy', a middle-ranking, middle-aged officer with greying hair, a beer paunch, and a permanently quizzical expression asked the questions.

"Are you Chwistek?"

"Yes."

"And are you the Chwistek who has been working as a policeman in this town?"

"I am."

"What is your race?"

"Catholic."

"Your race, not your religion, numskull."

"Polish."

He continued: "In your job you must know many secrets: you must know about Jews and other criminals who are hiding in this town and in the villages. Are you willing to cooperate with us and to give us the names and locations of these people ...?"

And then seeing Ludvig hesitate, he added: "Let me be clear with you Mr Chwistek. If you help us, give us your full cooperation – nothing less you understand – we shall spare your life and those of your family.

Your destination will be Sachsenhausen and not heaven, at least for the time being."

"Yes, yes, I can write it all down. Thank you. Thank you very much."

The words tumbled out and the relief was so overwhelming that he soiled himself. Later as he cleaned up he joined in the laughter of the town's new enforcers as if he had been given an award. The Germans were as good as their word. He cooperated with them over several days. On occasions he led them to places that they might not have found. People were shot and imprisoned as a result of this cooperation, and sometimes on sight.

It pleased his interrogators to interview Sophie immediately after her husband. She was asked:

"Do you know that it is an offence punishable by death to harbour a wanted fugitive?

"Yes, I do know; but so far as I know my husband is not a criminal. He is a respectable and honest man and has not broken Polish law in any way."

The reaction was quick and threateningly icy.

"Mrs Chwistek, Silesia is German. It is German law that applies here and I will tell you what it is. Do you understand?"

"Yes I understand."

"Tell me please, who else do you hide?" said the 'bad guy' speaking for the first time.

"You let out rooms. Who are the people in these rooms?"

Sophie said that they were lodgers and tourists usually staying for a night or two; and some were regulars who worked in the town. She explained that she kept a register as required by Polish law and that this was up to date and could be inspected.

She was told that her explanation had been noted but not accepted. "Mrs Chwistek, you have broken the law and you will be punished. You can leave now but soon we shall be in touch with you again." She hurried home to her worried children neither fearful nor contrite but angry and annoyed that she had been inconvenienced.

Several days passed before she heard again. A Polish policeman called to tell her that Ludvig had been sent to a camp in Sachsenhausen and to give her a letter. She was told that an Order had been issued prohibiting the letting of any room at the farm, or their use by anyone other than her immediate family, and that a breach of this Order was punishable by imprisonment. Without delay Sophie gave notice to leave to the two lodgers *in situ*, and they left in a hurry.

This left unresolved whether any action would be taken against them for the fence-painting episode. Another two weeks elapsed and Sophie thought they had escaped punishment. But then two large German military trucks drove up. Marksmen entered the farm, shot the livestock and rounded up those of the chickens and geese they could catch. The animals were thrown or lifted into the vehicles and then carted away. A German soldier gave them a separate letter ordering Mary and Adam to report at different times for onward transport as farm-workers: Mary to L., a distance of only fifty kilometres but in Germany; and Adam much further away in C. near the German town of Dresden.

Mary reported dutifully, bought her train-ticket with the money given to her, and proceeded in an orderly but tearful fashion to L. She was to work as a farm-labourer on a large German farm. There were some fifteen Polish girls and they were billeted in a large outhouse. Although prison-like with bunk-beds and straw palliasses, these living quarters were not uncomfortable. A wood-stove provided some heat in the winter, and they were able to cook most of their food.

While they worked long hours, and were tired at the end of the day, supervision was friendly and relaxed. The girls became good friends and the general atmosphere was not unlike a working holiday. It was a seven-day working week, but this was normal for a farm, and once every eight weeks they could take a weekend off. They were paid a nominal wage and, after necessaries, there was just enough money to buy a train-ticket home.

The girls replaced men serving in the German army and it was soon obvious to them that the neighbouring farms were underworked or idle. Mary settled down to familiar tasks. By popular acclaim she became the billet cook which removed her from work in the fields, which in poor weather was very harsh. During the day when she could busy herself she was happy enough; but at night the tears came, for her father, as she thought about the dreadful camp he had been sent to, and for her lost family.

Adam reported some days later to the police station. In the queue he met a former schoolmate and they both received money for a train-ticket. They went together to the station. As they stood on the platform his schoolmate Tadeusz said: "Fuck this Adam, I've no wish to go to fucking Dresden." He jumped onto the track and out into open country on the other side, closely followed by Adam; and collecting fishing-rods from Tadeusz's home, and well-fed on German money, they spent a day of freedom.

The day of retribution duly arrived and Adam reported back to the police station. There was no queue for Adam to join on this occasion. He was ushered into the back-room where fortunately for him a regular army officer was in charge on that day. Adam gave his explanation: "I can't work on a farm because my mother and younger sister need me. My father is in a concentration camp and my elder sister is working on a farm in L. now. We have no money and they look to me."

The officer looked at him attentively for what seemed to Adam to be a very long time. And then he said: "Turn round and face the window." There were French windows open at this time with steps leading down to grass. "Bend over." A forceful thrust from a booted foot propelled him downwards sprawling onto the grass. "Get yourself up and in here," was the next command: and he did so, hastily, shaken and in fear of what would come next.

The German was writing a letter of some kind, and was silent while he did it. Eventually he said: "What is your name? Adam? You are a lucky boy today. I have a mother and a sister. Tomorrow the officer in charge is single with no children at all – at least which he is willing to confess to. Report to this working-party tomorrow at the address on the letter. If you don't turn up we shall shoot all three of you." He grinned: "I'm not joking. Some of my colleagues enjoy shooting people."

Adam was not required to go to Germany – yet; he was able to work locally in a work-gang under the supervision of German civilian engineers. Their tasks were to widen and strengthen railway tracks and bridges to take heavy traffic: trains which would run east. *It seemed obvious to the Poles: Poland first and Russia next.*

He was collected by a truck in the town centre and dropped off there at night. The group consisted of young lads like himself and others too old to serve in the army: some were educated white-collar workers unused to manual work in the open and who found it heavy-going, while others like Adam were used to outdoor work and made nothing of it.

This motley crew became good friends and developed a cohesiveness which compensated for the disciplined and strict way they were treated; they were not free, but they remained human beings, with homes to return to and families who waited for them.

As he walked home one evening, Adam realised that the state of affairs where he could stay at home and work locally, was temporary:

there had to be a limit to the number of railway bridges in the neighbourhood that needed widening! He would be moved on out of the
reach of his home, without choice, and probably for the worse; but for
the moment he was happy enough.

He was a sort of slave now and the first lessons of slavery had been
hard. He realised that some of the things that he had done were stupid
and dangerous not only to himself but to others – Miss Zbucki would
not have approved of the painting of the fence. However, he thought
that he had resisted the slave-masters and, although punished, he had
done himself and his family some good. He was after all walking home
and not just picking turnips in a muddy German field!

He had challenged the system and changed his fate for the better. He
had discovered that his tormentors were human beings too, sometimes
very like him; they were malleable and, if he was careful and curbed
his impulsiveness, then he might make things work out.

For his sister Rosa, the signs looked not too bad. The school
remained open although many of the children and staff were gone.
There was a new Head Teacher, a severe German lady. She told them
that they were German now and for most of them there was nothing to
fear. Schooling was to change. Class sizes would be larger and fewer
subjects were to be taught. There was no need to teach some subjects at
all for in the jobs of the future there would be no need for some of the
skills they had learnt in the past. But they would all have the opportunity
of learning German. School-hours would be shorter and they would be
able to leave school at thirteen years of age which, she said, would
come as a relief to their families.

The new Head finished with a peroration. The Third Reich had its
enemies: communists, Jews, and other criminals. It was necessary to
deal with these people, and, indeed, anyone who opposed National
Socialism and it's Führer. She said: "Heil Hitler," and gave the Nazi
salute. Some of the children laughed. They hadn't seen anyone give the
salute before and thought it very funny. The Head blushed and looked
very cross. This was the first salute she had given in public, although
she had practised it before a mirror in her bedroom.

Rosa did not know what this meant for her. Would she be regarded
as a safe person with nothing to worry about when her father had been
treated as a criminal and put in a camp?

Her mother said: "That teacher is talking about Jews and real criminals: those sort of people are not safe."

" Jewish children do not come to school at all now," Rosa said.

"Well there you are then, that just shows you doesn't it?" was her mother's reply.

Miss Zbucki was no longer at school and Adam wondered about her fate. He could not imagine her working in a field or in a factory, if alive, that is. What was she doing? He knew that not everyone had survived, and it was known, although there were no radio broadcasts or newspapers to confirm it, that many people had been shot; clever people with professional skills, community leaders and patriots.

Among his workmates, there were some who had lost friends and relatives. Some people had been picked up at work or at home without warning, sometimes in the middle of the night, and no one knew what had happened to them.

Adam thought: "Well, perhaps, these people had been very foolish, or maybe they had done something wrong. They might have deserved to be arrested, and other people did not know the true reasons." But he was sorry for their relatives. Of course, it was unfair on them.

Was Miss Zbucki a criminal? He thought not. She was a patriot as he was, but she would have been careless and told the Germans about her true feelings. They would have punished her for that.

He thought of her soft hands with their long slender fingers and pink nails. How could they survive? Passionately, he wanted both her and her nails to survive. "If only I could help her," he thought. But he knew that he couldn't, even with his new found powers.

For the moment he felt happy, living for the moment, breathing good air in the open and loving the familiar people; but at that moment also he felt with foreboding the impermanency of it all. He licked his finger and held it up in the air to dry. "That is how it is," he said to himself, "that is history, and I am part of it."

In her kitchen Sophie finished her soup. There was no need for her to rush. There were no animals or lodgers to feed – and how quiet it was without them. It was not so long ago that she sat in this room full of dread and thinking about the awful disasters that were about to overwhelm them. They had been engulfed and, coming up for air, they had survived. Adam was still here, and Rosa: they could look after each other. Mary could look after herself, and she would be all right if she kept warm and fed herself properly.

Her heart was heavy for Janek and as for her husband – she sighed – she couldn't think about him. She would pray for him; but hope was her last enemy. Sophie knew that he might not return. She cried a little for him, as she had done on every day since his arrest.

The manner of Ludvig's arrest worried her, and she thought about it yet again. Someone had betrayed Ludvig to the police, but she did not know who it was. How did the police know that he was at Paula's? She felt fairly sure that she had not been followed on the train for it was small with few passengers, and she would have noticed these policemen. She was sure they were not on the train. These policemen came from Katowice. How did they know that Ludvig was in Paula's house and that he was wanted by the new authorities?

Had a neighbour become suspicious and reported Ludvig's presence? She found this difficult to believe. How would the police know that she would be coming at that precise time? Only her relatives knew the time of arrival. Paula insisted that she had warned her daughter to say nothing to anyone about Ludvig being in the house and, of course, her daughter did not know the planned time of arrival. Neither Herman nor her sister, who alone had known, had said anything to anyone, they had told her.

Sophie did not have a satisfactory reply to her own questions. She realised that denunciation was a feature of life now, sometimes because people were afraid of being branded as not cooperating and for others out of greed or a wish to curry favour. You could be shot for harbouring a wanted person. People were hidden and discovered and other people punished for it here in her own town.

Ludvig had been betrayed: she was sure of that. But who did it? She comforted herself with the thought that Ludvig was bound to be discovered at some time, and at least no one had been harmed for hiding him.

The family was very short of money. Adam had told her of a new plan he had for making some and she thought that this might work out. She knew she could rely on him. At least there were fewer people to feed. The neighbours had been supportive and were all agreed that they would look out for each other.

Last night there had been a clear sky and a full moon. The sky was full of stars. She knew that the light from these stars took many years to reach Earth. Adam had read somewhere, and told her, that there were millions of stars. He said that there was no constant mass of stars: millions were created and millions burnt up continuously.

Sophie found this difficult to follow. Could it be true that by the time you saw a star, perhaps a really bright star, that it had burnt itself out? And were these stars, that looked so fixed, really dashing around the universe with a future as uncertain as human beings?

She thought that was an important consideration: for if there was an inconstant state for stars, a sort of permanent state of flux, no matter how bright they seemed, perhaps there was a similar state for human beings.

She sighed again. "I don't understand it," she spoke aloud. But as she said it she knew that she did. "*Nothing would last forever, even for the conqueror. Your days and his were numbered: while there might be little that you could do today, it was certain that he would not prevail in the long term, no matter what he thought or did.*"

Sophie was comforted by this thought, got herself up and began to prepare the lunch-time meal, just as she always did.

CHAPTER 5

IN THOSE EARLY days of occupation and annexation, the inhabitants of P. entered into a new world, into an existence where their fate and everyday life was to be determined not by their energies and talents but by their ancestry and origin. In this Kafkesque new world an army of bureaucrats, making up the regulations as they went along, classified every citizen to new and baffling rules.

At the top of the new social pile were ethnic Germans who had full citizenship rights and benefited from lower taxation, jobs in the public service and the day-to-day deferment of others. Adam and his family came into a lesser category of volksdeutsch, third-class German status. They were dubbed State Citizens; in many respects their rights were similar to those of the ethnic German, but they were excluded from public service and membership of the Nazi Party. Their status was infinitely preferable to that of the Pole who had no citizenship rights; a Pole was excluded from any professional or public service, was paid less than his German counterpart for similar work, and paid higher taxes. A Pole had no legal right to own property and his house and personal possessions could be taken from him at any time without notice or compensation.

A Pole had to identify himself by a badge and give way to Germans in the streets and shops, when he was allowed to use them – some shops being designated for Germans only. A Pole had to show respect at all times to his German master by saluting a German soldier when encountered. Unless it could be proved that a Pole could not speak German, all communication with an official whether spoken or written had to be in German.

The professional classes in Poland were systematically killed or sent to concentration camps. A situation was rapidly created where no Pole filled a professional position in society, and with children not expected to be trained or educated for any advanced skill, the surviving Polish population was intended to become 'lumpen proletariat', so that a visitor might exclaim: "No wonder the Poles could not keep their nation, lacking as they do anyone with the capability to run the country."

The only group worse off than a Pole was the Jew, regardless of his national origin. In time the Pole felt himself similarly treated to the Jew but there was a vital difference: both groups might be robbed of all they possessed, uprooted from their homes and moved many thousands of miles into camps and restricted territories and arbitrarily shot; but most Poles avoided these disasters and there was no master plan in existence to destroy them all, whereas ninety per cent of Poland's three million Jews were to be systematically murdered.

This then was the new world-order in which Adam and his family found themselves. It was an order which destroyed the basis of trust between people: the initial camaraderie of Adam's work-gang turned to suspicion and awkwardness. Adam found himself earning more than men three times his age because they wore a Polish badge and he did not. Whereas he had nothing immediate to fear, they had everything; on several occasions men from some outlying areas failed to report for work and it was learnt later that they had been deported to the directly governed Polish territories so that German immigrants could take their homes and farms.

Whatever their feelings about their country, his workmates knew that they would be more secure and their families safer if they became German, and they discussed how they could become so. It was known that the authorities were indulgent about citizenship claims as the bureaucrats had targets for increasing the German population and, if you could establish a German relative, you might be reclassified.

Alternatively you might be able to prove a Latvian, Lithuanian or Ukrainian grandparent and reclassify your nationality that way; and, as the German authorities as part of their plan to destroy the concept of Poland played off one national group against another, this might work to your benefit. But would it? You couldn't be sure because the politics might change. Each man tried to do his utmost to protect himself and his loved ones; the everyday catch phrases became: "*Me first*" and "*I am one of you.*"

Early in the spring of 1940 on a bright sunny morning, spoilt only by a cold gusting wind from the east, Adam made his way to the town centre. There life seemed to go on as normal. The market was busy as usual but people were more sombre and the confusion of many tongues was gone replaced by German and, more subdued, Polish. Jews wore their badges and Poles went about their usual tasks, but warily although there was no immediate danger to *them*.

The German military had moved on, to be replaced by the new police force and in the background a small detachment of the SS with their distinctive black uniforms; but today there wasn't a policeman to be seen.

In the square he met many of his market-trader mates who exchanged greetings and entered into the usual badinage with him but without the gossip. It was no longer safe or comfortable to discuss the fate or probable destiny of missing faces and there was an unwritten compact not to do so.

As he pushed through the crowd of shoppers he felt something thrust into his hand but looking around he could not see who had put it there. It was a leaflet and, when later he felt it safe to read, he saw that it came from a Polish resistance movement, and that it gave advice to Poles on how to react to the occupation.

Poles were advised not to collaborate with the enemy in any way while avoiding putting themselves in obvious danger. His countrymen were urged to put their normal courtesy aside; if, for example, they were asked the way they should avoid giving it. And it was unwise to make a noise, to laugh or appear happy in the street, for this might be captured in a German propaganda film showing the outside world that the Poles were content with their lot.

Most important of all, they were to speak Polish. Even if they knew German and were addressed in it, they should reply in Polish, apologising for their lack of German and inviting the questioner to respond in Polish. Adam decided that he would take this advice and from that moment when confronted with the authorities he spoke only his own language. He felt easier in his mind once he had taken the decision, and later he knew that many of his countrymen had decided to do the same.

As Adam made his way up a small side-road which wound upwards from the central square, he felt a tug on his sleeve and an arm steered him gently into a small shop selling leather goods and souvenirs. As he expressed his surprise, Joseph put his finger to his lips to command Adam's silence and beckoned him into the small back-room of the shop. Adam looked over his shoulder to see whether he had been observed but, apart from the shop assistant going about his tasks oblivious to strangers, he could see no one.

Joseph did not look at all well; he was thinner and, for a young boy whose face had always expressed animation and fun, worried. He was feverishly excited and keen to talk; and as Adam was curious, he let him do so without his usual level of interruption.

Joseph told him that his family had lost all their businesses and property which had been seized and given to German immigrants.

"What about this shop?" said Adam.

"We have an arrangement. We passed the ownership of the business to an ethnic German on the understanding that we could continue to draw a small income from it and live in the apartment above the shop."

"We trust him," he said, seeing Adam's expression of disbelief, and nodding in the direction of the shop assistant.

"Look," he continued, "I am trusting you in telling *you* this."

And when Adam nodded, he continued: "We have no illusions. We shall be taken from here, from this town, all of we Jews and shot or put in a camp."

"Yes, we shall be," he said, as Adam murmured that it might not happen.

"My parents are not going to do anything to try to escape, they think they are too old and are resigned to what might happen, but Rebecca and I are going to try," and his voice dropped to a whisper.

Joseph's plan was to reach the Russian-occupied part of the country where he hoped to make himself obscure and useful. "*They might kill us but not because we are Jews,*" he said. He smiled and Adam was relieved to see it.

His sister Rebecca and he were to disguise themselves as best they could. Rebecca was a jolly girl with brown hair and a light complexion who might at first glance be taken as German; but Joseph was unmistakably Jewish. His plan was to dirty himself and to carry a tool kit in the hope that he would be taken to be a workman and so not attract any attention. A Polish friend was to drive them as close to the frontier as possible and they would walk the rest of the way.

Adam thought it might just work. He felt a pang of discomfort: there were at least two people willing to help these Jews. Why not him?

"Joseph," he said diffidently, "where are you going to head for, where will you stay?"

"I don't know. We have some thoughts about it: but we're not sure."

"Well, I am willing to give you the name and address of my relatives in Lvov. I'm not saying that they will help you, but they might put you up for a night or two until you find a Jewish family. I won't write it down and I don't want you to either. You must remember it."

Adam said the address several times so that Joseph could learn it.

As Adam left Joseph he was in turmoil. Had he made a mistake? Were his relatives in danger now? He felt that he should not have done anything but that it was now too late. Anyway, in all probability, they would not make it to the border so nothing would happen. He thought about Miss Zbucki. What would she think about it? He felt in his heart that she would have approved. But he had been impulsive again, he hadn't really thought it through, and she would not have thought much of that.

In the time he had available, Adam engaged in the task of rebuilding the family fortune. After the loss of the farm animals, their neighbours had rallied round to restore the position: one gave a pig, another some chickens, and the geese came back to their small pond. It was not possible to keep the larger animals any more because they had neither the time or money to sustain them. It was still possible to grow vegetables and the orchard provided good apples in the autumn. These foodstuffs were useful because in a local economy starved of money barter became common and the Chwisteks were able to exchange their products to meet their everyday needs.

They held a party to celebrate their restocking, but although they all made an effort it was a sad affair as their thoughts were of absent friends and of those whom they had lost – the dead and the temporarily absent. At the end of their celebration, when the immediate effect of the vodka had worn off, they cried for themselves and for others, and for their traduced and diminished country.

Adam created a new business for his mother, the liming of farm buildings. He was aware how desperately difficult this work was for her. It was physically hard and carried out in all weathers in cold and dirty surroundings, not at all the sort of work he would have wished for her. He did all he could to help her whenever he had the time, mixing the lime and accompanying her to the farms.

His mother became a familiar figure among the local farmers, who admired her for her tenacity; she acquired new friends who went out of their way to help her, so she thought that the good Lord had loved and cared for her in adversity.

Over the coming weeks Adam's work carried him away from home, too far to return every night. His gang were billeted in a variety of accommodation, most commonly a school hall or farm barn, and it was some three months before he was in his town centre again. On the outskirts of his town a new sign proclaimed it as Judenfrei* – and in the market-place no Jew was to be seen.

He made his way to 'Joseph's shop' where Joseph had predicted the fate of the local Jewish community. The shop assistant was in his place and greeted Adam. He said that he remembered Adam and his visit well and answered his agitated questions calmly and fully.

The assistant told him that about six weeks ago, and without notice, the town had been surrounded by a platoon of German Order Police; from Hamburg, he thought. They had cards with the names and addresses of local Jewish families. A house to house search was made by a detachment of SS and trawnikis.† Jewish families were driven out of their houses, with only hastily thrown together hand luggage, and assembled in the market-place.

Throughout the town screams and shots were heard. It appeared that the trawnikis had been given orders to shoot the very old, young children and the sick; but mothers with small children were seen in the market, so perhaps some of the beasts disobeyed orders, having children of their own.

In the market-place there were a large number of Jews, he thought over a thousand. They were made to parade; able-bodied men were put onto trucks presumably for hard-labour somewhere – nobody said where to – and the women and children were marched off to the rail station.

Adam turned pale and he thought he would be physically sick. His legs buckled and he fell forwards onto his knees. The assistant found him a chair and gave him a glass of water.

The assistant said with determination and conviction: "Look, there is a problem with these Jews. There are too many of them, and they own and run everything. Look at me? Would I be owning and running a nice little shop if there hadn't been plans to deal with the Jews? I'm not saying that they should have been treated in that way. *Don't get me wrong. I feel sorry for them but they did have it coming.* And it's our turn now to run these businesses. It's only fair."

* Jew free.

†Ukrainian prisoners of war released and trained for the nasty business of 'deportations'.

Adam swallowed hard. "What happened to the Pstrong's? What happened to Joseph?"

The assistant looked at him closely and hesitated before replying.

"I have nothing against *you*. You seem a reasonable enough boy to me, and I know you were a friend of Joseph's, but I have to be very careful about saying anything about *this* family."

Adam protested that they were not friends of his: rather that he and Joseph were at school together.

The assistant still hesitated.

"Well," he said at last, "I can tell you *this*. Joseph and Rebecca were no longer here when this happened. They hadn't been here for about two weeks. I don't know where they were or where they are now. As for his parents, they were taken away and I don't know where they are either."

And he wouldn't say anything more. Adam saw that the assistant had said more than he had intended and wanted him to go.

This story turned out to be true and was confirmed by his mates in the market and by his mother. His mates said that it was the most horrible experience of their lives. Old people and children had been shot and their bodies were left in the streets for days. At the railway station the Jews had been herded into cattle trucks that were far too crowded, like animals, and the guards had beaten and clubbed people without reason; they seemed to enjoy it, this beating of helpless people.

Some of the traders said that there were businesses to be picked up for very little and he should think about finding out whether there was anything for him. Was there? Could he? He was tempted but then he thought it was not possible. After all what was he but a sort of slave labourer.

He reproached his mother.

"Why did you not tell me?"

Sophie stroked his hair and comforted him.

"Adam," she said gently and softly, "Joseph is a very capable boy, he will look after himself and Rebecca. His parents will be in a camp somewhere, but they will be all right. Their position is like your father's. It's not good, of course, it isn't. But one day they will be released, when this war is over and everyone comes to their senses; they will come home, you'll see."

He knew that she believed it would happen and, as he did not want to upset her, he let it go.

For some weeks Adam was not his normal self. He was not so certain of himself and had lost his usual bounce. At lunch-breaks and in the evening he did not join in with the others, preferring to be on his own. Although he was not fond of reading, and read slowly and with difficulty, he began to devour any book he could get his hands on, and seeing this the older men lent him their own books and encouraged him.

He realised, without the help of Shakespeare, that there was more to the world than was dreamt of in his philosophy. He had to catch up, to bridge the gap, and literature held the clues. Sometimes he felt that he had become wiser and more knowing, and then something happened, and he knew his new knowledge wasn't good enough.

In June 1940, as Adam was helping to widen bridges in Byton some twenty kilometres from his home, the German armies were unleashed upon France. It was the apogee of German military triumph, and the Poles noted with distress, but wry satisfaction, that in this campaign it seemed that the French, Belgian and the British armies together had inflicted fewer casualties on the Germans than the despised Polish army of a year earlier.

The British seemed not to have recognised that they had been beaten and continued to mount sporadic bombing on German targets including Silesia. Adam's work gang was moved to G., an industrial town to the north west. British planes had bombed factories in the town and the German authorities decided on a subterfuge. It was decided to build a dummy town of wooden houses and factory buildings, laid out in rows and squares like real buildings, and with street and factory lights.

In G., a nightly blackout was enforced. The only lights visible to attacking planes would be the illuminations of the new town so, it was hoped, it would be their new town which would be attacked. The builders of this new wooden town drew great satisfaction from the construction work. They were proud of it. These wooden houses, were good enough to live in and it saddened them to think that they would be destroyed and that they would have to rebuild them.

The day arrived when, their work completed, the lights of their dummy town were left on. The gang were billeted in the town centre, and when in a few days time it was attacked, they approached their construction work the next morning excited to see what had happened. Not a single building had been bombed but there in the middle of their town attached to its parachute and blowing in the wind was a bomb. It was wooden with words in English painted on it. 'A wooden bomb for a wooden town,' they read, 'With the compliments of the Royal Air Force.'

Even the Germans laughed. The Poles said: "These British are a very funny people. They are hopelessly beaten but do not give up, and make a joke about it. What sort of people are these?" But it was a good joke and the men told their families, who told their neighbours and school friends, and they all concluded that the British had not given up.

Shortly afterwards, at Ehrenforst, where there was a prisoner of war camp, Adam saw some of these British at first hand. His gang was helping to construct a factory extension and British prisoners of war were helping with light work. The prisoners were issued with shovels and brooms and were meant to be clearing up after demolition work. What they actually did was to pick up rubble from one place and put it down in another; and then someone else would pick it up and take it back – and so on. The Germans did not supervise this activity and seemed to have given up on it. It was sometimes difficult to know who *were* the prisoners as the British were extremely rude to the Germans.

Apart from the desultory attempts to move rubbish from one place to another there appeared to be two main activities: making tea and playing cards. The English had made themselves a coal burner, having scavenged some metal and the coal, and on this they brewed tea. Every hour or so they downed tools and had a tea-break, which they claimed was their right; and during the tea-break they played cards. All this was accompanied by a good deal of what Adam learnt was swearing: it was all fucking Germans, fucking tea and sodding weather.

The Poles and the Germans were very impressed with this behaviour. They were a poor lot these English, physically unimpressive and even weedy, but they did not look at all like prisoners or a beaten race; deluded people, perhaps, but not defeated.

Although they had to be careful, the gang were able to talk to the prisoners and they found to their surprise that they included a Pole. This man explained that he was working in Britain when the war started and had joined the Royal Air Force. He flew a Spitfire over France and it was shot down. The gang wanted to know what he thought about the war.

"Would the British be beaten, like the Poles?"

"No, they won't be beaten. The difference is that Britain is surrounded by water and Poland by land. Britain commands the sea and the air. So it can't be beaten. Germany cannot beat Britain," he said with finality.

They knew that this did not mean that Britain could beat Germany but who knows, they said to each other, so long as the war goes on anything might happen. At the end of September they all became aware that the British air force had defeated the Luftwaffe over Britain and that Hitler had called off a planned invasion; and the British prisoners, who were jubilant, told them anyway.

Adam was encouraged. It was Germany's first defeat. Perhaps, it might turn out that the Germans could be beaten, the Polish prisoner might be right about the British winning in the air and at sea. Adam had seen a news film of the British fleet parading in British waters. He was very impressed. He had retained the images: these mighty ships moving towards you, silver-white and threatening, bobbing up and down in choppy grey seas and under clear blue skies. For comfort, he had got into the habit of bringing up these images before he fell asleep, and he often woke to the gentle movement of the sea and the blue sky up above.

Sophie became busy with her lime-washing business and set out from home to do this work on a regular basis. Her horse and cart became familiar to local farmers as she traversed the narrow country lanes in most weathers, and they came to accept her as part of the landscape.

She became aware at the same time of two things of importance to her. First, she caught sight of herself in a mirror and was shocked. She looked much older, her hair was greying and her face had become wrinkled from exposure to wind and the cold. Secondly, she was being observed. A local farmer had decided that his farm buildings required rather more liming than was strictly necessary and a business relationship was starting to develop into a friendship.

Peter Voller was an earnest dark-haired farmer in his forties and of a mixed Hungarian–Polish background. Above average height, he was slim, in pleasant contrast to Sophie's stocky Polish neighbours. His great gift was his occupation of space. He had a way of moving so that he was always perfectly placed: never too close to invade your privacy and never too far to lose the intimacy of his company. He was never clumsy: he did not bump into things or brush against them. He created by his very presence a wonderful sense of intimacy and reassurance.

Peter never said much, but you remembered everything he did say. He was always kind in his remarks: if he could not think of anything pleasant to say about a person or a situation, and usually he could, he would say nothing.

Sophie enjoyed his presence and took reassurance from it. Work done on his farm, he gave her the hospitality of his table and food which he cooked himself. He set his offering before her in a way she found thrilling, and which turned her from cowgirl to a lady of gentility.

She knew he was married but his wife never appeared nor was she missed or demanded by him. He asked her what she needed doing on her farm and then without notice he appeared with his tools at the weekends to undertake the tasks she had told him about, which he did perfectly and without payment. So he shared her table and an intimacy arose between them based on respect and the performance of simple household tasks.

After a while, and without anything being said to each other, she found herself thinking about him constantly, and missing him when he was not there. Peter thought about her too. Her presence was with him in early morning light, in the gentle rise of his green meadows, and in the wind sloughing in his trees.

Sophie decided do something about her appearance. She consulted her friend, Anna, who had once worked as a hairdresser, and who confessed that she too had 'let herself go', and they decided to do something about their appearance. Anna brought along some German magazines and they examined the hairstyles. Most of these were impossible and inappropriate in that they were 'coiffures' difficult to create or to maintain: but they gathered ideas from them.

Anna cut Sophie's hair to a more fashionable style and with the help of some beer, and the addition of herbs, Sophie's hair was brought to a better condition. Anna was able to obtain some face-cream and make-up from the beauty salon in which she had worked and they both started and maintained a beauty regime which included keeping out of the sun and the wind whenever they could. New clothes were impossible but they squeezed out some money to buy some good second-hand items and some boots.

Overcome by guilt at this self-seeking pursuit, Sophie bought some clothes for her daughter Rosa and Anna restyled her too.

Sophie looked at this new person in the mirror and was pleased at what she saw: but it wasn't enough. The house needed improvement and she cleaned and polished it. She made new curtains and cushions and changed the furniture around in the living-room until it was worthy of her new self.

Peter did some of the painting for her, which refreshed everything, and they took a pleasure in these changes as something they had done together. They smiled at themselves and into the mirror.

Peter became a more frequent visitor and dropped in unannounced and merged into the household activity without ceremony, becoming part of the household routine. Rosa liked him because of his immense practicality and good nature: he mended her dolls and bedroom furniture without being asked and in such a friendly and unobtrusive way that she felt under no obligation to him. Without being asked to keep a secret, Rosa said nothing about Peter and his visits although she was bursting to tell someone.

All that Mary and Adam knew was that their mother was getting on with things with the help of the neighbours, which was, of course, true. When without realising the consequences of it, Rosa had spoken of Peter in their presence, they assumed he was a friendly neighbour, which of course, he was. They thought nothing of it at all and did not even remember his name. They were pleased to see that their mother was happier and on top of things and to hear her singing in the kitchen.

Sophie thought that as the family approached the first anniversary of life under the occupation, they had reached a kind of normality. They went about their business without hindrance and maintained their solidarity. It was all quite possible. There was the menace and problems of the war, of course, but it did not really affect them; and, in any case there was nothing that they could do about that.

CHAPTER 6

THE PERIOD OF nomadic working based on leaving and returning home came to an end for Adam when without notice he was posted to N., a small industrial town some ten kilometres from Dresden. There together with another boy, Antoni, like Adam a new Polish-German creation, he arrived for duty at a newly-built synthetic rubber factory.

The general manager to whom they reported turned out to be a German Silesian – from the 'other side' of the Oder – of Polish origin and Polish speaking. A small, sturdy and energetic person, he was on the particular morning of their arrival pleased to see them: bursting into Polish, offering them chairs, and arranging for their refreshment.

Karl Hoffman, introducing himself, said that they should call him Karl and expressed the sincere emotion that he wanted them to be happy in their work. They would not be content, he continued, until they had found suitable accommodation and he was pleased that he was able to help them. He had some accommodation in his very own home for which he could vouch. He gave them instructions on how to reach his house and explained that his wife was expecting them.

Frau Hoffman, a thin middle-aged German, created an impression of permanent worry. She led them to a kind of summer-house in the garden – somewhat dilapidated and unused – and as she opened the door they ducked to avoid the pigeons, the established non-paying guests, who flew at them and beyond. "Well, boys," she said briskly seeing their astonishment at the offering, "there's a war on, you know. It will clean up. I will bring you some water and soap and you can make a start." It did clean up well although the smell and nuisance of the displaced pigeons was hard to shake off.

Frau Hoffman provided them with camp-beds and clean pillows and blankets and explained the household regime. They were to receive two meals a day in the kitchen and the food and accommodation charges would be deducted at source from their weekly wages.

They were to discover that the Hoffmans were Catholics and that by leaving it to the providence of God, and as the result of an active sex life, they had acquired six small children. Adam and Antoni were in the garden because the Hoffman's house, although capacious, was near to bursting to the seams: the eight family members lived cheek by jowl with four lodgers directed to the establishment, like Adam, from the factory. As it turned out, they were pleased to lodge in the summer-house free of the noise and confusion of the Hoffman's household ménage.

Working life at the factory was bearable. Mr Hoffman had stamped his personality on the proceedings. They all worked hard but not excessively so. The long working hours were expected to result in the achievement of certain production targets, and usually, and on the whole, they did. It appeared that the factory responded to requests from the authorities for higher output and achieved these targets also. Mr Hoffman involved his work force in discussions about these additional demands and, because of this, they did their best to help him; he was reasonable and so were they. This behaviour was not a commonplace at the time and the workers were grateful.

The factory had its informers: workers at various levels in the plant who reported back to the local administration and the security police: but everyone knew who they were and avoided the giving of offence or unnecessary or careless information about themselves or others.

In time the informers became discouraged because their bosses did nothing as a result of their regular reports: the factory did what was expected of it and performed and everyone's nose was clean. The factory performed well because of the benign and good-natured governance of Mr Hoffman who succeeded in annoying no one and remaining the kindly man he was despite the opportunity and provocation to be otherwise.

Adam entered into what might be called 'the university of life'. It was a large factory with several hundred workers but exigencies of war and National Socialist policy meant that those who laboured there were an extraordinary lot: you were as likely to work alongside a university professor as a labourer: and with a gentile as a Jew, as defined by the Third Reich; and among the mix of nationalities within the power of the State; and there were many more women than men.

Conversation was possible; as you worked, or in coffee-breaks and in the canteen at lunch-time and in the evenings. The canteen had a radio which kept you in touch with a wider world as seen through the eyes of the German authorities. Older workers knew how to sieve the propaganda for truth by the analysis of commission and omission and after a while Adam could do this also.

The canteen was an important place with major opportunities of exchange. To begin with it was for Adam an opportunity to play cards and, following his usual practice, he set himself an objective: in this instance to finance himself from his winnings so that he could send his weekly pay-packet home to his mother unopened; and with a very few lapses this is what he achieved.

It was necessary to rotate his playing circles so that others did not pick on him or resent his success, and whenever possible he chose the weaker players. Playing took up a large part of his free time and kept him out of mischief – and it built him a reputation as a success and someone to be looked out for. The practice also circulated him not only around the canteen but across the factory, wherever these activities were discussed, and as a consequence people took notice of him.

Socially Adam hardly existed. He was working long hours on six and sometimes seven days of the week, and arriving back late to his lodgings. Sundays in N. were very dull fare as the mainly Catholic popu-lation treated the sabbath as a day of rest. Apart from the occasional visit to a beer cellar with workmates of his age, where his drinking was limited by his purse, and a few visits to the social club of his local church, his leisure activities were severely limited.

In the unnatural and tension-ridden factory surroundings, however, things were very different. Relationships developed quickly and were consummated passionately at every conceivable opportunity and place: sexual gropings were a commonplace in the lavatories, empty offices or the cycle-park, and they were hardly to be missed. No one thought it wrong. They all knew that life was short. Away from family and friends, men and women sought consolation and reassurance that all might be well. As the Japanese would come to say and practice, 'There is no shame when abroad'.

Adam was tempted but did not know how to start. He was approached, started out and withdrew. He made some friends and within the bound-aries he had set himself his friendship was valued. What he discovered was that he responded best to older women and he came to value the warmth of those of German and, in particular, Jewish background: not that they were truly Jewish, rather they had Jewish relatives that caused them to be classified as Jews – a Jewish grandparent or parent – so that they failed the regulations and were treated as half or quarter Jewish and therefore not acceptable because of their race.

To Adam it was obvious that these girls shared his sense of family values, there was more to them, they were better educated than the Polish girls, and responded to him in a more feminine manner. But whenever he advanced, and at the moment of his acceptance and when the chance of adventure beckoned, he drew back. To the fear of sexual exploration, which was largely unknown to him, was added the feeling of shame and the risk of the ridicule of associating with a Jewess. He felt sure that they must feel this too – contact with a gentile would not be their choice in the usual way. In this he was wrong so far as the girls were concerned but he was too young and too inexperienced to know it.

He worked for a while with a Jewish girl from Berlin. Hannah was a pretty dark-haired girl in her thirties who had worked as a nurse before her summary racial reclassification. She was glad that nothing worse than forced labour had befallen her. She liked Adam in an uncompli-cated way, falling for his brash manner and Polish good looks. Her nursing duties had released her from many inhibitions and she was not shy in approaching Adam and in making clear that his attentions would be appreciated.

Getting an uncertain response and not taking hesitation for an answer, Hannah took advantage of a break for Christmas jollity. Finding Adam on his own in an unoccupied office, she pinned him to the wall unbuttoned him and brought them both to a climax: "Very good, Adam I liked that," she said, rearranging herself, and skipping away.

But she didn't approach Adam again and he said nothing to her.

It was Adam's first fully consummated sex and his head was in a whirl. He was relieved that he had performed and excited by the response. How could it be continued? And could it be? Did he really want to carry it on and, as important, did Hannah? He did not know the answers to any of these questions and it all seemed immensely difficult to him. How could he really? Hannah said nothing but she smiled at him and he knew it was all right by her. But nothing was said by either of them and the moment passed.

When it had become history, Hannah took him by the arm and said gently and sweetly to him: "Adam, it was lovely, I really liked it but it can't happen again. I shall get fond of you, and then where will we be. Impossible, you can understand that. You will find lots of nice girls attracted to you, safe girls that will not get you into trouble."

And before he could argue she kissed him on the cheek and moved quickly away.

Adam knew that she was right. Sexual relationships with Jews could get you into serious trouble. He was pained though by having to let go when it had only just begun. Why should it be wrong? He drew back into himself. If he couldn't have Hannah he didn't want anyone. Perhaps, if he liked Jews best he would never have anyone and his life would have been written-off. "What a waste, written-off at the age of eighteen," he said to himself.

In January 1942 something happened to their benevolent boss Mr Hoffman. His workers did not know the cause, or exactly what had happened, but Mr Hoffman was removed from his job and replaced by a very different person. It was thought that an enemy had taken advantage of some lapse or indulgence on his part and informed on him. In this respect it was no different from past complaints that had been made about him: but, perhaps, on this occasion it was more serious; or maybe, it was cumulative – perhaps you got black marks for each offence and when you got to a certain score you were removed.

Later the rumour spread that he had been falsifying personnel records and protecting people he respected from being transferred elsewhere. They thought that this might be true because it was just like him to do it and falsification of records was easily detectable in an inspection and regarded as a serious crime.

Mr Hoffman was transferred elsewhere and had to sell his house in a hurry. This would have required Adam to find new lodgings, but before the event he was summoned to the new manager's office and told brusquely that he was to be transferred to a factory in Krakov, in the directly governed territories, where they would know how to deal with him. "You are a trouble-maker Chwistek, and we don't want you here. Good riddance to you." Adam found out that there were others to be transferred so he did not take the rejection seriously, he was just sorry to go and for Mr Hoffman and his family.

Adam travelled to Krakov by train with six other boys. Arriving in good time they decided to sight-see because none of them had been to this beautiful and ancient town before. It was a sad and sobering occasion. The town itself had escaped the worst of the war and at first sight all appeared normal. But there were fewer Poles on the streets and a general air of despondency. German soldiers and policemen were everywhere and on several occasions they saw the black uniforms of the SS.

They came across the Jewish quarter, now walled up so that the inhabitants could not leave and they could not enter. They were turned back by armed guards but not before they had a sight of the new ghetto's crowded streets.

"Why are these Jews crowded together as prisoners?" they asked themselves.

"Because they are going to be worked as slaves and then killed," was the reply.

And some of them thought and some of them said: "And that's right, they deserve it."

While others, Adam among them, said or thought: "Poor buggers," and "I'm glad it's not me."

But the ghetto was the reason that they were there in Krakov at that time. Jews, it had been proclaimed, were to live and work in the ghetto and many important factories outside the ghetto were emptied of their Jewish workers. They and others were the replacements for the Jews. A shiver ran down Adam's spine: *it was not a nice thought that you were standing in for a Jew.*

The easy ways of N. were not duplicated in Krakov. They were billeted in an old Polish army barracks where they were locked in after 10.00 p.m. The food was poor and badly cooked. In the factory they worked long hours without a break and conversation while working was forbidden. The company's security guards patrolled the gangways and infringement of working rules were punished by beatings. Yet despite these unpromising surroundings spirits were not low and people found ways of circumventing the rules and humanising the surroundings.

Outside the factory walls much of the town was subject to restriction and curfew. This was not a free city except for the conquerors, and for Poles and Jews it was something far worse – it could be – and for many it was – a gateway to their death. And they saw this. They saw people being arrested, beaten up and ridiculed in the street and people shot dead and their bodies left in the gutter. "There but for the grace of God go I," they muttered as they scurried past.

These young boys believed that they had become inured to happenings in the street: "It is not our business," they said to themselves.

"There is nothing we can do." Then on one Saturday afternoon when they were leaving the factory to walk back to the barracks they saw a man spread out on a wall and being kicked and shouted at by a German soldier, not a particular soldier but an ordinary everyday one. As they approached along the pavement they saw that the man was Polish from his identity badge. Should they go back? They didn't. The soldier was demanding the man's wallet. Not his identity card but his wallet. They thought the Pole to be respectable – not a thief or a partisan – and a common fellow like themselves.

Without thinking Adam rushed at the soldier closely followed by the others. They pushed him to the ground and punched and kicked him until he was not moving any more. They shouted to the Pole to run and he belted into a side street, where they followed him running for dear life. No one followed them, there were no shouts, and the few bystanders in the street stood aside to let them pass.

For a long time at the factory they expected the authorities to arrest them: but no one came. Perhaps, they wondered, when they got back to the barracks there would be black uniforms and a van waiting: but there never was. Or, perhaps in the street they would come across this soldier again and be recognised: but they changed their route to and from the factory and never saw the soldier again.

They had got away with it. "How stupid we were," they said, "to have had this rush of blood to the head." They decided not to be seen together again and started to disown each other as a sort of defence against the likely investigation. As time passed they thought of themselves as heroes – partisans resisting the enemy. But Adam was ashamed of himself. The advice of the partisans was not to resist but to look after yourself and your family, so he knew he had been foolish. Miss Zbucki was looking at him. She nodded her head in disapproval but she smiled at him also. *So he knew that the resistance had been a mistake but not something wrong.*

In Germany and the occupied territories there was an acute shortage of labour. Jew and gentile alike thought: "They will not get rid of me because I am useful, they will need me." But little did they know at this time that they were destined to be murdered and that their absence would be felt but unheeded.

The barons of this new empire vied for acceptable labour; human beings were pushed and pulled across Europe at the will of the most powerful. While the military need was to move millions of soldiers and their weapons both east and west, other men were moving millions, on the same rail system, to their enslavement and death – against all reason and humanity.

It was a great relief to him, and some thirty others, to be called into the canteen and to be told that they were being released from their work at Krakov to work on building a new factory at Auschwitz. It would be near his home and he would be working in the open air again. After the four months spent working in Krakov anything else would be preferable. They learnt that some Jews were to be released from the ghetto to take their place in the factory. Apparently what was to be built at Auschwitz had a very high priority.

Adam was given a weekend pass to go home before he started his new job and it coincided with a visit from his sister Mary. He was back with a happy family again and amazed to find them all looking so well; as they were disconcerted to see him looking so poorly. They decided to spoil him and to try to bring him back to his normal self, although in the time available this was not going to be possible.

He started to tell them about Krakov but seeing their faces cloud over, he stopped. "Why make them unhappy," he thought, "when they can be joyful, for these moments of happiness are like water in the desert."

Rosa, bringing him coffee in bed, curled up beside him and chattered gaily about her life, her school and her friends, and then she said, dropping her voice with the importance of the subject which she could suppress no more:

"Mummy has a boy friend."

"What, what do you mean, a boy friend?"

Rosa told him about Peter and how he was often in the house doing things for Sophie and for her.

"Do you like him?"

"Oh, yes, he's very, very nice."

In the kitchen Adam said: "Tell me about Peter. Who is he? Rosa's been talking about him."

His mother blushed.

"He's a friend – a customer really – and he has helped with some jobs around the house. That's all, he helps out from time to time."

Adam saw that she didn't deny Peter and from his newly-gained sexual awareness he was both pleased and apprehensive for her.

Adam discovered that his mother had already started a conversation about Peter with Mary and that he had interrupted them. He left them to it and went for a walk with Rosa. He was pleased for his mother that she had someone to keep an eye open for her. "Why not, so long as she's careful," he said to himself. His experience had not taught him that falling in love was not about being careful but in being very reckless, in committing yourself to the unknown, and being moved by emotions you do not control.

He would have been more alarmed had he heard what Mary had told his mother and which on no account did she want Adam to know about. Mary had settled in well to her forced labour on the farm: she was popular and trusted by the farm-management, so much so that she often accompanied the farm-manager into town to buy supplies, and she had become fully responsible for the feeding of the farm-labourers.

Mary was happy in her work and had reached the stage that many young girls achieve in their life when they seem to blossom; her short black hair gleamed, making up in sheer good health for what it lost in amateur cut, her skin glowed with the exposure to good air and she had slimmed down by necessary attention to a more limited diet.

She was eminently noticeable and unfortunately she was noticed by the wrong person. When in a farm supplies' wholesaler, she encountered a shy young man, an SS officer in his black uniform with the SS skull and crossbones insignia. He engaged her in conversation, charmingly and with great deference and politeness. He introduced himself formally and bowed. His name was Heinrich Hildenfeldt and he came from Munich.

In a few short minutes Heinrich made her feel like a lady or what she imagined a lady might feel like. She didn't know really because no one had ever treated her in this way. He made her laugh. And then he had helped her carry her bags to the wagon and had clicked his heels and saluted her as she left. He seemed a very nice man she thought and not at all like the image of the SS which she had been given.

"Perhaps it is all propaganda," she thought, although she knew that it wasn't.

"You've made a conquest there," muttered the farm-manager disapprovingly. "You'd better be careful."

She blushed and looked quite lovely as she did so.

"Rubbish, of course not. We won't see *him* again." But she thought: "Well you never know. I wouldn't mind if I did. You shouldn't condemn a whole class of people. Of course, the SS are horrible and do the most dreadful things but that did not mean that all the individual members of it were bad. After all it was war and in war the most dreadful things were done by soldiers of all countries. One day soon the war would be over and everyone would change back to a normal life."

He did want to see her again and a few days later called at the farm. The farm-manager gave her permission to talk to him for a few minutes. They went for a walk which lasted for more than an hour. Heinrich told her about where he lived, about his family, and why he had joined the SS.

He said that he believed in the Nazi ideas of a new society, without racial tension and class divisions. A world of natural justice where Germans could live peacefully free of enemies within and without. "We Germans," he had said, including her. Of course she was a German too and he was speaking of the future of *her* country. Her heart swelled with pride. "What could be better than a mighty country living in peace and in justice for all its citizens?" she concluded.

Heinrich was a Catholic like her and told her that he believed in the values of the church, of the sanctity of marriage and the importance of the family. She was puzzled by this because she knew that Catholic churches had been destroyed in Poland and their priests imprisoned and sometimes shot.

She asked him about this and he explained that in Poland the churches had become the centre of resistance to the new ideas and had to be swept aside. There would be new churches, he explained, which obeyed the civil authorities. And this is what the Pope wanted. As he explained these things, she thought that all these actions must be right, and, indeed, inevitable.

Heinrich said to her that he had greatly enjoyed their conversation and that he hoped that they would be able to meet again. She had smiled at him and said that she hoped they would too, but she didn't know how. "How very nice he is," she said to herself, "and how very attractive." She hoped with all her heart that it would be all right and that something might work out.

Mary had been observed with Heinrich by some of the other girls and it soon became clear that they did not all share her vision of the Third Reich. That night, when they were preparing for bed, a group of girls surrounded her led by a sturdy fair haired girl from Czechoslovakia called Greta.

"Is it true, Mary? Are you seeing an SS man? The girls have seen you."

Mary was scared. The girls looked excited and threatening.

"No, no, you've got it wrong. An SS man saw *me* in town. I couldn't help it. And he came onto the farm and asked to see me, and I couldn't do anything about that either; but that's the end of it. Look, I'm not to blame. I can't tell the SS to get lost, can I?"

Some of the girls had seen her laughing and walking intimately with this SS man and so they didn't believe her. Mary tried again: "My family has suffered too you know. My uncle is dead and my father is in a dreadful camp."

She pleaded with them and they relented a little.

"No more, Mary."

Greta wagged her finger in Mary's face.

"If we see you with this SS swine again, we shall come for you. Do you understand?"

Mary did understand.

"If he comes onto the farm I shall refuse to have anything to do with him, but I can't prevent him coming."

"Of course you can. Do it or else!"

Sophie hugged her daughter. She had listened very intently to her daughter's account of meeting this handsome, exciting young German and of his courting of her. She remembered how she had felt when first Ludvig had approached her: how her heart had pounded, how she had felt so weak that she had almost fainted; and how she would have done anything to *be* with him and for him. And she thought of Peter and how she felt now, and how different this was – and how good it was, though not the same.

"Do what they tell you, Mary. Don't think about this man. No good can come of it," she said, as she wiped the tears from her daughter's cheeks. She thought of Peter. Could any good come from a friendship with Peter? And if the answer was no, could she give him up? And she cried and Mary wiped away her mother's tears.

They cried and hugged each other throughout the weekend and felt stronger and better by the time of their parting. And they hugged and comforted Adam. Auschwitz would be better they told him, and he could come home more frequently and be fed on home-cooking. Adam needed to believe them. "*Of course, Auschwitz will be better, it could hardly be worse,*" he said to them.

CHAPTER 7

WHEN HER FLOCK had flown off again and Sophie was on her own once more she thought rather sadly about Peter. While he had been a secret from her older children he had occupied an unchallenged position in her heart and in her thoughts. But now that she had been obliged to explain him and her own emotions, defining him and herself, doubts crept in: was she using him to fill in her emptiness, was he a creature of a particular moment and circumstance, or was it something more than this? It hadn't mattered before: it was enough that he was there when she needed him. But now it was self-conscious and she thought she would blush and stammer when next he came.

When he did come, however, it was different. She was bolder with him as if to test her feelings and to know his reaction: and without thinking, he responded. It seemed that they no longer took each other for granted, content to be with each other, easy in their ways: now they were more deliberate and considered and a tension had eased its way in without either of them wanting it. In some way she was challenging him, and she hated herself for it because she had liked the old ways. Peter did not think too much about it for he had already decided that he wanted this woman and that he would do what was needed to win her.

It took him some time to make his move because he did not want to lose her, but one day when they were helping each other clear away and they were unglamorously at the sink together he put his arms around her waist. She swivelled round to face him. Nothing was said. He kissed her and she did not resist. And as she kissed him she swayed back her face showing him that she had waited too long for this moment. He heard her moan and then sigh as if she had come; and as he looked at her, he saw that she was entranced and, to his astonishment, that she had come.

Peter was alarmed and confused at what had happened. He wanted her to sit down and calm herself; but she didn't want to be quiescent and embraced him again. Sophie kissed him gently and fiercely in turns and in these kisses he felt the longing and despair of the slights and loneliness of many years. While he wanted to believe that the longing and the passion was because of him – and him alone – he knew that it wasn't: but he hoped that at least some part of her response was aroused by him.

At last they pulled apart and calmed themselves. Needing something more than water they drank vodka. Very little was said. Sophie lit some candles and they sat at the kitchen table. She looked across at him, seeing his kind face and worried expression, and she stroked his face and smoothed the worry-signs. And he saw this lovely women, whose flushed and translucent face had been caused by him. It was a very emotional and precious moment; but when he had to go he was glad. He needed to think and to understand what had happened. Sophie did not need to think about anything for at this moment she loved this man and he moved her more than she could say.

They embraced each other gently before parting. Now that the Rubicon had been crossed they were in another and stranger land and neither knew what to do or say. Peter thought that he might lose Sophie almost before he gained her. How could he live up to such longing and desire? Nothing in his life had equipped him for high passion. All he knew was that he loved this woman, but he was frightened by what he had put in train.

Sophie thought of Ludvig. When she had lost him she had told herself that she would wait. If he survived the camp to return home she would be waiting there for him. About two months after he had been imprisoned she had received a card from him, from the camp, telling her that he was all right, that he was being well-fed and cared for and doing a worthwhile job. It seemed reassuring but she knew that the authorities forced prisoners to send these cards to their families to create a favourable impression of the camps to the outside world and to hide the reality that they were very rough places. You didn't know what to think and she hadn't heard from him since.

Sophie was a Catholic, not a practising member of her local church, but a Catholic nevertheless. Her marriage vows were for life and for her adultery was a sin. Of course, it hadn't come to this yet but it was in her mind. In the town she knew it to be a commonplace thing for women deprived of their menfolk to start new relationships. That might be all right for others but she had her own values, and she did not want the gossip and sniggers of neighbours and friends behind her back, let alone the reproaches and disappointed faces of those of her friends who were religious.

Sophie decided to make a confession at her church. Although she was not a regular attender, she did go to church on the main feast days, and she did respect and believe in the rituals. She told herself that she needed to share her thoughts and to be held to account for her feelings.

The church was off-putting, dark and empty but for a few poor souls praying, and it took some time before entry to the confessional box summoned a priest. The air was heavy with incense, which she had always disliked, and she became depressed while waiting and was tempted to leave. "Good Lord," she thought. "What on earth am I doing here?" And then a priest came and she slipped into the old and comforting words.

"Forgive me Father I have sinned," she said, drawing confidence as she went on.

"In what way my child have you sinned?"

"I have had impure thoughts father," and she explained.

"My child you have sinned and you are right to confess. It is hard for you, I know, but you must repent while you can. You must give this man up. You must not see him again else you will fall into the sin and shame of adultery from which I shall have difficulty in absolving you."

She realised that it was an inevitable response. Perhaps, she needed the advice before she could stop. She thought it must be so. She was very angry. How foolish of her to come. Now she had been told what to do she was bound to carry through the action of rejection, or by disobeying put at risk her immortal soul.

Her heart was heavy and so were her limbs, as if saying to her as she left the church that she could not cut off the lifeline that had been given to her; but these limbs carried her home and she knew that she would end the relationship.

Having resolved what she must do, Sophie lost no time in telling Peter that their relationship had gone too far and must stop. Peter received the information with stupefaction. He found it hard to speak, but then he said slowly and with great sadness: "I thought we were friends. I care for you. There is no harm in it." Sophie interrupted him and speaking more bluntly than she had intended said: "It won't stop there, it will amount to much more than that, and it mustn't. I love Ludvig and I must wait for him."

So he was defeated. Peter stood before her all square and as obstinate as a mule: but there was nothing he could say or do, so he left.

Peter did not understand. At one moment Sophie had responded to him passionately, so much so that he had been taken aback and had doubted his own capacity to react; and now, and almost immediately, there was a cold rejection. Sophie knew that she had done the right thing but it gave her no satisfaction. She knew that she was going to miss him dreadfully. The farmhouse was empty and cold to her, the tears came and the dread and despair. She did not know how she could cope without him and her good spirits had evaporated. Sophie said to herself: "Peter must be feeling very unhappy and angry and lost to me."

Mary travelled back to L. with a new resolve. The picture of this handsome young man with his charming ways remained: she couldn't stop thinking about Heinrich, and when she did she trembled. She believed that he must feel the same as she did, and that he was thinking of her. But she accepted that he was dangerous to her and that it would be sheer foolishness to persist or even tolerate his attention. And as she said this to herself her heart jumped and she knew that she wanted to be with him. She saw his handsome slim figure in his smart black uniform, with his head held high, and the slope of his neck as he bent forwards to acknowledge her. The image was so strong that she closed her eyes tight in the half-belief that when she opened them again he would be there; sitting across to her, and smiling. She was disappointed when she opened her eyes to find the space empty. How could she cut him off when the exploration of these emotions had just begun?

Her resolve vanished: 'We must go on,' she thought, 'I know he loves me.' She trembled with the strength of unknown emotions. "I mustn't," she said in reply. And then over and over again that she couldn't and she must, to the rhythm of the train, until she believed it: that the relationship had to end.

Stopping Heinrich was another matter. She decided to enlist the help of Georg, the farm-manager. Georg was a married man but he had a soft spot for Mary. She asked for his help in sending Heinrich away when he came again as she knew he would.

"Mary, do you really think that I can do that, send an SS man away and order him to keep off my farm? I'm flattered that you think I could do it, but I would be crazy if I did."

"I'm not asking you to do that," pleaded Mary getting tearful and clutching his arm. "Just tell him that I have asked you to tell him not to visit me, that I cannot see him – that I don't want to – so that he will go away and stay away."

Reluctantly, and against his better judgement, Georg had agreed. So when Heinrich did return, Georg was as good as his word and nicely and firmly asked Heinrich to desist: to leave Mary alone as she did not want to develop a relationship with him and that she had asked him to say these things. Heinrich laughed and stood very close to Georg, and then he said in a different and far less charming tone of voice: "Very interesting Georg, I will remember your little speech, now tell me where she is." Georg told him.

Heinrich confronted Mary in the farm courtyard where she was on the way back to the kitchen.

"Is it right Mary, you don't want to see me?"

Mary was frightened.

"I can't Heinrich I shall get into trouble, and you too I expect if you are honest."

"Mary, I am sincere about this, about you. I can get you off this farm, to something better where we can meet. I can do this if you wish."

Mary weakened. To be with Heinrich would be very exciting. She longed to be with him and shivered with the thought of it. Tears came into her eyes and she swayed a little towards him.

"I don't wish to Heinrich. I'm happy here."

"Tell me then that you don't care for me?" he continued.

"I can't do that," said Mary tenderly, leaning towards him and kissing him on the cheek.

Mary walked away but Greta coming into the courtyard had seen the kiss, and the brief embrace that followed, and she assumed that Heinrich's departure was because of her.

The girls enjoyed the last minutes of their day as they prepared for bed in their billet. Tonight there was less laughter and Mary's first intimation that there was something wrong came when she realised that she was on her own. Then suddenly she was surrounded by a group of girls led by Greta shouting and screaming at her that she was an SS lover, a traitor and a whore. She was thrown onto the bed and, with girls sitting on her and holding her down by her legs and arms, her struggles were in vain.

A scarf thrust in her mouth prevented her from screaming. Greta had some shears and they cut off her hair and, as she wriggled her head, the hair came away in lumps. Greta pulled up her nightdress and continued to hack away at hair. She wanted to scream and in trying to do so she started to choke. But they were not finished. While they had her night-dress up they used some farm creosote and branded her with a Nazi swastika. All the time they screamed at her and called her names. And then they went and she heard the laughter and shouts as they left the billet. She was alone sobbing into her pillow, where she remained for a long time before anyone was willing to help her and she could leave the room.

Eventually her friend Jana came into the room. Jana caressed and cuddled her speaking softly and gently and telling her that everything would be all right; wiping away the tears and then, when Mary could move of her own volition, she guided her into the showers. Jana had some scissors and gallantly redesigned Mary's cropped head into some-thing better and even fashionable, although Mary had to wear a head-scarf for two to three months to hide the desecration. Mary scrubbed away at the creosote and had some success although it remained a terrible reminder of the attack for some time.

It was nearly two hours before Jana could lead her back to the billet where they were both jeered at until some of the girls protested that enough was enough.

It was some time before it all died down. Mary could see that some of the girls were ashamed or sorry at what had happened and tried to make up for it. There was a move by some girls to remove Mary from her duties as cook and get her back into the fields. When Georg, with the support of most of the girls, would not allow this, cow dung and excess salt was put into the food to spoil it. But Georg found out who did it and there were punishments, so it stopped. And after a time no one referred to it and life went on as normal, or at least as normal as life could be under the circumstances.

Greta was not a bad girl. At the time she was overcome with rage; a red-mist of anger and frustration had descended upon her – and a desire to hit back and take revenge, if not upon the Germans, for this was impossible, then upon those who collaborated with them or who excused their actions. Greta came from the Sudetenland where her father had been a prominent social democrat and the mayor of his small town. In 1939 when the Germans had invaded her father had been shot dead outside her home by these very same SS as she had seen at the farm and the family had been left to recover the body and bury him. And she herself had been moved pillar to post in forced labour camps before finishing up on this German farm. Her experience was not unique for there were other girls on this very same farm who had similar experiences and felt as strongly as Greta did.

But when the anger had abated, Greta was willing to understand that Mary had been trying to do the right thing. She came to Mary to say sorry and to try to explain. Mary was pleased that she did: she harboured no anger or resentment and embraced her, kissed her, and forgave. But in her mind remained the thought that these companions were uncouth; and although she could hardly believe it, that the Germans she met were more civilised; they were clean, well-ordered and correct. These things, she thought, were virtues which she admired and wanted to emulate.

As Heinrich walked away from the farm that day he was annoyed. "My God," he said to himself. "Rejected, and by a little Polish girl. Nice enough, quite sweet really, but there is plenty more where that came from. I can do much better than that and not get no for an answer. After all there will be many more opportunities."

As Mary's train had made its way, Adam's had been arriving in Auschwitz, a small country town in the midst of rapid industrial change. Himmler, the Gestapo chief, had decreed Auschwitz to be a twenty kilometre long industrial development area, enticing Krupps with the promise of at least one hundred thousand Russian prisoners of war to build a vast new factory. These prisoners were to be housed in the existing camp at Auschwitz which was to be expanded.

As the train passed into the station, Adam could see these factories in various stages of completion. As he disembarked he smelt a curious smell which seemed to pervade the entire space in which he walked and breathed. It was both sweet and a stench. Adam remembered the burning of cattle on a neighbour's farm, and the smell reminded him of these burning corpses. It was not a smell that one could ignore or forget.

He made his way to the Church of the Holy Mother where he was to see the priest and to give him a letter of introduction. His mother had been disturbed by his account of the wretched life in his Krakov billet and had decided to help him avoid this in Auschwitz. A neighbour had a relative there and Sophie thought that it might be possible, with an appropriate letter of introduction, to get Adam lodged in the town.

The priest turned out to be an accommodating man and provided a suitable letter and was willing to give the authorities a guarantee of good conduct, and what is more to confirm that the relative was a valued church member. Adam had to give a guarantee of secrecy; that is that nothing he learned as a result of his work in Auschwitz would be revealed to any one at any time. As Adam had never before given such a guarantee he felt it to be peculiar.

As he left the church the priest put his hand on his shoulder and spoke very simply to him: "This is a very difficult town to live in at the moment Adam. Very difficult. It is wise of your mother to try to obtain lodgings for you. The Diels are good, loving people and they will look after you. There is not much love in the world at the moment; and we all need it. Don't forget to come – to the church that is. And speak to me if you need me. That is what I am here for."

So against the odds, and as a result of a certain impudence, Adam found lodgings with the Diels, who ran a delicatessen and bakery in the heart of the new town. The Diels were to become his friends and guardian angels during his stay in Auschwitz, and it was they, more than anything else, who saved him from insanity.

As he trudged through the town to find them he smelt the dreadful air and resolved to ask the Diels about it. In their establishment he found the wonderful cooking smells of new bread and cakes, a blessed contrast to those other disagreeable odours. When his time at Auschwitz had passed into memory, he was left with these smells; and he would awake with them in his nostrils; sometimes unable to get his breath at all.

CHAPTER 8

KATYA AND ALFRED Diel were fat and jolly and anxious to make him feel at home. While he waited in the back-room for Katya Diel to become available he picked up a wedding photograph. This showed a much slimmer Katya, a young and smiling dark haired girl, and he wondered about the process by which serious young girls became fat. Of course, the shop itself was a standing invitation to eat all those delicious things which did fatten you. In the window on marble shelves were hams and cheeses delicately presented and labelled; and in the shop itself were sausages, bread rolls, and pickled vegetables all so temptingly arranged so as to make resistance difficult.

Adam was to eat with the Diels and to discover that the meals were very large and regular. There were large steaks, stews with dumplings, rich and filling soups, and meat pies, all accompanied by groaning platters of fresh vegetables. To follow there were a variety of cakes and flans with cream and custard. Adam wondered how they obtained this plenitude in wartime, but was very grateful that they did.

Every morning Katya would provide him with a packed-lunch: pies, sausages, cake, fresh bread rolls and soup in a thermos and when he protested that it was too much, she would say: "Adam you are a hard-working boy and you do this work not just for yourself but for your family and for me. If there is too much share it among your comrades."

Tears came into her eyes as she thought of her own son serving his country in France, so many kilometres away, and she wondered if he was eating properly today. Perhaps, some other woman was cooking for him. She would be a French woman, of course, but that did not matter for women were the same wherever they were to be found.

As he knew her better, Adam ceased to think of Katya as fat and came to see her as a very attractive woman. She had such sensibility to everyone, and she remained very feminine, seeking and receiving recognition and approval. And she was very kind to him. He had been given her son's room in the attic under the eves of the property which like the rest of the Diel's establishment was impeccably clean and presented although sparsely furnished. Adam felt happy in this room from the beginning. He could hide himself away with only the distant sounds from the shop and the kitchen smells to intrude on his privacy.

A number of boys had been billeted in the town. They were picked up each morning by truck and deposited back at night. On their first journey there was some talk about what they could expect to find. They were a little nervous because they knew the camp was tough and that it contained Polish and Russian prisoners of war and – the rumours went – some of the prisoners had been killed.

A German sergeant on the truck explained: "There are three types of prisoners: politicos, opponents of the State, some of them German and Polish, people who couldn't see the error of their ways; then prisoners of war who were being asked to make a contribution; *and lastly Jews, who are not wanted by anyone and who have to work to justify themselves, and good riddance to them anyway.*"

The sergeant emphasised that they were not to be worried about anything. The work was straightforward. They were still clearing the site for building work and there were tasks to be done in widening roads and improving the infrastructure generally. The camp prisoners were guarded by the SS and they were not to speak to them or assist them in any way.

They were first on the site and allocated working areas and given shovels and pickaxes. They started working and, as they did, they saw columns of people approaching the site from the camp. The first of these were Russian women. They were dressed in prison uniform and looked all right, being cheerful and lively, and appeared to have been well-fed.

They were followed by a raggle-taggle of other prisoners of all ages and nationalities, including Germans and Poles. Some of these men looked dreadful: their heads were cropped, their prison garb torn and without exception they were emaciated.

The last column were Jewish, identified by their yellow stars. As they approached you could see that they had difficulty in walking; they

shuffled, and from time to time swayed. In their greying faces you saw
the abandonment of hope: these were dead men walking.

These columns were accompanied by SS guards with dogs, batons,
rifles and whips. The columns reminded Adam of the herding of cattle
down the country roads he was familiar with but accompanied by
gratuitous violence. Prisoners were not allowed to speak to each other.
If they fell down another prisoner was allowed to pick them up; but if
not, they would be dragged away and beaten-up until finally they
expired, or they would be shot.

There were working-breaks during which these prisoners were given
water and a lunch-break at which some type of gruel and a piece of
bread was given. The boys saw that the Jews were served last and that
the gruel ran out before they had all been fed.

The boys were greatly shocked and looked away. They were
forbidden to speak to these prisoners and they did not wish to be near
them, but there were common tasks and so some contact was inevitable.

At the lunch-break the boys sat on a wall and viewed the Dante's
hell before them. Adam opened his lunch-box with its fresh bread,
sausage meat and steak pie. He could not eat.

"Why do they starve them if they want them to work?" he said to
Tomas, a boy of his own age and from his home town.

"You mutt," replied his friend. "You don't feed people you are going
to kill, it's a waste of good food. And don't waste that pie," he continued,
seeing that Adam was not eating: "I'll have it you don't want it."

At the end of the day a truck drove on to the site. An SS man shouted
at them. "You men jump to it. Get on the truck."

They drove round the perimeter and across the site picking up dead
bodies, mostly Jews but other categories of prisoner as well. Adam had
never picked up a dead person and here he was shovelling up these
skeletons of men and occasionally dropping them in the terror and
disgust of it all.

"What will you do with them?"

"Burn them. What do you think the smell is?"

And then they realised what they had been smelling on the site and
in the town; the burning of human bodies. They pressed the sergeant,
on the way back to town, to explain.

"Well, you boys should not be concerning yourself. There has been
a serious typhus outbreak in the camp and clothes and dead people
have had to be burned to prevent its spread. It's a public health matter."
He laughed: "Don't worry, you will get used to it."

Reaching the Diels Adam dashed up to his bedroom and threw himself on his bed. Katya heard him sobbing and being sick in the lavatory on the upper landing. She came up to see him and cradled his head while he tried to tell her what he had seen. She hushed him as she would a very young boy and rocked him from side to side, and without speaking. Katya did not seem surprised or shocked. Her concern was for Adam. She rocked him gently for several minutes before he suddenly fell asleep. Katya straightened him up and covered him carefully before she left the room.

Over the course of the next few days the boys discovered more disagreeable facts about this camp. It was not a prisoner of war camp any longer, although there still were prisoners there; nor was it a punishment camp like Sachsenhausen which accommodated Adam's father, although people were punished; *it was something new – a death camp*.

The boys were able to speak to the German soldiers, and even the SS, and if they were careful, to the prisoners. The Russian girls, who were university students, told them that very large numbers of Russian soldiers who were in the camp had disappeared, and it was believed they had been killed; and the Poles told them that for the most part, the Polish politicos had been killed, and that they were new to the camp and expected to be killed also.

They asked about the typhus epidemic, and had it confirmed that there were not vast numbers of ill people. The Russians told them, and they had difficulty in believing it, that over the past few months the Germans had started to gas people in the camp and that Russians and Poles had been killed in this way.

What they couldn't understand was why if the Germans were short of labour, and of course they were because that is why *they* were there – and there were thousands of prisoners, including Jews, working in the new factories – why were they so intent on killing people?

Drifting over Auschwitz were clouds of smoke with their dreadful smell; and the day to day reality of their building-site was that people died of neglect and cruelty and their bodies were disposed of in the camp.

The boys reacted in different ways. Towards the end of the first week, most had become accustomed to the surroundings and worked happily away oblivious to the unpleasantness, just as their sergeant had predicted; and some of these began to copy the German captors by showing hostility to prisoners who got in their way, or even went out of their way to ridicule them. It was a minority of the boys who displayed or felt any compassion.

Each evening Adam lay on his bed thinking about the camp, endeavouring to understand, and trying to work out what to do; and every evening, Katya and Alfred heard the creaking of his bedsprings, and at night Katya heard him get up and move around his room. Once Katya heard him scream out and wondered whether she should go up to him: but the Diels decided to leave it to the weekend. *Adam thought of the German soldier in Krakov and what he had done. It was a foolish thing to do and could not be repeated. If he was not careful he would finish up killed.*

At the weekend Alfred found an opportunity to talk to him. He started awkwardly: "Adam, my dear boy, Katya has told me about your talk with her and of your difficulties. We want to help you, we will help you. Now do you trust us?"

Adam nodded that he did.

Alfred looked at Adam in a determined way.

"You must be very careful; and there are some things you must accept. Germany is building a great empire. As a Pole you know about that for Poland has had an empire in the past. You can't build one, you know, without war and a mess; just as you can't make an omelette without breaking eggs."

He paused.

"Isn't that right?"

Adam supposed so and Alfred continued: "Germany has enemies; enemies from without and enemies from within. They have to be swept aside if Germany's great civilising mission is to be achieved. Do you see what I mean?"

Adam said that he did see what he meant. He realised that he had heard those words before – on the German radio in the canteen.

Over the weekend Katya found time for him. They sat in the courtyard and drank coffee and ate cream cakes. Katya could be very funny and they laughed together at her stories about her youth. He realised that Katya had been adventurous and that even now she was a long way short of being a staid middle-aged housewife. Alfred had spoken to her, he was sure of that, and there was something more to be said. At last she said: "Adam is it all right now? Are you going to be able to cope with the work?" She looked anxious for him and loving.

"I don't know. I appreciate what Alfred said, but he is not doing it, is he? I don't see why these prisoners are being treated so badly. *We're*

Catholics, Katya. Aren't we told to love our enemies, to be good to other people?"

He knew this sounded weak but Katya couldn't answer. She thought of her own son and hoped that he was safe.

On Sunday they had lunch together. Alfred took up the subject again.

"Adam, you have to be very careful – about your work – I mean. Not only can you harm yourself but you could make things very difficult for us – Katya and me – and your family."

Adam looked astonished.

"How could I do that?"

"We have guaranteed you to the authorities, so you are trusted; but if you are a suspect person, well let us say a weak person, then so are we. One moment your family is thought to be loyal, to be German, with a son boldly serving his country as best he can, and the next moment your family is a traitor's family. You – we – them, could all finish up inside the camp. That is what your principles and your weakness would have achieved. Is that what you want?"

"No, of course not," he replied.

But he knew it was all wrong whatever they said, and that he could not stand it.

Alfred continued: "I went to Mass this morning, and afterwards spoke to Father Stephan – you know, the priest you met when you came. I didn't say very much. You know – a young man, away from home, lonely – doing difficult things. Nothing specific you understand but more like that we are concerned about your welfare. He said he would be pleased to see you for a chat. Only if you want too, of course," he hastened to add as Adam nodded his head.

"When?" asked Adam.

"Well, anytime really, but you are busy during the week aren't you?"

"You mean now, this afternoon?"

"I arranged it for 4.00 p.m. if that is all right by you."

So at precisely 4.00 p.m. Adam re-entered this small church, not this time with hope but with foreboding. As he waited he looked around him. It was magnificent. The altar was resplendent in real gold and the fine stained-glass windows seemed to soar to the wooden-vaulted roof. The walls themselves were covered with sombre religious paintings of the mediaeval period and around them were the stations of the cross. Above him was a fine wooden gallery and when he craned his head he could see the fluting of a large organ. All was wonderfully cared for, polished, scrubbed and shining.

Adam thought about it. This place did not achieve its splendours without cost. He imagined all those people rich and poor who must have contributed: all those appeals for money, and all those priests living off the sweat of the poor. "Well it's what they want to do, I suppose," he muttered to himself. "And it reserves their place in heaven so must be good value for their money."

Father Stephan greeted him with kindness and courtesy. He clasped Adam's hands with both of his and led him to one side to a small chapel where above them as they sat was a statue of the Virgin Mary and Child.

This time Adam observed him more closely. Father Stephan was small and portly. He was dressed in his priestly robes of red and black. Stephan's face was rounded with rosy fresh skin and he smiled a lot showing his teeth: but his smile seemed to leave his face in arrears, and not really to belong to him, so that on a closer scrutiny he seemed depressed and withdrawn. Father Stephan smelt badly. There was the mustiness of his robe, his bad breath and the smell of spirits – something heavy and disagreeable.

"Adam, my dear child," he said, "I would like to start with a prayer for you and your family, that they will come to know God's mercy and love, and that he will look kindly upon them." He spoke this prayer to the Holy Mother who gazed down upon them, and so quickly that Adam wondered idly whether she could be expected to hear it.

The priest continued: "Katya and Alfred are very dear people and Alfred has told me something of your difficulties."

As he spoke he slurred some of the words and Adam realised that he had been drinking.

"Tell me child, in your own words, about these problems."

Adam told him exactly as he had told Katya and the priest listened intently. When Adam had finished Father Stephan sighed and looked sad, although he continued to smile: "Adam you are an intelligent boy and I want to talk to you as one."

The priest told him about the position of the Catholic church and how dangerous it was for the church in these troubled times. He explained that the church had survived similar troubles in the past and that it was its duty to do so because God had given the Catholic church the responsibility of being his witness and the custodian of his love for the world throughout all time. "*And the way we do that Adam is to render up to Caesar what is Caesar's and unto God what is God's,*" he said.

He paused while drawing in a deep breath: "In Poland, Adam, the church is being destroyed, literally, closed down with the priests arrested and sent to camps. In the Auschwitz camp itself there may be some of my dear brothers in God. You may be looking at them tomorrow as you do your work; but God's church is universal and for all time; it cannot be destroyed by one regime at one moment of time. Similarly his love for human beings is for everyone at all times and you must not forget this either."

Adam responded: "Yes, father, I understand that," and bursting out before he could be stopped, he said: "*But what if Caesar's law is in conflict with God's law, and if God is so powerful and loving why does he permit such cruelty.*"

Confronted with St. Augustine's dilemma in the mouth of a babe, the priest hesitated before slipping into the accepted response. "Adam, my son, it is not for you or I to say. God has given us the church to guide us and we must obey. The Holy Father reminds us that the church must obey the State in things that are temporal. As a Catholic you must obey the Holy Father."

But seeing Adam's face, with its look of incredulity, he went on: "Adam this is not a moment for doctrine or foolhardiness but for common sense. You must look after yourself and your family and friends. Do good when you can and avoid doing evil. These days if you do a kindly deed do it quietly, exercise a little stealth, and expect nothing in return. And don't isolate yourself. Come to church and mix with other young people. We shall look out for you."

The priest put his arm on Adam's shoulder as they stood in the early evening sunshine on the steps of the church. And then he said: "*Understand Adam that you must not be sentimental about Jews. You know from your bible studies that it was the Jews who rejected Our Lord, and that it was because of this rejection that Christ was crucified.*"

"Why then was he called the King of the Jews?" was Adam's quick rejoinder.

The priest took it in his stride.

"Some German scholars believe now – I am not saying that they are right for I'm not a Hebrew scholar – that the Gallileans were not Jews, at least not proper Jews, and if this is so Christ was not a Jew either."

This assertion was so strange to Adam, so extraordinary, that he had no reply and moved to turn away and go. Seeing his discomfiture Father Stephan continued.

"I'm talking theology to you, Adam, and perhaps I shouldn't be, but you are a clever boy and I wish to help you if I can."

Adam wanted to leave but did not wish to seem rude.

"You say to me that God must be dead or totally indifferent to human fate if such cruelties as you witness are permitted by him to occur. *If God is dead, he has died of pity for mankind, not because he is oblivious to man's fate. God gave us free will and what did we do with it – what did we choose? We chose the anti-Christ.*"

Adam fidgeted and started to move away. This was all too much for him.

"So beware of pity. If you are asking God to pity us – to pity the Jews – we human beings may pay a heavy price for it."

Adam said: "I'm sorry Father I must go."

Father Stephan could not be stopped.

"*Both Christ and the anti-Christ are the same in this. Both ask us to accept that love is above pity. They wish to create and they need our love and obedience to help them do this.* You talk about Hitler being the anti-Christ and Nazism being evil. Well, if the devil and evil are alive and well so must Christ be, and as a Catholic you must believe and trust in him." Father Stephan ended on a note of triumph.

Adam was well down the steps when he heard the priest have the last word: "I shall pray for you, my son."

Adam hurried away. He had enough of all that. "What a load of nonsense this priest speaks," he said to himself believing not a word of it and having no respect for him. But as he left the church he felt better. It was not anything that the priest had said, for clearly he was scared out of his wits and as clueless as himself, but because he had the chance to speak about his problems.

He missed talking to his mother and sisters, although on reflection, he couldn't talk to them about these things. His mother would think of his father at Sachsenhausen and be frightened about his possible ill-treatment. Nevertheless, he expected that he would blurt out about it at some time because of the horror of it; he would have to share it with his mother.

But the priest was right about meeting people. It was difficult, however, for he did not want to mix with the other men because that meant not escaping the horrors of his day: and they would all have to drink themselves stupid.

He thought of Miss Zbucki and what she had said about the way Poles survived in the past. Was she in a camp like this and, horrors of horrors, was she at this camp? If he saw her in one of these columns of prisoners he would go quite mad. She had said something Christian, he supposed Catholic: "Love your neighbour and maintain your solidarity and love for your country." But what was his country now? *Should he love Germany? Perhaps, if he loved Germany he would be all right, but could he do it?*

Katya and Alfred seeing him happier were relieved. Katya hugged him and said: "We shall look after you Adam, don't worry. Rest now so that you can get through next week. A day at a time. Sufficient until the day is the evil thereof."

As he lay on his bed, half asleep, and reflecting on the week ahead, he began to evolve his tactics for making sense of it, but just when he thought he was succeeding an overwhelming sense of dread would consume him, which would require him to deal with the panic and then, and gradually in case the feelings returned, he would start all over again.

On the site he decided to concentrate all his attention on his mates and to block out the prisoners and the guards. Although he had to relate to the prisoners, to give and receive commands, he classified them in his mind as non-people; as pictures on a wall or robots, depending on the task. But there were times when he couldn't do that – and it became too difficult.

He began, despite his rules, to exchange a few words with a prisoner on a common task and discovered that the man was a Polish Jew and a university professor from Warsaw. They could talk in Polish.

"What is your crime, why are you here?" he muttered to him.

"I have committed several crimes; first I am a Pole, stupidly born at the wrong time and in the wrong place; secondly, my parents educated me, and foolishly I became an academic; and then I was born a Jew, and although willing to disavow this religion of my birth, I was told that renunciation would make no difference, that racially I would always be a Jew."

He started to cough and then stopped speaking.

Adam knew that he had to be cold and deliberate and he tried hard not to be emotional or angry. It was hard to watch the lunch-break queue for bread and soup when Jews were made to queue last of all and when you knew that there was no intention to feed them all, and to hear the laughter of the guards when they packed up with the Jews still queuing, and then to open Katya's lunch-box with its fresh bread, meat and cakes.

He decided to break up some of this food and to place morsels in his pocket so that he could feed the professor. "Put it straight into your mouth and eat it slowly but right away," he whispered, "or it will be spotted." He did this for several days, running the risk of detection or receiving other ill-judged pleas for help. He knew it was futile, but he could do it.

Towards the end of the week he lost touch with the professor and when he saw him again in the distance he was relieved and pleased that he could reserve some more food for him. But when he returned to the place where he was working, at an interval of no more than twenty minutes, he found him dead. No one had beaten or shot him, he wasn't diseased, he was just dead; undernourished and without hope he lay there with the distended stomach of the malnourished and the swollen ankles and bleeding canvassed feet of the ill-equipped labourer.

Was he dead when he fell or after he lay there? Who knew or cared? And no one would care now. He would lie there until the truck came round at the end of the day when Adam and the others would pick him up as rubbish and throw him onto the truck.

Adam wanted to scream but he couldn't. He turned round and looked away in impotent rage. A guard seeing his distress laughed and shouted some obscenity about a filthy Jew. He wanted to hit him but he didn't. At that moment a light went out in his soul. It was no longer possible for him to believe in this God in his heaven. What sort of a God was it that would permit this? He saw now that he couldn't help. He was powerless. He would look into the faces of the living-dead and he would do nothing, feel nothing, there was nothing he could do.

At the weekends he would help out Katya in the shop. He showered and groomed himself to be worthy of her impressive establishment. It was a relief to handle the foodstuffs and to chat with normal people. Katya dressed him in a blue and white overall and with his handsome head of fair hair, and his knowledgeable ways, he was a success with the customers. He was a success with Frau Julia Von Hempel who regularly bought food from the shop.

Julia Von Hempel was in her early twenties. She might well have been a model as she was tall and extremely fashionable. She wore her fine black hair in the braided style thought impracticable by his mother, and so immaculately in place that he thought it must take her hours to prepare. Her summer dresses were haute couture and not available in any local shop. He thought, when he first noticed her, that they must come from Berlin or even Paris.

Julia spoke well in carefully elucidated hochdeutsch.* She chose her words carefully and spoke softly and clearly. "She is very cold and correct," he thought, as he served her.

At first she did not look at him directly but he was conscious of her appraisal; she was taking in information and assessing him. And when she did look it came as a shock as he saw that she was bold and incredibly beautiful. He thought: "This is a woman that men would die for," and then he blushed at such a ridiculous and inappropriate thought.

As she turned away he saw how slim she was and that she wore silk stockings and high-heeled shoes. He hadn't seen a woman like this before. Katya smiled when she saw his discomfiture. "One of the many advantages of a well-conducted retail establishment, Adam," she mocked him kindly, squeezing his arm as she did so.

He didn't forget Julia. She was disconcerting in that although, of course, she was out of normal human reach, there was something about her, an insinuation of something other than inaccessibility. It was not only that she was on the street and in Katya's shop, but that there was something else; Julia showed a little more flesh than was strictly right for a young woman of her class and there was a boldness in her manner from time to time which hinted at some rashness or unconventionality. "Remember me," she seemed to say, when there was no need to say anything at all. It was not an invitation to flirt or be inappropriate towards her, but a hint of sensuality which at that first moment had included him. It was an unstated challenge to him that his experience had not encompassed and which, therefore, he did not recognise.

At the end of four weeks' labour, he qualified for a weekend pass and was able to go home. On the train he rehearsed what he would say to his mother because he was determined not to upset her by talking about the camp. But his carefully rehearsed words were no proof against his mother's capacity to see right through him. In no time she had him speaking freely: the words tumbled out of him like the undamming of a mighty river, shocking her and himself. His mother clung to him, kissing and stroking him and calling out Ludvig's name, as he knew she would. When he stopped they looked at each other in silence.

* High German.

And then he said: *"Mother I can't do it any more. What shall I do?"*
*"You must continue, for if you don't they will put you in this camp.
What good will you have done then?"* was the blunt reply.

He came back to Auschwitz by train on a fine summer evening into
the dark, grimy and smelly surrounds of Auschwitz station. He was
calmer and more himself. After all he was a lucky boy. He had his
family, and in Auschwitz he had Katya. There were enough good
things to keep him going. He marched out of the station head held high
and humming a popular German patriotic song. He was up to it again.
He felt manly. His family were right to rely on him.

CHAPTER 9

HERMAN DRESCHLER WAS having a good war. But his good fortune was the result of a great deal of thoughtful planning and, in his own estimation, good sense. Herman welcomed the invasion. As an ethnic German he was an enthusiastic supporter of the Greater Germany. He had resented the anti-German policies of successive Polish governments and, as a consequence, his support of the Polish state had always been fragile.

In the new state of affairs he and his family could assume their rightful position in society; first, he thought the ethnic German, then those of German descent, followed by the Pole, lastly the Ukrainian or Latvian – and then the Jew. Following the occupation and annexation he was quick to ingratiate himself with the new authorities and to find his new level.

He made contact with the police and the SS. Through his activities in the German club he was well-known in the town and therefore had a ready audience. He explained that he could be helpful: the abattoir kept him in touch with local farmers, and his shop with other citizens; he could be a source of useful information and he was willing to report anything strange that was going on. He established personal contacts with the authorities, all of whom thought he could be relied upon.

Herman was an imposing man of above average height and weight. While not handsome, he carried an air of natural authority which swept much before him. He was persuasive: so much so his wife was known to remark that there was nothing in this world that Herman could not do if he set his mind to it. But if you were less partisan, you might not believe in his powers, finding something rather disagreeable about the heavy jowels of his cheeks, the way he thrust himself forward, the insistence of his speech and his practice of always having the last word.

Herman needed all his powers of persuasion now. In return for his cooperation he wanted something in return from the authorities for it was difficult doing business. Many farmers were in dire straits; they could not afford to feed their cattle and were short of labour. He, Herman, could help them, by offering assured sales for their animals, once he knew that he had assured buyers for the slaughtered meat. Herman negotiated long-term bulk contracts with the army and police force which, while not on favourable terms, enabled him to make money.

Displaying great energy, Herman became something of a local dignitary, a person of consequence. He visited the farms and made supply arrangements with them, advancing loans to keep them in business from advance payments on his contracts, and using his contacts to help in the supply of scarce foodstuffs. This business was not built in a day or without unusual commitment. He was so successful that he had to invest to increase the capacity at the abattoir, and all this at a time when his competitors were going out of business.

And while he did this, he kept up a constant stream of information to his security service contacts: through Herman they learnt of individuals engaged in partisan activities, Jews in hiding, communists and other suspicious individuals who might be on a wanted list – intellectuals and professional people. He became a very useful person, indeed, and as his reputation grew so did his business.

In his security activities Herman kept a low profile: it was never known to the victims that their fate had something to do with Herman. In his everyday business dealings, Herman was slow to comment on political matters and when he did people were impressed by the balanced and worldly-wise attitude he displayed; in an intemperate world his mild and friendly approach to everyday concerns was welcomed.

Herman regarded himself as being a good family-man. By this he meant that there was never any trouble over money or other women. When he thought of his sister-in-law Sophie and her problems, he admired his own virtues: with the support of a good wife he had kept everything going in an easy and pleasant way.

On a higher plane of consideration, however, he might have been found wanting. He did not see much of his daughter and, if he had been entirely truthful, he did not greatly care for her – or indeed children in general. Children, he considered were for women; they meant more to them, and it was their task to bring them up. But in this he showed a good deal of practical good sense: he thought that his wife Paula was extraordinarily good at the job, he backed her completely in the exercise of it, and family-life progressed as smoothly and agreeably as his working-life.

Adopting Lucie, or to be more accurate, bringing her up was a practical solution to a problem. Paula wanted another child and he was determinedly against it; he couldn't bear the thought of the demands of bringing a new child into this world. Lucie was the ideal solution; a ready-made child, a companion to his own daughter and good-natured and orderly into the bargain.

Eyebrows might be raised in some quarters, and the matter had to be handled carefully, but it solved more problems than it created. It was for Paula to do the relating to her sister and her family, and he encouraged her to make the visits to P., and not the other way around. He could hardly be criticised for harbouring the family of a disloyal person, a prisoner's family, if they were never seen: and he could say to himself, with a sigh, it is the Christian thing for Paula to support her sister in adversity.

If he had been closer to his family and to Paula he would have known that all was not well with Lucie: she missed her family, the mornings when she had curled-up in bed with her mother, and the kitchen and farmyard games with Adam. And she felt badly about her father: how could they treat him as a criminal and prevent her seeing him? She wanted to talk to Paula about him but she knew it would not be welcomed. At school they had noticed that she was withdrawn although complaints could not be made of her. The school reports remarked that she was doing quite nicely but could do better: "Lucie should participate more in class," they said.

Lucie followed the progress of the war on the radio. She took sides: to begin with it was Poland, then France, and then it had to be Russia: but all her favourites were beaten and she decided it was too disappointing to have them because they always lost. The children in her German school had the best of it because Germany always won. But they were not on her side, she was clear about that: she wanted her father home and her family back again, and that would only happen if Germany were beaten. So Lucie developed, at the age of eight, a secret life in which her deepest hopes and greatest fears were hidden from the world.

Lucie did go home but not often and after a while she did not want to go at all: how could she be in the place of her dreams but without those most dear to her, her father Adam and Mary? She was angry with her mother. She was sure that it was her mother's fault that her father was not there, although she could not explain why this was so.

Every time she went back she hoped her father would be there: perhaps, it was all a dreadful mistake, he had done nothing wrong and had been released: and when he wasn't there she felt the disappointment so keenly that she wanted to leave immediately and not to go back again, or to believe in the miracle any more. And she did not want to speak to Rosa, whom her mother had preferred to her, and who now had secrets which she hinted at to her but never told.

Sophie looked forward to these visits and when they became more infrequent was sorry. She tried to behave well with her daughter and encouraged her to do normal things: to play with Rosa, to feed the geese and take the dogs for a walk. Perhaps, she had made a mistake in placing Lucie with her sister: but she thought not, she couldn't manage, she would be better off with Paula and after a while she would settle down. She worried about her but these were distant thoughts. "A great many people have become remote to me and unreal," she said to herself. And she judged and punished herself for it. It was as if she had a fixed capacity to feel things and when that had been reached she could absorb no more.

Sophie missed seeing her eldest daughter, Mary, now that she could talk to her as an adult. Mary had not been home for some weeks and then had written to her saying that she could not take any leave for a while because everyone was so busy. And Adam, dear boy that he was, had not been a comfort. She was deeply shocked by what he had told her about the camp at Auschwitz: but she wondered whether he was making heavy-weather of it, and doubted that it was really as bad as he described it to be. Anyway, she couldn't think about it. "It's no good worrying about things you cannot change," she said to herself time and time again.

Following his visit to his mother Adam had done his very best to settle down. He ordered his life by a regular routine. At work he avoided the prisoners, for no good could come out of contact. He helped Katya and Alfred in the shop and he took the priest's advice and attended the church social club where he met local boys of his own age. He sloped-off with some of these from time to time. He had very little money but he could afford the occasional drink in a bar: and he kept his hand in at cards, winning occasionally and getting some measure of personal admiration from other players. He refused to socialise with other men from work because he told himself life had to be compartmentalised.

But every day he felt himself die a little. Every day the sights and actions he witnessed and, despite his unwillingness, he participated in, diminished his faith in others; every day prisoners were beaten up, and a thousand cruelties and obscenities were acted out before him. He did nothing. He looked away, counted the time, thought of Katya and his lunch and the shop, and imagined himself fishing for trout on a cloudless day. He picked up bodies without seeing them and dumped them onto trucks; and got back to Katya's, to his whitewashed attic, as fast as he could.

One Friday evening Katya said: "Adam, Frau Von Hempel has placed a regular weekly order and wants it to be delivered to her. For some reason which I do not understand she has asked me to promise that you will deliver these orders. What an impertinence to tell me how to run my business. But there you are. Be a good boy and deliver it. And smarten yourself up before you go. We have a reputation to maintain."

The address was written in German on the back of a visiting card with guidance on how to get there and an instruction to go to the back-entrance. It was a well-scrubbed Adam that found the detached modern villa of the Von Hempels, modest by the standards of Hamburg, her home town, but conspicuously grand in Auschwitz. From the back-entrance you could see the camp perimeter, which was within comfortable walking distance. Adam had never been inside a house like this and his heart bounded as he knocked and waited.

The Von Hempels had servants but it was Julia who opened the door and invited him into the kitchen. She was formally dressed in a purple silk dress, which swirled as she walked. He thought that she must be going to some prestigious dinner or to the opera. He was overwhelmed, scared and anxious to leave so that she could go to this function, whatever it was. But she slowed him down by asking him to unpack the delivery and check it with her. Then as he moved as if to go she asked him for help in splitting logs in the yard, indicating that she would serve him a coffee when he had finished.

Julia was bored. Newly married she had been moved with her husband Friedrich to this hell-hole of Auschwitz where no doubt he had been involved in doing some terrible things. Then without notice, and no doubt because he was a rising star, he had been drafted into an SS regiment in Russia leaving her marooned: for the moment she could not go back to Hamburg and, of course, she could not go on to Russia.

Julia was the daughter of a career army officer. Her family had been dismayed by her attachment to Friedrich, a person of dubious class background, and even more dubious associations; but they recognised his abilities and thought that he would get on in this new Nazi State. As she was determined and they loved their daughter they gave her permission first to associate with him and then to marry. Julia loved the excitement of her new life and the power her husband came to exercise. She missed him and feared that she might not see him for some time, distrusting the talk of early victory in the East.

She was sexually bored and restless. In her position she had to be careful and any indiscretion within the closed circle of the SS would almost certainly become known. She was willing to pay for sex but, in practice, how could you do this in a place like Auschwitz? Anything sexual she did had to be under her control. It could not be a love affair but it had to be real sex with another human being: and more than the relief she got for herself in the shower.

Then she saw this handsome young man in the delicatessen. A sort of German but really a Pole and someone who could be made to do what she wanted. "Why," she thought, "I could have him killed if I wished."

Not that she did wish, for here he was in her house doing what she told him to do. There was more to this than she thought. As Adam looked at her he believed her to be younger than her age. He could see that she was nervous and that behind the imperious manner and class certainty there was self-doubt. He thought that if he said 'no' to her about something he wouldn't come to any harm. Adam did what had been asked to do and then had the coffee as he had been promised.

Julia asked him questions about his family and what he did in Auschwitz, and what he wanted to do. His answers were perfunctory. He did not ask any questions of his own because he was scared and wanted to go. Julia gave him instructions about next week. They did not shake hands because that would have indicated familiarity and equality. As he left Julia looked at him and he recognised what in another context he would have understood as a plea.

Julia was annoyed with herself. She had wanted some uncomplicated sex. How tedious it would be if she were to have feelings for this simple boy. And she hadn't got what she wanted: she had been left feeling like a gawkish schoolgirl on a first date. As she felt incomplete she had a shower and relieved herself. She had no one that she could talk to about this. The wives of officers on the camp were a vulgar lot and unsafe as confidantes, and how she wished she could go home away from this tedium. As she dried herself and felt her body she found herself doing what was not wanted, imaging herself doing it. She was disgusted with herself but that was how it was.

During the following week Adam put this disturbing encounter largely out of mind, but as the week drew to a close he found himself dreading any repetition and hoping that the order would be cancelled. On the day itself he felt feverish and excited and as he approached the house he wondered whether he could get away with leaving the order at the back door: but he decided against it and knocked.

This time Julia took him by the hand into the sitting-room where he sat awkwardly on a large white sofa in elegantly furnished surroundings. She started firmly: "Adam I am going to be honest with you. I have chosen you to do certain duties for me of which I have a need from time to time. I have great power you know and I can order you: but I don't want to do this. And anyway you will like it and you don't need to be ordered, do you?"

Adam shifted nervously on the sofa and wondered what the hell she was talking about. She was determined: "Now be a good boy. There is a shower-room on the first floor. Have a good shower and put on the dressing-gown you will find on the door. My room is opposite. Don't be long," and she smiled winningly.

He wasn't long and he found her there in a white silken nightdress which fell to her ankles, with her hair down and brushed out and smelling of something rare; and he did what she wanted though he was amazed by it and by himself. Julia enjoyed it because for the first time she felt wholly in command. This boy did not know what to do, but she did. She remained on top and taught him what to do and where and how to touch her. Friedrich was an experienced and accomplished lover but she never felt that he was really interested in her: and her pleasure had been accidental and not really sought by him, although she did not think of him as thoughtless.

Julia liked to come quickly – and she did: but she felt she could go on – and she did, coming several times. And when she was finished she fell asleep immediately, and when Adam woke he saw her sleeping like a very small girl with her arm crooked-up on the pillow and a finger in her mouth to suck. As he moved to get up and move away she restrained him for a moment, with her hand upon his arm: and then she let him go – without a word and without rising.

Adam was astounded by what had happened and couldn't leave fast enough. What had he been doing? How absurd and how dangerous – and how delicious. But that was that and he would not go back again. No doubt he had served his purpose. And then he was angry because this was the second time that he had been set upon against his will. Or if not against his will, because he could not quite say that for otherwise it would not have happened, without him initiating it. Perhaps, there was something wrong with him for if other men were to be believed they did all the chasing and the girls did all the pretending to run away. But he did not really believe them. It wasn't right though, he could see that; but of all the things that were not right this was the best. He wanted to boast about it to someone but he couldn't.

It took some time for Julia to get up. She was pleased with herself because she had pulled it off and it had worked out just as she had hoped. There was the disagreeable thought of whether it was safe. Not the sex because she had taken precautions but the secrecy of it: she should have said more to Adam about the absolute need to say nothing or do nothing that would lead to suspicion. Now it was too late for she was not at all sure that she could ask Adam to come again. It had been very satisfying, and really he had done most of the right things, but it was too dangerous.

As the week went on Julia wavered between common sense, which urged her to go back, and passion which urged her to go on. Being a sensible girl she decided to put back the decision and she notified Katya that she would not be needing her order over the next two weeks although leaving it open to resume; and Katya had told Adam. "Good," he thought with relief, but with a pang of regret. "That is the end of that adventure." But Julia's state of mind and need remained what it had always been. It pleased her to know that an encounter would happen again; but not for the moment.

Adam believed that there was something very definitely wrong with him. Apparently once was enough for women he became involved with. In the books he had read there were no characters like him and so he had no point of comparison. He examined himself in the shower and thought he looked normal enough. And he remembered Julia's green eyes when she came as they dissolved into a thousand fragments like the shattering of an emerald. It was wonderful and that moment alone would make all the effort and secrecy worthwhile.

When Julia had asked him about his work he had been ashamed to tell her; but when, hesitatingly he did, he saw that she knew, that she knew far more than he did. It was a relief to tell her and not to be judged, and he thought about that as he struggled on.

Peculiar things were happening now and some of the men spoke of whole trainloads of prisoners coming to Auschwitz and rumours of their death. They couldn't all be killed in the camp, he knew that, because there was a constant flow of new prisoners working on the site; rumour had it that women and children and old men who couldn't work were being killed.

Once when they were on their way back to the town their sergeant needed to go into Dvory station, a kilometre from the town, to make a travel enquiry. They got out to stretch their legs. A train was standing at the platform – a long train of cattle trucks with sealed doors. There were shouts for help, for water, and they saw that these cattle trucks were full of people shouting and waving their hands through cracks in the wagons. Some of the men tried to help by using water from the fire buckets but there was nothing to put the water in. Two of his mates ran back to the truck for their own beakers and did what they could to provide water but most of it was spilt.

Their concern was in a minority for most of the men did nothing and some of them laughed, while the sergeant said when asked: "What are they? Dirty Jews, of course, on the way to their death. Forget them, there is nothing you can do." But he did not say this harshly and Adam remembered later the way he did say it. Adam was ashamed of himself, for he had done nothing. He had thought that there was no way you could get water in a beaker through the sides of the truck. It couldn't be done. That was the practical conclusion. But when he looked at this desperate scene he realised that the truth was that he had ceased to feel anything. He was numbed down.

Later he considered it and made a decision: if he saw something like that again, and he could help, he would do so. He thought of Miss Zbucki – *he would help but he wouldn't do anything foolish.*

He asked Katya when they were alone in the shop whether she knew about the trains and that many people died in them before they reached the camp. She said she did know. When he was at the church social club he asked the same question and the boys said of course they knew but it was stupid to talk about it. "After all," they said, " the town was full of SS men drinking and talking too much. Anyone who was curious to know soon found out – and then they told their families and neighbours, assuming that they didn't know already – which you could be sure that they did."

So he concluded that people in the town knew about the transports and the vile way people were killed in the camp and none of them did anything. He thought: "If everyone who knew and was not a part of it did something, then it would stop." And then he realised that he was being stupid. People knew about it, even nice people like Katya, but either they did not want to do anything to prevent it, or really couldn't – *who* could really – do anything about it; and a lot of people approved of the killings.

People who cared couldn't be expected to do anything: realistic and sensible people accepted the reality of occupation and did nothing. *But he stuck to his resolution: if he could do something he would, whatever the others thought.*

CHAPTER 10

ADAM BEGAN TO think seriously about trying to escape from Auschwitz. It would not be at all easy. He might run away and hide somewhere but he would be caught: or if not his family would be harassed in some way. He couldn't do anything that would harm them. The war might go on for a very long time for the Russians had not been defeated, and he did not think that America and Britain would give up easily either. Perhaps, they would all negotiate an end having fought themselves to a standstill. None of this would help him, at least in the short term. There were a lot of factories being built in Auschwitz and he would not be posted anywhere else in a hurry, at least that was what his sergeant had said.

Some days now he had difficulty rising in the morning and Katya had to pull him out of bed. Once he missed the truck and had to walk to work. He was threatened with punishment and loss of his privileges. The threats did not make it any easier to rise and, although he could not diagnose himself, he was in reality sinking into a deep depression. Katya knew it but she felt powerless to save him: her normal remedies of holidays and a good family life were inapplicable now. She fed him, warmed him and kept him clean: but they both knew that he was ill.

Something was sure to break and it did. One September evening his work-gang was coming back to the town. They were late and the light was beginning to fail. At Dvory station the truck was halted by two armed SS men. "You men get down and into the station, you are needed." They did what they were told and were lined up along the platform at regular intervals. There were armed SS present but in fewer numbers than usual. His gang saw that the SS were very twitchy and nervous and their uncertainty was communicated to them.

Dvory station at his time was unprepossessing: nothing more than a halt with a small station building. It was double-tracked and on each side of the track a white-painted wooden fence was the only track protection. Some local people curious to see what was going on lined themselves up behind the fence on the station side. The SS men would have wished them to move off but there were too few of them to impose their will.

As they waited it was dark enough for the station lights to go on and some of the men lit up cigarettes. Adam thought: "Evil can arise suddenly from the most normal of situations." He looked around at the scene. It had a certain drama because of the soldiers and the waiting spectators but otherwise how ordinary it was. So what were they all doing here plotting some dreadful cruelty to defenceless people? He felt very bad about it and, as he looked, he could see others who felt the same.

They discovered that a train transporting prisoners was expected but that for some reason it was unscheduled or late; apparently there was another train at Auschwitz station which was being unloaded. The SS found themselves exposed and undermanned in having to meet the Dvory train as well. Adam thought: "*What sort of new empire is this which cannot even get the trains to run on time?*"

The men in his gang were very nervous because by now they had all heard of these trains and expected something dreadful. But whatever they had heard, and however imaginative they might be, nothing had prepared them for what they were to experience.

It was a normal-looking train with carriages. As it came into the platform they could see that it was crowded with women and children. They heard screams, the crying of children and the barking of dogs. SS men on the train were shouting out orders and, as if in union, in some sort of devil's chorus, the troops on the platform joined in. Women and children, closely followed by a few SS men, spilled onto the platform.

A great wail went up from local bystanders standing behind the fencing bordering the platform as they saw that these women and their children were in various stages of disrobing: some were naked, while others in what remained of their clothing, shirts and dresses, were being set on and the rest of their clothing ripped-off. These passengers had been taken by surprise; they had not expected the attack upon them by the guards and their dogs. They milled about the platform shouting and struggling, with the mothers keeping hold of their screaming children while trying to protect their modesty.

In the midst of this madhouse, now clearly out of control, came the sound of a shot. A woman had tumbled onto the platform fully clothed and, as an SS officer waving a pistol had sought to grab her, she had picked up some grit from a bucket on the platform and had thrown it into his face so temporarily blinding him. She snatched his pistol and shot him. There was blind panic on the platform with the SS running for cover and in this confusion she succeeded in shooting another in the leg before she herself was shot.

A little way down the platform a small child had been scrambled across the fencing to a Polish spectator: but before it could be smuggled away, it was grabbed back by an SS man, who smashed its head against the station wall killing the child outright.

Adam picked up a dress and thrust it at the nearest naked woman. He was standing by the station door and as he grabbed he succeeded in pushing her into the empty station waiting-room. No one seemed to see him do it; or if they did, it was assumed that he was struggling to keep the woman on the platform.

There they were, two panting and terrified human beings, staring at each other. For a moment Adam did not know what to do: then looking around and finding a wall-cupboard with a key in the lock he pushed her in, locked it and withdrew the key, while all the time he repeated in Polish and German: "Don't be frightened. I shall help you, come back for you." She would be all right. It was a large cupboard used for storing shovels and brooms: it was not airtight and probably he possessed the only key.

No one noticed his absence. Gradually the SS regained control and the women and children were loaded onto waiting trucks. The SS man was not seriously injured and was removed by his comrades. As he passed, Adam heard him moan: "What a disgrace. Shot by a filthy Jew." Adam's shaken gang got back onto their truck. There was no conversation: even the sergeant had nothing to say.

Within an hour Adam was back in his familiar bedroom and in an hour and a half he was back at the station. The woman was still there. Adam saw that she was a perfectly normal middle-aged Polish woman. He supposed her to be Jewish and when he asked her she confirmed it. She did not look very Jewish to him but he was not a judge because he did not usually think about whether someone was Jewish or not.

"What's your name?" he asked.

"Rebecca."

"Put these on Rebecca and follow me."

The dress was some sort of fit and he had brought with him an old pair of Katya's shoes and a head scarf which he hoped she would not miss. He had worked out what he would do. It might not work but it was the best he could think of. Amongst the spectators at the station he had noticed a married couple from the church. They were kind people who had given him some hospitality so he knew their home. It was dark now and their house was not too far from the station. They walked as normally as they could, with linked arms, and weren't challenged in any way. On arrival they pushed their way into the home of this retired couple.

Adam explained what had happened and asked for their help. The husband, Otto Dietrich, protested. What was Adam doing to endanger them all? His wife was clearly scared but, as she looked at this frightened and respectable Polish lady, she relented.

"Give us five-minutes Adam," she said pulling her husband into the kitchen.

Seated in the living-room they heard the couple's agitated voices. When they came back, she said: "We shall help Adam but you must trust us to do it our way. Leave this lady with us. She will be safe. But don't come back for some time."

"How long?" exclaimed the worried Adam not knowing now whether they could be trusted.

"At least ten days," was the reply.

The Jewish woman kissed him as he left and he thought that he would probably not see her again.

While Adam couldn't be certain of the outcome of his rescue operation, he was pleased that he had acted. As the days passed and nothing was said to him about the debacle at the station he knew he had got away with it. He thought that even if it went wrong and the woman couldn't be kept in safety, he was fairly certain that the Dietrich's were sensible people and he could keep out of trouble: *the outcome, he realised, was less important than the action*. It would be the *second* time that he had done something. In Krakov, he had resisted and escaped punishment, and so why not in Auschwitz?

After the requested ten days had passed, he returned to the Dietrichs. "You must not be angry with us, Adam," a nervous Otto blurted out, as he led Adam into the sitting room. Adam's heart sank. "What had they done?"

"Rebecca's not here, but she's safe," and he explained. It was too dangerous for them both to keep her in their house here in Auschwitz. It was not as if she had been missed and there was a search going on – he was fairly sure that this was not the case – but rather that the town itself was dangerous because of the large number of SS men on the streets. Anything could happen.

"Where is she?" asked Adam, anxiously.

"With my brother-in-law in M." he explained. He has a farm there and in return for a small payment he was willing to take her in and get her some new papers. She can work in his house. No one will ask any questions for the house is very remote, and she doesn't look Jewish. So, with a bit of luck she will be all right."

Adam realised that Otto had made a real effort to help and had taken risks. "I had to make two trips to my relative, Adam," he explained, relieved that Adam was approving. "The second one with Rebecca in the cart. I'm not a hero. I was very scared I would be stopped. She is a very nice woman and we wanted to help. But Adam you must promise me. Don't dare to bring anyone else to our house again because if you do we won't help."

Adam promised.

Adam was very pleased with himself. He had been proved right. *What he knew now, although he would not at that time been able to articulate it, was that solidarity was not enough. Of course, you had to stick together with your family, friends and mates: no one needed to tell him that. But solidarity did not involve moral choice, and because it didn't, it wasn't enough. And self-preservation and the acceptance of a new social reality was not enough either.* For a moment he knew this to be true: but what he was being asked to do was too much to endure.

Adam couldn't act the hero every day because he would be caught and punished and, as important to him, so would his family. And so the relief of his action, like the effects of a drug, ebbed rapidly away, leaving him with only a glimpse of how things might be different.

Adam believed now in what his instincts had told him – the efficacy of the individual protest. Human beings were not on their own in their essential humanity; after all whatever their motives, Otto and his family had helped. So other people felt like him.

The irony of his situation was not lost on him because he had received another order demand from Julia. He did not want it and he hadn't sought it but there he was, smartened up, excited and expectant, dealing with the enemy: the very sort of people who caused the problem in the first place with their desires to dominate other people and their racial nonsense.

Julia was very pleased to see him and he was, when he came into her house, very pleased to be there. He was less intimidated by her manner and, although he was dutiful and did what he was told, they were aware of a shift in the balance of power between them. She despised herself for intimations of feelings, yet unrecognised by either of them, that she wanted to please him. Adam for his part was more confident and displayed it sensing that the imperious Julia he had started out by admiring was, if the whole truth be known, as vulnerable and as lonely as he was.

And this time neither of them wished him to go quickly. Julia prolonged his stay by offering him food, not prepared by her because she couldn't cook, but at least planned in advance. She did not care for doing it but she spoke to him about her family and, in particular, her father and his distinguished military career, and she asked him more questions: all of which she had been anxious to avoid. Two young people who started out by using each other as a convenience were becoming something else: not lovers in the true sense but something more than two bodies obtaining physical pleasure. Neither wanted it, but they had become collaborators.

When they met for the third time they met as friends: there was laughter and confessions of a minor nature, and expressions of hope. This was surprising and disturbing for Julia because at this time she knew that she was going back to Hamburg. Her father had finally accepted that it was pointless for her to wait in Auschwitz for her husband's return. She was to go back home.

Speaking in an intimate tone, although remaining authoritative, she asked him: "Adam, if I could do anything for *you*, what would it be?"

"Get me out of Auschwitz."

She laughed.

"What would you be willing to do to get out? Would you be willing to serve as a soldier. How about the Russian front? Would you serve there? There would be no difficulty in getting you there?"

Adam thought not in Russia.

"If I could serve in an army honourably – not putting down my own people – not fighting at all really then I might like to be a soldier."

She thought it a tall order.

"At some time they will catch up with you and call you up, you know. And when they do you won't have a choice."

She was so relaxed with him that he felt brave enough to ask her questions. He picked up a silver-framed photograph in her bedroom.

"Is this your husband?"

She nodded.

"He looks a handsome and clever man."

"He is."

"What does he do in Russia? He has a high rank doesn't he. Is he a major? Isn't he very young to be a major?"

Julia laughed: "Do you really want to know what he does? Do you think you have the stomach for it?"

He signalled that he did.

"Well," she said teasingly to him and flirting with the words, "of course, *I don't know exactly*. These things are very secret you know. He is in charge of an Eisengruppe, they follow the regular army into Russia and deal with the undesirables."

Seeing him blink, she added quickly: "Of course you know about these things. He arrests Bolshevik officials and hunts down partisans and gets rid of the Jews."

And getting annoyed at how he looked at her, she continued:

"Don't give me those apple eyes. I don't like it any more than you do. It is the war. These things happen in wars and you and I have to see that they don't happen to us."

Julia changed the subject but not before Adam had seen how excited she had been by the discussion. Julia rubbed her finger slowly up and down the picture-frame. "It's a wonderful uniform, don't you agree?" she said playfully but testing him. "Wouldn't you like a uniform like this and the power that goes with it?" And then seeing that he was not so impressed, she changed the subject again.

He put these thoughts to one side because he thought nothing would come of it. Julia did not tell him that she was leaving, why should she? She thought: "He is a very nice boy, but I would very quickly get tired of him." And she persuaded herself that she was bored of him already. She left Auschwitz earlier than she had planned and wrote Adam a note which was delivered by a servant to the shop.

'Adam, you are a dear boy and I wish you well. As you read this I shall be in Hamburg with my family. So that is the end. I have spoken to an army friend of my father who is about to give you your heart's desire. You can be a German soldier in France: the plum post in the German army with no fighting at all – and with very pretty girls, so you won't miss me at all. Sincerely, Julia'

She gave him the name and address to contact.

It would be nice to record that this was true romance and that this young couple were to miss each other. However, that would not be true. An advantage of youth is that it is in its purest form unreflective. In a short time they had mostly forgotten about each other.

Adam did not hesitate to make contact with this military contact of Julia's – who turned out to be a colonel in the regular army: and it was after he had done something about it that he told his mother.

He didn't actually see this colonel who thought it more sensible to direct him to and through the normal recruitment process; but it was known that the colonel was taking an interest so the outcome was a done thing. The medical presented no problem and as he had no other obvious qualification, and there was no mention of his father, he sailed through. He was given generous treatment. He was to stop his work on the site and go home for a holiday where he would receive a letter giving him a date and venue for military training.

Outside in the street he began to sing out loud: he was free of Auschwitz and the nightmare was over.

At home his mother was supportive. "Like father like son," she said, for his father had served in the German army and had been captured by the British in France. He looked disconcerted and Sophie reassured him. "We have two hundred years of experience of Poles fighting in German armies, not that you will have to fight from what you say."

Adam thought that it might be best if he did a little fighting and then got captured by the British like his father. There was no need to be a hero and, if Germany lost the war, he could come back home again. No trouble. He was not going to think about it. He was away from Auschwitz, that was the important thing.

He was at home for three weeks and as happy as a sandboy. He went out with his mother on the cart and did the hard part of the liming work. He took in the fresh air from the familiar lanes. And his mother cooked him the familiar favourite dishes. He forgot about Auschwitz. That is he almost forgot for he had realised that he did miss Katya and the shop. She had hugged him when he left and he had promised her that he would stay in touch. They both knew that he wouldn't: that life would sweep him away and that he would not correspond.

But Katya was the only person in Auschwitz that he would miss and he found the time to write to her and to thank her from the bottom of his heart for keeping him going through the nightmare. Katya put this letter in her writing-desk with the letters from her son because this is how she had come to consider him. She didn't write to him because she found difficulty in it: and anyway she knew that it was not a matter of words.

After he had been at home for a while and had settled into this unexpected domestication his mother wanted him to tell her more about Auschwitz. "Don't worry about frightening me," she said, "I know that this camp is far worse than Sachsenhausen."

He started to tell her more but the words were hopeless because, for what he had seen and felt, there were no adequate words: at least if there were some he did not know them. He could not tell her everything because some events were closed up for ever: but some of the happenings were so traumatic that he could convey to her their horror, almost without words, until she came to see them almost as he had experienced them; and then she wept.

At this moment mother and son were very close. They ate together across the familiar kitchen-table as two old friends. Without recognising it consciously, Sophie was treating him as an adult. He saw that she was a lonely, worried woman; grieving the absence of her husband and three of her children. Adam asked about Peter and she told him what she had done.

"It's a great pity, mum," he said sympathetically. "Peter is a very good man."

And then hastily, surprised at what he had said: "Rosa must miss him."

"She does miss him" was his mother's gratified response.

"Rosa asks about him all the time. She wants to go and see him," said his mother, encouraged by his approval.

Sophie told him that she had heard nothing from Mary for nearly three months and that she had no reply to her letters. Adam said that he would write, and did so while he was at home. They thought of travelling to see Mary but in the time available they were reluctant to break the golden circle that bound all three of them before its time had come. Adam was not worried about his sister's silence. She would have good reason, he felt sure of that. But he was sorry not to see her and did not know when he would do so again.

When the letter arrived they saw that he would do a month's training in N. in Czechoslovakia. That was all right he thought, no harm in going there. But the letter said nothing about where he would be posted once his training was completed. They agonised over what, if anything, that meant. For the first time Adam had doubts. It was one thing to serve out the war on the French Riviera, or if not exactly that in some soft sort of way elsewhere in France, but quite another to serve on the Russian front. Going to France had been the easy option. But did he really want to serve his new masters by dying fighting the Russians or in some camp in Siberia if he were captured?

Sophie thought that Poles had no alternative but to fight somewhere and for some one; and not for your own country either, not for Poland. France was a civilised place. He would be all right there, but only a complete fool or criminal would let himself be sent to Russia, if he could avoid it.

Adam thought about his mother's statement that he was following in his father's footsteps. He hadn't realised up to this point that there was a comparison to be made, and he didn't fancy it; that is turning out to be like his father. He thought of Julia. Was he going to become a womaniser like his father? And would that be bad? Did women let you down really – in the end. Had Julia let him down? Talking to him about France and then playing some macabre black joke on him by getting him sent to Russia. Perhaps, all the men who got themselves involved with Julia got themselves sent to Russia! He didn't really think that to be true but it crossed his mind.

Sophie made him promise that if he had leave he would get back home before going to France, or if no leave, he was to write to her telling her what was going to happen to him. He promised, but he knew really that none of these matters would be determined by him. He was going to be swept away on the tide of history as Miss Zbucki might have said. Everyone was being carried along with no control of their own. He tried to remember a French revolutionary quote Miss Zbucki had told the class. Something to the effect that 'in a revolution no one can stand still'. It was true, as much of what she said was turning out to be true.

CHAPTER 11

IT WAS A fine October day in 1942 when Adam crossed the frontier into Czechoslovakia. He was tired and the steady slow movement of the train had lulled him to sleep. Outside the passing train were pleasant green fields and gently rising hills; and clustered whitewashed red-roofed houses and church spires spoke a message of normality. There he imagined men came home from a day in their fields to family meals, to women who loved and protected them; and children were placed abed and read to by the light of friendly lamplight; where they would all wake up on the morrow to a similar day and the reassurance of a life of normal rhythms; where babies were welcomed into the world, and the aged would leave it with honour and respect.

And as he thought of these things, and drifted in and out of sleep, he would laugh to himself, and sometimes out loud: not a nice laugh at all but forced. Into his head flashed other images and noises, so that near to sleep he thought himself to be quite mad and waves of panic flooded his unconscious forcing him awake. He saw again the prisoner beside him collapse and die compulsively spitting blood; he heard the crunch of a rifle splitting open a man's head killing him outright; and the sound of a baton drumming on a prisoner's emaciated ribs.

As he found the mechanism to switch off these images and sounds, he thought of Julia; he saw the narrowing of her green eyes as she approached orgasm, and the lift of her firm and shapely breasts, crowned as they were with purple nipples, like luscious and fully-ripe soft fruit. He attacked these images with a sense of decorum and propriety until he lost them.

And as he drifted in and out of sleep he thought this must be like going mad but he knew he was sane because he could feel the upholstery beneath him and smell the fresh bread rolls and cut meat of the passengers opposite him, which for a moment he felt must be Katya's. And then he was offered a bread roll; an offer from a friendly stranger repeated to him several times until he woke and accepted it.

When he left the train at N. he realised that there were many recruits like him on the train, some of his age and background and older men who were not called up at earlier stages of the war but who were needed now. They were met at the station by a regular sergeant who ticked them all off and took them by truck to the old Czech army barracks which was to be their home for the next two months. This was a substantial building modernised and freshly painted. The older men thought that everything about it was professional and that the Czechs had a modern army which would have given a good account of itself in 1938 if it had been allowed to fight.

But that was a thing of the past. Now N. was a small prosperous market town where the inhabitants mostly spoke German and seemed friendly and relaxed. These new recruits became aware almost immediately that they had been washed up in a peaceful backwater of the war. On the whole, and given that military camps do not exist to nourish the spiritual life of their occupants, this establishment was cheerful and relaxed. The German instructors, themselves drawn from diverse backgrounds, were people who had dropped out from frontline service: some were too old, some too unfit, and others politically unreliable.

While the official ethos was to fully train them as professional soldiers capable of serving the Reich anywhere they were ordered to do so, and their formal training programme was consistent with this, their instructors treated them as innocents who should be taught how to defend themselves in situations that might be desperate or unyielding. They realised that these regular German soldiers were not fanatics imbued with the Nazi theories of racial superiority, of which some of these recruits had seen a great many, but men who did not believe in the triumph of the Third Reich: they all to some extent accepted that Germany was in a war that it had been unwise to start and which it was unlikely to win.

Adam was immensely cheered by this realisation. It being so he could enter into the training and mix with his new comrades with good heart. What they were doing was learning how to defend themselves and, in being trained, they were in a funny way learning how to protect and fight for the things in which they really believed, or which they might find expedient at some future date to accept – an independent Poland, Czechoslovakia or Austria.

Of course, there was some political indoctrination. This propaganda was amusing to some of them; the origins of the war, the Jewish and communist conspiracies to conquer the world against which Germany stood alone as a beacon of European civilisation, and so on. These ideas washed over their heads: it was best to enjoy yourself while you could was the principal idea in which they believed.

But in one important respect, it was no joke. The Gestapo had produced a grotesque film about Jews as the justification for their persecution. The Jews were blame for almost every ill in society: for economic exploitation, the spreading of disease, and for undermining national solidarity by mongrelizing the German race. Even the most tolerant and easygoing were influenced in some way by the film: and for the anti-semitic among the soldiers, it stirred emotions to a frenzy of spiteful enmity.

His fellow recruits naturally divided into two groups: young men with similar backgrounds to Adam to whom this conscription was a great adventure which they might not have wanted but were determined to enjoy; and older men with families, who thought of very little else but their homes, who sought leave more often than it was offered and who listened anxiously to the radio for news of Allied bombing. These men did not enjoy themselves; they waited eagerly for the post, and pleaded illness and injury to avoid the physical rigours of the training. Adam thought: *"If this is the master race it isn't very frightening."* And as he was naturally better than most in doing the training tasks, he grew in confidence.

The military training itself was thorough. Adam learnt to be proficient in several weapons and became very fit. He learnt something of military discipline and its reasons; which they interpreted as doing what you wanted while keeping out of trouble. They learnt how to care for each other when in battle. Adam had no difficulty with all this; he could already shoot and had a good eye for it and a steady aim. But more important than this he found that he had natural leadership qualities quickly recognised by his comrades and which scored highly in his assessments.

As he passed through this course he saw himself approved of. His instructors would say things like: "If you want to know how to do that watch Adam." He had to be careful about that: not every hard-pressed recruit wanted to admire him, and as his self-esteem rose he became bumptious. He was riding for a fall. Fortunately he made good friends and allowed himself to be ragged and when he joined in the card games he tried hard not to be obvious about winning – and even lost a little to be politic. And as he was thought a good sport, he managed to walk his personal tightrope without falling off.

After they had been in training for a month these raw recruits were given weekend passes and allowed to visit the town. They were warned to be careful because although most of the townsfolk were friendly some of the non-German speaking Czechs could be hostile.

It was the first public outing in a German military uniform. Adam loved his uniform. Simple and rough cast though it was he felt that it defined him: he felt more powerful, a feeling reinforced in the town. Some people treated him with deference, which he liked; it aroused fear, which he enjoyed; and the girls reacted positively, which he thought promising.

Without thinking about it, his behaviour became more arrogant; in important respects he had always been bold, but this was something more. The inhabitants of N. had seen it all before and so they were not slow in putting this young upstart in his place. There was a possibility of trouble and Adam was saved from difficult situations not by his own good sense but by his friends dragging him away from them.

On his second weekend Adam got into a card game in a local bar. He had been drinking and his normal good judgement in selecting the players and in strategy was missing: he lost money and became cocky and aggressive. Looking around first to see whether the coast was clear, his fellow players, who had turned out to be Czech, decided to teach him a lesson: they jumped him, beat him up and with the assistance of the barman, threw him out into the street. His companion, a small and nondescript conscript, staggered out after him and, being the better of them both for wear, walked him back to the barracks.

He had been seen and reported. Consequently, he was summoned to appear before the captain responsible for his discipline and reprimanded. His explanation was accepted. There was no punishment and the captain, to his astonishment, winked at him while issuing his warning. His behaviour in the town, and his response to the captain, had been noted down as spirited. New standards were being applied to him and his hopes and aspirations soared. *Perhaps, he thought, I could succeed in the German army and get a really nice uniform with epaulettes and badges. But, of course, this was stupid, he knew that, and he didn't really want to do any fighting; he wanted the war to be over and to go back home.*

The boys knew that the local girls were impressed by them as young heroes in waiting; it gave them hope of immediate conquest. They were up for it, but that did not mean that it was easy to succeed. Despite the boasting most of these young soldiers failed their conquest and virility tests.

Time passed and there was only one remaining chance. On their last Friday a dance was arranged for those recruits who had done well. Some of the local girls were invited. This was a staid event and although there was some alcohol it was really a fruit juice and sandwich affair. It was highly supervised in that there were career soldiers present: but there were girls, no matter how sanitised the arrangements. There were snags: Adam couldn't dance and he lacked social skills. But latching himself onto Maurice, a doctor's son with some wit and charm, he hoped for the best.

The boys lined up along one wall with the girls opposite them. At a given signal the boys advanced. "Follow me Adam, I'll get you going," said Maurice darting towards the prettiest girl; blond and curvaceous, with what might be described as winning ways. Adam got the consolation prize of her friend.

At first he was disappointed. Her name was Maria and she could not be described as pretty. It wasn't either that she was plain: with a slim body, smooth brown hair falling almost to her waist, and an engaging smile, she was really presentable: but he was so hyped up and expectant that he needed something much more obvious.

But she did smile at him. "Hello Adam," she said, "show me then." And he did his best to show her although she was far more proficient than him. But as the evening wore on, and the country dancing swirled them apart he thought that he had lost her and that he had been inadequate. Later, the four of them did meet up again. He saw enviously that Maurice appeared to have made a conquest while he had made a mess of it.

Towards the end of the evening they danced again. He felt her body press against him: her breasts were small and firm and he liked them. He had consumed some beer and made some jokes, which she laughed at. They laughed a lot. And then she spoke to him very directly and simply. "Adam, it is so nice to be a German, my family are so proud of it, and they would be proud of you too, as a German soldier, if they met you. Of course, I know they haven't met you," she chattered on, "but if they did they would be delighted with you." He thought this was a strange way of talking but he liked her more now and pressed her closer to him.

And then suddenly it was all over. Distracted for a moment, when he looked for her she had gone. His heart sank. Just when he had got going, he had lost her. Maurice found him.

"Adam, great wasn't it."

He looked like the cat that had found the cream.

"Here's the arrangement."

The girls were to come to the Passing Out Parade the next morning and then they would find a place and time.

"I thought I'd blown it," said the relieved Adam.

"Not a bit of it, I hear you were a great success. You must have hidden talents," and Maurice punched him to show his approval.

The girls were as good as their word. After the Parade they went off together, the boys having been given leave. Maurice and Anneka went on ahead and Adam envied Maurice's poise and success with her. They took a bus up into the forest which surrounded the town and where Anneka's father had a wooden dacha. In the bus Maria took his arm so nicely and squeezed it so gently that he felt reassured and they spoke gaily to each other so that he was sure that she really liked him and that he liked her. Maurice and Anneka said hardly anything: they were too busy necking, kissing and giggling.

The dacha was small and sparse with only two rooms and a kitchen. While the girls prepared some warm food the boys lit a log fire, so very quickly they were all warm and well-fed. Adam offered to help Maria clear away and wash-up, and when they returned there was no sign of Anneka and Maurice who had commandeered the bedroom. Adam did not know what to do but for Maria there was no problem. She found some blankets and spread them on the floor before the fire and then she persuaded Adam to take of his clothes and to help her undress.

"Stay calm, Adam," she murmured to him. When Adam said something about protection, she said: "No need Adam, there's no problem at this time of the month and, even if there was, I would be proud to have your child. Be quiet, Adam, you talk too much," and she stopped him talking.

Adam thought afterwards that he had been a fool to think that Anneka could have bettered anything he had experienced, for Maria's calmness and sweetness must be unparalleled. She had given herself to him without reservation and timed her coming to exactly mirror his own.

She had clung to him in a state of ecstasy which pleased him. And when they had rested, she had wanted to continue and to bring him to release again, bringing to him the understanding of what had gone before. In the end he drew back when she would have continued.

His head was in a whirl. He had done nothing to deserve this; like Hannah and Julia before he had been pathetic, but despite that he had been chosen. This time he recognised that it was different because in other circumstances he and Maria could have been friends. He would have liked to be friends. But it was the war, throwing people together and whirling them apart. As he got up Maria pulled him back, kissing him again. *"If this is the result of war,"* he thought, *"let it roll on."*

It was the happiest day of Adam's life. He was eighteen years of age. He had become a German soldier and would succeed in this: and then this lovely girl had given herself to him without reservation and in the sweetest way. The dark days had passed away and he would be all right. Before they parted Maria gave him a silver pendant and a chain. The pendant contained her address, and she asked him, with tears in her eyes, to remember her; and he said that he would. *He felt a real man: that is what real men did, they kissed them, loved them and left them.*

Back at the barracks Maurice and Adam were able to exchange notes. Adam said: "The one thing I didn't understand was the bit on babies," and he told Maurice of the conversation.

"You are a baby yourself, you simpleton. The girls at the dance were specially chosen. Their fathers are all Nazi Party fanatics who think their daughters could not do better than to populate the new Reich. It's just as well that we are getting out of here tomorrow."

"Go on with it," replied Adam. "Pull the other leg."

Adam was told that the detachment of trainees were to go to France. The relief was enormous. What could be softer? No fighting, friendly people and a warm and pleasant climate. God was smiling on him again. Before embarking they were allowed five days' leave, which for him was a chance to go home. He thought of Julia. She had been as good as her word and he was sorry he had doubted her. She would have been pleased for him, top of his detachment and a real German soldier. For the moment there was no thought of Miss Zbucki, pushed out of his consciousness by these momentous happenings and undertakings.

He travelled back on the same route, perhaps the same train, by which he had come eight weeks ago. Now he had behind him the best military training a soldier could receive and was entitled to wear this uniform, which commanded respect everywhere. He was coming up to his nineteenth birthday and already he had been asked to do the harshest and most difficult tasks and had not been found wanting. He passed through the same peaceful and prosperous country, but this time without the foreboding and unpleasant dreams.

At the rail station at P. he joined a queue to catch the bus home. As he waited the conversation stopped. People waited quietly for the bus for some minutes without uttering a word. As he approached the bus someone pushed into him with a muffled apology, and a farm boot came down hard on his foot.

"So sorry," said the voice, as the unknown passenger pushed his way to the back of the bus.

"Nice day," he said to the old lady next to him. She grunted but said nothing, looking fixedly ahead of her. And as the bus stopped, and he got out someone spat at him, spoiling his pressed trousers, but he could not see who it was. Voices growled in protest as the bus moved away, but it was too late to identify anyone with the sound.

He stood there in this familiar road as the bus disappeared. The German army writ did not run everywhere, he realised. It could even be dangerous for him to stay where he was, and he hurried himself home. Knowing he was coming, Sophie had written to Mary pleading with her to return home for some leave and she responded. Mary's hair had grown now and some of the mental scars had healed. So he was greeted by all three of them with kisses and hugs and with Rosa riding on his shoulders he whirled round and round the kitchen. They persuaded him to get out of the uniform and into some old clothes. "When you meet people Adam," said his mother, "do not say anything at all about the army. It's best for them and you not to discuss military matters."

"What a fool I am," he said to himself as he got out of this uniform and sat on his familiar bed. "What an idiot," and then he thought of Miss Zbucki and was ashamed of himself. "*I am Polish. I must do my best in whatever situation I'm in, but whatever I do I remain Polish – it will be pointless unless I remain Polish.*" The self-confidence flooded from him, leaving him much where he was eight weeks ago.

Mary comforted him. "There is nothing to be ashamed of in being a German soldier, Adam. I've seen a lot of them. They are very polite and correct. There's a lot worse than them." Adam thought that to be true. At Auschwitz there was hardly a German voice to be heard; the SS guards were Ukrainian or Latvian, the scum of the earth, who enjoyed cruelty and punishing people. The professional soldiers like him knew this to be wrong. But what could they do? Nothing. Then he thought of what he had done and knew this argument to be wrong. But he was grateful to Mary for taking his side.

Mary meant it. She had compared the Germans with the people on her farm. After she had been attacked, she had become contemptuous of her attackers and thought of them as barbarians. She did not want the life they wanted for themselves. At the end of this war, when Germany had defeated its enemies – as she was certain they would – she would go to Germany. Perhaps, she might marry a German, for German men seemed to like her.

Mary had said nothing to her mother about the attack on her. She laughed off her short hair as the current style. And, yes, she had given up Heinrich. Sophie pressed her for she knew that all was not well with her daughter, but in the end she stopped, for Mary resented the questions and in the short time available no one wanted to fall out as there would be no time to mend fences.

Sophie said nothing about Peter other than that he did not come any more. But she looked sad about it and Mary, resolving to say nothing, saw that the bounce and glow had gone out of her mother, and that she was looking old again. These two women forced to confront each other with things of the heart saw the similarity of their emotions and the foolishness of falling in love in the midst of war: there could be no certainty in it and nothing but heartache.

Adam was sobered by the two women who were most important to him in this life. Mary was not her usual self and he felt sure that something bad had happened; and his mother seemed very lonely indeed. He liked Peter and he raised his name several times to show that he approved of him. She saw that he was being very loving and anxious for her and so told him about the visit to the church and what had been said.

"What do those crows know about life."

The words spat out of him as he recalled his own encounter at Auschwitz, and with all his new found knowledge he said: "Life is too short Mum. You deserve a good friend."

But he didn't mean anything sexual, finding it hard to believe that adults of his parents' age did that kind of thing. And it wasn't 'goose for the gander' either, as he thought of his father.

At different times Sophie took her two elder children to the station. In waving them goodbye she was aware that she might never see them again. She waited for some time on the platform until the last of the engine smoke had disappeared. Each time her heart was heavy and her spirit full of foreboding; and on each occasion she lay on her bed for a long time crying about her husband and for Peter.

CHAPTER 12

IN THE WINTER Sophie found it difficult to earn enough money to
support herself and Rosa: seasonal sales of vegetables and soft fruit
were no longer possible, and even the friendliest of farmers declined
the liming of their buildings. Without Adam's regular unopened wage
packets she could hardly have subsisted, and now that he was in France
this regular assistance had become more sporadic. She had taken to
visiting neighbouring farmers without appointment and, that was how,
without planning it, she had met Peter again.

On a narrow country road her cart was blocked by his tractor, and in
the ensuing confusion of manoeuvring to and fro they had to speak to
each other, and to laugh in their embarrassment and excitement. The
human heart in its vagaries has its own logic: Sophie was on a road
she might have avoided, as it was not the most obvious route to her
destination, and in taking it she was sure to pass near his farm. As for
Peter, he used this road more often than strictly speaking made sense.
He would gaze up the hill towards P. and sigh when he saw the road
was empty.

Shyly they shook hands and Peter kissed her on the cheek. He asked
for permission to visit her at the farm, and she returned the kiss without
a word. When she got home she washed her hair and changed into her
Sunday clothes, although it was a weekday and she had nowhere special
to go. She decided to visit her friend Anna and arrived there not able to
talk. But she asked her for another appointment and for her help in
rearranging herself. So without her saying anything about Peter, her
friend knew, and all Anna said was: "I will," and hugging her, "I'm so
pleased for you, dear Sophie."

Peter came back to Chwistek family life and everyone was the better for it. Rosa welcomed him with enthusiasm but with some anxiety about whether he was back to stay. She was easily reassured. For Sophie and Peter it was not entirely a matter of continuing. Now they were a little wary of each other and, having been hurt, a little cautious; the rush of spring had become high summer and there was a need to coast along for a while.

This time as she became easier in her mind Sophie wished to know more: she encouraged him to speak more about his family, and she asked him about his wife. While he wanted to respond and to be open with her, she saw that it was difficult for him: his face darkened and he moved about the room restlessly. She wanted to withdraw her question seeing the pain and disturbance it had caused him, but he waved her away in order to speak at all.

"Sophie I do have a wife, you are entitled to know, and I want you to know. I do not know where she is. I know that sounds ridiculous, but I do not know. *I've lost her.*"

"Lost her, what do you mean? How could you lose her?"

Peter explained. His wife had become ill – become depressed – and she needed special treatment. His doctor had been very good and had found a place in a nursing home near G. for her where she could receive special treatment – psychiatric treatment.

"She was not mad," Peter said anxious to reassure her, "but very depressed."

This treatment cost him a lot of money, at least a lot of money for him, and he paid the fees monthly. Each month the matron would send him a receipt and a short summary of his wife's progress. At the beginning of 1940 these monthly reports stopped and a little later when he queried this he received an official letter.

Peter pulled a letter out of his jacket pocket and Sophie read it. It came from the Regional Health Authority and was signed by a Commissioner of Health whose signature was unreadable.

It said:

'I have to inform you that the sanatorium to which you refer has been closed so that it can be refitted as a military establishment. The inhabitants have been evacuated to suitable premises to the east where they will be well looked after. Please continue with your payments as usual.'

"What does it mean? Where is she now?" asked a puzzled Sophie.

"I don't know. I wrote again, several times, and then I received this letter."

Peter gave her a second letter and with mounting anger she read it. It read:

> *'We have received several communications from you. We have explained that the subject about which you write is covered by military intelligence regulations. We remind you that to seek confidential information about military matters is a criminal matter which could render you liable to imprisonment. The evacuation of the patients was in their own best interests and their location cannot be revealed to you. You are instructed to make no further enquiries and to continue with your payments.'*

"What did you do?" enquired an incredulous Sophie.

"Nothing. What could I do?"

"And are you still making the payments?"

"Yes, I am. I haven't missed any payment."

"Do you understand what has happened?"

"No. I haven't a clue."

They resolved that something must be done. While not admitting it to themselves or each other they were recognising that until this matter was resolved there was no moving on for either of them.

They decided to visit the sanatorium together. While the decision to go was an easy one, the practical difficulties were immense. It would be costly; arrangements would have to be made to look after Rosa and the farm; and they would have to find over-night accommodation as it would be unlikely that their mission could be completed in a day.

The latter consideration raised the issue of where they stood in their relationship. Sophie decided to be clear: "Peter," she started in her usual confident manner, "I need you to know that nothing can happen between us until I know what has happened to *my* Ludvig. So long as he might be alive I shall remain faithful to him. I'm sure you feel the same about your wife."

He nodded.

"What has happened to Ludvig? Have you heard from him?" he said.

Sophie explained that she had received a card, and that she sent him regular food parcels and believed him to be all right. Peter thought that it was not for him to be pessimistic or to attempt to set the rules for their relationship; and so he agreed with her, and decided to take his chance.

When two people are newly in love even mundane tasks carried out together become an adventure. Here these two were on a long train journey, side by side, and after a while, hand in hand, sharing a meal prepared by her, and talking about all and sundry without a care in the world. On such a trip every little thing learnt by a lover becomes keenly acquired knowledge to be stored and treasured.

Sophie enquired: "Peter do you think that this war will end soon?"

"Oh, yes I expect so. In war the two sides exhaust themselves after a while and negotiate the end. That's what will happen this time."

And he continued: "Don't you think it is pretty normal. Life I mean. We go on as normal for much of the time."

She nodded.

"Of course, one good thing is that we are getting rid of the Jews."

Seeing her startled, he added quickly: "Not that I wish them any harm but, if we have a choice, I would prefer them to be somewhere else, not in Poland."

Sophie was thoughtful.

"But they are being harmed," she said. "Everyone in Poland knows that they are being cruelly treated and killed in camps. That's right isn't it?"

He agreed that it was right but continued calmly: "Don't you think that these stories are exaggerated: the Jews are always complaining. You can't believe what they say."

Sophie thought that she did believe these stories. She continued: "If these stories are right though, don't you think that when they have killed the Jews they will start again on the Poles?"

"Oh, no Sophie," he laughed, "why should they?"

"Well for the same reason really, hatred and greed."

"Well maybe there is something to that," Peter responded carefully and changed the subject.

These two had more on their mind than politics. For the moment there was the journey and the immediacy of each others company and then, as they approached G., there was the task ahead. It was best they thought to go first to the sanatorium. It lay close to a village three kilometres to the north of the town. A bus took them to the village and they took a pathway through a pleasant forested area where, in a clearing relatively remote among the trees, stood an entirely normal four-storey red-bricked building. The windows were covered with iron grilles and the door was reinforced in steel, both of which Peter thought new. The door was locked and they had to ring a bell. As they waited they noticed a brass plate on the wall which read: SS Abhurst, Regional Centre.

The door was opened by a middle-aged man in civilian clothes and they told him that they had come to see the superintendent of the sanatorium. "You had better come in," was the response. He ushered them into a waiting room off the main hall and they waited for what seemed to them a long time before he returned. "Follow me," was the command, and he led them along a corridor to what Peter remembered as the superintendent's office.

To Peter there seemed little change in the office itself: but there was no superintendent. Behind the desk was a black-uniformed SS captain and to one side a young female secretary with poised notebook and pencil. Sophie nearly died on the spot, her knees buckled and she swayed a little. Peter was struck dumb and his words when he could summon them were incomprehensible.

The SS captain said: "What can I do to help you?" and then, "If you want my help you must speak up. We are very busy here." So Peter spoke up and explained that he was concerned to know what had happened to his wife. The SS man who had been looking at them as if practising a reply said: "Where have you come from?" and then expressed his surprise that they had travelled such a distance. "It is a great pity, this journey, for I cannot help you. I am a military man, you see, and I know nothing about this sanatorium you speak of and indeed, until you told me, that there had ever been a sanatorium here."

They looked startled and he saw this as he continued: "So Peter, if that is your name, you must address your inquiries to the appropriate civil authorities and keep well-clear of the military." He had been very polite and correct but they felt menaced: this man was not to be argued with or believed. And in response to their half-hearted questions as to what civil authority, he responded: "That is enough of this matter I think. War is very confusing and great changes are going on. I cannot advise you and you shouldn't ask me. But Peter take it from me, if you will, you should forget about this matter. Your wife is being cared for, I have no doubt about that, and one day you will hear something from her."

The secretary ushered them out of the building. Shaken and disturbed and saying very little to each other they made their way back to the village and the safety and warmth of a bar.

"Well Peter, what do you make of it?"

At last warmed a little by some soup they were able to speak again.

"I don't like it. You cannot believe that man. He knows what has happened and it must be something very dreadful."

They chatted on trying to reassure each other and to work out the next step, for they were determined to keep trying. The bar was not crowded and the proprietor, noticing that they were strangers, and hearing some of the conversation, sat down at their table and engaged them in conversation. He seemed an approachable man so they told him from where they came and what they were trying to do.

The barman knew something, they thought, for he appeared disturbed by their account and a little nervous. He made as if to go without commenting but Peter treated him to a drink and persuaded him to stay and talk.

"You are very brave people going to that place. Not many people would go into an SS office and ask awkward questions."

"What do you mean, awkward questions?" said Peter.

"Well, questions that they don't want to be asked," and then hastily, "well any questions at all really. They don't answer questions, do they?"

"What do you know?" said Peter impatiently. "Do you know anything about these patients – what happened to them?"

"I can tell you that they were evacuated from that building some time ago. I don't know anything else. But the superintendent does. You could ask *her*."

As they expressed surprise, he told them that she lived on the outskirts of the town and, while he did not know her address as such, he described to them how to get to that area.

"When you get there ask again, anyone will know, and good luck."

The barman's directions were accurate and they found the superintendent's house – a substantial detached property standing in its own grounds and just as he had described it. Peter recognised the elderly, stout, and respectable woman who answered the door bell although she on introduction did not recognise him.

She did not wish to be identified as the superintendent of the sanatorium or to answer his questions and tried to close the door. Peter stuck a foot in and resisted her and then thrust himself through it closely followed by Sophie. The woman threatened to go the police.

"Do it." said Peter. "We would welcome it."

They all calmed down: no one wanted to go to the police.

"Come into the sitting room," she said.

And then she relented seeing that they were determined: "I don't know much but I shall tell you what I can."

She said that in May 1941 she had received a notice from the local administration that the sanatorium was to be evacuated to somewhere in the east and that at that date her services would no longer be needed. When she enquired about it, she was told that the military authorities required the use of the building. She was not told the patients' destination. The SS collected the patients in two special vans. At the time she thought these vans to be peculiar because the passengers were sealed in and the windows were small and rather high. There were nearly five hundred patients in the sanatorium and it took these vans some five days of three trips each day to transport them all out.

"Didn't you ask where they were going?" asked Peter.

She looked at him pityingly.

"I was busy with the patients. They were very excited. Some of them thought they were going on holiday and the SS soldiers laughed and said that they were. So everyone was pleased and impatient to get into the vans. I must say that these soldiers were very nice to the patients, reassuring them and settling them down. That's all I know. Since then I have been out of a job. My treatment has been a disgrace."

She went on about her favourite subject – her treatment – for a while before they decided that she knew nothing more and got up to leave. "Oh, yes," she said, holding them back. "I thought there was another odd thing about the vans, for the SS that is. Along the sides were printed, 'Louies Cakes and Delicacies.' One old lady had said: "Of course we're going on holiday, look at the vans!"

It was getting late and they were tired so it was agreed between them that it was all they could do on this first day. They found some modest lodgings and agreed to share a room. That was all they shared for Sophie took the bed and Peter a blanket on the floor and they fell asleep almost immediately.

Sophie slept well but when she woke it was clear that Peter had not. Yesterday had been a day of action and while acting he had little time to dwell on what he had learned. The night had been different. He had slept badly and woke early, angry and confused, and doubtful whether they could do any more. But over breakfast he calmed down and they decided that there was one thing further they could do: they would go to the offices of the local administration and demand to know the whereabouts of the patients.

It was not as easy as they thought to find a responsible office authority and it was their third port of call before they found what appeared to be an appropriate functionary. Local administration in the area was in a state of confusion. Since the occupation extra layers of accountability had been added and interlocking agencies blurred and delayed the making of decisions. Nowhere was this more evident than in security matters where the local police lacked any real powers, and the various sections of the SS, sometimes taking local decisions and on other occasions their orders from Berlin, exercised overweening authority in no way answerable to the civilian authorities.

In a modest grey functional building where worried looking Government servants bustled to and fro in a state of excited activity and confusion, they thought for a brief few moments that their questions might be answered. They had found the Department of Health and within it the functionary responsible for Mental Health, and within that, which was an achievement, the official responsible for sanatoriums.

At first the receptionist told them that it was not possible for them to see anyone without an appointment: they explained their position. The receptionist told them, quite rudely they thought, that the official they needed to speak to was at a meeting and would be unobtainable all day. They said that they would wait. Sophie asked for and was given the name of the person. After an hour of waiting it was suggested that they leave and they refused.

Their refusal caused a flurry of activity behind the desk and resulted in the appearance of a blue-uniformed Polish policeman. He was a tall, overweight man, with a shaven head. On first sight he seemed brutish but his manner as he spoke to them was polite and gentlemanly.

"I've been told to kick you out. What's your problem?"

They explained and he looked thoughtful.

"I tell you what. Do you see those stairs to the left of me?"

They nodded.

"Well if I walk to the other side of the entrance with my back to you and you go up those stairs to Room 512 it won't be my responsibility will it?"

He winked and confirmed the name of the official to them.

They found Room 512 and the official. It was a large room with six people working in it, and their arrival and their question about the presence of the official caused a disturbance. The worried looking official in question was an imposing woman of above average height and weight. Her fair hair was tied in a bun and her dress was masculine in effect. She identified herself, rose from her seat, and taking Sophie's arm led them both back into the corridor. "This is outrageous. You have no right to come into my office unannounced." She spoke in German and in an agitated whisper which ended in a hiss.

They were daunted by this powerful response to their audacity. Hesitatingly and in Polish they started to explain their purpose in coming. The official became increasingly agitated and annoyed.

"I cannot talk to you about it. It is a military matter you are raising and I have no authority to discuss it with you."

"*Who has the authority?*" asked Sophie recovering her courage.

The official looked around her in the corridor. There was no one passing. She hesitated, and for the moment they thought that she was going to reveal something. But she didn't, and then noises of people on the staircase hardened her attitude to them.

"In our department we have no knowledge of the matter you describe," she began to sound authoritative fearing that she might be overheard.

"And for all we know this sanatorium is operating as normal."

"What nonsense," exclaimed Sophie, "we were there yesterday and it was closed."

"You had no right to be there," was the exasperated reply. "It's a security matter and you are foolish to ask me questions about it. You must leave now."

She insisted on leading them back down the stairs.

She reprimanded the Polish policeman who explained that they had sneaked in when his back was turned. He said to them at the entrance: "Go to the small square to the right of this building where there are some benches. I shall be free in a few minutes and will come and talk to you." They did what he told them to do, and they held hands in the square comforting each other, going over together what they had been told, and making no sense of it.

This large shambling bear of a policeman joined them as promised. "I won't sit down," he said, "because I do not want anyone to see me with you. You can talk where you are sitting. Tell me your story again." Peter told the story.

The policeman said that over the last two years several people had come to the office seeking relatives and that there were rumours in the office about what might have happened to them. He looked very grave, as if he knew, and they feared the worst. And then Peter said: "And the really peculiar thing about these vans was that on the side of them was printed, 'Louies Cakes and Delicacies'."

"Oh dear," said the policeman. "I'm so sorry, I was hoping you wouldn't say anything like that."

And he told them this story. Some while ago the office had been visited by a senior SS officer, he couldn't remember his name or the date. The Director of Health Services had asked him to stand guard at his office door as a precaution – he didn't know what against – and he had heard part of their conversation. He took a deep breath. They talked about gassing people in vans. And then this SS officer had said to the Director, and he had heard this clearly: "I do not want you to think, dear Hans, that the SS has no sense of humour. The really nice thing about our plans is that the vans will have printed on them, 'Louies Cakes and Delicacies.' Amusing don't you think?"

Sophie screamed, causing bystanders to look at her. Peter buried his face in his hands and sank lower like a stricken beast. The policeman was alarmed: "I've tried to help you. For God's sake don't say anything to anybody – and don't come back into our office. I could be in serious trouble for talking to you. Go home now."

But they couldn't move. There was no comfort in knowing – and in any case they could not put this poor woman to rest. They would never know where her remains – if any – were to be found. These poor patients had joined the millions of others who had disappeared without trace and were assumed dead.

On the train back home, Peter had gone to sleep with his head cradled on Sophie's shoulder and she had not moved for a long time for fear that he would wake. She knew that he was dreadfully upset, consumed with guilt for putting his wife in this asylum and for his slowness in responding when he knew that something bad might have happened.

"Peter it is not your fault," she murmured to him constantly. "*You* didn't kill her."

"I should have done more," was the reply.

Peter thought himself a very bad and foolish person. He suspected his motives: perhaps, really, he had wanted to be rid of her, and that was why he had taken the doctor's advice to place her in the sanatorium. But then he knew that was not right, and he had done it out of genuine concern and care. But if so, why had he not acted more quickly? Could it be that he had moved on: that he wanted Sophie? But he knew himself to be an honourable man. And what about this nonsense of trusting the Germans and believing in the best? He hardened his heart. But most of all he grieved, overwhelmed by the horror of what had happened and his own inadequacies.

Sophie thought less of Peter. He had proved to be weaker and more naïve than she had thought before: but she loved him more, for his shortcomings had shown her that he needed her. She kissed him gently while he slept. And while he slept, she thought of Ludvig. Perhaps Ludvig was dead too. She had been sending him food parcels every few weeks with letters bringing him up to date with family happenings without receiving any reply. Did this mean that he was dead and that she was free? Sophie thought him to be alive. She didn't feel him dead – or want him to be so – and so she answered her own question. She wasn't free.

Had Sophie possessed magic powers at this time she would have discovered that her intuition was right: Ludvig was very much alive. At this time, when their train was wending its way back to P. in the failing evening light, Ludvig lay peacefully on his camp-bed. Not any old camp-bed, but rather a comfortable one, in a small room of his own. This bed had not easily been come by: it was the result of a good deal of effort or, to be more precise, what the prisoners described as 'organising'.

Sachsenhausen was a very hard camp: not a death camp like Auschwitz but a punishment camp of long standing. To survive at Sachsenhausen you needed to learn the rules very quickly and then 'to organise': that is to use the rules to your advantage. Prison was not an all-lose, no-gain environment: but it was one where the overwhelming majority did lose, and where the rules were designed to see that they did. At this moment Ludvig was not a loser. He might become one in the future, but for now he had started to climb the ladder to safety.

Ludvig had become what was called a blokowy: a masculine prisoner in charge of a block. From his doorway he looked down the block that was his domain. It was long and narrow. Down each side were some fifty bunks, three-bunks high, giving a total capacity of three hundred prisoners: sometimes there were less and sometimes more. At the far end there were some washing facilities and lavatories. It was spartan but clean: he made a point of it, his block was always clean. For the moment there was nothing to do. He made himself some coffee using his electric ring and his own provisions, took down a book from the rack above his bedhead and started to read.

Sophie felt herself to be closer to Peter as a result of their dreadful experience. She believed that Peter needed her. She decided that if

Peter still wanted it she would take this friendship further. But for Peter the result of the discovery of his wife's death was overwhelming. He wanted no more than to be on his own to come to terms with what had happened. He stopped going to Sophie's for a while to think it through and to grapple with the guilt.

CHAPTER 13

THE SACHSENHAUSEN CONCENTRATION camp, situated a few kilometres north of Berlin, was built as a model German camp in 1936, replacing an older one on the site dating from 1933. Sachsenhausen was designated by the Germans, with their passion for classification, as a Class 1 camp. The sign above the gate proclaimed Arbeit Macht Frei,* but unlike Auschwitz which had the same homily, the sign had a real meaning: in its early days many prisoners serving indeterminate sentences, including Jews, were released if they demonstrated that they had learnt the principles of being a good German citizen or, in the case of Jews, if some deal had been done, such as arrangements for their emigration.

In September 1939 when Ludvig arrived through the main gates he found himself in a fenced camp with modern barracks and well-maintained roads and pedestrian ways. It reminded him of the best of the army barracks he had experienced in his military career and commanded his respect. Although the gate-house was equipped with machine-guns, with lines of fire that covered the entire camp, he felt no fear: his heart leapt, and he said to himself that this was a place in which he could survive.

For several years of his life, during his military and to some extent his police career, Ludvig had experienced the liberation that comes from the removal of responsibility. In some sense a prisoner is like a military conscript: now it was his duty to understand and obey the rules and to survive. Wars did not last forever and prison terms would surely come to an end at some time. In the meantime he would be

* Work Sets You Free'.

housed, fed and clothed: there were no bills to be paid or family to be cared for.

These early hopes were cruelly tested. It was true that he was here to work and that the rudiments of care were present: but the camp was intended as a punishment and the means for doing terrible things were numerous and cruel. First, he discovered that Sachsenhausen was not one camp but many: there were over one hundred sub-camps in the history of Sachsenhausen where over five hundred thousand prisoners worked as forced labour. A sub-camp could be little more than a barracks adjacent to a factory where working and living conditions could be highly primitive.

Prisoners at Sachsenhousen were categorised and labelled. The inhabitants wore badges on the familiar striped prison uniform: political prisoners wore red triangles: homosexuals wore pink and Jehovah's Witnesses purple, Gypsies brown, the work-shy white, and the 'social misfits' black. A green triangle denoted a recidivist: a repeat offender. Non-Jewish 'race defilers' wore a triangle with a black border. Jews wore the familiar yellow but rarely yellow alone: with red political, green criminal, and so on.

Your classification was your milepost to death or release – and a sure indication of your treatment. From 1942 if you were a Jew your prospects were poor; separate barracks, the worst food and work, and the harshest punishments. If you did not die from the combination of malnutrition, excessive work, and beatings – and the resulting diseases – you might be arbitrarily shot or sent for gassing to a death camp such as Auschwitz. By contrast the political prisoners, of which Ludvig was one, were privileged and largely left alone.

A great many prisoners were killed at Sachsenhausen although we do not know, and Ludvig did not know, how many. Most of these deaths were of gentiles and the greatest number of them were Soviet prisoners of war; Jews were always a minority of the prisoners and, although by 1943 the camp had built a gas chamber, it is unlikely that any Jew was gassed at Sachsenhausen: Jews were removed to Auschwitz before the Sachsenhausen gas chamber became operational.

From the moment of his arrival, therefore, Ludvig was a privileged person and his chances of survival and release were better than average. The odds were subject to the arbitrariness of camp-life and a regime that had no regard for the sanctity of human life, although possessing one for rules and regulations. The operation of these rules and procedures were under the control of SS guards – model guards specially trained for a model camp. So highly regarded were these SS men that when Auschwitz was set up, its first guards were drawn from Sachsenhausen.

What was operated was a punishment regime. People were to work in a variety of factories around the site whatever their age or condition. These tasks were to be made as unpleasant and debilitating as possible. If your shift was to start at 7.00 a.m. you might be wakened at 4.00 a.m., and counted to 5.00 a.m. without receiving food or drink and in the open air whatever the weather. You were then marched to your work by 6.00 a.m. and made to stand to attention until work started one hour later. The next day might be normal, and you relaxed a little, to find on the third day that you rose at 3.00 a.m. All of this was accompanied by shouted commands of abuse, and beatings if you slipped or hesitated in any way.

There were a diverse range of potential offences and punishments and the consequences of even the most trivial could be disastrous. The most important event of the camp day was the roll-call when the count needed to be exactly right. The counts took place in open ground on at least two times a day, in the morning and in the evening, and could last from twenty minutes to three hours. However, they were also called at random times, at any hour of the day. Individual failure to answer the dreaded cry, 'Schnell, schnell. Appell, antreten'* could result in a severe beating or your death.

Bizarely Ludvig quickly learnt that bedmaking was a sacred relic of Nazi folklore; failure to make a bed 'properly', or beds if an entire block was involved, could result in your death, deportation, or a severe beating. 'Brontenzug'† could be imposed arbitrarily for not working hard enough. Disciplinary matters could lead to bunker punishments – locking into a small room for days with regular beatings – or locking into a cupboard in your block without food for some indeterminate time.

The consequences of what were considered as more serious crimes could be spectacular. Early in his camp life a random roll-call was held to publicly hang two men whose crimes were thought to demean the Reich; their fault was to be overheard singing the Internationale. An act of defiance? Probably.

The dreaded cries ring in your head. You get up, but too slowly. You are late. Three days without bread. What do you do? Steal some. Search

* Quickly, quickly. Roll call, line-up.
† A withholding of bread.

the other bunks for secret stores. Perhaps, someone will help you. Lend you some food. Or you look for your own secret store to find it stolen. The misery and despair is overwhelming. How can you endure these days and the people who have done this to you? Then your blokowy or kapo* tells you that your stinking lavatories – smelling to high heaven because of dysentery – are not properly cleaned – more punishment!

Ludvig is on his bunk. Saving grace – these straw palliasses are clean and comfortable, and for the moment he is not sharing it with anyone. You can sleep at the end of your day. He says to himself: "Let's be logical. What problems do I need to solve?"

Answer: "First. How not to be killed by work? Second, how not to be starved to death?" A working day could be twelve hours and six on Sundays, physically very hard, and in the open air in all weathers. A frequent group punishment was to make you work twelve hours on a Sunday, so you got no rest at all.

But some people had it very soft – why not me? – and how? The two problems were related. The standard diet gave too few calories to survive hard work. Quickly you lost weight and became enfeebled – became a skeleton person – a mussulman.† You would be judged to be unfit for work and murdered. He looked at his body closely. Had he become a mussulman? Perhaps not yet, but he was definitely much thinner.

There was no solution to his problems unless he could command some protekcja:‡ that is what he needed. If you had some protekcja you could be turned into a prominente overnight.§ "How do I get it, become it?" he said to himself. For a man of his experience these questions could be answered. "They were solvable problems," he thought. His police background and natural cunning was useful here. But there was a starting issue: in becoming part of the camp administration, whose side should he be on?

In a sense to be involved in the camp administration at all made you one of them: but there were degrees of belonging. If he became a läufer¶ he might be able to play it both ways. A läufer's job was not

---

* Work leader.
† A man so sick and undernourished that he could not survive.
‡ Patronage and protection.
§ Above others, and to be respected and obeyed: an authoritative person, well dressed and fed and with a place in this new world.
¶ Courier.

simple. A läufer took reports and messages around this complex camp. Ludvig spoke several languages perfectly: Polish, of course, but also German, Czech, French and Russian: and his police training enabled him to find out was happening, and thus he could become a conduit for information and gossip. "I could be useful to a lot of people," he said to himself.

To get a job as a läufer he needed a recommendation. He decided that the best route was through his blokowy. He did him a favour and asked for a reward. Discovering that his blokowy did not know the names of the informers in his block, and what they were getting up to – what they were saying about him – he investigated, identified the men and told the blokowy the results of his enquiries. The blokowy was grateful and impressed and duly made Ludvig the required recommendation. Ludvig got a job as a läufer and took the first upward rung on the social and economic ladder.

A läufer was given a kind of uniform with his job identification on the sleeve. Ludvig began to strut around the camp in full view of everyone. His food ration was increased and the camp kitchens did him favours. He put on weight again. Soon he looked more like his old self. He was a carrier of good and bad news and adroit in recognising its value, so he became not only well-known but respected. He was in a position to do good and help other prisoners or he could do them down. "Quite like old times," he thought.

He waited for the real powers in the camp, the political resisters, to contact him; and once they had checked him out they did so. The two political groups struggling for power within the camp were the German communists and social democrats. At the outset the social democrats, with their numerical superiority, held the advantage: but in the brief period of the Nazi–Soviet pact the communists were able to gain greater acceptability with the SS and from that point their determination and discipline earned them the pole position: an advantage which they never lost.

To the German authorities it always appeared that the communists were the major players as German hopes and fears were centred on the titanic struggle on the Russian front. The communists never weakened in their ideological certainty that the outcome of the struggle with the fascists would be the victory of communism. History, they believed, was on their side and they would triumph in the end. This belief and the self-confidence and organisation that it created was very impressive to the Germans: while these communists remained their enemies, they bore in mind that they were Germans, and that one day they might be their masters.

As the saying goes, information is power. The communists asked for Ludvig's cooperation, and he agreed. The request he was told came from the camp senior, Harry Naujocks himself. Ludvig was very impressed. It was said that Naujocks was so powerful in the camp that even the Commandant himself, Höss, who would find notoriety later as the Commandant at Auschwitz, could be persuaded to rescind an execution.

Ludvig became a loyal servant of the party. He dutifully carried back information which proved timely and accurate. At the same time Ludvig used his gathering influence to assist his fellow prisoners, particularly those he identified as communist or fellow traveller; it might be medical care, extra food, or some protection against bullying; and it was noted that he was especially kind in listening to their problems. Some of these problems he brought to the attention of the Party. In these ways Ludvig kept himself constantly in the minds of the Party functionaries and stored credits for himself for future use.

This new role for Ludvig was not without its disadvantages. He had to move about the camp in all weathers. He thought to himself: "This job is really for a younger man. I need to find a softer job." And then he realised that his job was highly dangerous: the role of the double agent is never easy, and the chances were that you would finish up by getting something of great importance very wrong, your credits would have run out, and that would be the end of you.

Ludvig decided to cash in his chips and seek support for obtaining a position as a blokowy. He made a formal request to the Party while his credit was good. The outcome was disappointing. He was told that he was serving the Party very well in his present position, and that he must accept Party discipline Anyway, there were practical difficulties. These openings were highly prized and fell vacant very rarely. He must be patient and continue to serve the Party. They would tell him what functions he should perform. In short he must wait his turn. He thought: "Waiting your turn might be a fine sentiment but I could be dead before it comes."

Ludvig realised that something more was needed to be done, and the opportunity was before him in his very own barracks: he decided to get rid of his blokowy. This was not easy to accomplish. The blokowy, a small fat middle-aged man with swarthy Georgian-type features, was relatively easy going and indulgent with very few enemies. This easygoing nature was his Achilles' heel, for the job could not be done to the satisfaction of his German masters without the imposition of punishments: weeks would pass without any and then, stung by criticism and fear, he would levy them right and left to the confusion and resentment of prisoners.

Ludvig decided to compile a dossier of the punishment of the political left in his barracks and their grievances. With a little imagination this was not difficult to do, and after a month or two it was quite impressive. Ludvig thought that it might form the basis for an argument that the blokowy was politically unsound.

In itself this was not enough. Ludvig then put together a more insidious list of allegations of the blokowy's indulgences, and an argument that his life-style and sexual behaviour was unacceptable. He maintained that he secured luxurious clothes and other valuables from the store and from prisoners by the granting of sexual favours; that he used SS showers twice a day, and that he and his clerk were seen coming from them wearing silk dressing-gowns and towels.

He set out a series of sexual allegations that the blokowy's relationship with his clerk, with whom he shared his room, was homosexual. In a camp without women, homosexual relationships were not uncommon. To the Germans such relationships were criminal, and the communists, with their puritan ethic, frowned on homosexual behaviour. Ludvig had no idea whether this allegation of his was true: maybe it was and maybe it wasn't, but he thought it arguable.

When he had got that far he tried out his allegations, without the paperwork, with a senior Party official. He was listened to very seriously and told: "Do nothing more. We shall carry out our own enquiries."

He felt sure that something more was needed and he decided to plant some documents. This was a highly dangerous thing to do but he was willing to take the risk.

At this time the matter most concerning the communists was the systematic killing of Soviet soldiers, of which there were large numbers in the camp, and regular large-scale arrivals. The communist intelligence system had proved inadequate, and the Party had been slow to recognise the magnitude of what was happening. The camp authorities had built a killing area out of sight of the barracks. A series of trenches had been created in which Soviet soldiers could be seated on benches. On an excuse of their height being measured as part of a health-check, they were lined up and shot in the neck through a hole in the wall. The bodies were disposed of in the crematorium.

To confuse the Soviet prisoners, their officers and commissars were shot first so robbing them of leadership. They were told that their comrades had been moved to other accommodation. Over a period of a few weeks, twelve thousand soldiers were killed in this way. As it became known, mass protests were made in the prison, and serious difficulties were created for camp security. The Party was outraged that their Soviet comrades had been killed, and mounted their own internal investigation into the inadequacy of their response.

After these happenings, and in the course of his work, Ludvig got his hands on two memoranda from the SS administration. These documents, harmless enough in themselves, if read together could be interpreted as forecasting the killings.

Choosing a moment when the blokowy was absent from his room, Ludvig hid the documents under the mattress of his bed, and immediately told the Party of his suspicions that the blokowy had known something about the killings in advance. The Party made a search and found the documents.

The Party decided that a trial should be held. After curfew the blokowy was confronted with party functionaries who escorted him to another barracks where the great Harry Naujocks resided. There, crowded into a small room no bigger than his own, and a good deal more sparse, his trial took place. This was a Soviet-style trial. The hearing had no legal authority other than the law of the jungle: it obeyed no rules of evidence, there was no representation for the accused, and the complainant was a judge in his own cause.

Despite these handicaps the blokowy handled himself well. Sweating and nervous he might be, but he was innocent of the charges, and like others throughout the ages he felt this to be enough. He reminded them that although not a Party member, as a social democrat he had been anti-Nazi all his adult life. He said it was absurd to think that he picked out Party members for punishment, and that any fair-minded person looking back on all the disciplinary matters that he had dealt with would see that he was even-handed. "No, he was not a homosexual. No, he had no homosexual relationship with his clerk." And to the most serious charge of all: "It is a monstrous suggestion. Of course not, it is crazy, these documents must have been planted."

During this examination the presiding 'Judge' had said nothing: but once the accused had been led out of the room to await the verdict he expressed himself forcefully.

"This man is an honest fool. I don't think he has done anything

wrong and in all probability he has been set up. This Ludvig person –
he seems a likely lad. If he has set this up he has certainly done a good
job."

They all laughed. Their verdict was a simple one; they preferred to
deal with Ludvig, and so they switched the jobs; the blokowy was to
do the job of läufer and Ludvig was to be appointed the blokowy.

This promotion Ludvig felt should be his apogee. He had seen many
men overreach themselves by aspiring to positions that they were not
suited to perform. The higher you climbed the more enemies you made
and he thought: "Making a mistake in this place could be curtains for
me." To the politicos, however, he was now a useful comrade, and,
perhaps even one on the climb and to be looked out for.

So once more Ludvig's star was in the ascendant and his life materi-
ally altered. Now for the first time he could demand his food parcels.
He discovered that Sophie had not forgotten him. The earlier parcels
had long since been disposed of, but he could see from the postage
dates of what was left, that she sent one parcel a month.

The benefits of his position were manifold: with more to bargain
with he could obtain cigarettes regularly, and smoke them in this really
quite pleasant little room; and although he was still required to work,
he was in a position to take the soft jobs and work fewer hours.

What he enjoyed most was the resumption of control over people.
As he looked down his barracks he saw that this flood of people were
under his patronage and influence. Never before had his writ spread so
far. Matters of life and death could be determined by him. "Not that I am
going to do anything really bad, at least if I can avoid it," he said to
himself. "I will be tough but fair."

Of course, he could be bad if he wanted. He knew that he would
have to behave harshly because it was expected. As defined by the SS
a certain level of punishment was required. He did not see anything
problematic about that; the prisoners were inured to it and complaints
about them were easy to conjure up.

In addition, however, there were life-and-death matters, serious
misdemeanours and 'debility as to work', in the official jargon. A man
too ill or incapacitated to work was a useless burden to be disposed of
and he was required to be ruthless and to report it. "Not pleasant," he
said to himself, "but I can do it."

As Ludvig relaxed on his bed he thought of his family. He had heard
nothing about them. He hoped, of course, that they were alive and

well: but he felt nothing. Looking back over his life, deprived as he was of sight and sound of his relatives, they became unreal: a distant memory of another life that probably could never be revived. He sighed as he thought about it. What was this struggle about? One day it would come to an end, hopefully with a German defeat, but the damage would have been done: his family would not have been preserved, and the easy life of friends and comrades was gone forever.

It was around this time that Sophie gave up on him. If Peter's wife could be murdered right under his nose, so to speak, what chance could there be for Ludvig at the mercy of German swine. She felt sure that if he had been alive he would have found a way to get in touch with her. Part of her still felt that he was there and she should wait for him: but until when? The war went on and on and time was passing for her. She needed to love, and Peter needed her to love him. She had a real flesh and blood man on her very own doorstep.

She made a decision. No more food parcels. No more idle dreams.

CHAPTER 14

ADAM'S NEWLY-FORMED division of three battalions assembled in Dresden over a three day period at the end of November. Adam had been posted to its mortar battalion. He felt proud to be a part of this fighting unit and confident of its prowess. His new-found comrades seemed to him to be good chaps and they soon slipped back into the cheery camaraderie of their training days. He was fortunate to depart on the first day because on the second Dresden was hit by a heavy Allied bombing raid which put the rail station out of action for several days and caused heavy troop casualties.

They were sobered by attacks such as these because somehow they had it in mind that they would not be required to fight and, if they did, that it would be a ground battle which, of course, they would win. Now suddenly they had lost thirty to forty of their number without a shot being fired. As the train left the station they saw the very heavy damage caused to the town by bombing, a picture reproduced in every industrial conurbation they passed through on their route across southern Germany to Marseilles in the south of France.

Many of the new recruits were young boys, either ethnic Germans or third degree Germans like himself. It was hard to be starting out in a defeated army and especially one which was determined to fight: in which the professional soldiers believed it was their duty to do so and a matter of honour. Perhaps, he thought, there would be no bombing in France: if France was an ally of Britain it would not be bombed. But his lieutenant said that they should not count on it.

They found it confusing. As they travelled they were told that they were going into the unoccupied zone of France because this part was no longer reliable as some of the people were supporting the British and Americans in their invasion of the French colonies in North Africa. Adam thought: "It becomes more confusing by the hour. *Here am I, a Polish farm-boy, who until the war began was never out of his country, and now I might be killed by an American bomb in Africa.*" That is if he got there at all because on two occasions the train was stopped and remained without lights and silent in the pitch black as bombing took place around them.

Adam asked his lieutenant what they would be doing in France. He thought the question to be amusing.

"Well Adam we are there to maintain security. Not policing, the French do that themselves: but external security against our enemies. Hopefully we shall not be invaded – although we might be. But we must remain vigilant."

"Against whom?"

"Well against the resistance movement. And the British who parachute spies into the country. That sort of thing."

Marseilles took their breath away. Adam was amazed by this large bustling sea port and its cosmopolitan population, where north Africans with their multifaceted tribal groups mixed freely with the French; and where café life with music, girls – all kinds of girls – and gossip, seemed a million kilometres away from the war and the miseries of eastern Europe. But in the beginning they were to see very little of Marseilles as they were trucked away to barracks a few kilometres outside the town.

They arrived to the confusion of events. Suddenly there were too few Germans: the Vichy government's so-called alternative army was being disbanded and there was a need, as their lieutenant explained, to make themselves seen. The three companies of his battalion were to take part in an exercise, 'Operation Visibility', to enforce on the public consciousness the presence and power of the German army. But before this task could begin for Adam, there was something else far more dramatic to happen in Marseilles itself, for which there was a special briefing and training.

Their lieutenant gathered them together to explain the task and their role. Lieutenant Zeisler was a serious young man in his thirties and a professional soldier. He started slowly: "Men. You are new here and have no experience of Marseilles. I must tell you that it is a very dangerous place. There are resisters in this town and a number of our soldiers have been killed and kidnapped. Of course, we have reprisals where this happens – ten of them for every one of our comrades. But this does not stop them."

He paused. He had lost his audience, some of whom gasped. He continued, anxious to allay their fears: "Don't worry you will be fine if you obey the rules when you are in Marseilles. In particular, never less than three of you together at any one time: and always armed."

He continued: "Then there are the spies," he laughed nervously. "Thankfully it it is not my task to tell you how ludicrous this spying is – French resisters, the Vichy Government, the Vichy police trying to catch the resisters, and the Jews – there are a lot of Jews in the town and no one seems able to catch them. Then there are British and American spies – we have more of them since the north African invasion. Then the so-called Free French spy on other Frenchmen here. All this spying does us no good at all and we must bring an end to it."

Lieutenant Zeisler quickened his delivery with the passion of his subject: "These people hide in the old town – in the Old Port to be precise. It is a rabbit warren of secret places and tunnels connecting house to house and street to street. It is easy to escape through these tunnels and dangerous for us to follow our suspects. These people are armed and trained to use their weapons. Well, we Germans have had enough of this. We are going to stop their tricks by blowing up this old town. That will put an end to it."

In this operation the engineers were to wire-up the streets to be destroyed and the SS and the Gestapo were to provide the inner-ring through which the population of the Old Port was to be filtered as they left the area. Their task – their battalion – was to form an outer screening-ring to pick up anyone suspicious who escaped the first line of search. In their training these anxious boy soldiers were reassured: their tasks, although important, were nothing at all really. Their training dealt with the methods of making a search, on how to spot a suspected person, and how to deal with surprise attack – not that this was at all likely.

And so on a cold day in January shivering with anticipation and expectation this blow to the enemy was delivered. It was the German tactic on these occasions to seek the benefits of surprise and to use overwhelming force. Engineers and bomb experts in the dead of night, and while the population slept, wired-up the entire area to be demolished, working quietly and efficiently under the protection of the SS who created the checkpoints through which the population had to pass.

Adam and his comrades established their checkpoints around the area, working in groups of three, during the hours of darkness. The population awoke to be greeted by megaphones, street by street, shouting for them to evacuate; the dreaded shouts of schnell, schnell rang out again and the tramp of SS boots in the streets, up stairwells and in shop doorways terrorised the innocent and the enemy alike, forcing them out of their homes and hiding places.

At first things seemed to be going well. Soon the streets were full of frightened and indignant people who had gathered there with what few personal possessions they had been able to throw together. But panic followed, and cries of indignation went up, when explosives were detonated and people saw, or knew if they could not see, that their homes had been blown-up.

All of this took time and for much of it Adam and his comrades, a fellow Silesian Pole and an ethnic German corporal three or four years their senior, were bored; lolling about on their street corner, smoking and kidding about. Their lieutenant had said that the rats who came last were the most dangerous. Those who believed that they were going to lose their liberties and, perhaps, their lives were the most desperate.

Some tried to leave by the sewers and they became aware that they were being by-passed and escapees were coming out behind them; others were willing to fight it out and came out firing, and on the second day Adam's fellow private was shot in the leg and had to be replaced.

As people came through the checkpoints many were arrested and removed to camps in special coaches hired for the day from their French owners who drove them and helped to get these prisoners securely on board. Adam overheard a heated conversation between the drivers and the SS about the operation taking too long and that they should be paid overtime.

"God almighty," said the corporal."What sort of people are these?"

"So much for this so called French Vichy Government", they said.

They despised this regime and thought it right that the Germans should govern the territory. "How can we though?" said Adam to himself. "There are not enough of us."

"And what if the British and the Americans were to come? We Germans cannot fight everyone?" they said to each other. "Best get rid of these enemies while you can," said Erik.

Some escapees came out of the buildings along the street they were guarding.

"How the hell they managed to get out of the Port and this far escapes me," said the corporal. When they weren't satisfied with their papers they referred them to the nearest SS unit. They saw some of these people arrested.

"What happens to them, corp?" asked the naïve Erik.

The corporal drew a line across his throat.

"Kaput, Erik. Behave yourself," and he laughed.

When the corporal was otherwise engaged, Erik was responsible for inspecting papers. It was getting dark when he stopped a group of four people, two adults and two young children, leaving a building in their street. "A Jewish family for sure," thought Adam. Their Jewishness had been registered in their passports. Adam stood back leaving Erik to deal with it. His heart churned as he thought of Auschwitz and what had happened there to the Jews. He wanted to be sick. He stood aside for fear that he would be noticed. He couldn't see properly: black patches obscured his vision and blurred the images.

He heard this family pleading with Erik but could not make out the words. Erik shouted at them in Polish and in German. He swore at them: "Fuck off, get lost, I haven't seen you. For God's sake don't thank me. Disappear, vamoose."

Adam felt Erik put his arm round him.

"I couldn't do it Adam. That family were refugees from my home town. We support the same football team! How could I?"

They looked around. No one had seen them – and there was no sight of the Jews.

"Erik," enquired Adam, "where do we send these Jews?"

"Drancy, a camp at Drancy. And then they are settled in the East." He whistled.

"You know what that means Adam, Auschwitz. Everybody hates the Jews."

"You don't hate them," responded Adam.

"I do really, at least I don't like them, Adam; but that's not the same as saying I want them killed, is it? I'm sorry for them."

These duties at the Port lasted several days. They learnt that over a thousand people had been arrested including six hundred Jews. Everybody was very pleased it had gone so well. The lieutenant congratulated them all. "Well done lads. You were splendid. That will teach them not to shoot at us, and plot against us. The French know that we are the bosses and that their stupid and greedy politicians are wasting their time. No one is going to take any notice of them now."

The lieutenant overstated the success of the operation; many people on the lists were not captured and others were thought to have escaped. While the captured were being processed others had to be rounded up. The risks of such an operation had risen sharply because the local population were very angry and all illusions of Vichy independence had ended with the German occupation and British and American success in north Africa. Never mind about that," their lieutenant had told them. "Rommel is not defeated yet." It was true but they wondered how long Rommel could hold out.

Adam's operating unit, Erik, himself and the corporal were thought to have done a good job – to their surprise – and were kept together for the next phase. They were to work with the French – sometimes the police militia and at other times men in plain-clothes. The French had lists and a work plan and for Adam and his mates it was cushy; they squeezed into an unmarked black Citroen and drove to various villages and farms. Their task was to provide armed protection in case of resistance – although the French themselves were armed – and sometimes to guard back-entrances to the buildings while the French went in by the front.

Sometimes the wanted people were not there, the buildings empty, and the occupants protested that they could not explain their whereabouts. "Liars," muttered the French. "We'll get them next time." Sometimes it was easy: the wanted people came meekly and were taken away in a second car, and on they all went to the next address. On occasions there were fights and beatings-up. When the suspects came out they were dishevelled, bruised and bleeding.

The corporal began to object: "Is this hard stuff really necessary: these people don't look dangerous to me."

The Frenchman in plain clothes said: "If we soften them up now they cause less bother later on."

He spoke softly and easily leaning back in his seat to look at them and with a smile and a question of his own: "You're not telling me, are you, that you Germans have scruples?"

There was no answer to this.

The round up lasted two to three weeks. They did not go out every day: and when they did it was usually one call – but sometimes it was two. When it was two they had a mid-day break in a bar or restaurant. One of the Frenchmen spoke some German in a thick Marseilles accent and they got him talking.

He spoke about his business and how well it was doing.

"What is your business?" enquired the ever-learning entrepreneurial Adam.

"Well several businesses; there is the protection business, and we own property – apartments, a casino and other things," he tailed off.

"My family is very successful in Marseilles, very successful – we are grateful to you Germans."

They never stayed long in these places and on occasions left abruptly.

"Not safe," or "No longer safe," they were told, and they were up and into the car very quickly. Adam had heard that German soldiers had been shot in bars in Marseilles and so he did not wish to hang around. *Miss Zbucki came into mind. Speak Polish. That was the thing to do. When people heard him speaking Polish they treated him differently. He was like them: taken over for a time but not forever.*

Erik was quicker off the mark in working it all out.

"Mafia Adam, they're mafia."

"Mafia?"

"Yes. Rounding up Jews is a mafia business in Marseilles. That's what they mean by protection; so much per head."

"I can't believe it," exclaimed Adam.

"You are telling me that the French Government uses gangsters to round up French Jews to send them to a Polish death camp. I don't believe it."

"Believe what you like, but it's true," said the worldly Erik.

Adam and Erik had become a good pair and good friends. Adam's sense of adventure – recklessness to Erik – amused Erik as it carried him into adventures – scrapes – he would not have contemplated; while Erik's quick wittedness and intelligence enabled Adam to see things from a quite different perspective and to get out of the high-risk activities that so diverted him. Erik was one of those people who always knew what was happening; intelligence, information and gossip were his specialisations. If you asked him something he usually knew the answer; and if he didn't know he could find out. These qualities made him indispensable to a great many people and a person to be relied upon.

Early one morning they went on a short journey to V. a small village ten kilometres to the north of Marseilles. It had been raining and the skies remained obstinately grey. In this half-light the prosperous village looked wonderful to Adam. He thought of Poland where the villages were a good deal less affluent and his heart turned over with the grief of it. These calls were often early in the morning when there were few people about – no one at all thought Adam as he looked up the winding village road where no one moved and where there were very few lights in the houses – and where the suspects could be taken by surprise.

"Stay by the car," said their mafia friend. "These are Jews and should come quietly, they usually do."

Adam heard repeated knocking on the door. There was a light on in the appartment above a small village store and the sound of movement. The mafioso called to the inhabitants: "Madame, police, open the door. We know you are there. Open the door, there is nothing to be gained by delay. If the door is not opened we shall break it down."

The door was not opened for some time. The knocking although persistent was not loud; the mafioso did not want to make too much noise or to knock the door down for fear of arousing the attention of the neighbours. After some minutes had elapsed the door was opened and they could thrust themselves inside.

The Germans waited outside. Shots and raised voices could be heard and then the crashing of furniture, screams and crying. The mafioso came out. "We don't have them all. We must do a search. We'll look inside and you get round to the back and search the outbuildings. Quickly, quickly this is dangerous."

The dreaded words rang out again and the Poles froze to the spot, reluctant to get involved.

"Who are we looking for?"

"A grandfather and two children, quickly, quickly."

They got round to the back. There was not much to search; a garage and a rackety shed. In the garage they found a car. Quite a nice car under wrapping. The corporal pulled off the covering and opened the car doors to admire the interior."Very nice," said the corporal, "I'd like one of these. It doesn't appear to have been used recently. Search the shed lads while I see whether I can start it."

They left him to it.

The shed-door had a key in the lock.

"Very careless," said the prudent Erik.

When they opened the shed-door they found two young children crouching at the back of the shed, scared to hell and ready to scream.

" Sshh," said Erik putting his finger to his lips.

He hesitated and looked at Adam.

"What shall we do, Adam?"

Adam uncharacteristically did not know what to do.

"Nothing, just nothing," came his reply at last.

Putting his finger to his lips again, Erik pulled Adam from the shed, locked the door and pushed the key under it.

"They can get out later. Let's go."

The corporal was still in the car.

"Bugger," he said, "I can't start it. Pity."

They went back again to the front in time to catch the mafioso leaving the house.

"Anything?" enquired the mafioso.

"No," said the corporal. "We all searched very thoroughly and there is no one, no one at all."

"Not to worry we shall find them. We must get out now, it's not safe."

In the Citroen the corporal said: "There was a nice car in the garage. Pity it's not being used."

"It will be, never fear," was the mafioso response. "Get it out of your mind. We shall collect it later and anything else we fancy."

"What all of it? Do you get all of it? Doesn't it go to the authorities?" said law-abiding Erik.

"Are you out of your mind. What do you think a civil servant could do with the stuff. We are the disposal experts. If we don't do it the villagers will loot the house. Spoils of war, you see."

He looked at them amused by their disapproving reaction.

"Big deal, eh. You have to be a German do you?"

He did not expect a response.

They were relieved when these visits came to an end. But their chances of settling into the town had gone. Now it was time for Operation Visibility and that was to be centred on the city of Montauban many kilometres to the north. Suddenly and with no notice they were off making as much noise as they could summon on the way and achieving the greatest possible visibility: that was the point, making the French believe that the German army was present in great numbers and everywhere when in reality they were very thin on the ground.

It was two days to settle in and then they were off again – and again – round and round in circles – stopping overnight and then moving on. The trucks stopped outside the small towns and the men got out. They marched into the centre of the town making as much noise as possible and timing these sorties for the early hours when people were getting up and late at night before they got to sleep. Round and round they marched, and when they stopped the empty trucks took over roaring about the streets until everyone noticed them. "These German troops are everywhere," said the locals in astonishment, "and if they are here in our small town they must be present in very large numbers in the big cities."

There was not much fun in it but it was better than fighting. Not that it was risk free. Moving in motorised columns late at night was danger-ous: you could be ambushed by resisters or you could be bombed – and they were. In February, when darkness came early and when they were approaching the small town of S. through lightly-forested terrain, resisters opened up from behind the trees. The advance motor cycles and the first two trucks were hit. A lieutenant ran down the line of vehicles ordering them to reverse and troops to go down both sides of the road to return fire and to thin out among the trees.

For the first time Adam found himself under fire. While his heart beat faster, he felt no fear, as he charged into the trees with his comrades against this hidden enemy. But then suddenly the firing stopped. The resisters had fled into the darkness. They were ordered to cease fire and to return to the road: there was no point in chasing an enemy in the darkness when he knew the terrain and you were clueless.

There were five casualties two of which were fatal. On this occasion the SS escorted them into the town and by lunch-time twenty of the town's male population, seized at random on the streets, had been shot in accordance with the threat: ten of you to one of us. They did not see these shootings as they had already moved on.

In March while in a barracks at the town of C. they were bombed. The attack came at two o'clock in the morning. The air raid warning gave them barely a minute to scramble into the cellar. There was no anti-aircraft fire – the town was too small to be prioritised for air cover. The building was partly demolished but no one lost their life. As they crawled their way out over the debris they felt it to be a victory: cheering broke out as they greeted each other like long-lost brothers. Later that evening they got drunk – even the lieutenant had too much to drink.

But, of course, it wasn't a victory. Like the French, they said to each other: "If this is what they are doing to C., goodness knows what it is like in the big cities." And then they grew silent because they knew what it was like. Now they knew that getting killed was not something that only happened to the enemy or the Jew, it could happen to you.

As they swept around their circle they returned to Marseilles, and paused waiting for new orders. It was a welcome break and a chance to unwind and assess things afresh. Adam and Erik sat outside a bar in early spring sunshine, stretching their legs, and with tunics unbuttoned at the top. The bar owner spoke some Polish. When he did not understand he nodded his head and smiled. This morning, unasked, he had given them croissants – fresh from the oven with a smell so endearing that you felt hungry even though you had already eaten.

"Not easy, this soldiering lark," said Erik distracted by a passing girl, who smiled at him tossing her head.

"That's what we should be doing at our age, chasing skirt. Oh, to be twenty, in France, and surrounded by pretty girls, some of whom smile at you."

"It will get worse," said Adam, suddenly disconsolate and thinking of home.

"You bet," said Erik. "Any time now we might wake up to find the British and Americans on our doorstep. Real fighting. We shall have to use these mortars we lug about with us. And the natives are getting restless. We couldn't sit here but for knowing this bar owner."

Erik waved at the barman to express his gratitude for the croissant and he waved back. Adam thought that in his moments of crisis he had always come up with something to deal with the problems. He felt lucky. Here he was in this place. How did he get here? He had been carried across Europe by a vast wave of human disturbance: and he had ridden the wave until he had come crashing down. You couldn't get back onto the wave to surf some more because you had been beached already. Or could you?

Erik said: "We're not on the winning side. We need to be on the winning side."

Adam agreed with him.

"Easy to say," he responded.

CHAPTER 15

FOR THE MOMENT the higher-ups did not know what to do with them. So they sent them on leave. There were three hundred of them all boarding a normal passenger train leaving Marseilles for final destinations across Germany. Laughing and singing they elbowed and pushed themselves onto the train filling every space. Still more pushed onto the platform: they were pulled in, spilling onto the floor and occupying the luggage racks. Still more of them came until at last there were no more crevices to be filled: and all in the most boisterous and cheerful spirit. The relief was enormous, to escape the war and to return to loved ones: to be followed by the nervousness of not knowing what they would find.

It took Adam two days to arrive back: days of hilarity and joshing – and then the quietness of the familiar small-town station – his station – and the familiar buildings of his town. He stood outside the station, removing his knapsack while he waited for a bus. A man he knew greeted him in passing. Tears came into his eyes and quite literally his heart heaved with the emotion of it.

He thought: "All over Germany there are people like me. Waiting, parting, coming back: all my mates standing outside stations like this one, with mothers, sisters and girlfriends, weeping and cuddling them." He found himself trembling with the emotion and stupidity of it.

For Sophie his arrival home was a miracle. By definition miracles are rare but in a Catholic community they are believed in: and while she had no expectation, she was certainly prepared to experience them. Each time that Mary and Adam returned home she thought it to be the last time and so their welcome was something special. It was a long

time since she had seen Mary and her occasional letters were not reassuring, raising more questions in her mind than answers to her questions. There was nothing she could do about it lacking the time and
money to visit her daughter.

Rosa remained a robust and happy child but she missed her father and
Adam dreadfully: there were nightmares and shared beds and anxious
questions: a warm bed, good hot food and plenty of cuddles was her
mother's recipe: "Everyone deserves at least two good cuddles a day,"
she would say. And to herself she said: "What about me?"

Well there was Rosa but no Peter. Since their epic journey she had seen
nothing of him. What was the point? Internal torment and the decision
to give up hope for Ludvig and nothing in return for it. Of course, it was
not arithmetic – you give up something and God gives you back something of at least the same importance – of course not; but nevertheless
it was hard. "Is God in his heaven at all?" she thought blasphemously.

She despised herself for these doubts. A good Catholic woman should
put her faith in God and seek his grace. While his purpose for you might
be obscure you could feel sure that if you trusted him and sought his
mercy, things would work out for you. Still it was hard. And she worried
about Peter. *"Once a woman starts to care for a man,"* she thought, *"the
heartache is not far behind."*

She felt guilty. In the eyes of the church she was married to Ludvig
and would remain married to him even if he were dead. Of course, if he
were dead and she waited a few years the church might give her dis-
pensation to marry again if she wanted to – needed to – and lacked the
strength to continue on her own.

She was right to be worried. Peter was consumed with guilt and
suppressed rage. Time and again he went over the way he had sent his
wife to an asylum: desperately he had tried to shift the blame onto
the doctor who had advised it, the priest who had condoned it, and the
relatives who were not there for him when he and she had needed
them. She was very depressed that was obvious – but not always – and
she had stayed in bed a lot, leaving the housework and her domestic
tasks undone. She had refused to leave the house or to see her friends
and neighbours, sending them away when they called and shouting at
them to leave her alone. But she had not been a danger to herself or to
anyone else.

The doctor said that she was ill, clinically ill, and for her own sake
needed treatment and special care. *"Peter my good fellow,"* he had said
meaning to be kind to him, *"these days people are depressed."* He had

put his arm around him in a sympathetic gesture. "It has to be your decision, Peter," he had said. "A decision for both of you."

The priest had advised him to pray and seek God's will. He had prayed and whether God had noticed his prayers he knew not.

But being a fair-minded man he could not shift the guilt onto doctor or priest: he Peter and no one else had taken the decision. A less kind man might have put up with her, being less involved and less affected. In a very long relationship we can become less tolerant, harbour more resentment of the things we do not like, angry at lost hopes and disappointed by diminished passions. Had that happened to him? It was true, he admitted, that there were times when he had half-thought that she might die in an accident or illness and that he would be better off if she did. There might then be romance in his life again. But that did not mean that he wanted her dead. Of course, it didn't.

Now he behaved like his wife. He did not want to get up in the morning – although he did: he did not want to see his fellow farmers or his neighbours – although he was civil to them when he met them: and he did not think he was entitled to love – because he had failed in it, failed to give love to someone who deserved it at the time when it was needed. In all this his mind did not take the obvious route, the obvious conclusion clear to others. *He had not killed his wife. The German SS had murdered her: stuffed as they were with hateful racial theories and willingness to indulge them by murderous activity.*

He could not grieve for his wife because of the horrific nature of her death and his inability to deal with its causes. A glass wall surrounded him through which he saw a reflection of his life: he was conscious that others were smiling at him, reaching out for him, but that he could not respond: he was disconnected from them. Each day was a torture to him and the condition he was suffering from was remorseless and without relief. Even if he had known that winning the loving care of a good woman was there, within reach and his for the asking, he could have done nothing.

Sophie was amazed at the son that pushed open the farmhouse door in April: so grown-up looking, so handsome and confident, so full of energy and good spirits. He had flourished in the few months since she had seen him. She was full of questions; about France itself, where had he been, what had he done, who were his friends – and were there girls and were they serious? There were precious few answers and none were really expected – but there was a lot of laughter and larking about.

Mother and son fell into the old pattern and rhythms: working together around the house and in the fields, visiting some neighbouring farms and behaving as mates: in this very short period of time, it was if nothing had happened, the clouds of war and occupation, the cruelty and loss of life, dropped away.

Spring had renewed the countryside and the cherry trees were in blossom: but to the experienced eye much was not right, the farms often lay neglected as if in mourning for their lost Polish guardians, uprooted and deported hundreds of kilometres away, while the new German owners, who had paid not a penny for them, struggled to start anew in strange and alien surroundings: not real farmers at all scorned the locals.

Rosa had become the repository of family secrets. She listened behind doors and on the edges of conversation. She stored information and sifted and checked it: she saw that much was not right and, though usually wrong in her opinions, and impotent to influence events, she tried to change things.

It was Rosa who told Adam about her mother and Peter making a visit by train to a sanatorium and finding out something dreadful – although she did not know what it was – and coming back dreadfully upset – and then not seeing Peter for a long time. Then having told her story, Rosa sat back to see what would happen. Hopefully, there would be a good conversation and she would find out something, and then, perhaps, Peter would come back home again for good, which is what she wanted.

She was to be disappointed. The conversation did take place but Sophie and Adam went for a long walk across the fields, from which she was excluded. Sophie told him every detail of her trip with Peter, and of the impact on the both of them: and Adam listened with mounting disbelief. He questioned her account. After all it could hardly be imagined. Finally, he put his hands to his head to stop it bursting: he screamed so loudly that a flock of crows wheeled from their protective cover in a vast flock, darkening the sky above them like death itself. His mother poured out her heart to him and he held her until her agitation subsided, and then walked with her slowly, his arm around her shoulder.

It was coming up for four years of horror and disbelief. Perhaps, for some this horror did not touch them. But, they thought, that could not be true for many. After a while the mind was numbed: all these monstrous crimes and injustices became almost acceptable – after all they were happening every day and were part of the landscape. What could one do but grin, shrug your shoulders and walk on: cuddle your child, help your neighbour and take the dog for a walk?

Sophie said to Adam that she believed that his father was dead. A victim of the mindless killing and abuse of the camps. He reassured her that not all the camps were the same and that Sachsenhausen was not a death camp. "And you know that Dad is a survivor. He can look after himself." he said. Adam told her about his captain and that he spoke Polish. "I'm in good favour, Mum, I'll ask about Dad and see if he can do anything to help." She was comforted a little: at least that was something that could be done.

Adam decided to go and see Peter and went off on an old bicycle. He could hardly recognise him. The farm and Peter were badly neglected. He was dirty and unkempt with sunken cheeks and dishevelled uncut hair. He walked and moved very slowly as if in the grip of a disabling disease. He spoke very slowly, hesitating and mumbling – getting his words wrong with each syllable being wrung from him. He did not want to talk about his wife, and when Adam persisted in his questions he stopped him by taking hold of his arm, gripping it so tightly that Adam cried out with the pain. And then he drew back, pushing Adam away, the effort being too much for him, and tears trickled down his face.

Adam had seen this expression of Peter's many times: they were etched into his memory and into his nightmares. These suffering faces devoid of hope and impulse to live were the faces of the dispossessed and persecuted. He had seen them in their hundreds at Auschwitz and now he saw it on his own doorstep.

Adam did not want to give up on Peter and he went to see the neighbouring farmer whom he knew slightly.

"Nothing to reproach himself with there," said his blunt speaking neighbour. "Nutty, she was, and a great burden to him. Course, I do understand that he is grieving for her. That's only natural. I'm sorry that I haven't done more to help him. I'll try to do something."

His wife was more practical: "I'll call and get him cleaned up, Adam. And when I'm next in town I'll call in on the doctor and get him to visit. He needs some proper help."

On his return Rosa found out where he had been and made him talk to her about his impressions. Rosa was insistent about knowing what was to happen next, and Adam told her. "Mum let us go and help him too," Rosa burst out. Sophie protested it was not necessary and held out against her demanding daughter: but not for long. Without saying anything to Rosa, and while she was at school, she began to help. Whenever possible, she made her way to his farm and gently and firmly got this man back on his feet again.

When she came first he said nothing: tears came to his eyes and he kissed her and held her hand. She thought that the look on his face was as any farm animal: not without a certain intelligence and animation, but dumb and expectant. And she treated him as a dumb animal: he was fed and made clean by her; she saw that he exercised, and then that he worked. She demanded normality and in the end she got it: she demanded recognition, respect and love, and in the end she got that too.

It was to be a long time before all this was achieved and the balance of the relationship changed: and Adam was not to see that because his short leave came to an end. Once again Sophie had to see him off: the sandwiches, pies and fruit for the journey had to be gathered and prepared, the bus journey – hand in hand – endured. Each time they thought: "Is this the last time?" and if not: "When will we see each other again?"

On this occasion there were the usual hugs and entreaties to write, but the dangers now were to them both: in the east the German armies were falling back under massive Soviet pressure, and soon Poland's ancient enemy would be knocking on the door: and to the west, Allied armies were gathering in Britain and north Africa to invade France. They were not to know that their embrace would have to endure as a contact for over a quarter of a century.

Each time that the train journey west was taken across Germany into France, it took longer and was more perilous. Allied bombing of German industrial targets was now intensive and continuous and the railway system itself was targetted. Yet despite the gravity of it all, these young German conscript soldiers reassembled in France in high spirits.

This time they had moved north again and had set up a tented camp outside Montauban to avoid becoming a bombing target. That is the common soldiers were in the tents and the officers were billeted in a chateau owned by the local mayor. While the mayor no doubt had no choice in the matter he was known to have far-right sympathies and was eager to please his German guests. As important to the conquerors, he had three very pretty daughters one of whom had her French army officer husband in England, to where he had escaped in 1940. These very delightful girls were – so rumour had it – as anxious to please in their own way as their father.

The tents stood in an open field in the grounds of the chateau and were, therefore, vulnerable to attack. It was more than a theoretical danger for the activities of the maquis in the countryside had grown in intensity and effectiveness. External defences had to be created and staffed and Adam, under the supervision of the corporal, was given the task to create a secure bunker in one corner of the field open to an obvious line of attack. Digging the trench was straightforward enough but it needed to be supported by wooden battens. Where was the wood to come from?

Adam started a foray of the chateau outbuildings. Sure enough he found the wooden planks he needed and calling for help in moving them he started the task of gathering them outside the outhouse. His shouting had alerted the chateau inhabitants and soon Adam was confronted with no less a person than the mayor himself. Adam looked up and there advancing upon him with aggressive intent and shouting at him in German was this large Frenchman.

Afraid of no German, and secure in his position in French society, this very large man stood in front of him and bellowed to his face: "What the hell do you German swine think you are doing stealing my wood." For an instant Adam perceived this menacing large man as his father with his punishment strap. In an instinctive response Adam lashed-out with a punch to the mayor's face, the effect of which was surprising. On his right hand he wore a large and elaborately shaped bronze signet-ring – ironically the sole momento from Julia – and as the mayor swayed to avoid the punch he suffered a glancing blow across his cheek. The signet-ring cut long and deep into his cheek from which blood spurted and streamed.

The mayor slumped onto his knees with the shock and surprise of his injury. Adam could now see that people were moving towards him from the chateau, and then he was confronted by his captain and lieutenant – not properly dressed – and some strangers who meant nothing to him.

"God, Adam, now you have done it," said his corporal reaching the building first. His captain viewed the scene:

"Corporal arrest that man," was the captain's reaction.

Arrest was not too onerous as it meant that he slept in a special tent with his corporal as surety for his good behaviour: but as for his punishment?

"I'm glad I'm not you," observed his corporal.

Next morning his corporal greeted him. "Schnell, schnell, get yourself prepared, you're wanted in the chateau." He was marched there by two provost sergeants, into a room where he was confronted by a very senior officer – a colonel – or rather *the* colonel responsible for the entire Division. At the time he did not realise that the colonel was visiting, checking up on the state of readiness and morale of the company, and that the conduct of this inquiry was incidental to his purpose in being there.

"Chwistek," began the colonel, "you realise that this is a very serious matter."

"Yes sir."

"I am willing to hear your side of the story. Speak up, man."

Adam explained that he had been asked to build the bunker and the difficulty he had experienced: that a man he had not recognised had accosted them, tried to stop them and called them German swine. He had a peroration: "Colonel," he said. "I am a conscript but so long as I wear this badge it is my duty to maintain its honour."

"I see Chwistek, well spoken. That will do," said the colonel struggling to keep a straight face and then addressing the provost sergeants.

"Take him away. I will give my verdict in due course."

Several hours went by before the corporal entered the tent and with a chuckle said: "Look to Adam you are off to Divisional headquarters. To see the tailor," he thought the whole matter to be very funny and couldn't stop laughing.

The tailor was to the point.

"Take off your jacket while I sew it on."

"Sew what on?"

"Your stripe, of course."

Back in the camp there was a special assembly addressed by the colonel. He said: "This man Chwistek is a credit to the German army. He was given a vital task to do and when there was a misguided effort to prevent him doing it and the honour of the German army was denied, he struck back. In this he is a lesson to us all. If all of you men acted as lance-corporal Chwistek, we would have no worries about the fighting spirit of this Division."

There was a good deal of joshing and kidding to be suffered. Erik said: "Drinks on you from now on, Adam. Corporals pay and all that." And he pulled him to the ground and started to wrestle him. His lieutenant said: "What a lucky fellow you are, Adam. We shall all have to notice you from now on. But don't go angling for a visit to the chateau now, will you?" and he cuffed him playfully around the head.

Adam was proud of himself. "I really am a fine fellow," he said to himself. "I wasn't scared, well not much anyhow, and now I shall have to be respected."

Now was his chance. He sought an interview with his captain and explained in Polish the position of his father. His captain humoured him and was willing to converse in Polish. Speaking now as an expert in perorations Adam concluded: "It is simply unfair. Here am I serving the German army in good faith, and as the colonel has said with distinction, and my father is in Sachsenhausen and no one knows for how long. Can you get him out for us?"

"What, single-handed Chwistek?" the captain laughed and so did Adam.

"Well leave it with me. I will do what I can. I'm not making any promises, but maybe something can be done."

CHAPTER 16

IT CANNOT BE said that lance corporal is a very elevated rank or that the promotion had altered his life. Apart from the ragging, however, there was a small but important change in his situation: given the pressure on numbers he did sometimes find himself the senior in small teams of men with the responsibility for actions, of deciding what to do, ultimately resting with him. The issue of moral choice, although Adam did not put it to himself in this way, could not always be avoided.

Adam contrived to work with Erik whom he trusted.

"It is ridiculous me being the corporal," he told him. "It's you who should be doing this job."

"Of course," was the reply, "there's no justice in this world. We superior beings are here to serve," and punching him, "I shall stay by your side."

Erik was as good as his word.

They were painfully aware that German army resources were highly limited to face the growing threats upon them. Their officers grew despondent with each new reverse on the Russian front and with the north African disasters. In May when the last German resistance in Africa collapsed the air of gloom spread and descended on them all. Previously the propaganda within the army had been exultant: each victory or advance was celebrated while each retreat was said to be tactical and would lead to victory in the future; but now there could be no illusions.

Wherever their abode was fixed for any length of time, newsreels in brilliant black and white photography were shown to them of the supposed German triumphs accompanied by the playing of patriotic music and speeches. But in contrast they had their own experience. Around them the Vichy regime was in decline and the ongoing cooperation of the French citizen could no longer be relied upon. In everyday exchanges people were rude to them and it had become dangerous for a German to be on the street after dark.

In June three of their number disappeared without explanation. As there were no corpses the blame could not be laid at the door of the resistance and, therefore, no retribution was exacted. The talk among the ranks was of desertion but no one knew for sure. On other occasions it was clear that it was active resistance: bridges and rail points were blown up, convoys were fired upon and trains derailed. The SS retaliated where they could find the slightest reason to do so, and sometimes without any reason at all; but the retaliations now were of little effect and arguably strengthened the increasingly common resolve of the French citizen to resist the occupation. Not that there were not collaborators: some were paid and others did it out of the desire to injure others. The time for the settling of grudges was a long time from ending and denunciations remained a national sport.

In this changed situation, and in preparation for an invasion date not yet known, British and Free French agents were increasingly parachuted into France to make contact with the resistance groups. The breaking up of the resistance networks and the capture of these spies became a vital German priority. While this was the responsibility of the Gestapo and the SS, manpower shortages made it necessary to use the Army and Adam's company became involved.

The capture of spies was not as simple as it might seem and the men selected to do it required training. These encounters took place at night. Intelligence was not always exact or comprehensive and the reported place for a drop was often wrong. Sometimes the information was correct but the drop had been cancelled because of bad weather or for other operational reasons: and sometimes the information was deliberately wrong, and the drop had taken place but elsewhere.

Then the spies had to be captured alive for interrogation by the Gestapo. "Poor buggers," they said, "but it's war. Better us than them."

Capturing them alive was not so easy either. They were armed and in a position to fight back. Better to die in a shoot out than at the hands of the Gestapo might be their conclusion. And then there was the resistance who might be there in hiding and in a position to fire on them from prepared and hidden positions.

Spy-catching was not a glamorous undertaking. You lay in a wet ditch for hours, sometimes for the whole night, listening, waiting and watching. If nothing happened you travelled back to your mates feeling very stupid and demoralised. There was a worse feeling: you might have captured someone or one of your mates might have been shot. Although you were supposed not to think about it, you did: a spy was a human being and now unmentionable things were being done to him or her from which they would never recover and if they did blurt out what was demanded of them to save themselves further torture, they would be shot anyway.

Late on a June night when the last of the skylarks hovered in belated search for food and when the first of the owls, equipped for the fading light, waited to take over, Adam found himself behind a screen of trees to one side of a large meadow laid out to pasture. It was a clear night and the moon already shed its softening beams, illuminating the pasture, while the sun still lit the sky in red and orange.

On any night but this lovers would have been kissing in the lane or a walker with his dog might be found on a pathway; but tonight the pathways had been blocked off some way from the scene and his comrades in various places around this great meadow discouraged the stray walker without causing alarm. At some time tonight, they had been told around mid-night, a British spy was to be dropped in this area and no resistance activity was expected.

It was around one o'clock when in a clear sky they saw the billowing of a dark-fabric parachute falling rapidly towards the drop zone. There was a light breeze and despite the efforts of the parachutist the 'chute drifted towards the trees and came to a halt no more than one hundred metres from them. They had been taught that in these circumstances you do not give the enemy the chance to get out of the harness or to recover from the impact of the fall. Without another thought, Adam, closely followed by his comrades, broke cover, running towards the parachutist as quickly as he could.

The parachutist saw them coming and was out of the harness very quickly. Without any further glance he ran as fast as he could towards trees to the right of them. Adam running faster gained on him and shortly before the safety of the trees rugby tackled his prey bringing him to the ground. The parachutist wriggled round to face him. To his astonishment it was a woman, a pretty dark haired woman, breathless, frightened and pleading with him in English.

He sat back up, astonished and ashamed to be sitting on her. His comrades were still some thirty metres away. There was a brief moment in which he might have let her go. She asked him again, seeing him a young boy and disconcerted. She could have sprinted into the trees and in the dark they might not have caught her again. He thought about it. He might have done it. But he didn't. He grabbed her round the waist in a crude bear-hug trying hard not to look her in the face. When his comrades arrived he let them drag her away. She struggled as she was pushed into a familiar black Citroen. She glanced back, her face white and frightened in the moonlight. It was the last he saw of her: but he never forgot.

He was a hero again, slapped on the back, and commended by his superiors. He was mentioned in dispatches and then told that he was a likely-lad. But as he lay in his tent, unable to sleep, and when the sounds of his comrades were reduced to the comfort of their snoring and heavy breathing, he did not feel himself to be a likely-lad. He saw her face, frightened and pleading. He told himself that he really did want to let her go; but he couldn't. He would have been humiliated if he had. What was happening to her now though? He imagined it. Of course, he should have let her go, come what may. He prayed to this absent God, in whom he had lost faith, to forgive him.

He tried to forget it and largely succeeded; but he decided that if he were offered further promotion he would refuse it. You did not need to be an intellectual to work out that the higher you got the more frequent the decisions you had to make where you might or might not do something and then be held responsible for it: and decisions not just affecting yourself, but others who looked to you for an example.

It was a relief to get away from Jew-hunting and spy-catching and to do something practical. No one knew when or where the British and Americans would invade, but that they would come was a certainty. A desperate rush to improve the sea-defences around the northern coast now started. They moved to Brittany and then around the coast-line to the north wherever defensive structures had been created or were needed.

It was a beautiful summer with sunshine and clear blue skies. Working along the coastline and camping in the fields was like a holiday. For most of the time they worked like navvies stripped to the waist, wearing only shorts and skin-dipping at various times of the day in the pleasant swell of the sea. In the evenings they walked into the villages and small towns like gods: bronzed and fit. They came to see and conquer and sometimes they did.

Their spirits rose. The locals were all friendly and the girls even more so: you could hardly blame them, husbands and boy friends were absent, perhaps, permanently so, and often not heard from; and in strode the gods, charming and polite and definitely up for it.

"From what I can gather from Delphine," said Erik, who had been quick off the mark on more than one occasion, "these locals do not want an invasion disturbing their lives and destroying their houses." While others thought that if you could crack down on the resistance groups, who were really causing the trouble, all would be well.

What they were doing was mining beaches. This was not popular with the locals at all because it rendered the shore line unusable.

"Not everyone wants to fish or swim," said Erik.

"Why Delphine doesn't," chanted his mates.

They were not to be cast down and worked with a will. At low-tide they waded out into the sea and hammered in stakes with the points at angles to any approaching enemy. Sappers then attached mines to the stakes which at high-tide were invisible. They built concrete bunkers for machine gun emplacements on the dunes and sealed off the beach with barbed wire.

Locals were sequestered to assist in this mammoth task but rarely turned-up, and when searches were mounted could not be found. They set out to cover almost one hundred kilometres of beach defences and from time to time those much further away in northern France.

It was not a task that went unnoticed by the enemy. The German Luftwaffe no longer commanded air superiority and as they worked British reconnaissance planes droned overhead photographing the work and recording their activity and progress.

As part of the defensive fortifications there were anti-aircraft batteries and machine-guns mounted up in the sand-dunes but, where they were working, this was all set up on a minor scale, and the big guns were not operative without a great deal of effort. They looked nervously at the skies and hoped that their minor war efforts would be disregarded by the enemy and that they would not be punished for them.

The view from high up in the dunes was idyllic. The sea stretched blue to a misty horizon, while the pastel blue sky became brilliant overhead. The long sandy bay curved to either side and fine sands more white than yellow played with a gentle surf. Craggy grass-covered dunes, now scarred by the newly-erected barbed wire, were limitless to the eye.

The men below, spread out over a hundred metres, worked contentedly, contained in their tasks, and their voices and laughter, and from time to time the sound of their horseplay, rang out in this vast empty space rivalled only by the screams of the sea gulls.

Death struck suddenly. Wheeling to approach out of the sun, and not seen or heard until very close, a British Mosquito fighter-bomber swooped down low and raced across the bay firing its guns repeatedly before wheeling away across the sea. It had happened with brutal suddenness. From the dunes they could see the pilot: they could smell the plane: it was almost as if you could touch it.

There was panic below. Several men had been hit and efforts were being made to save them by dragging them out of the water across the sand to the relative safety of the dunes. Most of the men ran for their lives. Adam, taking a deep breath, submerged and swam out to sea. When he broke surface he took in all the air he could and repeated his movement away from disaster. The Mosquito approached again and this time machine-gunned the dunes. For a third time it approached, firing as before, but as it passed it dropped a single bomb which scored a direct hit on a gun emplacement. It was this bomb which killed Erik. Normally to bomb a sand-dune is a useless activity as the bomb would have little effect, the sand muffling the explosion. Unless you received a direct hit the worst you might expect would be to be buried by sand: but this time metal from the gun emplacement sprayed out for many metres and Erik, hit in the head by a metal fragment, died instantly.

Adam was met by a scene of great confusion when, in his own time, he swam back to shore. The casualties, of which there were many, were given some emergency treatment, loaded onto trucks and motored over fifty kilometres to a military hospital. Some died on the trucks because of the delay in treatment. The surviving company, shaken and dishevelled, were taken back to camp.

Adam felt himself inadequate in this situation. For a farm-boy it was unusual, he hated blood; and picking up corpses and dumping them onto trucks brought back the hated images of Auschwitz, which continued to haunt his dreams. Once back in his tent and in his bed he fell into a deep sleep from which he had to be roused many hours later. He had been missed in a roll-call and now had to be counted in.

He was more than counted in: he was promoted yet again. It was his battalion that had suffered the casualties, and it was withdrawn from duties to make up its numbers and to re-form. Before they left his lieutenant summoned him and congratulated him for his courage and resourcefulness under fire. He muttered, being really ashamed, that he had done nothing. He had rushed away from the disaster that was to consume his mates, and swimming back at his leisure he was too late to help the critically wounded. His lieutenant said that they had lost a corporal in the incident and that Adam had been promoted to take his place. There was no argument about it. He was promoted and that was that.

Adam was distraught at the loss of Erik. He realised, and had to admit to himself for the first time, how dependent he was on him. It was Erik that calmed him down at moments when his impulsiveness threatened to get him into serious trouble: it was Erik who was willing to listen to any amount of his claptrap: and it was Erik who stood by him whatever the crisis. Now he would have to manage on his own. He would have to grow up some more and quickly if he was to stay out of serious difficulty. He thought of his promise to himself that he would not take any further promotion, and how weakly he had responded to it when it was offered, and he despised himself.

There was a funeral service for the men killed in the attack. Afterwards it was possible for the men who mourned to have private time with the Army chaplain and they were urged to do so. Adam told the chaplain about Erik and how he would miss him, about his anxieties for his family and, as he grew in confidence, about his doubts about this war and its likely outcome.

The chaplain was a well-ordered professional sort of person who had spent a long time in the German army. He explained to Adam the duty of a soldier to serve loyally and to obey without question the orders of the civil authority. Seeing his doubt, he continued: "You have moral responsibilities Adam. Please don't think that you should have to do evil things. I don't think you will be asked to do these things. Stay loyal to your comrades for their safety may depend upon you and pray for an end to these hostilities so that you can return to your family."

In his own quietude Adam recognised that these words were insufficient. He had already reached the conclusion that solidarity and discipline, although necessary, were not enough. The mad world they were in was too much for the chaplain and his beliefs. The chaplain could not help anyone.

Adam spoke to the other lads, particularly those with a Polish background. They were to a man very upset and hopeful of the victory of their ancient enemy, Russia, in the East: victory which would give them, if

Russia were to believed, and Britain and the Americans were strong enough, an independent Poland.

Back in Marseilles they had a period of rest. They drifted back into the familiar bars and held their animated conversations in Polish. The barman in their favourite rendezvous continued to wave and smile at them. On their third visit he signalled to a man sitting on the terrace who appeared to be listening to their conversation, and he rose and came over to them. He spoke in perfect Polish explaining that he *was* Polish and had emigrated to France over ten years ago. He sat down at their table and made himself agreeable, but he glanced around as he spoke as if anxious not to be seen talking to them.

"Gentlemen," he said at last getting to the point in a rather rehearsed manner, "forgive me for saying this but do you not think you are in the wrong army? If I can help you in this please speak to the barman." And before they could respond, he rose quickly and left the bar. They looked at the barman. He smiled and waved and gave them the thumbs up.

"What the hell did he mean?" they said to each other. To which the answer was: "We can help you to desert." They did nothing."Too dangerous," they thought, but on the other hand it was dangerous to stay in the German army. They were too scared to do anything.

And then they were beaten to it: four men were reported missing. They might have been shot but the rumours were that they had deserted. "They will come back in a sack," said the lieutenant. They waited for the sack and heard and saw nothing.

"If they can do it so can we," they said to each other, and the die was cast.

They returned to the bar and it was arranged for them to meet, what had turned out to be a resistance group, in open land outside the town. Arrangements covering the desertion of four of them were made and immediately put into effect. On a rendezvous late one August evening they exchanged their uniforms – which were subsequently burnt – for workmen's overalls and embarked on a three-day journey to the Normandy coast.

They travelled only at night, sometimes in the back of a truck covered with beetroot, sometimes on foot when it was too dangerous to stay on the road. On one day they stayed in a farm barn, which reminded Adam of home, and on the last night, rather grandly in a chateau.

Everywhere they were treated kindly and with enthusiasm. While disaster might have struck them at any moment, there were no alarms. With the boldness of youth they were not scared, and when they finally made it to the safety of a fishing boat and beyond German-controlled waters they sang patriotic Polish songs and greeted the stars.

Adam was ecstatic. Hadn't he told them all it would be easy? And, of course, it was. He sat back and looked at the night sky. Perhaps, Miss Zbucki was looking at this same sky. He hoped she was. And if she knew, which of course she couldn't, even supposing she was alive, she would be proud of him.

They sailed on unchallenged by friend or foe into Portsmouth harbour. They were expected. The resistance group had got out a message of some kind to the British Government who had arranged a reception party: two very old soldiers, who turned out to be in the Home Guard, and a policeman. Not the sort of policeman they were familiar with but a smiling British policeman who courteously arrested them as illegal aliens, and who asked them would they kindly accompany him to the police station, where they spent a comfortable night in the cells.

CHAPTER 17

IN SEPTEMBER 1943 Herman sold his business in Katowice for a handsome price to the only potential buyer in the market place, took a job as a veterinary inspector with the local administration, and joined the Communist Party. In so doing Herman showed his flair and fine judgement about the likely course of military and political events, his rapaciousness, and the ability never to allow issues of principle to get in the way of the actions required to look after himself and to prosper.

Herman reasoned it out to himself as follows. The Germans would be defeated and the Soviets would win a crushing victory in the East. Since the German defeat at Stalingrad at the beginning of the year an ultimate Soviet victory was inevitable, although the timing of it, given German fanaticism and fighting powers, was difficult to predict. The lesson of Polish history was that once the Russian bear had you in its grasp it never let you go: Poland would be a communist State whatever the West thought. Were they going to go to war with the Soviets for the freedom of Poland? He thought not.

Of course, it was all very unpredictable. The West might make peace with Nazi Germany and then turn on the common – Soviet – enemy. He thought not. These Western countries were very soft. They would want to get back to their trading, to their families and to the easy life he imagined they lived. Anyway, they would want to take revenge against Hitler and his cronies for all the deaths and suffering – and lost profits. Already he was thinking as a communist which was essential to his survival. No, he didn't see it. If Churchill would not negotiate a peace in 1940 when Britain had lost, why would he negotiate one now when they were winning?

So if there was going to be a communist regime in Poland he had to be trusted by it, be part of it. What he would have liked to do was to join the Polish Home Guard which the Soviets were recognising as the 'official resistance' but he did not have the guts for it. He persuaded himself that it was because he did not want to cut his ties with the SS. After all he could be wrong, perhaps the Germans might win, or hold on for a long time – in either event he would continue to need them. In reality he did not have convictions at all and was frightened by the thought that he could be killed or captured and tortured.

It was better, he thought, to play both sides, while preparing to join the victors. He went to see his SS contact and explained that he wished to continue his services in a different way. Would it be helpful to the SS if he joined the Polish Workers Party?* He was willing to make regular reports on their activities in the town. Would that be useful? The SS trusted him a little. He had a good collaboration record and had been reliable over a long period. "Yes, it would be useful," they told him, and offered him their continued protection.

His story to the Party was rather different. He said, "Look, I can be helpful. I know a lot of people, they have used my shop and have done official business with me. I know people who work in the Administration. I know their secrets. You know, wives and sisters who have been up to things that they don't want their husbands to know about." And he rubbed his nose. "Naturally you will have your own contacts," he continued, seeing their doubt and hesitation and knowing he had acquired a certain reputation for double-dealing, "but you might find that I could be very useful."

The Party didn't trust him but decided to use him for a while. Maybe they would have to spit him out later or just get rid of him.

He sold his business partly because of his judgement that it was the last time he could find a buyer at a sensible price, but also because he needed to end his trading with the German army. And then he had to sell – although he hated the thought – because there was no future in being bourgeois. In all this he might be wrong, and he realised it, but it was his best judgement at the time.

He did a deal with the buyer to avoid tax. He prepared special accounts which showed the business to be loss-making and accepted a nominal transaction price. It was *this* price that he declared to the tax authorities. Then he received a back-hand cash payment. Not that he

* As the Communist Party was called then.

wanted money in a currency that might become worthless. The task now was to turn this money into tangible assets – gold, silver and jewellery – that would stand the test of time. This was not so easy and the penalties for illegal trading were severe. *"What a pity we eliminated the Jews,"* he said to himself, *"this is just the task for them."*

He had to find an intermediary to do a deal, and then to do it in a place well-removed from him; and he did it in Vienna where he had some contacts. It took five days and thirty per cent of his substantial lump sum to convert the currency into precious metals and jewellery. In anticipation and well in advance he had bought a steel strongbox and he filled this with his special hoard and buried it in the garden of his new house in the dead of night. At no time was his name associated with any transaction and, as he made no journey of his own, he avoided the risks of carrying cash and precious objects on his own person.

He sold his house and declared the transaction to the authorities but didn't buy another. He rented a modest but sufficient cottage to the north of the town which he repaired and refurbished to a pleasant but unostentatious level of comfort. His salary as a veterinary inspector was modest but the money from the house sale could be drawn upon to live comfortably.

Herman then removed his daughter and Lucie from the fee-paying German school and sent them both to the local state school where they received an infinitely worse education with large classes, poor teachers, and educational progress at the speed of the slowest child. Paula and the children were distressed and upset by the change. "I will make it up to you," was his response. And he arranged special instruction at home in key subjects to ensure that the children continued to make progress.

In the course of two to three months Herman had reinvented himself. Gone was the successful businessman and suspected German collaborator and in was the well-respected and valued public service worker: owning nothing and ideologically on the side of the new and coming masters. He was pleased with himself. *"Admittedly God took only seven days to make the world and it has taken me three months to change mine,"* he said to himself, *"but it is a complete reinvention and in good time."*

He became a diligent and valued employee. He took veterinary examinations to become fully-qualified and cooperated fully and loyally with his Department. To the farmers he showed compassion and constructive support. He was slow to put-down or condemn livestock; constructive in advising on preventative measures; and always cheerful and in good spirits. The rumours about his collaboration ceased and after some time everyone thought and spoke highly of him.

Around this time Paula took Lucie on a visit home. Paula and Sophie had a heart to heart while Lucie played with Rosa. It had taken some time for Sophie to forget the circumstances of Ludvig's arrest but Paula and Herman were so adamant about their innocence in the matter that at last Sophie had put the matter aside and had resumed full friendship: while not entirely happy, she could not in her loneliness and isolation fall out with her sister, who gallantly looked after Lucie and was so keen to be helpful.

On this occasion, Paula explained the changed circumstances of her family and Lucie's schooling. Sophie expressed her surprise. Paula responded: "There has been a great change in Herman. He is now open about his opposition to this war. He has been misunderstood you know. Of course, it is true that he wanted Silesia to be part of Germany. Well, he admires German efficiency and as an Austrian he feels himself German: but he has never supported this stupid war with the Russians, which could kill us all in the end."

Sophie thought otherwise but she was not a political person and so said very little in response. She looked at her sister across the kitchen and asked herself whether she really liked her, surprised by the thought. They were an interesting contrast these two sisters: Paula being fair haired to her sister's dark looks and smaller than Sophie, so that for a stranger they would seem not to be related. Sophie saw a sounding vessel: a person with no strong feelings of her own who absorbed her emotions from others and who bore the imprint of the last person who had sat on her. There she was waiting, amoeba-like, to absorb the next emotion and the next fashionable opinion. "How unkind I am," she said abandoning her doubts and changing the subject. Sophie wanted to talk about the things that really mattered: about the scarcity and price of food; about Rosa and Lucie, and Adam and Mary; about hearing nothing from Ludvig and something from France which worried her badly. She wanted to talk about Peter, for she had no one to talk to about him, but she dare not.

"What," said Paula brightly, "have you heard from Adam?" Sophie fished through some papers on the sideboard and found a postcard. She gave it to Paula and then promptly burst into tears. The card was from the German military command in France and read:

'We regret to inform you that your son Corporal Adam Chwistek is reported missing.'

"Corporal," said Paula, "You didn't tell me."

And then hastily seeing that her comment was not the one called for by the occasion: "Only missing – that's good isn't it? Not killed or captured or anything like that. He's sure to be all right. You know Adam, he can look after himself."

She supposed that he could: but she thought that there must be partisans in France as there were in Poland. They could kill him and bury the body. And she cried some more. If he had deserted, and she supposed he might have done, he would be shot on recapture. She couldn't think about it. All she could do was to pray.

"How can you find out?" said Paula trying to show practical concern.

"I don't know. Perhaps Herman might know. Someone said through the Red Cross. How do I contact the Red Cross?"

Paula didn't know but she thought that Herman would and promised that she would ask him.

"And Mary. How's Mary?" Sophie said that she had gone through a very bad spell but she thought she was all right now. In truth she didn't know because Paula hadn't been in touch and she could only hope for the best.

Paula thought that her visit was a great success. "Lot's of good gossip." Sophie was not very happy about things at all. "What was all this stuff about Herman? Goodness knows what *he* is up to." Sophie thought that it hadn't helped her to talk about Adam and Paula. The more she thought about them the more she worried.

Sophie could not share her feelings about Peter with anyone except Rosa and then only to a very limited extent because of her age: although she thought for a twelve-year old girl Rosa probably knew more, understood more, than she credited her with.

Peter was in a long slow recovery from his depression. Sophie nursed him and fed him like a child. At first he was reluctant to visit, but he came more often now – so that Rosa could help. She was so full of life and love that he had to respond to her innocent demands for his attention and approval. For a time it was only Rosa who could bring a smile to his face.

As he came more often and grew more confident they slipped back into their old ways of easy companionship. He noticed when she made an effort for him and she responded when he paid attention. And then one day it all changed. They were standing looking out of the window across the meadow and he put his arm round her waist and she turned to him and they kissed. Not a passionate kiss but a long, gentle kiss, which warmed and disarmed her. So when he lifted her into his arms and carried her upstairs to her bed she did not protest. It seemed the most appropriate and natural thing to do. They lay there after the act. The heavens had not moved but these two people gave each other physical intimacy which made them both more complete.

There was no more discussion about intimacy and no more mental agitation about whether they should. It was accepted by them both that they did: that they were a couple. There was palpable relief. After waiting so long, life could now move on for them both. Peter's recovery continued and he became more of his own true-self once again, and Sophie went about her duties with a light heart. Rosa was a like a kitten who had found the cream. So in this way the three of them comforted and encouraged each other, and all three felt valued and cared for.

On her farm Mary went about her usual tasks with care. Much of the self-confidence and ebullience which made her so highly attractive had been knocked out of her. She was reluctant to express opinions and slow to make friendships. No longer the star she drifted out of the firmament while others glistered and played out their concerns.

She was not, however, without an ally and in time a true friend. Georg, the farm-manager, who admired her from her first day on the farm, and who had encouraged and spent time with her from the very beginning, had become a good friend.

That is how they thought of their relationship. Not farm-manager and farm-worker, not working colleagues, not acquaintances – but friends. He had seen her at her most vulnerable and without hesitation had befriended her, while she seeing and being understanding of some of his personal problems, had listened to him and given support and surprisingly good advice for such a young person. The age gap was such that he could have been her father, certainly he had paternal feelings for her, and in him she saw and felt the best of her own lost father. But the difference in age seemed of no consequence. They sought each other out and enjoyed each other's company not imagining a day without the presence of the other.

Georg and Mary had known each other for over four years when the New Year of 1944 was ushered in. The farm-hands were in high spirits for it was clear to them all that the war was coming to an end and while the circumstances of its ending and their fate was unknown they had high hopes of rejoining their families before the year was out. They celebrated the New Year in the large farm barn with music, the patriotic and folk songs of many countries, and food and drink.

There was a restlessness to shake off the tyranny of their entrapment. Crude jokes were made about Hitler and his Nazi cronies and their ultimate demise, and even the Germans present laughed at them – something that none of them would have done on any previous occasion.

Mary danced with Georg.

"Where is Magda, where is your wife?" she asked, not seeing her.

"She does not wish to come, Mary. She's rather sad. She doesn't welcome these disasters like some of you do."

Mary quietened for she knew that his wife had lost relatives killed in air raids. He continued: "She would not laugh at these jokes. She loves Hitler. For her he is God. He can do no wrong. But let's not talk about it and spoil our evening."

Later when they were standing together at the makeshift bar he did go on talking about it:

"Magda wants us to sell up – that is if the farm is saleable at all – and go back to the west. It was a mistake coming here in the first place and I will be forced out of it at some time. Maybe something much worse will happen."

Mary looked at him anxiously.

"*Will we be safe?*" she said.

"I don't know. I've been thinking about it. At some time I think I will let you girls leave and go home while there is time. If Russian troops know that there are girls up here, whatever your status, I don't think you will be safe from them."

Mary felt a pang of despair and a feeling of panic. She shouldn't have said it, and she regretted it as she did: "What about *us* Georg? What will happen to *us*?"

For a moment he thought she was talking about the girls, and then he realised Mary was meaning the two of them.

"Mary, dear, there isn't an *us*. I'm a married man, there can't be an *us*."

And then seeing the tears in her eyes he kissed her on the cheek, in a fatherly way, and teased her, showing he cared.

Mary slipped away early and retired to her bed. She said to herself that she had been drinking and that this celebration was bound to be too much for everyone. She tried to remember his every word and gesture after she had blurted out her remark and went over it time and again in her own mind. "He hadn't minded," she thought. "He liked it really." Although he had teased her it was not a rejection. She hadn't been rejected. And it was out in the open and couldn't be ignored. "*What a gambler I am*," she thought, amused by herself, and thinking of her father and Adam playing cards. "*It must run in the family*."

Georg looked carefully at his wife that night. She remained a very beautiful woman and with her fair hair so very carefully arranged, her beautiful full lips and fair complexion, and her elegant dress – he smiled at this aspiration for the good life – he could remember why he had wanted her in the first place and why he had allowed her to determine their behaviour. It was Magda with her instinct for the main chance who had wanted to settle in the east in the new German territory.

"Think of it Georg, just think of it?" she had pleaded with him, her blue eyes shining with the excitement of a small child: "A large fertile farm for free and the gratitude of the Führer and the Party. We wouldn't look back."

He protested that he knew nothing about farming.

"Darling there is nothing to it. You can employ people and you – we – shall learn about it."

"What a fool I was to allow myself to be governed by this avarice and these false dreams. We shall pay a heavy price for them," he said to himself. He thought of Mary and what she had said to him. He was glad she had said it and at that moment it crept into his mind, and stayed there, that there might be an *us* and that he wanted it. For the moment nothing could happen but there would come a moment when he might choose: come the new circumstances there might be a new life.

That moment of choice did not come quickly. In that very same month the mighty Russian armies crossed the eastern frontier, or what the Poles thought of as the border – the pre-war border, but not the border resulting from the Soviet–Nazi pact. To the south in Italy, British and American armies, supported by Polish soldiers, closed in on the Germans. But the Germans did not give up in Poland or Italy. They fought ferociously and tenaciously and it was to take a year of bitter fighting to force all the German troops out of Poland.

Now that the relationship was declared Georg and Mary needed to get on with it but that was not to be. As the war ground on there was no honourable way for them to develop a life together. The risk for them

both was that their growing passion for each other, deprived of fulfil-
ment, would atrophy, shrivel on the branch, and come to nothing. In
affairs of the heart, however, things do not stand still, there is a
dynamic which leads on to conclusions.

For Georg the effort to make something of his married life, which
might have saved it, was not made; and Magda, deprived of love and
attention began to contemplate life without him. They did not row, but
acted with resignation. It became accepted between them that when this
dreadful war came to an end they would go their own way. Magda knew
herself to be an attractive woman and did not doubt herself. Once back
in Berlin, Munich or Hamburg there would be excitement again.

In her own mind she began to prepare herself for this new life. She
lost weight and paid more attention to her appearance. So successful
was she in these efforts that for a time she enticed Georg back into a
sexual relationship which he had abandoned. Magda entered into sex
with a new ardour and not a little skill. Georg was pleased and impressed.
He thought for a while that it might work out between them. Magda too
deceived herself for a time. She was practising for her new life: keeping
everything in shape for somebody else. Later when she thought about
it, she was pleased. "After all," she persuaded herself, "I've put a great
effort into this relationship, and it is good and civilised of me to end it
in this pleasurable way."

Mary noticed a difference in Georg. He was paying more attention
to Magda and less to her. Although he told her not, she thought that she
was losing him. There was nothing that she could do – wanted to do –
to assert herself: so she waited, hoped and suffered. The moment for
choices would come. She was determined to wait for him and in the
meantime not to make his life more difficult.

Mary had no one to talk to about Georg. Heinrich had been such a
bitter experience to her that she did not trust any of the other girls. And
how could a daughter, in the circumstances her mother found herself
in, take this love affair back to her: she would only worry about it and dis-
approve. "I will not have this thing between Georg and me disapproved
of," she told herself. "It would be more than I could endure."

Mary deprived herself of the comfort of her home where, if she had
but known, there would have been warmth and compassion for her: a
mother anxious to share her own love affair with another loving person:
someone who would not judge her harshly: a mother who would above
all others welcome the support and endorsement of her daughter.

At this time, in Sachsenhausen, Ludvig began to suffer extreme stomach pains and after ignoring them for a while was obliged to consult the camp doctor. Stomach upsets in the camp were legion and at first nothing much was thought of it. He was given some stomach powders and they seemed to help. His work as a blokowy was not arduous and the condition did not affect his ability to work.

Ludvig had not been able to advance any further in the camp hierarchy: he lacked the intelligence and strength of purpose which marked out the high-risers, and in their absence his efforts were thought to be duplicitous. He bumped his head against the same limitations that had dogged his police career. Ludvig accepted his shortcomings and devoted his efforts to staying afloat and alive. In these efforts he succeeded. Once he had stopped trying to climb he ceased to be a danger to the aspirants: and he had the shrewdness to make judgements about them and to do favours for the most likely. His low cunning enabled him to watch his back and on the few occasions that he made mistakes he had enough favours to draw upon in the hierarchy to avoid their consequences.

The stomach pains did not disappear and the camp doctor having tried various medicines had seemed to shrug off any further responsibility. When Ludvig asked him to put a name to his condition, he had replied that it could be one of a number of ailments and that he lacked the facilities or the time to do anything more for him. Ludvig continued with some medication but the condition remained.

It came as a surprise to Ludvig when he was summoned to the camp administration block and told that he was to be discharged. He was given seven days to clean himself up and then issued with some clothes from the store. Whose clothes they were he did not know and did not care to think about. But they fitted him and after camp uniform he felt himself a lord. He was given a rail warrant and assured that his family had been informed of his release. On a bleak January day in 1944 the camp-gate swung open for him and in icy rain he passed back out of the prison.

He had no sense of elation. He walked with some physical difficulty to the rail station and embarked on the arduous journey to his home town, and to a family where in recent times, apparently, no one had cared enough to send him a parcel or a letter.

His feelings were mixed and troubled. The camp had been his home for over four years and whatever the harshness of the regime he had in a way been protected. His place there may not have been of the highest, but he did have one. He could call some shots: he had some influence.

In the end the authorities had fed him and looked after him, no matter how poorly; and for the first time in his life he had acquired a dramatic stage for his skills. All these blessings he was about to lose.

As he sat on the deserted station platform, Ludvig felt a better man for his experience in the camp: he had flourished in imprisonment. Now he was a free man he felt uncomfortable and out of place. He feared his freedom which, after all, and in many respects, had not worked out too well for him in the past.

CHAPTER 18

ADAM AND HIS comrades spent a pleasant night in the police cells and in the early morning they were led out one by one into an interview room where they were confronted by two plain-clothes men, one who turned out to be from the Home Office and the other from Special Branch. Having established that German was the common language, the interview was conducted in German. Adam's German was good but it was clear to the questioners that it was not his first language.

His story was straightforward enough and after a while the atmosphere was relaxed and jokey. Nevertheless the inquiry was thorough and the two men were there all day, checking and cross-checking the four stories and satisfying themselves that they were genuine deserters. Finally, they were all called together and were told that they were believed and that arrangements had been made for them to be collected and taken by train to an Assessment Centre for the Polish army in Kirkcaldy in Scotland, if they agreed. As this could not happen for another two days, they spent the nights in the cells.

Although they had been believed they realised that they were not yet in the clear. Their Polish countrymen would soon suss out the pretenders, and then they thought, it might all get rather unpleasant. Not that that applied in their case, of course, but they could imagine it. The train journey was long and tiring. There was no buffet and, although they had been provided with two packed meals, after a sixteen hour journey they were hungry on arrival in Kirkcaldy. The Pole who had accompanied them had chatted easily about his experiences. He was a pilot injured while flying and unfit for active service. Now all he could do were liaison duties.

They were interviewed by four or five people over another five days and after a while even they thought that they might be frauds. They were certainly not treated as heroes and their natural bumptiousness was deflated. And then after some sort of conference had been held it was all 'hail fellow well met' and drinks in the bar. They had been accepted and all was well.

There was an immediate issue of basic survival. It seemed to them that it was always the case in life. They were accommodated and fed and given one pound. What else would depend on the decisions they took and what they did.

In the main common room they saw that their fellow Poles were playing cards. For the last five years a major component of Adam's income had been his winnings from cards. Here was a chance to 'get ahead of the game'. The first problem – and opportunity – was the coinage. These Polish boys were playing for sixpences. There were two coins which seemed the same: the florin was worth four sixpences and the half-crown, five. After a few drinks he was sure that these lads would be unable to tell the difference.

He changed his one pound note for sixpences and joined in. This time his object was to make some significant money. These lads were not particularly good or particularly sober. He started to win and when he did he manipulated the coins so that for winnings in florins he took half crowns. In that way his winnings were multiplied by twenty-five percent.

In the ten days that they were there he won steadily without anyone catching on. With his winnings he bought himself an excellent pair of shoes, went to a cinema where he watched an old Hollywood movie, and frequented the bars. It did not seem to him that there was a war on in Scotland: the shops were full of goods and people went about their usual tasks in a cheerful manner.

At the end of ten days decisions had to be made about them. What sort of soldier should they be? There were two issues; first, if you were a prudent sort of person you tried to avoid getting killed. It seemed to them that Polish soldiers were asked to do very dangerous things and it was wise to try to avoid being a straightforward Polish infantryman. But, secondly, and as important, was what you were paid. The highest rate of pay seemed to be that of a commando whose starting wage was £5 a week. This seemed to Adam to be an incredibly high amount. He had never earned anything like this. And you could do better than this once you became proficient.

It seemed to them that it was a pretty sensible thing to be a commando.

Of course, you had to do dangerous things but not all the time: and then you went on missions and were taught special skills to make sure you could handle them. So these four lads decided to be commandos and to undertake the special training required.

The next months were the happiest time of his life. He was sent on commando training with a dozen other recruits to a British training camp at Achnacarry in the Highlands which the Poles were able to share. It was a twelve-week course: perhaps, the toughest course devised for specialist soldiers. But no one considered it a hardship.

Poles who had arrived at this point in their lives had done so by diverse routes, but they had in common a love of country and high hopes that the war would work out well for them in the end. Then the camp was in glorious countryside, which reminded him of Zakopane in his own country: rolling grasslands and rising hills and mountains purple with heather, and fast-flowing rivers and large lakes in which, from the road-side, you could see the fish jumping as if begging you to take your chance at catching them.

They fed and slept well and were surrounded by friendly people. On winding tracks in late autumn sunshine people stopped them, insisting on shaking their hands: friendly hands clasping their own, arms gripped to show their acceptance, and slaps on the back. In pubs and inns complete strangers invited them to join in the games and the girls smiled and engaged them. On hikes they were invited into cottages to share meals. The cottagers did not have very much but whatever it was they wanted them to have a part of it.

The training itself was intense. Although Adam believed himself to be fit, he was often found wanting. Long hikes over hills carrying very heavy packs in all weathers, sleeping rough on the hillsides, and living off the land, started to sort out the 'wheat from the chaff'. All the exercises were conducted with live ammunition which was unnerving for the recruits with no battle experience.

When they lived rough they had to live off the land with the only food being the animals you could catch. As Adam was a country lad, he had no difficulty in catching rabbits and other small furry animals, which made him a popular person with whom to bivouac.

A commando they learned was a person who arrived at night out of a mist and killed his foe quickly and silently before stealing back from where he came. As it was described it sounded both romantic and frightening. They were taught how to kill a man with a knife in the back or a garrotte. And then there was boat training out on the lake, which everyone enjoyed. The commando had to be able to understand boat drill and manoeuvre a boat to land on a heavily-defended beach.

Not everyone was to get through this course, and not only for physical reasons, but Adam was determined to be one of them. The nice guys and the nervous did not get through at all. And then, those that might succeed, needed to be mechanical or technical: to look after their own weapons and any others that might come their way, to communicate on walky-talkies and by radio, and to understand and use codes. Some of the requirements came easily to Adam but others presented him with difficulties.

They were taught things which held Adam in good stead for the rest of his life. A commando had to be well-disciplined, clean and precise in everything. He must behave in an honourable way to friend and foe and take a pride in his fighting unit, exhibiting a willingness to live and die for it. Commandos were smarter and better soldiers, and had to look good on all occasions.

Adam slipped back into the easy ways he had enjoyed in the German army. He started to make good friends and there was the easy companionship of buddies: card playing, pub drinking and, in his case, fishing and hunting. Scotland was just wonderful for fishing and wild life. As they were paid very little while training, he supplemented his income when he could by a little business of his own. He would get out of the camp at night to set a rabbit-snare or collect his catch and to do some fishing. He found a local inn that would take his catch and with a nod and a wink the transaction was conducted. "Food shortages! What shortages are you talking about?" The innkeeper was grateful.

He loved these night forays to the forest and to the river. The night had its own life and if you were quiet and part of it a whole new world opened up for you. Sometimes his mates urged him to accept their company and once or twice they came with him. But he discouraged them, and lied to them, keeping his movements secret. He preferred his own company: to go about his tasks in his own way. They were impatient to have things happen, whereas he knew that it wasn't like that. He was content to sit by the river for hours without a catch. What he knew was that if you were in the right place at the right time with the right tackle and bait you would catch a fish. And what more pleasant time could you spend than on a green, mossy bank with the sounds of wind in the reeds and the fir trees, and a fast-flowing river under a silver moon?

As he walked back to base from one of these night expeditions in the early morning light and softly-falling rain he considered and compared his two favourite activities – fishing and card playing. It seemed to him that they had a good deal in common: first, you had to choose your place very carefully and exercise great patience; good preparation and sound strategy was important, and learning how to win in the most unlikely of circumstances; and then it was wise not to be too greedy, he always threw something back as a good-luck gesture and in the knowledge that you might need this good fortune at some other time.

As for the girls, friendly they might be, but there were difficulties. There was the language. He spoke very little English and they seemed to talk none at all. He did not know what language they were talking but he could not understand a word of it. And then they were heavily guarded. The people seemed to be highly moralistic and you did not often find a pretty girl on her own or out late at night. They had to satisfy themselves with game playing, which while amusing and diverting, did not get them very far.

He decided that although he wanted to pass the course he did not want to do too well. The lads discussed this among themselves. The issue was that of their destiny at the end of the course. What would happen to them? The answer seemed to be that they could be involved in some very dangerous fighting. They would be regarded as 'crack troops' to be given the most frightening and difficult missions.

The Polish commando, they discovered, was paid less than his British and American counterparts which raised the question of whether they could transfer out. Polish commandos received their finance from the British and it seemed that they were regarded as a cheap option. Poles, it was thought, were so in love with their country and so anti-German that they would do very dangerous things for almost nothing. Adam did not want to be killed on foreign soil for hardly nothing: there was probably better ways of getting killed.

During the course they had a lecture from a visiting senior American officer. He spoke about the progress of the war from the American perspective and the activities of the American Special Forces. He was an approachable person and they were all impressed by him. Afterwards he made himself available in the mess bar, a primitive place but at least somewhere where you could mix and have a drink. The lads quizzed him about how the Americans worked and, although he had to be careful, he answered questions frankly in a very pleasant manner.

Adam thought, "That's the place for me. I should be in the American Special Forces."

He asked: "Can a Pole join the American Special Forces?"

"Yes, of course, we have Poles in every branch of the American and British armed services," was the reply.

The American wrote his name and address on a piece of paper for him and added: "If you want to know more, contact me there."

Adam carried the address away as a trophy and worked out how and when he could get to London to talk to this man and discover the lie of the land.

First, there was the need to pass this course and get himself accepted by the Polish commandos and in the end he did this with style. Then he had to act quickly before anyone could arrange a posting. It was down to the inn for the use of the telephone. In broken English, carefully rehearsed in advance, he spoke to a secretary, who made him an appointment.

He had very little money.

"Can you send me a rail voucher?" was his request.

"We can do better than that. A rail voucher, yes, and a reservation at a small hotel we use, no charge of course, for two nights. We shall want to have a good look at you," was the reply.

He needed some leave, but that was no problem because now they were all on leave for a while, and off he went. As he sat on the train he thought: "This gets better and better, even the Americans want me now," which was a somewhat premature thought.

He wore his carefully pressed khaki Polish military uniform and his army boots shone with a glow that no mere civilian could match. "It can't get much better than this," he thought, "if only my mother could see me. She would be so proud." For a moment he thought of how he felt when he wore his German uniform for the first time. It depressed him a little – this need to have a uniform to feel like a king.

A rather attractive young girl on the opposite seat smiled at him encouragingly and offered him some tea from a flask. "The way it will get better," he thought, "is to improve my English. And how amazing it is that in war-time, whatever the country, there is always someone to share food and drink with."

Adam was mightily impressed with London. The only other large capital he had seen was Paris, and that experience was very limited as he was passing through. This was something else. London gave him an immediate sense of being in a world capital and part of a world power. You could sense that this was the centre of an immense empire: there were numerous memorials to it, the streets were cosmopolitan and the vast buildings with their purposeful busy officials suggested activity on a great scale. He thought that if you could describe Paris as a feminine city, and it was certainly beautiful, you would think of London as masculine: authoritative, worldly and reassuring.

The offices of the American Special Forces (SF) was in Bryanston Square behind the Cumberland Hotel and within spitting distance of Marble Arch. Adam felt in the middle of things. This was a city at war, you could see this from the bomb damage and protected windows, and the muted shop-displays showing evidence of austerity and shortages. But the spirit of people on the streets seemed very good: people were kind to him and helpful in giving directions, sometimes going miles out of their way to make sure that he didn't get lost.

His morale rose steadily and by the time of his arrival he was positively enthusiastic and willing to agree to anything. The selection process, however, deflated him. He was interviewed several times and asked what appeared to be the same questions by different people. As he knew little English these interviews were conducted in German except for one friendly exchange in Polish. He sat an intelligence test where the instructions were in Polish, which cheered him, as it indicated that other Poles must have taken the same route.

Not all these interviews were very friendly. He had been pressed very hard on his experiences as a German soldier and the duties he had performed in France and he avoided answering some of the questions. He did not want to talk about Jew-hunting or catching British spies. For all he knew these spies and their operations might be known to the people in front of him. He was not ashamed of his record – *hadn't he tried to save some of these Jews?* But he sought refuge in the fact that he had no choice but to do what he was ordered to do: *he had to obey orders.*

He was asked about his experiences at Auschwitz. He started to tell the interviewer about the camp: the state of the prisoners and the cruelty of the guards, the stories about the gassing that was going on there and the burning of bodies. As he spoke the words tumbled out of him. He described the scene, the collecting of the dead bodies and the smells all over the town. He spoke about the train transports and prisoners being stripped naked. He couldn't stop: but he was halted.

The interviewer shuffled his papers. He didn't want Adam to go on with this story. He didn't believe him. Who would believe it? As Adam spoke he had great difficulty in believing it himself. The interviewer raised his hand to signify silence: "Thank you for that account," he said. "War is a depressing experience and I can see that you found this camp very terrible." He looked embarrassed as if the subject was in bad taste.

The interviewer paused and Adam blurted out: "So will you make a note of it and get this account to a senior person?"

"Yes, I will," was the diffident response, and Adam saw him write a note.

Back in the hotel on the first night, he dreamt of the young girl he had captured with a rugby tackle. He saw her terrified face clearly as he looked down on her, an image he had experienced a thousand times; he heard her appeal to him and saw his comrades running towards him across the field in the moonlight; and he woke sweating with a sense of dread and foreboding. He soon shrugged it off. It was all much too exciting to dwell on this memory. But he wondered whether it would be wise for him to confess to these things and whether it would it be forced out of him anyway?

But he said nothing and the moment to be completely frank about everything passed by. And then there was a disappointment. He had a final interview which seemed to go nowhere.

"Am I accepted?" he burst out.

"Not yet," was the reply. "We would not offer you a place with us without the agreement of our Polish colleagues. They may have plans for you. Anyway, we shall need to see their assessments of you to find out about your strengths – and weaknesses too, I expect. You will have to be patient with us. It shouldn't take too long. Try and see something of London before you go back."

He needed no prompting on that score. There was a very attractive secretary in the outer office of about his own age who had given him the eye and who on approach offered to show him around. They managed a pleasant evening despite his poor English. But that is all it was, to his disappointment. I really must improve my English otherwise I shall never get going with them, was his conclusion.

Despite the war there were things to do in London. He had seen a film and if there had been time he could have gone to a theatre. He had ate out in a restaurant and had walked in a huge and very nice park where he fell asleep on a bench in the sunshine. For a moment, when he woke, he did not know where he was: but wherever it was he was pleased to be there. The dread of the day ahead – his usual feeling – was gone, and he was happy. London was the place to be, he thought:

but then he hadn't done well in the tests, he supposed: he couldn't be thought to be academic, it had always been something of a problem for him. Should he have been more frank? After all they must know a lot. He slept and sweated on the train journey back although there was no heating on the train.

It did not take long to get a response and in a few days time he had an invitation to return to London for a final interview. He was to see a serving officer, a major at the Centre.

The secretary gave him a beaming smile and the thumbs up as he went through the door and he supposed in an instant, and was wrong to do so, that it was a formality.

The major was friendly but rather stiff and formal.

"What I would like to do at the outset," he was told, "is to go through with you the results of your tests with us and the assessment report from your Polish colleagues on your training with them. Is that all right with you?"

It was and he did.

Apparently it had been concluded that he was not a team-player and though he possessed the necessary level of fitness and courage – there was no doubt about that – and was proficient in weapon-handling and survival techniques, there were some question marks about his impulsiveness. Apparently, it was thought that there was a fine line between the ability to take initiatives in dealing with the unknown and unexpected obstacles and events and the taking of too many decisions: too little and you would not survive, too many and your unit might not survive. The major looked up from the paperwork: "We concluded, and I am sorry about this, that we could not offer you a place with the American Commandos."

Adam showed his disappointment and got up to go. He was very unhappy about this unexpected outcome and did not know what to say. He supposed that these assessors knew what they were doing and had got their assessment right. Of course, his impulsiveness got him into trouble: they were right about that.

"Hold on," said the major, "I haven't finished. What we all concluded is that you were likely to be highly successful in our clandestine activities. Not fighting as a commando but acting behind enemy lines either on your own or with a comrade. These activities are organised from this building and, if you are interested, you can talk to someone and we may be able to get you a decision very quickly."

Adam said that he was interested and was given another interview by a distinguished man in civilian clothing who was not a soldier but some kind of civil servant. This man explained to him in graphic terms the work of the Special Forces and the role of an agent. This type of work he said required very special people with rare qualities of courage, people capable of acting coolly in situations of great danger, acting alone and relying on their own resourcefulness. "Adam," he said, addressing him directly, "I have looked through your file and I have no doubt whatsoever that you are such a person. We would like you to join us. What do you think?"

Adam was pleased and astonished.

"Yes, I would like to join," was his immediate response.

"Good," the interviewer was pleased. "But before we close this off, I want you to think very carefully about it. It is – it will be – a job of great danger to you and may cost you your life. You should discuss it with your close family. Of course, that is impossible for you isn't it? Well, I shall provide you with someone. We have a chaplain we use here. He's a jolly good fellow. I shall find out whether he is available. All right? We shall arrange it."

In the availability of this chaplain, Adam was very fortunate. The chaplain was an active priest in the Church of England, liberal, worldly and warm-hearted. He had a sensible discussion with him. The chaplain who was not trying to influence him in any way concluded by saying: "Right Adam, that is all the time available to me at the moment. But if you join I would like to see you again and you might want to talk through some of the things that worry you, that have happened to you over these past years. I shall be pleased to help."

So Adam said: "Yes," again, to the major.

"Think about it and ring us in three days time," was the response. "And if you are of the same mind, you can join. But remember that these conversations are not to be disclosed now to any third party. Do you understand that? Good. We look forward to hearing from you."

In three days time Adam rang as requested to accept the offer but was put off once again.

Adam put the matter out of his mind. That was that he thought. The next stage in his training was learning to parachute which took place at Horstead in Sussex within commuting distance of London. There he qualified for the special wings which showed that you had been successful in at least eight jumps. You were dropped in open country and with a map and had to find yourself back to an agreed assembly point. It was an important skill and once acquired you were paid more!

The instructors were Polish-speaking British soldiers. They had good contacts with the Americans it seemed and American officers often visited their centre. To his astonishment Adam encountered the American officer who had interviewed him in Bryanston Square and he contrived to speak to him. "Yes, I remember you," he responded. "Shouldn't you be with us? Weren't we going to do that?" He promised to look into it. A few days later Adam received a written invitation to join the American Special Forces at the end of his course.

It was January 1944 when Adam moved to London to attend the American Spy Centre, for that is what he was going to be – a spy. A few months ago he was waiting in French fields to catch British spies and now he might be dropped back into these very same fields to be caught by his former colleagues, for all he knew.

The year opened to thoughts of great hope and optimism that the worst of this war was over. Adam took up lodgings in Bryanston Square in the very heart of the capital and was paid what seemed a small fortune of £58 a month which would go higher as his training was completed. It was like being a student. There were other lodgers like him in Bryanston Square. Each day they attended lectures. Each day they did the things that young male students did: they ate and drank too much, they sought out the sexiest and most accessible girls, and they were foolish, sometimes very foolish indeed.

They were adopted Americans. Not for them the shortages of war. They could shop in the American Shop in Edgeware Road where everything was available to them and not just only food but luxuries: cigars, vodka, and silk stockings to impress the girls. It was all very cheap. "It must be wonderful to be an American and have this stuff all of the time," he said to himself.

But unlike students their studies had a very serious and imminent intent. This purpose hung over them like a long postponed visit to the dentist. Adam was given specific training for this visit. He studied languages: English, of course because he would receive orders in English but also German. Adam's German was very good indeed, but it was not perfect. He would always have an accent. This did not matter too much so long as his German was generally acceptable, and with practice he would be able to pass himself off as a German-speaking Czech.

There were several of them in this category and they took instruction together. There was a shock for them: the instructor was a Jew. This man, Jacob Lipson, had fled from Germany in 1936. He spoke perfect English and was an academic sort of person. In better times he would have been called Herr Professor or Herr Doktor in Germany and much revered. He came right out with it: "Class, my name is Jacob Lipson. Please call me Jacob. I am a German Jew, is that a problem for anyone?" No one answered.

"Well that is very good of you. From where I sit you look a very nice lot. But I suspect that you are too kind to me and that some of you are uncomfortable at being taught by a Jew. It's all right, really, perhaps, it might be the case that I have my doubts about some of you. Had you thought of that? No, I guess not. I mention it now because you should know that it is *my* mission here to try and save *your* lives. When we are finished together your German will be so perfect that no one will be able to say that you are not German by listening to you. Of course, you might think that I was doing this for the money. That would be untrue for I could earn much more by doing some other job, but I could say the same about you couldn't I? That you are here for the money. But I wouldn't say that because I would know it to be untrue."

He paused for breath and to gather himself for the peroration: "What I suspect is that we are here together for the same reason. We wish to bring to an end a terrible tyranny which has devastated *my* country and your own – yes, Germany is *my* country – a tyranny which has destroyed *our* families."

He paused again and looked at them fiercely. "Yes, I see you agree. Well I'm glad we have got that out of the way." From that moment he did not have the slightest trouble with anyone and being an outstandingly good teacher very quickly had their respect.

CHAPTER 19

ADAM BEGAN TO hold regular sessions with the chaplain in his church in west London. The chaplain took him into his home and introduced him to his family, his friends and to the church members. Whenever he could, Adam attended the church social club. He began to discover, as immigrants do, fellow countrymen, fellow Poles. London was full of them. There was even a Polish Government in London, a Government in exile. It was spoken about and you could meet the members of it at social gatherings and read about them in Polish newspapers and newsletters.

He discovered that Poles and uniforms were liked in London and that subject only to his military status he could go anywhere and do anything. On the buses the conductresses chucked him under the chin, called him dear, and refused to take his fare. He had money in his pocket, not a lot of money, but enough. Although the war was hurrying him along, there were pauses and a time to think.

Adam started to address with the chaplain the nightmares of the last four years. Hesitant at first, he needed the reassurance that their conversations were entirely private and that the chaplain was bound by the ethics of the church not to reveal anything to anybody. Adam told him about Auschwitz and the affair with Julia: about trying to rescue the Jewess; about Marseilles and the blowing up of the Old Port: about the Jew-hunts and the capturing of the British spy (disguising his part in this): and the hiding of the two children in V. And he told him about Miss Zbucki.

The chaplain said very little. It was his task to listen and he was very good at it. But moved by Adam's account of Miss Zbucki he proffered a rare comment: "Miss Zbucki sounds like a very wise and loving woman, Adam, you were lucky to meet her. I'm going to pray for her and I suggest that you do so as well. After this war is over, we shall need Miss Zbucki and others like her to rebuild our world and make good the damage. I hope that she has survived, Adam. Unfortunately, the very best of us do not always survive. The wicked seem to have better durability."

In the Reverend Timothy Kitson, Adam had found a good friend and over time he became a father-figure to him. But unlike a father he hardly ever gave advice as such, nor did he deliver any lectures. If he had done so, he would no doubt have been disregarded. He had the happy gift of listening and in a sinuous and perceptive manner turning around your comments to illumine and explain them. This resulted in you arriving at the most remarkably helpful conclusions, and in being complimented for your wisdom and astuteness if you spoke about them. In this he reminded Adam of his sister Mary: but, of course, the subjects they spoke about were very different.

As Timothy Kitson had only daughters he was able to adopt Adam as a kind of honorary son, and Adam became part of a gregarious, friendly ménage of women, young and old.

Being adopted by this family enabled Adam to start the process of assimilation with things British. Mrs Kitson had said brightly: "Well Adam, now that you are here what do you think of Britain and the British?"

With practice he had been able to précis the response to: 'Kind people, dreadful weather,' having read and adapted Gogol's comments about about Russia: 'Two problems: fools and bad roads.' Later he would add comments about France, 'Wonderful country, marvellous climate and good food. Pity about the French.' It was good for a laugh.

In his limited English he couldn't express what he really felt and meant. He found Britain to be a *remarkable* country. It was, he thought, truly democratic. Here in the middle of a war Parliament subjected the leaders of it, the great Churchill himself, to scrutiny and censure. The press and radio, though naturally patriotic, reported the war, so far as he could see and certainly in contrast to German radio, with frankness and honesty. In Germany, Hitler was never seen in public; whereas in Britain, Churchill and the King and Queen stayed in the capital, sharing the fate of the common people, and were seen on the streets all the time. So far as he could understand it, the roots of this democracy were very deep and had existed for a very long time. Of course, it was not perfect but it seemed to him that British people could change the things they didn't like without the interference of dictators. Above all the British seemed to like the Poles. "Adam," they would say to him, "we came into this war to help your country be free. We shall not let you down." It was nice to hear this and he felt that Britain was a true friend of Poland.

You could enjoy yourself in London and he started to work out how he could do it. The three Kitson girls, aged sixteen, seventeen, and eighteen, were willing to help. The elder, Gloria, had joined the British army and had a host of bright young friends away from home for the first time and up for fun and adventure. They knew where the good parties and dances were being held and how you gate-crashed them in the absence of an invitation. Swept along by their enthusiasm and friendliness these Polish boys were rarely short of an invitation or a venue.

While the Kitson girls were highly respectable and not out for short-term sexual adventures, their friends were often more adventurous. Adam tried some and enjoyed the encounters but invariably found his way back to the safety of a more respectable harbour. Gloria would say to her friends: "You must meet Adam. He's a bit of a rogue if you let him be, but a very good sort at heart. He's not nearly as bad as his reputation."

"That sounds interesting, we could give that a go then," was often the reply, with a giggle.

A favourite venue was the Hammersmith Palais. There on a Saturday night to the sounds of a 'Big Band' you could ballroom-dance and, from time to time, jitterbug. The girls could wear their party dresses and the boys were expected to make an effort to look respectable in suits and brilliantined hair. The Kitson girls came in their own little gang and looked after each other, so a small gang of soldiers in their smart uniforms was just the thing.

There were drawbacks to these arrangements, the principal one being that you could finish up with a 'dog'. There came the awful moment of the last waltz: you might have no partner at all, which was sort of humiliating, or – and worse – be stuck with someone you most definitely did not want to see home. While that was how the mating game was played, it usually resulted in a lot of horse-play and fooling about and very little action.

If you were bold and didn't mind the likely rejection you might have a go with the older girls, many of whom were in uniform. These girls were very forward and were likely to be living in lodgings in Central London away from their families. But the competition was fierce and the likelihood was that they had come with some smart officer or were going to leave with one. Then there were the Yanks of all ages and ranks with more money than sense and flashing it around.

To be honest with himself, which he wasn't with his mates, he really preferred the Kitson crowd and people like them. They were really very nice girls – like his sisters – and you felt safe with them. It was true that you were not likely to get any of them into bed, and actually you would not want to, because it was generally accepted that you limited your activity to a good snog: but you got affection and familiarity without too arduous a challenge and commitment. In the morning it was hard to remember what had happened the night before. You felt that you might have been hugged by all the Kitson girls – and you probably had been.

They went on for some months like this, training during the day and playing at night and at the weekend. Everyone knew that an invasion of mainland Europe was being planned but no one knew exactly when or exactly where. London and the southern counties was full of encamped troops most of whom seemed to be American. At the Spy Centre it seemed to the boys that until this invasion took place it was unlikely that they would be used as they had been told that they were to be dropped into a place where they could help ground troops.

Getting a grip on the work of the Special Forces was difficult for the Europeans among them. It seemed that there were operations every-where but in Europe: in the Middle and Far East, in Africa and in Asia, and in places they had never heard of. To Adam's mind what was im-portant was to get back into France and to trounce the Germans: that was the only way to get an independent Poland: and to get back into Germany and Poland before the Russians, because if you weren't you could beat the Germans but finish up without Polish independence.

But where were the British fighting? Everywhere *but* in France. Even when Rommel had been thrown out of north Africa, what did the British and the Americans do? They invaded Italy of all places. You wouldn't beat the Germans by crawling up the spine of Italy. Sometimes they wondered whether they would ever be used: whether all this training and preparation was for nothing.

Impatient to do something Adam made a request to be used in France where there was a lot of activity. He was sure that he knew much of the territory the agents were being dropped into better than most. "No chance," he was told. "Your French is not good enough. We have all the agents we need for France and all entirely fluent in the language." He was urged to work hard to improve his German so that when he was used he would not be a danger to himself or anyone else. All of which he supposed must be right.

And then at the Hammersmith Palais on a blind date he met Eva and he didn't care at all about not being used right away. Not that it was like this from the beginning because she was very unimpressed with him and refused to see him again. Eva had been reluctant to go on this date and had been talked into it by her friend anxious to keep going with a young Pole without compromising herself. While Adam was impressed by this dishy well-dressed young girl – she was eighteen at the time – she was distinctly underwhelmed by what she was confronted with. Admittedly he was very handsome with wavy fair hair and steely blue eyes, above average height and in a very smart uniform: "But God," she thought, "how arrogant."

Adam thought: "She is on this date with me. What a lucky girl she is." This approach was doomed to failure even if Eva had been other than a self-confident young girl with her head in the right place. Her friend Rose on the other hand had a very nice young man, Eva thought: polite and intelligent and speaking very good English. After a few minutes she whispered to Rose: "Let's swap. Victor for Adam." "Not on your Nellie," said Rose grabbing her date and swirling away.

It was a most unpromising beginning: Eva would not be escorted home and muttered inconsequentially when Adam wanted to see her again. "Bad start Adam," said Victor, telling him the facts of social life in Britain.

But Adam did meet her again at a party at the Kitsons. This time, in the jolly surroundings of the Kitson family, Adam did not make such a fool of himself. Other girls were pleased to talk to him and the Kitson girls prevented anyone from being too pompous. So he got a four-somes date for walking in the park and the hiring of a boat. They all got wet and there was a good deal of laughter. Eva conveyed that she was not a girl to be messed about and, yes, she did find him dishy: and Adam succeeded in being his usual bouncy confident self and that, yes, she was a sweetheart. So on this more realistic basis Adam fell in love and Eva was carried along with the excitement and diversion of it.

The adult world might have considered that this was no time to fall in love. After all this young Polish boy was entirely uprooted and what did one really know about him? And because of the secrecy of his job he could say very little to them about himself. Even his name was false because all the people on the spy course were given new names so that no one knew the true identity of any other. Adam was given the surname

Alexander, but to an English person there was no way that this could be his real name.

Affairs of the heart, however, cannot be arranged to suit the authorities and elders of this life. All over London young men and women whose futures were uncertain met in the midst of the dangers of life and fell in love, behaving as if today might be their last on Earth which for many was exactly the position. It was no time to hesitate and to mess about: if you were in love you had better get on with it.

One day Timothy Kitson, seeing what was happening between these two young people, took the opportunity to talk to Adam. When pressed, Adam admitted that he was very keen on Eva. "And it is very obvious, Adam, that she is keen on you. That makes you responsible for her, doesn't it?" He agreed that it did. They discussed what that might mean and for Eva not just for himself.

He had been attending the Reverend Kitson's Church of England in Hammersmith, but moved by his conversation with him he decided to go to a Roman Catholic Church and make a confession. He confessed his feelings and his impure thoughts and received a penance. He found it an empty occasion and as he walked away he decided that he was no longer a believer, because the Roman Catholic Church had let everyone down.

Later in the isolation of his room in Bryanston Square he felt himself at peace: he had needed to make a confession and to be told that God had forgiven him. The Church of England was very pleasant but you were told to go out and do better, which somehow did not give you the same relief. He realised that he had not felt like this for a very long time, if ever before. Timothy Kitson had asked him to take responsibility for someone else, not a member of his family or a fellow Pole, not a comrade who he was bound to support, but an English person who he had met only a few weeks ago. He wanted to work out what this meant and how to be responsible. He got down on his knees and prayed for every person of importance to him. While he could not kid himself that this was an act of religious observance, it did mean something to him.

To this point nothing explicit had been said by either Adam or Eva to each other. Now Adam decided that he must say something. He wasn't very good at it. There was the problem of the language: even if he had known the right words he would have been unable to articulate them. But he tried. What Eva understood was that his job was very dangerous and that he might be asked to do something before the war ended that might result in his death. Adam said that this being so, perhaps, it was not fair to go on seeing each other in the way they were. And, as an afterthought, he told her that he loved her.

She put her arms around him and kissed him as she had not kissed him before.

"Silly boy," she said, "and I love you. You must come and see my family." And she arranged it to the astonishment of her father and grandmother who were now presented with this Polish boy to appraise, care for and worry about as if he were their own. And with immense goodwill, whatever their reservations, this is what they did.

He came to tea, hair slicked-down, and very smart. He told them about his family in Poland. He explained what had happened to them and that he had been called up to serve in the German army from which he had escaped as soon as possible. They remembered that he had clicked his heels when he introduced himself, and that they had thought that this was exceptionally polite. They saw that their daughter loved this boy and so decided to love him too.

Eva had been brought up by her father and grandmother on the death of her mother. Her father, Harry Randall, worked as a taxi driver and kept unsocial hours. Loving his daughter, he did his best, but it could not be said that he was a great influence in her adolescence.

Harry Randall was born into a large London working-class family and had not experienced a lot of upbringing of his own having been orphaned when nine years of age and brought up by his eldest sister. As a child, he could not help but to assume that he was an afterthought, being the youngest of eleven children, and now sleeping on a kitchen-floor. Life had taught him to be wary and to avoid, where possible, the taking of responsibility – and now, here he was, with the task of caring for a teenage daughter.

Harry had concluded that life was not fair but that it was open to the working man, at least in Britain, to do something about injustices. He became a sort of socialist and joined the Labour Party. He had his reservations about the war which he believed was the last death-rites of the capitalist system, and had some distrust of British politicians who had, he maintained, failed to prevent it – and might not succeed in winning it. And what was it to be won for – why, for socialism – and here in England's green and pleasant land.

Harry was small and wiry with a head just too large for his body and a nose just too large for his head. He was in a constant state of animation and concern for someone or something. It came as a shock to him when war came as it was his belief that working-men were basically good and would resist the war-mongers. When war came he had tried to enlist but was turned down on health grounds, suffering as he was, from the after-effects of gassing in the first world war – a conflict he had volunteered for at the age of sixteen by lying about his age.

Sometimes in the streets, and in his taxi, people called him a coward for not serving in the armed forces – angry and despairing of the fate of their own loved-ones – and after a while he had stopped explaining. In his own mind he was confused about the war and worried about its consequences. Of course, now that it was here, he wished it to be vigorously prosecuted and won – but won for him and people like him.

Harry had inherited a cheerful disposition; he was friendly and gregarious to all in good times and bad. Not blessed with much of a schooling, he had decided to educate himself. He read widely and nourished his curiosity. Thus he had an opinion about everything – although not always his own – and the appetite for expressing his views. On his bookshelves, Charles Dickens and Thomas Hardy co-existed with Upton Sinclair and the *output* of 'The Left Book Club': joviality and dogma were both there – as in him – and in never-ending struggle.

While Harry was strong on the principles needed to govern the postwar world he was a good deal weaker on how to manage house-hold affairs and feed and bring up a teenage daughter. Fortunately, much of these matters could safely be left to his mother. Frances Randall had been raised in the school of 'hard-knocks': she knew how to manage on too little money – putting aside the cash to pay the regular bills in carefully labelled jam-jars in the larder – and protecting them against unauthorised raids. She cooked acceptable and nourishing meals from the most unpromising of scraps – and she managed a demanding household budget without getting into debt. 'Look after the pennies and the pounds will look after themselves', was her motto. So successful was she in the practice of this principle that there was a family holiday in each of the war years and never a penny borrowed or a bill late in payment.

Frances did what she could to bring up her grandchild but in matters of the heart Eva had to find her own way and, where men was con-cerned, she was very cautious. All her training at school and in the home directed her to making a good home and to the mastering of household skills. She had become a sound cook, knew how to sew and repair, and was very ready to be a good wife to a suitable man.

At this time it was commonplace to marry young and to embark on raising a large family right away. Eva was prepared for this and wanted it. So when Adam, this dashing Polish soldier came along she was very ready to succumb. While her father was willing to give his daughter her head, *his* caution, which he expressed to her as being the difficulty of understanding this Polish boy, caused him to hesitate. The family had seen nothing like Adam, could hardly communicate with him because of the language difficulty, and had no frame of reference by which to judge and assess him.

They were conscious also that this boy might not survive the war: they did not want their daughter to be heartbroken and, perhaps, to be bringing up a child without a father. So while giving his daughter his approval her father urged caution: and being a sensible girl, and knowing she would have her way in the end, she accepted his advice. Adam seeing that the way might be clear for him stopped seeing other girls and accepted that in social terms he was committed to Eva. The other lads ribbed him about this and prophesied that his goal of abstinence would never be realised

In early summer they contrived a holiday with Rose and Victor who were going strong. They shared a caravan at Felixstowe. Her father had made Eva give a solemn undertaking that nothing would 'go-on' between them: "Of course not, silly," she said lightly. "What do you take me for?" Eva made Adam give the same undertaking and reluctantly he agreed.

It was a difficult undertaking to keep to as Victor and Rose were at it like rabbits.

"Are you taking precautions?" enquired Eva.

"No, we don't do it when it is likely to produce something," responded the unscientific Rose rather vaguely.

"Well I haven't noticed *that*. Promise me you will not do it when we are in the caravan," persisted Eva.

"Well it's not like that. I'll do what I can but Victor is difficult to stop once he gets going. And let's face it there's not an awful lot to do in Felixstowe."

Adam and Eva went for walks, played the pin-tables in the arcades and rode the dodgem cars. It rained a lot and they kept under cover sheltering on the promenade and drinking cups of tea in a steam-filled cafeteria where they wrote, 'Adam loves Eva and Eva loves Adam', on the window and waited for the words to disappear.

They would have liked to go swimming in the sea but barbed wire and sea-fences kept them off the beach and all they could manage was a walk along the promenade. In the evenings they went to a pub and drank weak wartime beer and played darts. Adam found a card game and had to be dragged away before closing time, and when he had become boring, but not before he had won some money. It was not Monte Carlo or even Marseilles. But when they were asked: "Did you have a good holiday?" they said as one that they had a very happy time.

CHAPTER 20

IT SEEMED TO Sophie that her home was a kind of railway junction. Sometimes the traffic was heavy and at other times nothing moved at all. The timetable was erratic and you were never quite certain of the time of arrival or what train it would be, but that there would be an arrival at some time was certain.

In March 1944 no arrival of interest to Sophie was expected. Life was quiet and peaceful. She and Rosa saw a great deal of Peter who was getting better. Not that he was his old self and they remained concerned for him. Peter took few initiatives and needed coaxing to come to see them regularly. Sometimes he seemed absolutely fine but on other occasions he lapsed back into melancholy. He usually responded to requests to come and be part of this fractured family. But sometimes he promised to be there and didn't turn up: and then he came as if nothing had happened and no promise had been made in the first place.

On his own farm, his neighbours noticed that his farming had become careless and unpredictable: the animals were not always fed or milked on time and their protests could be heard over long distances. The farm became uncared for and neglected. His neighbours did their best to encourage and help him and he seemed to respond. But after a while they felt less sympathetic, thinking that it was time he pulled himself together. "After all," they said, "he cannot mourn his wife forever. Times are bad and it is difficult enough for us to keep our own heads above water," and so they intervened less frequently.

He seemed to respond to the coming of spring and to the ending of the long hard winter, so they put their thoughts of him to one side. Peter felt himself in a long dark tunnel. He pushed himself towards the light. On occasions he felt close to its ending and his spirits rose. With a little more effort he would burst out of the tunnel and be free: but then suddenly he saw that he was no nearer and he despaired of ever getting out.

When in an optimistic phase he drew nearer to Sophie; they had happy moments together and times of intimacy. He knew then that he had something to contribute even though he was not a good person. But even at these moments Peter knew that he did not deserve happiness because he had been responsible for his wife's death: he had not been punished for it and, therefore, could not expect to be happy with someone else.

Sophie was thinking about Peter, a little sadly, when she heard the latch to the kitchen door being lifted. Over the last few years all sorts of people had passed through the door – known and unknown – pleasant and nasty, and hearing it she suffered a tremor of fear and anxiety. In walked Ludvig and the shock was so great to her that she fainted, coming round on her bed where he had placed her. She clung to him then, sobbing and repeating time and again that she had believed him dead.

"Didn't you receive the card?"

"What card?"

"Telling you about my return. You were sent one. Didn't you get it?"

There had been no card, which was not a surprise as postal deliveries were chaotic. Now Sophie was distraught and the questions poured out. Why hadn't he written? Did he get her parcels? Was he well? Why was he released, and was it for good? Some of these questions could be answered and some not. His release was for good so long as he behaved. And as part of good behaviour he was not to talk of Sachsenhausen: he had to sign a document to that effect, so he could not answer all her questions. She asked: "Are you well?"

"No, not really, "I have a stomach problem." He said that he did not know what it was but, perhaps, now that he was at home he would get better.

"And now, please, can I go to bed. It has taken three days to get here and I have spent two nights on station platforms. I must sleep."

Once he was in bed Sophie felt very weak. She couldn't say that she was glad about the return: she didn't know what she felt really. But she knew her *duty*. Now that he was back she would be a good wife to him. There couldn't be anything else. She had made it clear to Peter that if Ludvig returned she would stand by him. He would understand, he seemed to accept it, he must accept it.

Then she was in a panic. Peter mustn't come in unannounced or hear about Ludvig's return from anyone else. "They are such gossips, these neighbours," she said to herself. Now and then, while Ludvig slept, she took the horse and cart and drove as quickly as she could, in a state of heightened anxiety, to Peter's farm.

She found him in the farmhouse sitting in the dark. She burst in and fell on him like a wild beast, sobbing and shouting, pleading and cajoling and professing her love. But telling him that it had to be the end and that she must look after Ludvig.

Of course, she must, he knew that. And how lucky she was to have Ludvig. If *only his wife* would lift the latch. He often dreamt of it. It had all been a ghastly mistake. In his dreams she had been moved to another sanatorium. She had been well-looked after and had got better. When she came back into his room she was smiling: this was the woman he had fallen in love with and who had given him happiness for over twenty years.

Ludicrous though he knew it to be, he thought that if Ludvig could come back then so could his wife. He felt great happiness and consoled her. "Goodness," she thought despite herself, and misunderstanding him, "he is not even sad. He must not love me. I must have been mistaken," although she knew that she was not. But she felt a sense of relief that, perhaps, he would not take it too badly – although at the same time she wanted him to be heartbroken at the loss of the love of his life.

If she could have had what she wanted, she needed him to say that he was heartbroken, that he could and would manage without her, but would keep her in his heart always, taking no other to him, and that he would wait for her. If it didn't work out with Ludvig she wanted him to be there for her, waiting patiently, intact and available. She wanted him to say in a convincing manner that he would remain loyal to her. She coached him, waiting for these words. When they did not come she hugged and kissed him and told him that he was the love of her life. But he knew that he wasn't and that Ludvig, her first real love, would always have the first place in her heart no matter how he behaved. In the end she had to leave Peter without the reassurance she needed.

As she hurried home to be there before Ludvig was about, she knew that she had done the right and only thing, and it pleased her that she had behaved so boldly and decisively. She would keep an eye open for Peter and help him if she could: that would not create a scandal. She began to feel happy: now that her husband was back again life might begin to get back to normal. And he *needed* her, of course, she was *needed*, which was the main thing.

Back at home she found Ludvig in the kitchen sipping weak tea. She looked at him carefully for the first time. He was not skinny so she supposed he had been well-fed. His hair was cropped very short, which did not suit him, but she supposed this to be a prison requirement and that in time this would come right – although it was a pity that he had gone grey. He had a stoop which was new and seemed to cough a lot: but with fresh air and exercise she supposed the cough would go away.

But when she looked more closely she was not reassured. She thought that he looked ill: his face had greyed and he had red blotches under his eyes. And there was something about his face and his expression that she didn't like, although she had difficulty in defining what it was. "I'm a fine one to talk," she said to herself, "what must I look like to him after these years." But he had thought, and had said to her, that she looked very well, and to himself he supposed that life must not have been too hard for her if she looked like that.

She took a good look at herself in the mirror and quite liked what she saw. Middle-aged, yes, she thought, but quite reasonable with it. Since Peter had been in her life she had cared for herself: her skin and hair looked good and there were not too many lines. She smiled and the image smiled back. Not too bad at all she thought: "Well done me, and well done Peter."

When Ludvig smiled it appeared that he did not own it: the smile was at the front of his face but you felt that it might drop-off at any moment. And then she realised that he looked shifty: he did not look straight at you when he spoke, as if he was trying to hide something from you. He had an appearance of constant anxiety. Sometimes this was an active look flitting across the front of his face but more usually a settled disturbance like a deep and permanent shadow which put part of his face in darkness.

Ludvig did not say very much about the camp but what he did say made her very unhappy. He admitted to a number of very bad things happening. What she understood was that until he had started to co-operate with the authorities – he didn't say how – he had fared very badly indeed: a lot of people had been killed in the camp or had died from too little food or overwork. Ludvig didn't know why he had been released. She pressed him a bit but grew no wiser. "You shouldn't have been there in the first place," she said indignantly. "Perhaps, in the end they realised it." He supposed that they might have done.

She was worried about his health and thought that he was very unwell. She got him to visit the doctor in town and waited while he had a thorough examination. The doctor looked at him very gravely. He concluded: "Ludvig, you have been through a great ordeal. It is bound to have affected your health. There must have been a great many very serious diseases in that camp and you have probably caught something. I don't know what, and we haven't the facilities any more for me to find out. I can't get a blood sample analysed in a lab or arrange for an X ray. We can prescribe something for you, which should be helpful for the stomach pains, and you must come back to see me, say, every two months, so that we can monitor what is happening to you. Try not to worry."

"That's not very good," said Sophie, "not to know what is wrong with you – but at least we have the prescription." Back in the surgery the doctor wrote up his notes. He concluded: 'Suspected stomach cancer. Nothing to be done.'

Ludvig's health seemed to improve once he was back in a domestic regime and he was able to do a little light-work and so to take the strain off Sophie. Rosa gently and tentatively at first re-established a relationship with him and they took to taking walks together with the dogs. She said nothing about Peter towards whom she maintained a strict loyalty and was careful in any answer to a question. Rosa asked her mother whether they could visit Peter and was disappointed to be denied.

Ludvig wanted to know about the children. He laughed to hear that Adam was in the German army.

"Like father like son," he said, "and where is he?"

She showed him two cards, one from the army in France saying that he was missing and another received from France and dated before Adam made his escape. It said:

"By the time you receive this I may be laughing in England."

He laughed again.

"The rascal has deserted."

Sophie had not thought it.

"Is that what it means. Oh good. He will be on the winning side," and she felt a great sense of relief flood through her.

She told him about Mary, but revealed none of her secrets, and about Lucie. He was thoughtful about Lucie and sad that she was not with them and vowed that he would go and see her. After the first bout of questions he said nothing more although from time to time he said something which showed that he was thinking about them in his own way. And they did go to Katowice to see Lucie.

On this visit Ludvig went for a long walk with Herman and when they returned the family saw that they had been arguing, and that Herman was red in the face. On the way home Sophie asked him about it. He wouldn't answer questions and just muttered violently: "How I hate informers, collaborators and placemen. Everywhere you go these vermin are to be found and I despise them." Sophie did not want to fall out with her sister and dropped the subject.

Ludvig had been home for about six weeks when they received a visit from Peter's farming neighbour. Seeing Ludvig there he hesitated and was uncertain what to say. Sophie led him into the yard. "It's bad news Sophie. I'm very sorry. Peter's dead. I know you were fond of him." Sophie went a deathly-white and he held on to her. He explained what had happened. Yesterday he had been alerted by the noise from Peter's livestock. When they investigated they found Peter hanging from a beam in the barn. He had committed suicide.

Sophie wept and there were tears in the farmer's eyes. "I thought you should know because as far as we know there are no relatives and we have to bury him." He explained that there was a problem about the burial. As it was a suicide, Peter could not be buried in consecrated land and by a priest. The neighbour said: "My wife and I have discussed this and, if you agree, we think it best to cremate him." He continued: "We have a small copse down by the river and we thought that we might inter his ashes there with a small headstone and pay our last respects there. What do *you* think?"

Sophie agreed but she thought: "*You could be an absolute monster responsible for the deaths of thousands and the Church would solemnly bury you with full honours, but if you were a victim and took your own life, you could be treated as a common criminal and denied a proper going.*"

They cremated him two days later, put his ashes in a vase they had bought for the purpose, and buried it in a small grave dug by his neighbour. It was a pleasant little copse and Sophie thought that Peter would have been pleased to find this lying place. There were five of them: the neighbour and his wife, Sophie and Rosa and a seed merchant from the town who knew Peter well. They held hands and sang a hymn and the Polish national anthem. The seed merchant, who had a way with words, made a short speech saying what a good man Peter was and how he would be missed.

The neighbour had made a wooden cross – a very nice one with ornamental carving which must have taken time and care to do – and he hammered it into the ground with a shovel. And that was the end of Peter. Sophie and Rosa held hands together on the way home and Sophie heard her daughter sobbing into the pillow in the middle of the night. Ludvig saw their distress, which was very obviously a lasting one. He wondered about it, but decided to say nothing.

For some time Sophie expected to receive a note. She could not believe that Peter would have parted this life without leaving her with some explanation. She searched the farm, but there was nothing. Each day for some time she expected to receive a letter from him through the post: but nothing came. So she blamed herself for his death. She should have done something. She could have visited him, spoken to him or let Rosa see him. Any little act of loving might have saved him. It was all her fault and now she would suffer for it.

Once Ludvig had regained a little strength he slipped back, so far as it was possible, into his old ways. He went into town very often and established contact with those of his old friends and acquaintances who were still around. He frequented the bars in the evening and dined out somewhat on his experiences, which he spiced up as he recounted them. The audience had to be selected very carefully for these tales and he had to keep his voice down in case an enemy overheard him. After a while the stories became very polished and he emerged in his own mind as something of a hero.

Despite the physical effects of his incarceration, he remained a handsome man, gregarious and worldly-wise, and he was thrown back into a world of fragmented families, of homes without fathers or brothers and of lonely and desperate women struggling to pay the next bill. For a man interested in women, and after nearly five years of deprivation, the world was suddenly full of opportunities.

These were not opportunities that could be realised without money. He began to deal a little. Establishing what was mostly in demand, he started with a limited sale of foodstuffs and worked his way into other forms of trading. If you were resourceful you could find out human weaknesses and exploit them a little: a squeeze here and a suggestion there garnered the odd cash surplus, and one thing led to another. In this town, he boasted to his drinking partners, there is not a single family without secrets they wish to hide.

It was not that he needed to do much; and he lacked the energy and good health to dash around as he used to do. "What a pity I am not

twenty years younger," he thought, "we live in a world of great promise."
He was driven in what he did by the thought that he might have died at
any time over the last five years and could do so at any time now. He
was not well. Sometimes he had great difficulty in getting up in the
morning. He was often in pain and had problems in eating. "Live now,
for tomorrow we die," he said to himself.

There was no sweeter way to spend his remaining time than in the
bed of an attractive woman and he had no difficulty in finding one.
These days he thought, I am a kinder man, I shall do what I can for them.
His definition of those needing help included Sophie. He accounted for
himself to her so far as he was able; assisted her with her tasks whenever
he could; and brought regular money into the house. She thought that
he was drifting back into his old ways but she was happy." "He loves
and cares for me," she said to herself, "and even if he is dallying with
others he comes back here to me and warms my bed." She vowed to look
after him better and to care for him through this illness. Despite the odds
they were happy and in their own ways indispensable to each other.

They still had their radio. In July news came through about an uprising
in Warsaw. Reading between the lines of the propaganda it seemed that
the rising was on a significant scale. With Soviet troops poised to enter
Warsaw from the east it seemed for several days that the Polish resistance might succeed in asserting the rights of Polish people to influence
their future. What they did not know was that the Soviet Union had no
intention of entering the city until the rebellion was crushed, and would
steadfastly refuse the use of the airfields it controlled to Britain and
America so that Allied efforts to help the resistance would fail.

It was difficult to understand quite why the Germans, who were surely
losing the war, would go to such pains to resist the rebellion at all costs,
and then to raze the city to the ground. Even more horrible and inexplic-
able, the Germans then began to kill the inhabitants of the city in the
streets and in the death camps. The horror of it filtered through to them
very slowly; but when the population knew what had happened a dreadful torpor and sadness affected them all and the entire nation grieved.

After the battle had come to its grizzly conclusion they had a visitor.
In the evening, when Sophie was alone, there was a knock on the door.
A man in his mid-forties, dressed in workman's clothes, asked to be let
in. He looked desperately tired and hungry. He introduced himself in
German as a friend of Ludvig's from Sachsenhausen and begged Sophie
for shelter and food.

Sophie hesitated, remembering the Gestapo order at the outbreak of the war forbidding her to have lodgers or accommodate strangers on pain of severe punishment. She compromised by letting him rest and feeding him but then insisted that he stayed in the barn until Ludvig's return. In the stable she found some old horse-blankets which she reasoned he could have found for himself if he had not entered the house. Now she was in a position to deny knowledge of his presence should someone come searching and find him.

Next morning Ludvig sought him out and verified his story. It was true that this man, an Austrian named Wilhelm Muller, was at Sachsenhausen with Ludvig. He told them an incredible story. The moment the Warsaw rising began a senior SS officer came to the camp and a roll-call was held of selected criminal and political prisoners. A remarkable offer was made. They could take part in the putting-down of the uprising in Warsaw as ordinary German soldiers and, while no promise could be made, consideration would be given to their release from Sachsenhausen after the task was completed. This officer said: "This task is not for the squeamish. If you are not up to it stay in your block. I can give you an hour to make up your mind, and we shall remuster here."

There were anxious discussions. Some people said that to participate would be madness: all they had to do was to wait and the war would be over in a year or two. The braver of the communists thought that if they got to the front they could surrender to the Russians. While the criminals thought that there would be rich pickings.

"And you, what did you think?" said Ludvig mouth gaping in amazement at this bizarre event.

"I thought that if I could get out of the camp I could desert and work my way back to Austria."

Ludvig looked at him more carefully. He looked dreadful with his shaven head and several days of stubble. Wilhelm had difficulty in standing let alone walking and his clothes were worn and ill-fitting.

"Where did you get those clothes?"

"I broke into an empty house and stole them, what else could I do?"

He shrugged his shoulders knowing himself to be an honest man.

"So what happened when you got there?" Ludvig asked:

"Well, there was an SS Brigade which did the heavy fighting. It wasn't a cake walk: the blocks were very heavily defended. Then there was something called the Kaminsky Brigade, I don't know much about them except that they were a horrible lot, and Ukrainians, mostly drunk – they always get into the act. But we were attached to the Dirlewanger

Battalion: not just men from Sachsenhausen but from Auschwitz, Buchenwald, Dachau – you name it, we had them all. These men – and his voice tailed off – they were brutes. I can't tell you what they did. It's too horrible. I just had to get out as soon as I could." He was very tired and couldn't tell them anything more and they did not press him.

"He can't go anywhere for the time being. We must feed him and give him some rest." Sophie was firm. They kept him for several days until he could walk again. Then equipped by Sophie with a pair of reliable boots and some bread, cheese and fruit, he left in the night to try to make his way to the Austrian border.

The experience had sobered them. They stayed at home for several days doing simple routine tasks about the home, talking quietly and simply to comfort each other, and drawing strength from as much normality as they could muster.

CHAPTER 21

THERE WAS A great stir of excitement at the Spy School as the Allied landings in France took root and British and American troops inched their way across France. At some time soon, Adam and the other German-speaking spies knew that they would be pitched back into Germany. While not being told his assignment, Adam found himself in a group given special training at a British rail company and so he assumed that railway sabotage might be his selected lot. He had enjoyed his time of forced labour on the rail system in Poland and it amused him that it was now holding him in good stead. Now he was learning not how to build and repair but to make inoperative or destroy.

At Eva's home her father Harry kept a large-scale map of France and Germany on the wall. Different coloured pins recorded the progress of Allied troops: red was for the British, orange for the Americans, yellow was for other Empire troops, and black for the Germans. One day he put blue pins up which he said were for Polish commandos: "There you are Adam," he said proudly, putting his arm round Adam's shoulder, "that's where your lads are: and very good they are too. I shall keep their position up to date for you, but it's difficult because we do not usually get news about them."

Eva saw the map differently: each inch of progress brought the date nearer when they would be parted. Adam would be dropped on the wrong side of these pins and she would hear nothing of him for a long time. At least if he had been a Polish commando she would know where he was, get an occasional letter from him and if, God forbid, something went wrong, she would hear about it.

For Adam it loomed like a black cloud. You knew that it was inevitable, that is unless the Germans collapsed: it was a necessary thing, somewhat nasty, and drawing closer each day.

"Are you scared, Adam," Eva asked him, anxious herself.

"No, not scared. How would you put it in English? Perhaps, apprehensive, expectant. Oh, yes, and excited. I'm excited."

Back in his room in Bryanston Square he reconsidered his answer. Was he scared? Had he ever been scared through all those experiences over the past five years? Perhaps once, when the English plane had attacked them on the beach in Brittany and he had swum out to sea. And then not for himself, for he knew he would be safe out in the bay, but for his other comrades and, in particular, for Erik. He was right to be scared for Erik. Somehow the war took away everything that was dear to him, the brave and the good, like Erik, and spared the others, like him. He felt waves of sadness engulf him at his loss. He had needed Erik then and he needed him now.

He thought that somehow things were expected of men that were not required of women: earning a living, making your way, doing things you had never done before. At least that was true *for him*; growing up much too fast, pitched into doing these manly things without a chance to work it all out. And that's why he wasn't scared, he had always done things, sometimes very difficult things, without thinking about them at all. "*Ignorant* that's what I am, not scared." he concluded.

They continued to gather at the Kitsons but less frequently because their friends had been dispersed. Gloria had been promoted and they all teased her about her smart new uniform and her newly acquired gravitas; while others, men and women, were serving in France. But when Gloria was back on leave they often met up and tried to capture some of the more carefree fun they enjoyed before the war had reached out for them.

On one of these rare weekend parties, Adam and some of the other Polish boys were joining in as usual. Adam had thought that he might not go for Eva, stricken with a bad cold, had called-off. But in the end he did. There was the usual crowd but with a smattering of older people, now billeted in London and footloose and, for some, fancy free.

The boys surveyed the prospects. In the kitchen, Victor shared with Adam some suitably spiced fruit juice – the Kitsons were not too hot on alcohol and you had to smuggle in your own and mix the drinks. Victor said: "The hot tip for the evening Adam, is that fair haired girl in the blue dress. Some of the lads say that she tries you out by touching you up. Not that I know, of course, as I'm committed to Rose."

Adam went back in and viewed the scene. Susie was quite trim and she certainly seemed to be putting it about a bit. Victor winked, urging him on. Adam decided to do nothing, but he looked and Susie, getting bored, and seeing this handsome uniformed boy giving her the once-over, moved over to him and insisted, against his protestations that he couldn't dance, that he dance with her.

He was disappointed: there was no touching up. She danced too close and she talked too much but she was jolly and open with him. They got on well and continued to dance together. Adam thought: "This is a very sexy girl. She is certainly interested in me." Susie told him something about herself, that she was married but her husband was in France. She worried about him. She danced even closer to Adam, so close that you couldn't put a pencil between them.

Then the music stopped and the '*monstrous regiment of women*' took over. Gloria intervened and insisted that he dance with her now. She didn't dance at all close and spoke to him about Eva. And when the music stopped Gloria said that she wanted to show him something. She took him into the study and showed him pictures of her chums in her regiment and from her training school. They were there for some time and when they got up to rejoin the others there was no sign of Susie. He enquired as to her whereabouts. Victor said: "You've lost your chance there Adam. I saw her talk to the Kitson girls and then she went." And then the party wound-up too and all the other prospects were gone as well.

Adam was staying the night and had plenty of time to think about the party. Of course, the Kitson girls had seen Susie off. He was annoyed. What right had they to do it? And then he was glad: firstly, that he and Eva were being looked-out for, and then that the Kitsons were his true friends. At breakfast all was forgotten and forgiven and nothing was ever said. He knew that in his absence they would befriend Eva so far as they could and that the protective circle around her had grown.

Back at Bryanston Square he was ribbed about his lost opportunity and his reputation was at risk. "Well," he declared, "it's simple. Eva and I are going steady and I have no interest in any other girl." Which was the first time that he had said it out loud and not wholly true: of course, he was interested in other girls but, damn it, in the ultimate and when it came to the crunch, he had no appetite for adventure with them.

In the canteen there were two subjects of conversation: the war and sex. What they had in common was that for them there was little action on either front. They complained that they might be plunged into the former with catastrophic consequences without experiencing the latter. There was, of course, the opportunity for a quick-fix with a Mayfair prostitute: there was a line of those every evening in nearby Park Lane. After a few beers they initiated their fellow virgins for a few pounds: but that was not really what they meant.

They dreamt of the respectable girls back home, some of whom would be waiting, missing and even longing for them: and they grieved for their lost families, all mixed up with memories of festivals and parties, and smiling brown haired girls willing to dance with them and talking and singing in their own language. How absurd it seemed to them to die in some foreign field without fulfilling these dreams, as their fathers, or so they imagined, had been able to fulfil without question.

In their free time Adam and Eva walked together through the London parks and squares, holding hands, laughing and making tentative plans of things they could do together, as if this war did not exist, as if the gigantic clash of huge armies, and the confusions and tragedies of whole populations such a short distance from them, had no reality. And they were not alone for other couples like them were stumbling their way through strange languages in their efforts to express the most simple and most complex of emotions in the shortest of time, on the very same grass and benches as themselves. They drew comfort from these unknown couples in that they were not alone in their happiness and despair.

In October Adam was summoned to attend a briefing with his major and to be introduced to the wireless operator who was to accompany him on the mission. Their task was now defined: to make their way to Osnabruck in northern Germany and to take up work on the German rail system. They were expected to report back on train movements and carry out what acts of sabotage were feasible.

It was as they expected. They were given cover-stories and personal histories which they were to memorise and be tested on. They were to be German-speaking Czechs, railway workers fleeing Sudetenland to take up work in Germany for fear of the advancing Soviet armies. They were given three weeks to prepare and urged to get to know each other as well as possible in the short amount of time available, although their true identities were not to be revealed to each other, an ignorance which might save lives.

Adam had immediate reservations about his partner, Felix, a Czech of around the same age as himself: a self-contained, intense and rather studious boy, with poor German and a predilection for the bottle. They role-played, taking turns as interrogator, and Adam was not impressed: Felix was pedantic and over-anxious in his responses. Adam grew more and more uneasy and at the end of two weeks decided to complain about Felix. He sought a meeting with his major and explained his reservations.

The major listened very carefully to him, making notes from time to time.

"Right Adam, I'm glad you came to see me and you have explained yourself well. Let me summarise your arguments." The major was lucid. "What do I make of them? Well, it seems to me that you dislike the fact that Felix is very cautious and slow to come to conclusions. Unlike you? Is that right?" Adam murmured his assent. "Well that's the point isn't it? We selected him because he was not at all like you. You can be very impulsive – rash if we are to be entirely frank. While Felix is very well-organised and considered. Not at all like you, if you are honest about yourself. Providing you respect him, and you both listen fairly to each other, you will get along splendidly: you will complement each other."

Adam saw the point and although he was unconvinced he accepted it. The major said: "On the other hand your point about his German is well-taken. He will be all right so long as you take the lead and when-ever possible you should speak for him. I shall make it clear to Felix, and bear in mind that he may have his reservations about you, that in the final issue – and assuming that you listen very carefully to him – you have the last word. Is that acceptable to you?" Adam said it was very fair. As he said it he had a flashback to Miss Zbucki's words, "Respect your neighbour as yourself." "OK," he said to himself, "I will, but I'm not going to let the fool kill us both."

Adam found time to visit Eva's family before his mission started. Although he could not give them any details they knew that something was up: Eva had been heard crying in her room and she was anxious that they give him a proper going-away lunch which she was to cook herself.

While the meal was cooking, Harry took Adam for a walk and a fare-well drink at his local pub. There was backslapping and free beer from the regulars. The news about the war was good and the assumption was that it would be over in no time at all now. When asked, he gave it as his cautious opinion that they were probably right, and there was more cheering that he was a jolly good fellow. He thought to himself that if they were so certain about the inevitability of the triumph they might like to jump in there with him. It didn't seem to him that there was hardly anything more to do.

He was well-fed and it took a long time to clear the table.

"Let the condemned man eat a hearty feast," said Harry cheerfully.

"Dad, don't," cried out Eva, hitting him.

"More like the last supper," riposted Adam, avoiding Eva's blows.

They kissed and hugged each other as a real family.

Harry said that he must look after himself and not take unnecessary risks and that they would take good care of Eva. Grandmother gave him a large piece of fruit-cake wrapped in a spotless white linen napkin and exhorted him to take good care of it because you never knew when you might need some food: an exhortation with which he heartily agreed.

They all thought that it might be the last time that they would all be together until this war ended. Eva hated this thought and, although she knew that she shouldn't, called into Bryanston Square the next day to say her last farewells. At the Spy Centre they had all been advised to get their affairs in good order. Adam explained that he had left all his worldly goods to her, which so far as she could ascertain was around £80. Eva gave him a present of a silver watch, which she had bought with partly borrowed money that would take her many weeks to repay, and insisted that he wear it. It reminded him of another girl in another place who had done and said a very similar thing. Adam hadn't the heart to tell her that the watch would have to be left behind because it was traceable upon examination back to London.

And again they thought it to be their last meeting.

The following evening Adam and Felix were taken by military vehicle to Northolt where an American Flying Fortress was waiting to drop them into Germany. It was raining and the weather was forecast to worsen. "Nothing yet, guys," said the pilot. And they were allowed to use the sergeants' mess, where they waited for several hours while the rain streamed down the window-panes. Then a message was couriered over to them: "No go tonight, guys. Get back to your base and we will be in touch."

Back they went to Bryanston Square. It was three days later before they were allowed to try again. In the meantime they played cards in the canteen and Adam lost money while Felix won.

This time they took-off in cloudy skies which cleared once they were over France. The pilot chatted to them. "A good night for flying boys, but I'm glad that I'm not in your shoes." He asked them questions about their families over the deafening roar of the engines, and about how they had got into the *spying business*, and he whistled at their taciturn replies. Not put off he proceeded to give them his family history and his opinion on a wide range of subjects. Their stomachs churned over and they sweated profusely not really listening any more.

As they crossed the Rhine the sky was clear and the air was lit up by anti-aircraft fire tracing the sky beneath them. Urgent discussions took place in the cockpit and the navigator came back to give them a verdict. "Sorry guys this fire is too intense and we have to go back. We have to get you lower down to manage a drop and it's just too dangerous for you and the kite."

In the ride back to Bryanston Square they cursed and swore. "These bloody American cowards. First it is too cloudy and then it is too fine and all to save their own skins," which was unfair of them, and on reflection they recognised it as so. But for the moment they had to cope with the adrenalin pumping around their bodies. All that preparation and for nothing. They vowed a useless vow that they would not sit in a plane for the third time unless they knew that a drop would happen.

Although he should not have done it, and it being a Sunday, Adam slipped out and made his way over to west London to see Eva and with the limpest of excuses swept her up to spend the day with him. They took a boat on the Serpentine and being a sunny day spent the afternoon in Kew Gardens. Neither said much and there was no talk of the war. At the end of the day they found a restaurant in the West End, and with a little under the counter persuasion and the greasing of a palm, a good bottle of wine was produced and they celebrated a stolen day.

This time neither of them wanted to part and they drifted back to Bryanston Square where they had fresh coffee in an empty canteen. The 'no visitors rule' had been dropped for a few days as the inhabitants of the building were all at some stage of being dropped into Germany. When they had finished drinking endless coffees, Adam took her by the hand and led her up the backstairs to his room where she stayed the night. In the morning Adam explained about not being able to take the watch with him and asked her to keep it safe for him and with a quick kiss she stole back downstairs and caught a taxi back home.

All that huffing and puffing about whether she should or whether she shouldn't and in the end it was so simple and inevitable: and she was glad that she had. She rubbed her hand over her stomach, as if trying to ensure that he remained there, and felt for the watch. It was better now. She had shown him that she really cared and she hoped that the knowledge would stay with him wherever he was and whatever the danger.

The next day Adam and Felix set off for an American base in East Anglia where they waited twenty-four hours for a flight. For the third time of asking their enormous plane soared into the skies heading for France and danger. For the third time they chatted inconsequentially to an American pilot telling them about his life, why America was great, and why America would win the war. They wheeled across the Rhine snaking silver beneath them and again the night was lit-up by tracer bullets.

Again the crew consulted about what they should do, and once more a cautionary voice gave them an opinion.

"Look guys, I know you have had disappointments before and we want to get you down, believe me we do. But this fire is getting more intense. We have a choice here: we can turn back or we can drop you short of the target. It's your call, what do we do?"

Adam asked him. "How far off the drop area?"

"Well we might make fifty kilometres."

"OK, we do it," said Adam without consulting Felix at all, and they scrambled to get into position, all the while cursing under their breath against all things American, and then they projected themselves into the unknown.

CHAPTER 22

THEY DROPPED BY parachute into a black void. The first few seconds while he waited for the chute to open always terrified him and this time waiting for the familiar jolt seemed an eternity. As he fell he screamed into the night: "Bloody Americans. They're all cowards." And he went on repeating it until – warning himself – he regained control. To his right he saw Felix drifting slightly away from him and he adjusted his downward path to draw nearer to him.

While it would be an exaggeration to state that his life flashed before him, his spy-catching activities in France did: he saw the agonised face of the young British girl pleading with him, he heard the feet and shouts of his comrades running across the field – on such a night as this. Was he about to get his comeuppance, was there someone waiting for him below?

And then the ground came towards him and he landed with a squelch up to his ankles in mud. They had landed in a marsh. In the faint light of a partly obscured moon it stretched all around them, a vast area of treeless-grass and mud with nowhere to hide. Felix joined him and out of harness they sought to gather themselves, cursing the pilot and bemoaning their situation.

Now that they could see a little better they picked out a narrow path which wound itself across the marsh into the horizon, and they made their way to it. Burying the 'chutes and hiding the evidence of them presented difficulties, with no trees or scrub to obscure the site. At least in the soft ground they could dig a hole: Adam with his hands and Felix triumphantly with a plastic shovel, produced and assembled from his baggage.

The one advantage of the landing was that the area was entirely without habitation and the likelihood of the drop being observed or them being spotted on the ground was remote. But they needed to be holed-up somewhere as soon as possible. Their luggage, a suitcase each, had survived the drop and Felix announced that his radio set was undamaged. There was no alternative but to walk and after consulting the map and concluding that they were a good seventy kilometres from Osnabruck they set out along the path in what they thought was the right direction.

It was a long walk and slow-going. The dawn was breaking before they hit a minor country road and the safety of some pine trees where they stopped and rested for a while. They slept a little, and it was in clear daylight that they consulted the map again and picked out a possible route. They breakfasted on the small amount of food they carried and it was mid-morning before they joined the road. It was not long before they met other travellers. To their relief they were greeted normally enough as part of the landscape and soon they had the confidence to pass the time of the day in the manner born.

They took lunch in a newly harvested corn field with their backs to a hedge and the cover of an oak tree. It was not long before they were greeted by a farm-worker in the field and engaged in a lengthy conversation. They rehearsed their cover story. It aroused no particular comment or doubt.

"Osnabruck," the farm-worker commented, "you're a long way from Osnabruck."

And then he disappeared to be followed back a few minutes later by the farmer himself. He too was a pleasant enough fellow. After sizing them up, he said: "You two boys look a bit tired to me. Would you like to stay a night at the farm? We can make you very comfortable for a modest charge and to be honest with you we need the money. What do you say?" They looked at each other and Adam said that it was very kind and that they would stay the night.

There was a little bargaining to be done and once Adam had got the charge reduced they moved off in the farmer's truck.

"Here," he offered, "let me put your cases up onto the trailer."

"Take this one. It's the heavy one," responded Adam, giving him Felix's, the heavier of the two because of the radio, and winking at Felix.

"Yes it is heavy. What have you got in there, a bomb?" quipped the farmer.

"Yes, that's right," said Adam, laughing.

Felix hissed at him: "You idiot."

The farm was a modest red-brick building sparsely furnished but clean. They were accommodated in a spacious barn on straw mattresses with fresh clean covers and warm blankets: but were to be fed and could wash in the farmhouse itself. The farmer had introduced himself as Ulrich, and then to his wife Gunda. As they gathered for an evening meal they realised that it was a stroke of good fortune to have met them: Gunda was a splendid cook, and although the ingredients of the meal were simple, the cooking was supreme. There were several courses and the pleasure was so intense that little was said until only coffee and cheese remained before them.

"That was so good, Gunda," said Adam finishing at last and leaning back in contentment. Gunda smiled at him. She knew she was good and there was nothing to be said about it by her. Adam looked at her carefully for the first time. For a farmer's wife, accustomed and inured to hard work and to outside activity in all weathers, she was in remarkably good shape. She was above average height and remained slim while being just a little too muscular to be thought a lady. Her skin remained pale as if in defiance of the weathering process, which could not, he thought, be by accident. She had shoulder-length fair hair that was well-combed and brushed; and her whole demeanour, like the farm, was one of delectable if spartan freshness and appeal.

She saw him look at her and met his gaze boldly.

"It is difficult," she said.

"What is?"

"Looking after myself while working on the farm," was the reply as she stretched out two well-shaped and manicured hands.

"Just look at what it does to my hands."

They looked. Felix filled the silence.

"But Gunda, your hands are so elegant."

She simpered.

"It's very gallant of you to say so."

Of course, she knew him to be right, but it was not for her to say. She gave him 'seconds' as a sign of her appreciation.

Ulrich wanted to talk about real things: the things *he* was involved in. He complained that you could not get labour. There were a lot of Poles and other foreigners in the area but the large farms were given preference for the real workers. Many of the people available to him were illegals who had left their work without permission and were now waiting for the Russians to come – and no doubt they would help them when they did to fight good God-fearing Germans.

He was left with the granddads and the children when they flooded out of the cities to avoid the Allied air raids. What good were they? No interest in working hard, and back to their homes in the city as soon as they thought there was a bombing lull. Gunda thought, but didn't say it, that it was their manners that were at fault – all this shouting and rudeness. It might be the thing to do in town but not here in the country among respectable people. She supposed that it was not the sort of thing to say nowadays.

They sympathised with Ulrich and asked whether the air raids caused serious damage and where the Poles were billeted. He told them of the whereabouts of the camps and advised them to steer well-clear of them because of their danger: all kinds of people, and they were likely to turn on you.

"Does everyone put-up these refugees?" enquired Felix innocently.

"You must be joking. They're supposed to, but the posh avoid it; you know a few marks here and a call to a school friend there."

"It's always the same," they agreed.

"Do you think we can win this war? It's looking bad isn't it?" said Felix playing dumb. Ulrich sucked on his pipe and did not reply immediately. It was such a pleasure to be asked for an opinion.

"I'm not a Nazi supporter, you understand. Never was, never will be. Hitler got it wrong. Invading Russia, what a stupidity. I said so at the time."

Gunda, washing up dishes heard this. "What a hypocrite," she said to herself. "No one was more fervent a supporter than Ulrich and then when things go wrong he lies through his teeth. And it's most unwise. True they seem nice boys, indeed very nice boys, but they were strangers: you shouldn't say such things before strangers. Who knows where that might get you?"

She sat down at the table again. "Ulrich stop talking about politics. Let them tell me something about themselves." And they told her their cover stories and she sighed and asked more questions.

In an interval, when she was not there, Ulrich leaned across the table and said earnestly: "You must forgive her – all this family talk – we lost our two boys in this war."

They told Gunda how sorry they were. "Would you like to see some pictures," she said and got them out without waiting for a reply. One boy had been lost fighting in France and she showed a picture of him in his army uniform smiling pleasantly at the camera. Her other son was killed on the Russian front. He stared out at them in his SS uniform with its death head insignia, and without a smile.

"An SS uniform?" said Felix enquiringly, continuing in his dumb role.

"Oh, yes, special training. Not everyone can get in, you know."

Ulrich butted in quickly: "But killed fighting in the line, like anyone else."

"Oh, yes, I understand," said Adam responding to him.

Gunda thought that these nice boys appreciated her and she smiled a lot. When they retired for the night she rebuked Ulrich for his careless and disloyal talk and retired to her bedroom. She looked at herself in a full-length mirror passing her hands over her hips and smoothing-out her hair. She thought: "I'll just see how those boys are getting on and give them some extra blankets because the nights are getting cold."

She pushed through the barn doors just as Felix had closed his case after their first broadcast back to London. They were flustered and Gunda thought: "They like me but are too modest to say so, but how vexatious it is that I have to talk to them both together."

She confined herself to pleasantries showing these boys what she believed to be the best side of her nature and making them feel at ease. When Felix excused himself she took Adam by the hand and looking at him earnestly said softly: "Adam, my husband and I no longer share the same bedroom and you would be welcome to come later on." Thinking she had an agreement, she told him how to reach her bedroom, smiled sweetly, and made her way back. In her bedroom she took particular care in her preparations, dressed in her very best nightgown, and settled down to wait for his arrival.

Adam told Felix about this possible new adventure.

"Don't you dare, Adam," said Felix pushing at him.

Adam said very weakly: "I don't wish to disappoint her."

But with Felix so forceful in opposition he decided to do nothing.

Discretion having been the better part of valour, they decided on an early morning retreat and got themselves back on the road at first light. After they had been walking for a few hours they turned on to a busy main road. There was nothing unusual about their appearance or in walking along the road as it was common practice to do so: all manner of people, the rough and ready as well as the respectable, traversed it and the foot-weary greeted each other as part of a common fraternity. And then when they were becoming tired they were offered a timely lift. A truck stopped and a cheery builder offered a ride.

"Here. Let me help you with your luggage," and he got out of the truck to lift down the tailboard.

"Take his," said Adam pointing to Felix, "it's heavier."

"If you say that again," exclaimed the outraged Felix, "I'll throttle you."

"All right boys," said their driver half-hearing them.

And they said that they were, and that it was very good of him to stop.

"I like a bit of company," said their new acquaintance introducing himself as Hugo.

Once started there was no stopping Hugo and he talked about anything and everything. After a while it was obvious that their participation in the conversation was not really needed; they were catalysts to a flow of comment and diversion. Early on they encountered a military convoy travelling west. For one ludicrous moment Adam felt he should duck. What would he do if by mischance he met his old comrades moving up to the front. Of course, he told himself, the thought was absurd, but he looked the other way nevertheless.

"Poor sods," said Hugo. "Not a chance."

"Well at least they don't have to go east," observed Adam.

"When they get there they will," retorted Hugo.

"I shouldn't be talking to you boys like that. Defeatism that is – and you can get shot for it." He glanced sideways at them.

"You could be the Gestapo in plain-clothes for all I would know of it." They laughed.

"That will be the day," responded Adam.

There was a pause before Hugo started-up again.

"You would think wouldn't you that I would be very busy. Me a specialist in building things and all those bombs and guns knocking them down."

They nodded that they would.

"Not a bit of it. You can't get the materials you see, and even when you have them no one has the money to pay you. You wonder about it, you know. There are so many air raids that it hardly seems worthwhile putting things up carefully in the German way – solid and lasting for centuries – when they are likely to be knocked down again in no time at all. Still I mustn't complain. I still make a living."

"See that large house," said Hugo pointing to a mansion on a hill to the right of them. "Could take a lot of refugees that could – and they're supposed to take them. But I bet you anything that they have got out of it. Friends in high places, you understand." They muttered that there was one law for the rich and another for the poor.

"Too bloody right," said Hugo.

Feeling more confident of them, Hugo said: "Seeing that you're not the Gestapo, I'll tell you a joke. Stop me if you've heard it. Well, you know that Hitler is not seen much these days."

They nodded.

"And that his book is called Mein Kampf.* Well the reason he's not seen is that he is busy writing another book. Do you know what it is called?"

"No," they said.

"Meine Schuld.† Good, eh, true."

They laughed.

"OK, you can arrest me now for the joke."

Short of the Polish camps their cheery companion had to drop them off because his journey took him off in another direction. "Good luck boys," he called after them, "for God's sake don't take my vehicle number."

After a few kilometres they stumbled across the Polish camps, line upon line of wooden huts in a barren field. "Looks like a pig sty," said Adam, "and unfair on the pigs." In one of the huts there was a reception point and they paid for overnight accommodation and sought out the best bunks they could find.

Each of the huts consisted of two rows of bunks, two high, and separated by a narrow corridor. At the end were some wash facilities and latrines smelling to high heaven. In the centre of the camp were some common eating facilities where some primitive meals were served. They held their noses and selected the best bunks of those that were empty and available.

Later that day the camp came alive with workers coming back from the fields and from the factories in the towns. Adam's preferred method of introduction was a good game of cards and he had no difficulty in finding one. Felix having no interest in the game went for a walk and drifted round the camp before taking a coffee and engaging himself with anyone who was willing to talk. Adam set himself his most common card strategy – modest stakes, careful playing and not winning too much or too often, while making money in the end.

Both of them asked questions as carefully as they could: but not as it turned out carefully enough. The camp had its own social structure,

* My Struggle.
† My Mistake.

which was protective, and its own enforcers. Adam and Felix started with a disadvantage: they had not been in the country long enough to be dirty and, despite the efforts made on their behalf in London to dress them down, they were too well-dressed.

A resistance movement had started in the camp and by the morning the rumour had spread they were Gestapo in search of intelligence. The enforcers of camp authority arrived and questioned them about who they were and their purpose in the camp. They went through their cover story and after a while their questioners moved off.

"We didn't satisfy them," said Adam a little grimly.

"They have bigger fish to fry than us," responded Felix.

They had a more immediate problem – lice. The billet was swarming with them and by the morning the lice were well-advanced in the task of eating them alive. In the wash room they stripped, and helped each other to wash-down and remove the lice, and changed into their spare sets of clothes. "Right, we're out of this place," said Adam, "while we're still in one piece."

The small railway station which was the link to Osnabruck was overflowing with workers on their way to the factories in the towns, and displaced foreigners on their way to mischief and self-survival. As they made their way on to the platform it became evident that their reputation had gone before them: they heard warning whispers of 'Gestapo' and the way opened up before them. The train when it arrived was already overcrowded and in the rush not only were the seats filled up but all the standing and clinging room: men clung to the doors and the couplings between the railway carriages.

"Sod it, Felix, follow me," came the command, "if they think we are Gestapo that is what we shall be." Adam clutched his pistol in his trouser pocket to make it clear that he was armed and bellowed the instruction to make clear their way and then to surrender seats for them. It worked like a dream: seats were given up, people moved away from them and amidst the general babel they rode silently into town.

Fortunately it was a short journey, for it was difficult to keep a straight face. When they were deposited on the station platform Adam dissolved into laughter and Felix, despite his disapproval, could not help but to laugh too.

"God, Adam you will get us killed."

"Not a bit of it," was the reply. "Fortune favours the brave."

"What next?" said the unconvinced Felix.

"Follow me, I'm hungry. They're bound to have a staff canteen."

Adam marched them into the main station building and found the canteen. It was small and well-occupied and serving good food.

"Great, this is for us," Adam said to the protesting Felix.

But there was a problem: the canteen refused to serve them because they were unrecognised and lacked the appropriate permits. Adam drew himself to his full height and explained in his most authoritative voice that they were important rail workers recently arrived from Berlin who had as yet not been given the right documentation. The manager hesitated and Adam delivered his coup de grace: he asked for her name and said that there would be repercussions. He looked threatening and she gave in.

"Next time, please, show me your permit. We have to be careful. Anyone could walk in here off the street."

Adam said, rubbing it in: "It should be obvious to you that we are not *anyone*." She apologised.

At the table Felix protested again: "Adam you must stop this behaviour you will get us into serious trouble."

"Not at all. It is much safer here than in the street and we need a good meal. Eat up, you never know where your next meal will come from."

They ate up and the manageress came to their table and on being asked if everything was all right they ordered beers, which were supplied to them with a smile and without question.

The first test of their documents came next. They found their way to the stationmaster and requested work. This man was a hard-pressed railway professional. He looked at them and then at their documents and then back at them again. He hesitated before asking his questions.

"Why," he said, "has it taken so long for you to get here from the Sudetenland. I assume that these stamps have the right date."

Adam responded: "Ah, well we had to come through Berlin. It was in a terrible state because of the bombing and we were asked to give a helping hand to clear things up. What could we do?"

"Oh, well I suppose we mustn't be selfish. From all accounts their situation is more serious than our own."

He looked at them again.

"OK boys, these documents seem to be all right. Be good boys, go into the main office and they will issue you with the right papers."

Riding his luck, Adam asked about the availability of accommodation.

"Right. You are in luck there. We have some cottages in H., some five kilometres to the north of here and some space is available. It's safer you understand to be billeted out of town because of the air raids. There is a bus service. It is easy to get there."

As they moved out of the stationmaster's office he said: "You will have to take your papers to the local Gestapo office to get yourself registered. Nothing to worry about there, they are used to dealing with us."

Felix caught Adam's look of apprehension and once in the street asked him about it.

"Well we are fools," was Adam's response. "It was the first time that I noticed it."

"Noticed what?"

"Our documents. It is the same writing on them both although the documents state that we are from different places. They are signed-off by the same person."

They stopped walking. Getting these documents past a tired old railway manager was one thing but through the Gestapo quite another.

The problem with the documents was the only cloud in a very blue sky. They had struck lucky. The village of H. was an ancient and prosperous settlement which served as a dormitory for the privileged workers in the town. The railway company, acting with perspicuity, had bought a row of thatched cottages and had spent money on their modernisation. They were allocated a room in a three-bedroomed cottage, less grand than the others, but well-equipped and furnished.

The senior resident, a middle-ranking rail manager of advanced pretensions, showed them their room, gave them a list of house rules, and told them how fortunate they were to have these lodgings and that they had better behave well or they would lose them.

They surveyed their assets. The room was pleasant and they had a lockable wardrobe for their luggage and the precious radio transmitter. The bedroom door could be locked but they thought that the house cleaner, named on their written house rules, would have a key to the room. She must be considered a potential risk. They considered the presence of other tenants not to be a problem and this proved to be right. These men worked long hours, and spent their leisure hours in sleeping, in the local bars or card playing: their non-sleeping time in the cottage turned out to be non-existent.

The village itself was highly desirable: it had two bars, several shops and a post office and, with a bit of luck, attractive girls. Felix issued one of his warnings: "Don't be an idiot Adam, stay away from them and keep out of trouble," but even as he issued it, he knew he was wasting his time – he was talking to himself.

All in all they felt that the first part of their mission had been successful. They were able to radio London that they were in Osnabruck, employed by the railway and securely billeted.

Adam asked Felix a question: "Is it safe to radio from this cottage?"

"I think so. I doubt very much whether there is any organised attempt in this area to pick up radio signals and we would be discovered only by the accident of someone overhearing"

"What do you mean, you think so?"

"Well I am pretty sure, but we can't be certain. It's far safer to make a short coded transmission from the cottage than anywhere else. If we are wrong about this we shall have a knock on the door. Best sleep with your pistol under the pillow."

Felix looked pleased to be giving judgement in an area of his competence.

"I hope you are right but very few transmissions to London and very short. Agreed?" said Adam, reasserting his authority.

And it was agreed.

CHAPTER 23

THEY REPORTED FOR work the next morning. Anxiety about the problems of work registration had haunted them overnight and they took the first opportunity to get it out of the way. The local Gestapo office was a short walk from the station. It was a small building but prominently located on a street corner. Inside a receptionist kept them waiting before taking their documents and passing them on to the duty officer. On her return she told them they would have to wait as everyone was very busy.

They settled down to wait rather as you would on a visit to the doctor or a dentist. The waiting room was very ordinary: green walls and wooden benches with the compulsory picture of the Führer on the wall and various threatening notices to accompany it.

It had always amused Adam: this talk of the master race and racial purity accompanied as it was by pictures of fair haired amazons: and in contrast the mean racially degenerate picture of the first-world-war corporal: someone who was not German at all.

But in the names of such things and in rooms like these – ugly, boring and banal – crimes against the innocent were occurring all over Europe. Not that they were innocent, and Adam felt in his inside pocket for his pistol. He was not going quietly to his torture or death.

Despite themselves they began to sweat as the clock ticked on. It was, of course, part of the method – keeping you waiting, that is – they knew that, but on the other hand the delay might be because they were checking out the documents.

An hour passed before they were admitted to the duty officer's presence. He didn't look up and continued with writing a memo of some kind. Of middle-age, he looked competent: his uniform although not new was neatly pressed, he was well-washed, and the precision of his haircut suggested regular grooming. Adam's spirits sank: this man did not make routine mistakes. And then the duty officer looked up and shuffled the papers in front of him.

"You boys are from the Sudetenland?"

"Yes," was the reply from Adam who was determined to do the talking.

"And you have got jobs here in the town on the railway?"

"Yes, that's right."

"I see no problem in that."

He stamped their documents and dated them before their very eyes.

"I hope you enjoy your time here."

He gave them their documents and ushered them out.

Outside in the street, and away from the building, they were beside themselves, hugging each other and whooping in relief.

Adam cried out: "Can you believe it. He didn't read the documents at all. The words he used came from the receptionist. He hadn't read them, the lazy sod. So much for the efficiency of the Third Reich."

"If we're not careful we shall win this war," Felix responded.

The hurdle jumped they settled in to being loyal and indispensable employees of the railway. The training in London and the forced labour they had both experienced on the railway held them in good stead and distinguished them from the forced and occasional labour around them.

They were helped in the route to acceptance by the fact that some of the managers were their neighbours in H. and gave them occasional lifts to and from work. In particular, their operations manager often gave them lifts and, enjoying their company, chatted to them in an open manner.

This man, Otto Schneider, was in his fifties and had worked on the railway for over twenty years. Appearances were important to Otto and by regular savings, and a certain opportunism, he had acquired one of the latest Mercedes cars. They expressed their admiration for the car. Otto looked at them. "Well boys, I'm not a Nazi supporter, and we are going to lose this war, but I will say one thing in their favour, they certainly got rid of the Jews for us. This car was owned by a Jew and I picked it up for a song."

Adam closed his eyes and sank back in the opulence of the leather upholstery. He saw the columns of emaciated prisoners wending their way towards him, the shouts of schnell from the guards, and the crack of whips and the drumming of batons on bare ribs: he remembered the stench of the dead bodies at the end of the day and throwing them onto trucks, and the brutal jokes and swearing. He was not sure whether he would be sick over this sweet-smelling, and masculine-reassuring leather; and he opened the back window to gulp in some fresh air.

Otto was a jovial and friendly fellow and Adam did not want to fall out with him. Quite the contrary for it emerged that Otto was a keen card player and, once Adam had expressed an interest, he invited him to a session in his own house – Felix too if he wanted. But he didn't – and made his excuses.

"You're a fool Felix not to join in. What better way is there to gather information? All those managers drinking beer with you and chatting about their day," said Adam later when they were alone.

"I agree. It's a really lucky break, a great opportunity for you: but I'm not a card player, so I have to find other ways," was the reply.

Adam settled into a routine of regular card games at a variety of houses in H. Although 'talking shop' was banned, in practice it was impossible to gather without talking about the challenges of the day and of days to come. And it was not only what was said at these gatherings; friendships were formed, and he became a familiar figure to be taken for granted as part of the surroundings; things were said indiscreetly in his presence, which should not have been said at all.

There was a regular flow of information back to London. Well done was the response, keep it up. "All very well for them," said Felix "but every broadcast puts us in danger."

Felix did his best to relax. While Adam was playing cards he read in the comfort of the cottage. Discovering a small collection of books left by his predecessors he read steadily through them. When the weather permitted it, he went for long walks, missing his farm dogs back home. These walks brought him to the attention of Elizabeth Schwartz their housekeeper, who seeing him pass her cottage on the way out of the village, contrived to invite him into it for a coffee on his way back.

The invitation was indiscreet, for Elizabeth being a childless widow in her thirties, was seen by the women in the village as something of a threat to their married harmony. Although not a beauty Elizabeth had her charms and what is worse did not see herself as sexually dead or in hibernation. Felix was pleased by the invitation and found Elizabeth very agreeable. Of medium height Elizabeth was slim for country tastes – skinny said the other women. "She keeps herself very well," thought

Felix admiring her as she leaned towards him to serve some home-made pastries.

Elizabeth dressed as if she was a sophisticated town dweller, which would have been suspicious in any village less prosperous than H. The village elders thought that she must have wealthy admirers – how else could she live so well on a war pension alone – although they could not put their finger on who these admirers might be.

Elizabeth was not wealthy but she did have a gift for making the best of herself. In truth her outfits were very limited but she had a multitude of scarves and belts, and a variety of ways of arranging her hair, so that each day she looked a little different. The changes reflected her moods; and as she was generally of a cheerful disposition, and anxious to be noticed and to relate, her presentation of herself was both pleasant and endearing.

Felix found her to be well-educated and able to discuss literature with him. She was amusing with plenty of good stories to recount. He was bold.

"Can I visit you again?" he enquired of her.

"Of course, I would be very cross if you didn't," she dimpled and leant forwards, brushing against him and smelling divine.

Felix told Adam about this encounter. Adam was pleased for him but protective.

"Good on you Felix, but be careful, I think she could eat you for breakfast." Which was percipient of him for if Felix had looked more closely he would have seen that Elizabeth was not the agreeable innocent he thought her to be.

Elizabeth was avaricious for what pleased her and determined to get it. Once she had set her heart on something, nothing in the world would prevent her efforts to achieve it. If Felix had looked closely and had taken a cooler assessment he would have seen more than pools of enchantment; not only the mop of curly black hair and the pleasant oval of her face; but the thrusting forward of her chin; and that she stood too close to you, and inclined her face towards you, in an uncalled-for sort of way.

Elizabeth was alone in the world and did not like it. She needed – she told herself – a man who would be worthy of her, and who would look after her. Men she knew were weak and fickle creatures and her chances of securing the right one in the chaos around her was slight. In the meantime she had desires, like any woman, she told herself. Oh, to find a strong man who would sweep her away and be adequate to her passions. All of which was a very tall order for her. Sometimes she doubted whether it was possible and her resolve dissipated into way-wardness and led her into situations she wished to avoid.

For the moment it was pleasant to talk to Felix though if the truth be known she found Adam to be more to her liking. She asked Felix about Adam but, as he was not forthcoming, she decided to do something about it herself. Elizabeth did not like cards: she hated the smoking and drinking and the bad language. But she knew these games went on and Adam was often present. She approached Frau Schneider and asked her whether she needed assistance with the catering on these occasions. Frau Schneider was not too bothered but needing a good gossip she accepted the offer of help for one evening.

In the meantime it was necessary for Elizabeth to cool-off any un-necessary ardour or expectation of Felix's. She stopped answering his evening knocks on her door, even when her living-room light was on and it was obvious that she was at home, and after a while she succeeded in discouraging him and he gave up bothering her. He told Adam. "You are well out of that," was the response. And at that moment neither of them thought anything of it.

Then at the Schneider's, Adam caught sight of her, although in the excitement of the game he gave her little thought other than she looked rather sweet. Which was too little reward for the attention she had given herself, for she was wearing her very best dress, covered only by a very pretty apron, and had spent a long time in her preparation.

Elizabeth was rather annoyed by the experience. The card games had been as boring as she thought they would be: clouds of foul-smelling smoke and a lot of bad language and not a civilised word for herself: and Frau Schneider asking interminable busybody questions with no good gossip to contribute in return. "There just has to be a better way," she thought.

London was impressed by the intelligence they were providing but reminded them of the importance of sabotage.

"*What*," asked London, "*are you planning?*"

"*Nothing at all*," said Adam, knowing it *not to be* an answer. "If we have any sense. It's all very well in the safety of your office in London to ask such a question, but acts of sabotage are a sure way to get your-self killed."

They decided to do nothing, to keep up the information flow and to hope that the question would not be repeated. London did *not* forget and the question was asked again.

Then an opportunity arose to perform a simple act of sabotage and they decided to chance their arm. They were working on the track five kilometres to the east of the town. They worked late to strengthen the line, work which was needed they were told because a troop train was expected to pass through in the middle of the night. Being late they took some tools back with them on the bus. It was not uncommon to do so and they had done it many times in the past.

Once darkness had fallen and the village was quiet they slipped out across the fields and made their way to the track not far from the scene of the repairs. Their plan was to remove a section of the rail so as to decouple it. It was not an easy task because the joints were rusted and, although they had the right tools, it was difficult to unfasten the bolts. The track was deserted and it was cloudy, but nevertheless they were aware that the longer they worked there the more vulnerable they were to an accidental sighting.

In the end they had to be satisfied with shifting a small section of rail out of alignment. They reviewed their work.

"Not good enough," said Felix disappearing among the trees by the track side. Adam waited. There was a call for help from Felix. He had discovered some logs among the trees and they hauled them along the track some fifty metres away from the realigned section and placed them in a pile across the track.

"What do you think Adam?" enquired Felix seeking approval.

"I really don't know. But it's the best we can do," came the reply.

They made their way back to H. without, to their knowledge, being seen; and then upstairs to their room without interception.

They didn't sleep and reported to work early.

"Bad news, boys?" said their manager. "We have had a derailment – unfortunately of a troop carrier – and all hell has broken loose. It's all hands to the pump to get it repaired and the train on its way."

"Any casualties?" Adam enquired.

"Yes, there are a few. It's not much of a derailment really, but we must get this train back on the rails."

When they reached the site the work had started. The train was upright and one damaged carriage had been removed. It took over a day to repair the track and get the train on its way, so they had held it up for about thirty-six hours.

"Not much of a contribution," said Felix, "but enough to satisfy London."

And they reported it to London.

"Now," said Adam, "for the retribution."

Adam asked his works manager, who had been instructed to make an immediate investigation and report, what he believed had caused the accident. "Hard to say Adam. There is little doubt that the track needed repair or replacement. You know that yourself because we have been working on it. But we found logs on the tracks. Vandals? Kids playing on the lines? Who knows?"

The stationmaster received a visit from the Gestapo. The question they posed to him was whether there had been sabotage. He gave them his works manager's written report, the conclusions of which were that under-investment in track maintenance and running the railway beyond its true capacity were the causes of the accident. Although unhappy about the conclusions they went away.

The works manager under questioning from Adam as to the outcome of the investigation, gave him his own reasoning. "If we said it was sabotage, or that it might have been, we would have them crawling all over us. There would have to be culprits and, if they were not to be found, an example would have to be made of someone. That person could be me. After all, I am responsible for the maintenance programme. It might be the stationmaster. He would be the Wagnerian candidate, the grand gesture. Who knows, it might be you Adam. But be sure of it, someone would be made to suffer."

They had got away with it, and they told London of the outcome. The response was that given the success they should have the confidence to do more. They remained reluctant. The war was drawing to a conclusion, the information passed to London was obviously helpful, and they were entitled to survive. On the other hand their spirits were high. If they had got away with it once, why not a second time?

Adam came up with a second plan. It was to be their last act of sabotage. Over the course of a few weeks, Adam became friendly with a signalman. When working late he had acquired the habit of visiting the signal box and sharing a coffee pot with him. The signalman worked long hours on his own and welcomed the company. Adam visited a local doctor complaining of an inability to sleep and was prescribed a sedative. He was warned: "This is quite powerful stuff. Only use it if you remain sleepless over several nights and don't let it become a habit."

The plan was very simple: to cause the signalman to fall asleep on duty. They chose a night of heavy traffic. Adam called in as usual. The signalman was busy but chattering away about his family, the long hours and what he hoped to do at the weekend. Adam made the coffee putting some of the liquid sedative in the signalman's mug. Later he said: "Adam, I'm feeling sleepy, pour me another coffee, there's a good chap." The dose was repeated. Adam washed up the mugs and waited.

It took thirty minutes before the full effects were felt and the signalman could struggle against sleep no more. He fell to the ground and remained there. Adam had a small bottle of vodka and, opening the signalman's mouth, poured as much of it into him as he could without drowning him. He left as quickly and as carefully as he could, and got back to the waiting Felix without being seen. They played the radio loudly and ate noisily in the kitchen to the objections of their fellow lodgers, and then retired to their room too excited to sleep.

The results were spectacular. An express train travelling at speed crashed into a goods train stopped by a red light at the station platform. There were numerous deaths and serious injuries and a number of lines were closed for several days. It was many hours before the signal box was searched as it had been assumed that the failure of the signalman to respond to calls was caused by communication damage resulting from the crash.

The signalman was found sleeping on the floor of the signal box. He had been drinking and had failed in his duty. When questioned he could remember nothing of the evening or of drinking vodka. His failure to be frank with the Gestapo investigation and to admit his shortcomings was held against him. In mitigation the stationmaster stressed his very good record and the long hours he had worked because of staff shortages. He was ordered to be shot. His family and colleagues made desperate efforts to save him. Then without explanation the sentence was commuted to an indeterminate stay in a concentration camp and his family had hope that an early end to the war would see his release.

Felix told London. They were congratulated and told to keep it up. In the security of their room they discussed the signalman and his fate. Felix needed to be philosophical: "Our war is very dirty, isn't it, the signalman was a sort of friend and we betrayed him. If you had to do it would you have killed him?"

Adam was in no doubt; "Of course I would. If we held troops up for three days – of course I don't know whether we did – but supposing, we prevented Allied troops being killed by them for three days, didn't we? It could be a lot of lives not just one."

Felix supposed that it was true. He continued: "But he was a nice bloke with a family doing no harm to anyone, just doing his job as a railwayman."

"Yes, but that is true for all those civilians killed in Warsaw, London and elsewhere. They're all nice blokes doing their jobs and playing with their children, aren't they? And what do you think that these nice German blokes would do to us if they discovered us as spies?"

There was no answer to any of these questions but Felix was glad that it was Adam who was doing the dirty stuff.

Although he shrugged it off, Adam was not indifferent to Felix's qualms. He thought afterwards – and wasn't it often the case – that the telling point was forgotten at the time: he could have said that the outcome for the signalman was not too bad: that his father had spent over five years at Sachsenhausen for doing nothing while the signal-man would soon be released. But the sabotage was traumatic in its effects and he found himself wanting to retire to his proven healers, the countryside around him and fishing.

As the dangers grew for his German neighbours it seemed to him that they were kinder to each other. He found a fishing companion who lent him a rod and in their precious time they sat for long periods by a peaceful local river. They caught very little but neither of them cared about that.

Elizabeth having failed in her initiative at the card game continued to feel lonely and scared. Better a friendly chat with Felix, she thought, than no one at all. She waylaid him again one evening and apologised very nicely for her churlishness for which she blamed the war. Felix was pleased to receive so pleasant an overture and the two of them fell into their old habits of drinking coffee together in the evenings. In resuming this intimacy Elizabeth did not reveal the hidden desire to be closer to Adam. Little was said about Adam and they enjoyed their time together without any discussion of him.

Elizabeth asked Felix whether he thought that the war was lost. He said: "It looks bad doesn't it, what do you think?"

"Well," she said, "it might not be. Hitler is a great man, we all know that. In some ways, I think we have let him down. Now we are at the mercy of the Red Army. He warned us about it didn't he: that Germany was the last stand of Western Christianity against the barbarian hordes from the East."

Felix swallowed hard while Elizabeth searched her book case.

She went on: "I think that although the British and Americans will not admit it, they admire Hitler too. Have you read it, 'Frederick the Great' by an English author, Thomas Carlyle. He admired Frederick. Do you think that even at this late hour by an act of faith and an iron will – like Frederick – we might still succeed?"

Felix held her hand, worried for her:

"No," he said, "I must be honest with you, I don't think it, I don't think it all. The circumstances are quite different. The British and the Americans have come too far together, suffered too much, to be separated now. We can't win."

Felix squeezed her hand and she responded. He was really a very kind boy, she thought. She cried a little and put her head on his shoulder and permitted him to comfort her for she was very scared and very upset.

When she had recovered a little she told him about her husband and that he had been reported 'missing and presumed dead' in Italy. "Oh then," said Felix encouragingly, "then there is hope. Look on the bright side. The war will come to an end and you may see your husband again."

He was so positive that she dried her tears and found him another pastry. She gave him a little kiss when they rose to part: not a passionate kiss, not an invitation to something else, but a gentle, warm kiss with very soft lips, because he had been a friend and had listened to her.

Adam asked him about his progress with Elizabeth and teased him about it. Felix blushed a lot. He said very weakly: "I think we have become friends."

"That's a bad sign. There is no time for friendship. Go for it," was the worldly response.

Felix thought he might; but Elizabeth knew her men. She kept him within the bounds of friendship: whenever he threatened to overstep the mark, she restrained him; whenever she felt vulnerable, she withdrew. And after a while they became good companions and Felix accepted that they would be no more than that.

CHAPTER 24

SOPHIE VISITED PETER'S grave regularly. She tidied it with a small pair of garden shears and changed the flowers in a vase she had taken to the site. She straightened the cross when it was needed and sat quietly under the trees. Sometimes she sang to herself and she imagined that he heard her and on each occasion she asked for his forgiveness. She was not the only person to visit for she knew that the neighbours came as well, clearing the leaves and keeping it tidy when she couldn't, and she was pleased that she was not alone in remembering him.

Ludvig knew of these visits and had worked out for himself what must have happened between them. He was disturbed by the revelation of the relationship going on in his absence but accepting of it. In this he surprised himself and upset his life-long conviction that there was one rule for women in this world and quite another for men: his own philandering was one thing, and his wife's isolated betrayal quite another.

He realised that it must have been hard for her and that it was reasonable for Sophie to fear him to be dead. And then on his return she had given Peter up immediately and in relationship to him had been all that a wife could be. But more than any of these considerations he was coming to terms with his own mortality. He had passed through a valley of tribulation and now he was confronted with a serious illness. While he could not admit to himself that he was dying, he was conscious of other forces at work: he needed to make his peace with others and himself.

He and Sophie had reached the peace they needed. She said nothing about his absences, which in any event were growing less frequent as his health deteriorated; and he ignored her unexplained trips in the cart and the tears on her return. There were times when he retired to his bed and she nursed him. Nothing much was said but it was understood that she would stand by him and see him out of this world as she had guarded him in it.

On this particular morning he had kissed her when she left and she knew that he would be waiting for the lifting of the door latch on her return. She was emotional today and tiptoed back into the house. There was a murmur of conversation in the kitchen which she did not recognise and when she entered it a young man in the uniform of a Polish army officer rose from his chair at the table.

He greeted her and at last she recognised him.

"Is it Joseph?"

"Yes, of course."

"But Joseph you're so smart and so military."

He laughed happily even though he knew that she meant that he didn't look Jewish: gone was the black cap and the ringlets. He hugged her and smiled.

"We all have to survive, somehow, Sophie. Ludvig knows as much about that as anyone," he said generously, bringing him into the conversation.

It appeared that the conversation before her entry had been mainly about Ludvig's travails: Joseph had waited for her because he could not say everything he wanted and needed to say without her. The realisation of this pleased her, flattered her, and while she busied herself with forgotten hospitality, Joseph told them his story.

He explained to them what Sophie already knew – having heard it from Adam – that he and his sister had left the town in a commercial van before the Germans had arrived leaving their parents behind. As he reached this point he halted and became emotional. Sophie interrupted: "Forgive me Joseph I don't wish to interrupt you but what has become of your parents?"

Joseph replied, speaking very carefully: "I think they must be dead. I don't know for sure but I think so."

Sophie covered her mouth with a hand and uttered an involuntary cry.

"What happened? I know it is hard for you, but tell me."

"Well it was something like this. When the Germans came, and as we expected, all our Jewish businesses were confiscated. All the Jews were given street-cleaning jobs. You might have seen them, Sophie, on one of your trips to town." Sophie nodded that she had seen it. "And then one day all these Jewish families were arrested, quite suddenly one morning, and too quickly for them to take personal possessions with them, put on a train and sent to a ghetto in Trzbinia. Some people from this ghetto have been in touch and we know that my parents were there and that they survived the dreadful crowding, disease and hunger of the ghetto."

"Then in July 1942 there was a *selection*." Sophie interrupted him again to ask what was meant by a *selection* and, as Joseph hesitated, Ludvig explained what it was. Joseph continued: "The able-bodied people, those who could work, were sent as forced labour to Germany: the others, old people and children and the sick were sent to Auschwitz."

He stopped. Sophie burst out again. She was very agitated. She explained to Joseph that people from Auschwitz, prisoners, had passed *their* way when the Germans had evacuated the camp; very sick people and in a dreadful state, under-fed and diseased. A large number of them – about a hundred – had taken shelter in their barn and she had done her best to feed them and to enable them to rest.

Sophie exclaimed. "Joseph, oh Joseph, I do hope that your parents are not like *that*."

Joseph gulped and Ludvig interrupted. He said: "Let him explain in his own words."

Joseph continued: "It's much worse than that, Sophie. Hundreds of thousands of people, perhaps millions have been killed in this camp: gassed and burnt or simply dead from starvation and disease or from beatings."

Sophie covered her face and began to moan.

"It can't be right," she said.

But she remembered Adam's stories: accounts which she had felt must be exaggerated. And Adam must have been there outside the gates when all these dreadful things were being done inside.

"*How do you know how many?*" she said .

"Well, a Russian soldier told me that there were warehouses stuffed full of clothing from dead prisoners and that they had counted over 800,000 pairs of shoes at Auschwitz-Birkenau."

They all fell silent. And then Sophie asked: "And you and your sister, Joseph, what happened to you both?"

Joseph explained. The van driver had taken them to within five kilo- metres of the Russian border where he deposited them in the middle of the night. It was raining heavily. They worked themselves down to the banks of the River Bug. There they sat under a dripping tree. It seemed a hopeless situation. The river was full and wide and it was too dangerous to attempt to swim it. While he was willing to try, perhaps foolishly, his sister was not a good swimmer and couldn't do it.

They walked along the bank towards some houses that bordered the river. It was the dead of night but a dutiful guard dog became aware of them and started to bark and then, as if by signal, other dogs joined in. They stopped and waited for the noise to abate. Perhaps, the wind had changed. He didn't know. But when they moved again, the dogs were silent. Moored on the river bank at the foot of one of these houses they found a small rowing boat. They pushed it out into the river and rowing hard reached the other side. They had drifted downstream while crossing which suggested that an attempt to swim the river would have been disastrous.

There they made their way to a main road and hitched a ride by truck to Lvov. Joseph explained that Adam had given them the name of Sophie's relatives' in Lvov and that they had made their way to her relatives home. Sophie expressed her surprise and pleasure. "And did they help you? I do hope that they did."

"Yes, they helped. I think that they were a little nervous about it but they gave us three nights, and in this time we were able to seek out a Jewish group who helped us from then on. So we were very grateful to your relatives. They were very generous to us."

He continued: "The Jewish group gave us false papers. There were a lot of them around. So many Jews had fled or been killed that there were enough papers for everyone foolish enough to want Jewish identity cards." He laughed at his own joke. "There is, of course, a lot of anti-semitism in Russia: but it is not systematic and in theory – to officials – it does not exist. All men are supposed to be equal and there are many Jews in positions of authority and influence, and in the Red Army – like me."

Ludvig stopped himself from blurting out the Nazi message that Soviet communism was part of the world-wide Jewish conspiracy, which he knew was nonsense really.

Joseph continued: "We made ourselves useful giving piano lessons and translating documents, even teaching Polish. It's amazing what the Soviet functionary is eager to learn. So we coped quite nicely until the German invasion."

He paused and took some coffee. Sophie impatient to learn more, urged him on.

"And what did you *do then?*" she asked.

"Well we went to Moscow. It's a large place and you can get lost. We were given some good contact names. And we thought that if Moscow falls then the war is lost and there is no future for us anyway."

"You were very lucky people," said Ludvig. "Moscow nearly fell."

"Too true it did nearly fall. Rebecca and I joined in the efforts to save Moscow. Everyone did something. But it didn't fall and we made new friends, influential friends, who helped us. We met a very senior military man who did the bravest of things, laughing about it all the time. He had a very large and friendly family. Although they had very little living space themselves they gave us shelter and shared their food with us. They were wonderful. In return we taught them to play various instruments and did the menial tasks around the apartment. But whatever we did for them was nothing to what they did for us. Their influence and power put a protective screen around us and saved us from scrutiny. *They saved our lives.*"

And then Sophie and Ludvig thought that Joseph had started to ramble and they were concerned for him. He spoke of Miss Zbucki, the history teacher at the school, and what she had taught them. Something about loving your neighbour not requiring you to like them or to be the same as them, but to respect them as human beings, to honour them if you could but, if this were too difficult for you, to tolerate them.

So they stopped him at this point. Sophie cooked for them and they ate a pleasant meal by candle-light. They found Joseph to be his old self. Eager to talk about everything, inquisitive and amusing. As they relaxed Ludvig could speak about his experiences. Joseph prompted him by gentle questioning. This encouragement, a little alcohol, and the presence of friendly faces induced him to say more than previously he had thought wise.

Sophie thought: "How interesting. Every time we can get him to speak about Sachsenhausen, a little more comes out; and when he does speak about the camp, it is so vivid, even though he uses very few words. When he starts talking, we cannot stop him, and it is an uncensored flow in which he tells you the most startling things – happenings – *so strange and terrible that they must be true.*"

At these times she felt protective about him because she knew that unscrupulous people might try to use what he said to their advantage and against his. But then it was so fascinating that she did not want to stop him either.

Ludvig told them about the different categories of prisoner in his concentration camp and, that although there were some Jews, most prisoners were not; and which categories got killed and why they perished. He told them something of how people survived: what they had to do, who had influence, and how they acquired it. He explained that some prisoners had the power of life and death and that by the time he had left the communists were in control of prisoner representation. "More than that really," he said, "by the end the Germans were demoralised and seemed to accept that the future lay with the communists and their allies."

He told them about the killing of Russian prisoners of war and the thousands who were killed and the wailing that went on in the camp when batches of prisoners were to be deceived and then shot. Joseph asked him questions about the Russian deaths: how many and when, whether all ranks were killed or only the officers and whether he thought that any of the Russians had collaborated to save their own lives.

Sophie said: "Tell him about Wilhelm." Ludvig explained about the political prisoners, mainly communists, being given the opportunity for some form of release if they joined the SS in mopping up resistance and punishing people after the Warsaw rising. He told Joseph about Wilhelm's escape, how he had stayed a night and had left for the Austrian border. Joseph took a great deal of interest. He asked for the names of people and checked the spelling of the names. He wanted to know who had deserted and to where they had gone.

Joseph asked a number of probing questions and Ludvig became apprehensive. "Why all these questions?" he asked himself. And then he asked Joseph: "What do you *do* in the Army?"

Joseph hesitated before answering.

"I'm an Intelligence Officer. I monitor, translate and interpret reports."

"Reports of what exactly?"

"Oh, the war, political happenings. That sort of thing."

This exchange put a damper on the conversation and despite all Sophie's efforts to revive it the bonhomie had ended. Joseph accepted an offer to stay for the night and they decided to call it a day.

At breakfast next morning Sophie chatted on about Adam, Mary and her two younger children. Joseph hearing that Adam had gone missing in France said: "Don't worry about that. He's very resourceful and can look after himself. He'll turn up." Ludvig was silent and Joseph noticed it and went out of his way to be pleasant. Ludvig was familiar with the way communists had spoken in the camp and the way they had of ingratiating themselves and getting information out of you which, as sure as beans, would be used against you.

Ludvig decided to come right out with it.

"Joseph, excuse me asking. Are *you* a Party member?

Joseph said that he was. After a moment of silence during which they absorbed the information, Joseph began to explain.

"No need to explain," said Ludvig, anxious not to be dragged into a conversation he might regret.

"No, I want to explain to you both. I might be wrong but what I feel at the moment is that communism is our best hope, particularly here in Poland. Tell me what political movement or body of belief is international, non-racial and classless in its approach, and committed to economic progress and social justice?"

He walked about the room like a real agitator. "Here in Poland we have been crucified by our multiple loyalties and class-ridden approach: Pole against German, Ukrainian against Latvian, aristocrat against peasant and industrial worker, and Catholic against Jew. All these enmities and conflicts have made us easy prey to our enemies: they have turned brother against brother, and neighbour and friend against each other. Communism stands alone against all these evils."

Now that he had begun he couldn't be stopped.

"I know that Soviet Communism is not perfect, and there have been many mistakes, but they are behind us. The war has made a difference. We stand closer together now each man for each other." He paused a little surprised by his own fervour. "And I wish to be completely honest with you. I am grateful to the Soviet Union for what they have done in liberating us from the fascists and for accepting people like me – Jews like me."

Ludvig restrained himself to a few words.

"Joseph you are a young man and your grasp of history is not as sound as you think it to be. Once the Russian bear gets hold of you he never lets go. And despite what he tells you he is not hugging you to death for your own benefit."

Joseph shrugged his shoulders and looked embarrassed. He did not wish to argue with them. He was grateful to them both and wished them to think of him as a friend. But he said: "*Better a communist Poland than no Poland at all.*"

And Ludvig indicated his dissent.

All Sophie's efforts to turn them back to good humour were useless and Joseph left them in a stilted way and to feelings of disappointment and ill-ease. Their belief that things had gone wrong between them were confirmed for a few days later Joseph returned accompanied by a Russian officer, a full captain, and an upright young man of military bearing.

Joseph introduced him to them in Polish and explained that there was nothing to worry about, and that the Russian was a friend of his – a Jew like him – and that he needed to ask them a few questions. The Russian made an elaborate speech in which he praised Polish patriots and professed the full friendship of the Russian people. Joseph translated. As Ludvig was fluent in Russian the translation was not needed by him: but he decided to keep quiet about his knowledge of the language so that he could hear the asides between the two of them, and the differences between speech and translation.

Then the officer cut to the quick. He needed to know the names of the Sachsenhausen prisoners assisting the Germans at Warsaw and, in particular, of the communists. He wanted to know their ages and the places from which they came. Ludvig was asked to write down the information. The truth was that he knew very little, and all of that had been told to him by Wilhelm. He kept saying this to the Russian and the reply was always the same. Please write down the information. In the end Joseph had to tell the Russian to stop.

The subject then turned to the killing of the Russian prisoners of war. Ludvig was asked to write down his account paying particular attention to numbers, dates and the names of collaborators and to sign and date the statement. It was a short account and the officer demanded more. Ludvig became angry and demanded to know what right he had to request the information in the first place.

In Russian Joseph advised his Russian friend to stop. Displeased the Russian clicked his heels and thanked them. Joseph looked embarrassed. Sophie said angrily: "How could you Joseph. We are your friends. You should know better than to subject us to this questioning. You have abused our hospitality and we are ashamed of you."

When they had gone, Sophie did not know what to do with her anger.

"It is all your fault," she railed at Ludvig, "with your politics, and raising these awful matters. It never does any good."

"You should say that to Hitler and Stalin," was his response. "What do you think that they would say to you? Of course, Sophie my dear, pray tell us what you would like to talk about?"

But she knew what *she* meant: she valued Joseph *as* her friend which, despite the evidence of the conversation, she knew him to be.

A few days later Joseph returned on his own to say goodbye as he was moving on. As Ludvig was out they had the opportunity to talk as friends. She asked him about Rebecca and whether she had any plans. "I don't know. She is very happy where she is. Musically you know she is very talented – better than me – and she is part of a group of gifted artists. Maybe that is what she will do: follow a musical career. Russians are mad about good music and she will be appreciated."

He asked her about the prisoners from Auschwitz she had accommodated.

"Joseph if only I had known about your parents I would have asked them whether they had met them, knew anything about them."

"It's kind of you Sophie but it would have been very unlikely. Prisoners did not survive very long, and from what I hear many were killed on arrival."

"Well Joseph you never know. Your parents are fine people, surely God will have smiled on them. I shall pray for them now that I know they need my prayers."

"And what will you do after the war, Joseph?" she asked him. He didn't know and then he said very sadly. "Will I be wanted here? These poor people from the camp, that you sheltered, not all these survived in all honesty. Of course, there are good Christian people like you to help but I have heard some terrible stories. Some returning Jews have been beaten up and killed by ordinary Poles. Killed for nothing really because they do not have any money. I have heard shocking shouts from houses and in the streets: *"What, you Jews still here, I thought the Germans would have done us a good turn and finished you off."* He stopped.

"Joseph, there are always going to be people like that and you must ignore them," Sophie responded. "If we get a decent government all this racial rubbish will stop. You'll see." She squeezed his arm encouragingly.

"Sophie I want us to be friends. To stay friends," Joseph continued. "We don't know what will happen after the war. Hopefully it will be all right. But I want you to know that if it turns out that I can help you, I certainly will. Funny that, don't you think? Coming from a Jew."

"Not funny at all Joseph," she replied, "coming from a very talented and good boy."

Joseph laughed and said: "You sound just like my mother."

Sophie looked thoughtful and after a while gathered the strength to ask him a favour. She told him about the Russian occupation of the town and what had happened to many of her family and friends: of how the Russians had swept through P. like a swarm of locusts stealing and pillaging everything they could get their hands on and the suffering they had caused.

Joseph looked ashamed.

"As I understand it," he said, "the Germans did little to defend this town. It's not really defensible because it is so easily surrounded and so simple to enfilade through the fields."

"I'm not talking about fighting," she said, "or even stealing the animals and any possessions they could move. *I'm talking about what they did to us.*"

Joseph blushed.

"Tell me, if you can," he said gently.

Sophie went on: "When we knew they were coming, we women hid – in the cellars, attics and barns. We lit candles and placed them in the windows and put crosses on the doors to show that we were good God-fearing Christians that wished them no harm. Not that an unbeliever would take any notice of that. Then the men tried to distract these Russian boys – for that is all they were really – and sometimes, with some vodka and gifts, they did distract them, and sometimes, alas, they didn't."

Joseph looked very uncomfortable. Sophie went on: "A gang-rape by several brutal boys is not a matter of pleasure having no consequences."

"No, no I understand that," he said hastily and interrupting her.

"Some of these girls are so badly injured and scarred by it that they will never have children now. Physically, many are so damaged that they can't."

Joseph took refuge in practicalities.

"How can I help?"

"Tell them, your political masters. And ask them to get it stopped."

He said that he would try but thought it unlikely that it would do any good.

"Anything else?" he said weakly.

"Yes, there is," she said gathering full steam. "Our boys, in our family I mean, sons and nephews, forced into the German army, they will be captured if not killed. Can you help us by protecting these boys. We don't want them on a train to Siberia."

"I may be able to do something," Joseph said with greater conviction. "Ludvig is something of a local hero. You know – resisting the Fascists in a concentration camp. It helps. Give me what names and addresses you have."

He made a careful note.

"I'll put Ludvig in touch with the right person and we shall do what we can."

She decided that she would not tell Ludvig about Joseph coming

again, although she would give him the contact name: she did not want
to get into an acrimonious discussion and to have her friendship spoiled
by political posturing. Would she see Joseph again? Perhaps not, but if
not she wanted to remember him in her kitchen, taking coffee and
talking gently about his parents and his hopes for a better world.

At supper Ludvig said: *"That Jew-boy is riding for a fall.* When the
Russians have finished with him they will spew him out. You will see
that I'm right." And when she was silent he said: "You shouldn't have
encouraged him with hopes of his parents' survival. They're dead.
People don't survive Auschwitz."

She said: "I know that's wrong because we have had survivors in our
barn."

"Not his parents we haven't," he responded.

"You must not misunderstand me," Ludvig said, after a pause, "I'm
sorry for the Jews, but it is a good thing that most of them have gone
from Poland. Now we are a Catholic country again and everyone will
believe the same thing. That's a good thing isn't it? You must admit it
is, after all you are a Catholic. You know, the one true religion. I'm not
saying that they should all have been killed, but it is a good thing that
they are not here."

He helped himself to some coffee and she said nothing.

Now that he had started on her he could not stop. "What does he want,
my blood?" she thought.

"This nonsense about Miss Zbucki. What do you make of that? Not
having to like your neighbour but to respect him. Who the hell is our
neighbour, anyway? Are the Germans our neighbours, are the Russians?
Is it good scripture? And should it be taught in our schools?"

As he paused for a reaction she got up and said to him: "Do you really
want to know my opinion?"

He nodded assent.

"I think that Miss Zbucki is a very fine person: and that Joseph and
his family are very good and gifted. I think that if people like them
ruled the world, we would all be fine: that there would be no wars, and
the world would be a better place to live in: and I think that you are a
loud-mouthed bigot for all your fine phrases. And now, because I love
you, and in the spirit of Miss Zbucki, I am going upstairs to change
your bedclothes so that you can lie in your own bed."

"You know nothing. Nothing at all," was the retort.

CHAPTER 25

O N THE FARM in L. Mary sat down to write her mother a long letter. She felt guilty at not going home to see her father on his return and to rejoice with them both. Of course, she was glad about his release, but since she had drawn closer to Georg she had felt awkward about her father: Georg being very respectable and her father in a concentration camp. "These are horrid feelings," she told herself, disappointed for having them. In her letter she wanted to be bright and breezy so that her mother could share the contents with her father, for at that moment it was the best she could do.

She started by telling them that they were especially busy on the farm as their numbers had dwindled. Some girls had absconded, which was against the law, but no one seemed to care or do anything to bring them back; and then an older man, and two boys not yet sixteen, had been called up into the army in the attempt to make up the numbers in the struggle to protect the motherland. By this she meant Germany, and she wrote it even though she knew that her parents would think it wrong: for them the motherland was Poland.

Mary wrote a very long letter full of the kind of gossip she knew that her mother enjoyed. She wanted her mother to say: "What a jolly letter, how well Mary is getting on," and to dash down the road with it and show it to the neighbours. In this objective she largely succeeded. But then as she finished and posted it circumstances changed: changes which could have been anticipated but not their speed.

Mary had found herself thinking she was part of a couple, even though nothing formal had been agreed between Georg and herself, and increasingly she thought of her loyalties as resting with Germany. She realised that it was important to work these loyalties out very quickly because they were going to be tested. 'Are you with us or against us?' was going to cease to be an abstract question. It annoyed her that nothing could be decided: while Magda remained with her husband arrangements were in aspic. Every day she hoped for news that would enable her to be open about where her affections lay and each day passed without a resolution.

As the Russian armies drew closer these decisions could be postponed no longer. Magda was the first to break cover. One day in January she absconded leaving a note for Georg which he showed to Mary. It read as follows:

> *Georg,*
> *When you read this note I will have gone. Do not try to follow me or find out where I am – it would be useless. I have a friend. He is a major in the German army and he has promised to look after me. You have been very foolish in not selling the farm and I have left you without any money, only my clothes, many of them old. You should be ashamed.*
> *Magda*

Mary looked at him enquiringly.
"Well are you going to try to find her?"
"No."
"Are you sad?"
"No, it's a relief."
Mary was disconcerted. She thought: "If he can shrug *her* off so easily while seeming to be attached, what might he do to me?" He kissed her as if knowing her thoughts and said: "Now we can get on with *our* life and we must be quick about it."
Magda was right about the farm: it was too late to sell it. The locals knew that at some time a Polish farmer would squat on the farm and get it for nothing.
"Well to be fair to Magda," commented Georg, "she was right about selling the farm. Now she and her boy friend will get nothing. They will have to steal something from someone else. I expect they have worked out what to do."
Mary was cross with him. and accused him of not looking after their interests.
"We shall need some money," she said pleadingly, "how shall we manage?"

"We'll be OK," responded Georg, relieved to have got rid of his wife so easily.

Georg had left it late to protect his workers. Now he called them together and told them to leave the farm, to go with his blessing: to get back to their families or to some other safe place as quickly as they could as the Russians would be there in a few days time. In answer to questions, he explained that it was unsafe to delay. Once the Russian army knew that there were girls on the farm, they would come after them, and that with the Russians, unfortunately, gang-rapes were common and that there would be nothing he could do to prevent one happening on the farm.

The Czech girl, Greta, acted as a spokeswoman. She said: "We are very angry." There were shouts of assent."We shall talk about it in private and then give you our demands." They assembled in the kitchen. They all needed to go to the south or the east: back into Poland or to Austria or Czechoslovakia; back into the path of the advancing Russian armies; and none of them felt it to be safe to do so.

Some of the girls had picked up news of Russian statements that their army could do anything they wished to the civilian population in Germany in revenge for the terrible cruelties inflicted upon the Russian people. They told each other: "Common knowledge. Never trust a Russian."

The girls were very practical. They demanded money and transport.

"What transport?" said Georg expressing astonishment. They had worked it out.

"The tractor, the farm cart and that little carriage you keep in one of the sheds – and the horses to pull them."

"OK, you can have the transport," acquiesced Georg.

"And we shall need some money. What can you give us?"

"That's more difficult. Hold on and I shall see what I can scrape together."

He disappeared back into the house and appeared a few minutes later with some notes and coins.

"Here you are. This is the best I can do."

Grumbling about his meanness they took it.

"Come with me and I will help you with some fuel and harnessing the horses," Georg said.

"And with *some food*," Gretta demanded.

"Yes, with food. You should have been a politician," said Georg grudgingly and with admiration.

The girls had a further meeting to allocate places on the transport.

Three of the bolder girls, led by Greta, decided to take their chances of travelling back to their homes, took some money and their food rations and started out on a journey by road and by rail, while the rest divided themselves between the various modes of transport and set out in the 'wrong direction' to the west and into the German heartland.

"What about *us*?" enquired Mary anxiously as they returned to the farmhouse together. "Well," said Georg, "follow me down to the cellar." There from a locked cupboard he pulled a suitcase out into the light.

"Ye of little faith," he said mockingly, unlocking it and pushing up the lid with a flourish. "I have not been idle over these past months."

The suitcase was full of money and precious objects: not a little gold, and some expensive looking jewellery.

She gasped.

"How did you do it?" she exclaimed.

"With difficulty. The less you know the better. All you need to understand is that it is legal and, if we are careful, and look after it, we shall be able to resettle."

Georg told her that they would use the truck and that he needed her to help him prepare for a very long journey. He wanted to go as far west as he could, out of the reach of the Russians, and to hole-up somewhere safe until the fighting stopped. It took a long time to load the truck. Apart from bedding, food and clothes they took some household articles and furnishings – and then as much of the valuable items of furniture as they could load.

Mary grew anxious. They were taking too long and it would be sheer foolishness to be there when the Russians arrived. But Georg persisted with his plan and at last they moved off down the long winding pathway and then onto a main road where they could quicken and move out of the danger zone.

Mary asked: "Where is your suitcase?"

"Left behind. Not the contents," he hastened to add, "but the case. Don't ask me to explain. It is safer if you know nothing."

They were some fifteen kilometres into their journey when a detachment of Russian troops entered the farm. They were disappointed to find it empty, as the locals had indicated that there could be some good sport, but pleased to find a good billet and plenty of food and livestock.

Magda at this time was well on the road to safety and going west. She had taken great pains to look her best and in her luggage she had the means to maintain it. She was dressed in a smart and fashionable sheepskin coat. "It is a pity," she thought, "not to have obtained a *real fur coat.*" She knew that her friend would have wished her to have one; but in L. it was difficult to obtain luxury goods, and it was the best he could do for her at the time."

She was especially pleased with her hair. A natural blond, she had been able to enhance it with some peroxide which she had been able to buy locally once her friend had been able to demand it for her. Now, with the use of a little brillantine, her hair shone in a most becoming fashion. She had been able to have it lightly permed and was careful to place her fur hat on her head so that this crowning glory was not disturbed in any way. Her make-up had been applied in the modern style and suited her, although for some tastes it might have been thought overdone.

The *coup de grâce* for Magda, so to speak, was her stockings: sheer silk stockings which hissed seductively as she slowly crossed her shapely legs. She took great care not to snag them in any way. Before she started her journey she had inspected herself in a full-length mirror. She was pleased with what she saw. The image was not perfect and there were a number of alterations she wished to make: but she had made a good start. For the first time for many years she was drawing nearer to the person – the image – which she knew was the true Magda. Oh, what a relief it was to be with a man who truly appreciated her.

The three Czech girls had set out for the rail station where after a long wait they had boarded a train going south. The ticket-seller had told them that he could not guarantee the train would get to its final destination. Greta had said she understood that. The official insisted on explaining the position. "You must understand that you will have no claim against the company if you have to disembark before you reach your destination."

"Bloody hell, these ants will continue going about their daily tasks until they are stamped on," said Greta to the others.

The first part of Magda's journey had been in a staff car which her friend had arranged for her. Now she was in a passenger train which, given wartime conditions, was comfortable, although without refreshments. "Thank God for mother and her very wise upbringing of me," she thought, as she brought out the lunch that she had prepared for herself. She leaned back in her comfortable seat as the train wended its way to what she imagined would be the life of leisure which befitted her. She crossed and recrossed her legs as slowly as she could so that she could hear the gentle hiss: it was to her a symphony of sound unparalleled by any other.

A few kilometres from Berlin and in fading light the train came to a sudden and unscheduled halt at a small station. Leaning from the carriage windows passengers could hear the sounds of an air raid and rising smoke could be seen on the horizon.

Then came the unmistakable sound of low-flying aircraft followed by the most enormous explosion. Magda's carriage rocked upwards and sideways but miraculously stayed upright: the glass blew in. Instinctively Magda had frozen with her arms around her head. Screaming and shouting passengers struggled with each other to get out of the train and Magda got herself up and to the carriage door competing with the other passengers to get out. "God is merciful," she said to herself. "I am entirely unhurt."

And then she stumbled onto the platform and struggled to her feet. Exactly at that moment the attacking aircraft, having discharged its bombs and banked to make a further run, roared low along the station platform in a machine-gun attack. Magda was hit as she got up from the platform and died immediately.

Greta and her two companions made good progress. Although the train stopped and started it crawled towards its destination and after seven or eight hours of interrupted progress they reckoned that they must be some two hundred kilometres from the Czech border. Then the train stopped and a guard told them that they could go no further as the Russian army occupied the territory and fighting was going on. The girls decided to get off the train and to take cover.

Among some trees, but hidden from the track, they held a conference. Greta told them that having come so far and being so close to the border they must go on. The other girls were frightened and inclined to go to the nearest village and seek refuge. A compromise was reached: they would go on, travelling only at night, but if they reached a friendly-looking village they would seek shelter. And they waited for darkness before moving and ate the rest of their food.

On the first night they travelled twenty kilometres. Greta broke cover early the next morning to buy food and they rested all day. They travelled across fields trying to keep the roads in sight so that they continued to move south. On the third day their physical condition had deteriorated and they were reluctant to move out to continue the journey. With tiredness came carelessness and a critical error of judgement: they stuck to a roadway to ease their tired limbs and were spotted and arrested by a Russian patrol.

There were six Russian soldiers none of whom could have been more than twenty years old: simple Russian boys from somewhere in central Russia. They were greatly excited by their capture, chattering to each other and laughing. On the edge of a village these boys found an empty cottage, forced the girls inside and, at gun point, raped them. That is three of the boys raped them while the others, resisting the cries to join in, at first watched and then went away.

The boys committing the rapes had a competition, the objective of which seemed to the girls to be the number of times they could rape all the girls in one session. They would rape, go away, and return tanked up with vodka. These girls were strong and healthy but weakened by the journey of the last three days, they were relatively powerless to resist.

Yet despite their weariness, they did what they could. Greta scratched her assailants and attempted to gouge their eyes, while another girl landed several blows with a chair. The boys seemed to think that this resistance was part of their game and responded with heavy blows. It took several hours of ceaseless assault before a victor among the boys was declared and the rapes stopped.

The bedroom was locked and the weeping girls compelled by fatigue and their injuries fell into an uneasy sleep. They were woken by one of the boys who had not been involved in the rapes bringing them some bread and coffee and extra blankets. He tried to talk to them and they thought that he had apologised.

Early in the morning Greta, who knew some Russian, heard raised voices from the kitchen beneath them. These boys were discussing what to do with them and one of them, she could not tell which one, wanted them killed.

Then there was shouting from the road outside and the sound of vehicles stopping and commands being given. From the window they saw a line of military vehicles and in front of the leading jeep they saw and heard an elderly German, shouting first in Russian and then in German.

Greta said: "He seems to be telling them about us. He's saying it is a disgrace and demanding that they do something. God, what a brave man!"

"Who's he talking to," said the others.

"I don't know but he is very senior."

Then there was a knock on the front door and the bark of authoritative questions and commands. There were sounds on the stairs and then a knock on their door. When Greta replied, a senior Red Army officer came into the room: not an imposing bemedalled one but senior nevertheless.

He looked at them very carefully and asked a number of questions: who they were, the circumstances of their arrest, where they wanted to go to, and so on: and then, and in embarrassment, whether they had invited sex from these soldiers. As he did so the incongruous nature of the question when confronted with wounded and abused girls was obvious to him and he said: "Forgive me, please. I have to ask these questions."

He went downstairs and there was a long interval of raised voices below. He returned and told them that the Red Army extended its profound apologies. He would assist them with transport to cross the border to their homes. Disciplinary action would be taken. Clicking his heels, he asked them to gather themselves, and that transport was available.

The boys were lined up outside. A number of military vehicles were in the street and German villagers had gathered there. The officer called out a name and the boy who had declared himself the victor was brought before him, his arms tied behind his back, and made to kneel – facing away from them all. The officer drew his pistol and killed him with a single shot through the back of his neck.

He addressed them all: "Let that be a lesson to you all. The honour of the Red Army is not built upon the blood of innocent women." The body was thrown upon a truck and they climbed onto another. The villagers clapped the departing convoy.

The officer was as good as his word. They were put on a train to Prague with an impressive document guaranteeing them good passage. On their journey it was examined several times and accepted always without question. In Prague they had enough money to catch buses and local trains. They had no further trouble and made it back to their homes.

Mary and Georg in their journey to the west made good progress in the truck. There were shortages of fuel and the petrol stations were closed but Georg had stored petrol cans in the truck: enough he told her to reach the English Channel.

The roads were crowded and they were frequently pushed off them by military convoys. They took turns to drive and sleep with the intention of moving to safety within a day or two. Whenever possible they kept to the minor roads in the hope that they would not be stopped. By perseverance and good navigation they made good progress on the first two days.

"So far, so good," said Georg a little too quickly. "These soldiers of ours seem to be maintaining good discipline and remain in control."

"But they're not too impressive are they, young boys and grandfathers, they seem to me," was her response.

And then almost immediately they met their first road block and were confronted by a combination of a grandfather and young boys. These soldiers asked them where they came from and where they were going and the purpose of their journey. Georg told them the true story clearly and succinctly. The older man walked round to the back of the vehicle and looked inside. He said: "I'm not very impressed. Why didn't you stay and fight. We must all fight now for the freedom of our country. We can't let these Bolshevik swine govern us, can we?"

Georg explained once again. The senior man looked at him and said in an enquiring voice: "I'm not too *inclined* to let you pass."

"What would *incline* you," said Georg reaching for his wallet.

"Well that is up to you. I can tell you that they do not pay us much or feed us well in the latest ranks of our army."

Georg gave him some money. The man was unimpressed. Georg gave him his wallet. And they were waved on.

Mary was indignant. Georg laughed. "They were small denomination notes. Plenty more where that came from," and she realised that he was prepared for the jouney with more than one wallet. "Never underestimate a grandfather, especially when he is hungry," said Georg exultantly. "Which talking of food, *I'm* hungry." He stopped the truck at the nearest safe place and disappeared into the back of the truck where he rooted around for some time before reappearing with food and a grin on his face like a naughty boy.

The next encounter was a more serious test. This time there were more soldiers with greater needs. They were after serious money, refused the proffered wallet and began a slow and thorough search of the truck. "We're in trouble now," whispered Georg.

But when the angels are smiling on you no harm can come. During the search the blockade was approached by some military vehicles. Harsh words were spoken and outgunned by the rank of the senior officer confronting them, these soldiers abandoned the search of the truck and the blockade was lifted.

They were soon well beyond the German front lines and approaching the point at which Georg was beginning to feel safe. He explained to Mary that the safety point was a matter of judgement, he might be wrong, but that now he was looking for a place to stay. They stopped for the night, driving the truck off the road so that it could not be seen by passing traffic. They slept in the truck and tired though they were, enjoyed the best sex they had experienced together. Wakening, still twined together, stiff but joyous, with the winter sun shining benignly upon them, they felt for the first time that life had begun for them.

They took advice at the next village on local farmers looking for workers and by asking the right questions of the right people in the right way were given worthwhile recommendations. It took them a day and three meetings before they found the right nesting place: and then it was obvious and the farmer and Georg fell into each other's arms.

The farmer was desperately short of labour, not any old pair of hands, but experienced and reliable people. What he could offer was a pleasant bedroom in his farmhouse, a regular wage, and a secure shed for the truck. The farm was mainly arable but with a mix of livestock: sheep, cattle, pigs and chickens. It was remote: deep among the hills and reachable only by a narrow winding track. Except for a visit to the farm, there would be no point in braving the track which was barely passable at all in the winter.

Yet despite its remoteness the farm was prosperous: natural rich loams and expert cultivation over the years produced good yields, and the standards of husbandry were high. Here they could be safe. Mary gazed back over the pleasant landscape down to the valley below, and her heart lifted. It was a good place to begin their life together and to live out what remained of an unsuccessful war.

There is something irresistible about young people in love – Mary at least came into this category – and the farmer and his wife warmed to it. Their own passion may have diminished over the years but the presence of these two lovers starting out in their life together stirred in them the long-lost feelings of their youth. They forgot the disappointments and setbacks of the years gone by and even rivalled the newcomers in the desire to enjoy each other.

And as they all got on splendidly together, the coming spring lifted their hearts and the farm resounded to sounds of laughter and high-spirits. They worked hard, ate and drank well, guarded each other, and warmed themselves, not only by the evening log-fire, but in each others company.

Down in the valleys of this prosperous countryside, war was waged: towns and factories, railways and ports, men and machines were decimated at great loss of life: but here in the hills, when they turned their radio off, little or nothing was known. Occasionally the stream of a high-flying plane tracered the blue skies and they heard the distant sounds of guns and bombs: but they seldom looked up, and only rarely stopped to contemplate who was being killed on that day. They concentrated on common tasks and good moments shared.

One day someone would tell them that the war was over but they doubted, at that moment, that it would make much difference to their lives. They were dimly aware that at some future time they would have to venture into the lost world below and far away from them: but they had no wish to contemplate that time or to bring it closer.

CHAPTER 26

IN THOSE LAST few weeks as the ring closed upon Germany and the war shifted to the defence of their own homeland, a noticeable change in mood came over the good folk of Osnabruck. The air of resignation, even indifference, remained; but it coexisted with other feelings: of pride in country and a determination to be worthy of it, and a drawing together in communal solidarity – of a feeling of a common destiny and fate, of being in it together. Reluctantly Adam and Felix came to respect these changes and in some peculiar way to be part of them.

Talking together in the privacy of their room they were of one mind in the thought that too much had been asked of *them*: they had been undertaking their assignment over too long a period of time, partly by design but mostly by accident: it had taken too long for Allied forces to fight their way across France into Germany. In this time they had become part of two communities: the world of the railways and their workmates there, and of the village of H., where people greeted them in the street, and where neighbours invited them into their homes.

In these places people trusted them and had come to rely on them. And gradually, despite themselves, they had been drawn into relationships that meant things to them, which involved their hearts and their dreams, as well as their material well-being. At this time they were both twenty years of age and separated from family: torn and plucked out prematurely from all that was dear to them, from all that they needed to make the transition from youth to manhood.

Now as the dangers came closer they were required to betray these new relationships and to abuse these new intimacies, when their own fears called out for the normalcy of daily routine and the comforts of belonging and receiving and giving love.

This shared fear and the dread of dangers to come brought Elizabeth and Felix closer. As Elizabeth looked out for him, and hugged and kissed him, Felix wanted to be able to tell her that he was at one with her while he knew there would come a day when she would know that he had conspired against her. All their training told them to avoid such situations. Adam said bluntly to his friend: "Stop seeing her *now*. You will regret it." But at this time each man sought his own comfort and solace.

Felix's reticence, and his reluctance in answering questions about Adam, distressed Elizabeth. Now when she cleaned their room she looked about her and sought what information she could. There was nothing: the other tenants had family portraits and personal items which gave vital clues to their history, but these boys left no clues, at least none which could be seen. They kept their luggage and spare clothes in a locked wardrobe. She made discrete enquiries and obtained a spare key. There was a further disappointment: the cupboard contained luggage that was firmly locked.

Elizabeth got the cases out of the cupboard and onto the bed. She turned them over and over again and tried to establish what they contained. One was heavier than the other and contained some heavy object which moved. She did not know what it was.

Every day when she cleaned their room she tried to open the cases, and always they were locked. Then one day she saw that the clasp to the heavy case was open. She lifted the lid and found the radio. She sat down on the bed and pondered the significance of the discovery and, with mounting excitement, she stopped work and went home. When the boys returned they found both the cupboard and suitcase unlocked. In her confusion, Elizabeth had forgotten to re-lock both the case and cupboard door.

The conclusion they reached was that someone had broken in and they waited in trepidation for a sudden visit and their arrest. Nothing happened. Elizabeth became unavailable and Felix's late-night knocking at her door went unanswered. They considered the matter. Adam wished to be decisive.

"It must be Elizabeth. We must get rid of her, it is too much of a danger," he said. Felix refused to have anything to do with it.

"This war is coming rapidly to an end. If she has worked it out, she won't do anything and then it will be too late."

Adam disagreed.

They left it awhile and the war grew nearer. Then they could bear the risk no longer and the two of them called on her. Getting no answer and seeing a light they went to the rear door. It was locked but when they knocked Elizabeth answered it and welcomed them in. She was in very good form and in a curious way she acted as if expecting them.

Elizabeth offered some hospitality and on this occasion it included wine and entertainment. She played the latest hits on her phonograph machine and a party atmosphere was engendered. There was none of the dismal talk of the war and of impending doom and, though their mood was sombre enough, as was their purpose in coming, they relaxed and enjoyed themselves.

Adam had never been in her room before and he looked about it with interest. He was impressed. It was well-furnished with some modern pieces and pleasant pictures and *objet d'art*. He asked about them and she told them that her husband had brought them back from Italy when on leave. There were womanly touches: she had carpets and cushions and the ultimate signature of respectability – curtains. The room decorations reminded him of other rooms he had seen, of Katya's apartment in Auschwitz: it was bourgeois like Katya's, and immaculately clean, but unlike her room it was bookish and arty.

Elizabeth was not interested in conversation about her *objet d'art*. She pulled Adam up out of his chair and insisted that he dance with her. And then it was conveyed to them, and Felix did not know quite how, that it was Adam's company that was needed and not Felix's, and he retired from the house with relief and waited up for Adam.

Adam had decided that if he was not certain of Elizabeth's silence – and assuming that she had worked out what the radio meant – that he would kill her; and he carried a knife for the purpose. Elizabeth was not thinking of the radio. After a while she retired to her bedroom and reappeared in a different dress and asked him to dance with her again.

And then she wanted more of him. Adam blurred from wine and vodka was confused. He did not want her, and had business to resolve, but then the closeness to her, and the way she clung to him made it impossible to ask the questions he had rehearsed, and without the answers he couldn't kill her. So he did nothing. He danced a little, gave her some modest kisses, told her she was wonderful, made a few feeble excuses and left.

"Good God, Adam, you've made it worse," said Felix on Adam's unexpected return.

"I'll go." And he went back to Elizabeth's and didn't return until early morning.

"What happened, where have you been?" enquired the anxious and sleepless Adam. Felix grinned. He was pleased with himself.

"You made her as high as a kite. I picked her up and took her to bed."

He almost purred: "It was fine. Believe me. We'll be all right. Trust me."

At this time Elizabeth wept into her pillow. She had surrendered herself to Felix and lost her hard-earned respectability. She hadn't meant to do it, and she didn't really want to: and she hoped to God that no one saw anything and if anyone had that they would be silent about it.

Felix was a nice boy, and had been sweet to her, but there could be no future in it. "At her age," she thought, "she should know better. *As for the radio, what did she care if they wanted to listen to illegal broadcasts. Lot's of people did, and it was none of her business.*"

On the following weekend one of their neighbours asked Adam whether he would take her alsatian dog with him if he was going on his usual walk. This was a boisterous young dog and difficult to handle, but he was pleased to take it with him: somehow it didn't seem a real walk at all without a dog. He thought about the incident with Elizabeth and blamed himself for the indecision. Probably, their hesitation would have no consequences, but it might have done: the truth was that they had become too close to these people. What sort of spy was it who had neighbours and took their dogs for walks?

Felix had this irritating tendency to ask him questions, sometimes important questions, to which he had no answers. He could never have killed Elizabeth, or any other villager for that matter – unless of course they were about to kill him – and he supposed that before you killed anyone in cold blood it was necessary to hate them. He didn't hate any of them. He didn't want rail workers to be machine-gunned or villagers to be killed in air raids; he just wanted this war to come to an end and to get back to England – to get home.

He thought of Eva as he often did. Sometimes she came to mind during the day when he saw something which he knew she would have liked for herself, and in the context of what they might do together, and always he thought of her last thing at night. He remembered the days they had spent together: of visiting Kew Gardens, the holiday in Felixstowe and the walks in the London parks.

After a while, and when he was distressed, he was able to relive these occasions minute by minute: what she wore, what they talked about, the weather, and each and every incident of the day. With concentrated effort he was able to recover the memory of their travelling companions, what they had for lunch and the smells and touches of the occasion. He could say to himself: "Today we are going to take the 8.28 a.m to Southend-on-Sea," and gradually he came to be able to recall everything about that journey, and knew that its recollection would take the next hour and a half.

Instead of dreading the night and what it might bring, he began to welcome it. He rehearsed his menu of journeys during the day and selected the one he was going to recall that night. Once selected he could look forward to it and the nightmares could be crowded out.

As he thought about the incident with Elizabeth, he realised that he could not be interested in her, even for the simple question of having sex and chalking it up as a conquest, because of Eva. It was a bore. A year ago he would not have hesitated and now it was not possible. He was committed to Eva and emotional involvement with someone else was not in the cards.

So he told Felix that he could not be interested in Elizabeth because of Eva. Felix said: "Pull the other one." Adam was pleased he had told Felix because it created an air of expectancy, and removed some part of the pressure on him to perform.

Now the war came to Osnabruck with a vengeance. Heavy bombing hit the local factories and road and rail communications. As fast as the Allies put the rail system out of commission, the work-gangs, of which they were both an indispensable part, restored normal service. They rejoiced at the attacks and celebrated the repairs. Felix was restless, "Can't we get away from this now, Adam? Get away into the country-side. Haven't we done our bit?"

Adam thought not and, more important, so did London. Accurate information on troop movements was as important as ever – and they were told that this information would save lives.

Despite the dangers, the difficulties and daily losses, railway workers reported for duty in impressive numbers. Felix reported to London that, despite the undoubted bombing successes, the morale of citizens and workers remained high. While he had not experienced the London blitz, Adam thought that the reaction of the besieged and battered populace of Osnabruck must be similar to that of the people of London.

Perhaps, Adam thought, everyone was like that: Warsaw, Bucharest or Dresden, you name it: people rose from the wreckage of their homes, crawled from their cellars and got themselves off to their bombed-out factories to work: somehow they provided for themselves and their families. According to the military strategists they were supposed to despair and to turn on their political leaders and overthrow them – but they never did, anywhere.

The talk now was of the danger of foreign workers. At the peak of their use by the Third Reich there were over seven million of them. Allied leaflets had urged these workers not to endanger themselves by useless uprisings but whenever possible to leave their factories and to take refuge in the countryside. In this way the German war effort would be undermined. The railway lost key workers and suffered like other employers the vandalism and pilfering of an increasing number of men on the loose without the means to support themselves.

In H. women were encouraged to carry pistols and to practice in their use. While there might not be a general uprising of these foreigners, they were told, they should keep in mind that desperate and displaced persons on the run without any loyalties might be very dangerous. The citizenry did not know whether this was true, and there were very few incidents to support the propaganda, but they accepted that precautions would be wise.

Elizabeth showed Felix her pistol and he persuaded her not to be foolish. The pistol would be a danger to her and she must not think of using it. They laughed about it, and she put it away, but she remained pleased that she had it.

The moment that they had all dreaded or rejoiced-in came upon them. In late March fierce fighting to the west and north of the town was reported. The rail system had largely ground to a halt. While trains still moved it was not always clear from where they came or to where they were going. Wagons were moved into sidings with their loads intact. Workers deserted their posts and those that reported as usual hung about talking and making their own coffee while management sought to find tasks for them.

Troop reinforcements moved westward, some through their village. These troops were no longer part of the triumphant passage of crack regiments with their armoured vehicles hardly scratched by warfare: but lightly-armoured and weary columns of apprehensive men, often of granddads and young boys. The streets were no longer filled by cheering crowds and the throwing of celebratory flowers; there were few spectators, and they watched silently with hardly a wave.

Adam and Felix were turning up at the rail station as usual and reporting back to London as much as they could on the movement of troops, but as the fighting drew nearer they stopped and stayed at home. The rail station had become a point of resistance and a detachment of soldiers had been sent there with a view to fighting in the city itself. In the ears of the soldiers rang the injunction to fight for every inch of the motherland.

The demand was hollow. Outside the town was gathered a mighty force with complete air and armoured superiority. This force was upon them and the German soldiers knew that resistance was useless. The ranting went on but no one listened. These soldiers did not want to desert, but they expected the officers commanding them to do no more than to go through the motions, and then to get them out of the town as quickly as possible. Nevertheless, there were enough fanatics around for it to be dangerous for workers to be at the rail station: the spying job was done and they had to sit at home and wait.

They waited some time before they thought it safe to venture back into the town, and then, when the thunderous sounds of war receded and passed them by, they made their way back into town on foot. On the outskirts they were stopped at a British road blockade by cheerful soldiers in green berets and asked for their purpose in travelling. In perfect English they asked to be taken to the Company headquarters, and no they could not explain their purpose. They were checked for weapons and escorted by a bemused British tommy to the makeshift headquarters and to an equally puzzled adjutant.

The surrender procedure was simple. They gave the adjutant a British telephone number which they had memorised and, after some supplementary questions and a good deal of time to find the right person, their identity was confirmed. The adjutant had no experience of what to do with surrendered spies but in the spirit of British pragmatism created some emergency documents for them, and issued them with flak jackets and honorary green berets. He then found a debriefing officer for them to talk to and they were toasted in tin mugs of workman's dark brown tea.

The lieutenant allocated to them was not much older than themselves. He was a conscript and, after they had told him what he needed to know, which wasn't much, he was anxious to speak about his own experiences. He told them that it had all been much worse than he had thought. Fighting across France had been fierce and crossing the Rhine difficult. The regiment had lost many men killed and wounded. All that talk at home about easy victories and all that pressure from the Americans to go for all out aggression all the time regardless of losses didn't help. The Germans were good soldiers and did not give up easily.

They asked him: "Don't you think it's over now?"

"Almost, but that's when it's most dangerous for you. You relax, thinking it easy. Then boom. Some sniper blows your head off. When we entered the first German towns there seemed to be no resistance. White flags were hung from the houses. You strolled along thinking all was fine. And then some mother fucker fires at you from the very same houses. You can't be too careful. And if you are to come round this city with me it's no use wearing a beret, you need a helmet."

And he got them helmets before they moved off in his jeep.

They showed him the sights and the main buildings in the city. There was no fighting going on. People were moving around as normal, curious about them, but indifferent.

"What now boys, what next?" said the lieutenant.

Adam felt exultant and the adrenalin was rushing.

"Well," he said, "to the victors the spoils. Come we'll show you."

They took him in the direction of their village and then down some side tracks to their neighbouring farms.

"This is where we replenish with some good fresh food," they told him. There was no resistance from the farms, and they stocked up the vehicle with cheeses, eggs, fresh vegetables and chickens trussed by their legs and squawking on the back seat.

"Where next?" said the lieutenant, enjoying it.

"To our village if you don't mind. So that we can pick up our gear."

"Look," the lieutenant said, "in our regiment there are very strict regulations about looting. I don't want to loot but there is no harm in a few souvenirs. This village which you say is so wealthy, do you think I could take a few wrist-watches from your neighbours? I don't want to cause any trouble."

They told him that they thought it would be all right.

They came to their village. It was empty and quiet. It reminded Adam of the French village he had entered early in the morning nearly two years ago, the arrest of the Jewish family there, and the discovery of the two children and Erik's protection of them.

They went into their cottage and recovered their personal possessions. While they did this the lieutenant went into the neighbouring cottages. They were back in the street in a few minutes with the lieutenant pleased with his trophies. But already a small group of people had gathered in the street. When they were seen coming out there were some jeers from people who recognised them.

And then running down the street, and shouting obscenities, was Elizabeth. She came to a halt some twenty metres before the jeep. She spat at them, panting from her exertions: "Traitors, cowards, scum." Her face was distorted by her frenzy and her eyes were literally bulging. Adam, scared, was rooted to the spot, but Felix moved towards her. He said something to her but she screamed again telling him to keep his distance. And as she screamed she drew a pistol from her apron pocket, aimed it, and fired, not at him but at the vehicle. The bullet missed them and smashed the windscreen.

Elizabeth threw the pistol to the ground and hurled herself at Felix, beating her fists on his chest, screaming and crying. Felix restrained her and for a brief moment she put her head on his chest, sobbing while he hugged her gently. Then she broke away and a neighbour came forward to lead her to safety. Elizabeth looked over her shoulder as she lurched unwillingly away and screamed something at them which they did not understand.

Felix picked up the pistol and put it in his pocket. While he did so, their neighbour with the dog came right up to Adam and stared him straight in the face. She was white with the intensity of her rage. She said to Adam, without fear: "You two scoundrels should be ashamed of yourself for betraying our trust."

Adam looked straight at her. The words he wanted to say would not come to him. He wanted to tell her that she was a stupid woman: that her idea of solidarity was a pathway to the graveyard: that unthinking loyalty to a maniac with despotic desires on other people's property and lives had led to the death of millions, including their relatives and friends: that it was loyalty to a madman. He wanted to tell her about his father languishing in a concentration camp, and his uncle who had been shot like a dog; of the Jews, Poles and Russians, dispossessed and killed in camps, and the obscenity of the deeds done in the name of their beloved Führer.

But none of these words would come out. He pushed her aside and walked to the jeep. There to the protests of the lieutenant he seized hold of his tommy gun. He waved it in the air as if to threaten the small number of people who had gathered in the street, and they began to run away dispersing as quickly as they could. He went into the cottage that had been his home for the past few months. From the street bursts of gunfire could be heard and Felix, fearing something had had happened, ran into the cottage, closely followed by the lieutenant with a drawn pistol.

Adam was sitting on the kitchen floor still grasping the gun, head bowed and weeping. They could see that he had entered every room in the cottage and fired a burst on the gun, and there was damage everywhere. "Christ," said the lieutenant, "what the fuck's happening here? Let's get him out." Felix led him out, and they got themselves out of the now-deserted village street as quickly as they could.

"Just don't tell me what that was about," yelled the indignant lieutenant, above the roar of an accelerating engine. "Tell me how I can explain this," he pointed to the smashed windscreen and the empty gun magazine.

"No trouble," said Felix, in command: "You say that as you reached the village there was continued resistance. We were fired on and returned the fire. All of which is true."

CHAPTER 27

THE TIDE HAD been turned back but as the German occupation came to an end the Russian began. Not for Poland the luxury of liberty to be celebrated in the streets but a desperate struggle for power by which an ideology, and its new Polish adherents, were to gain ascendancy by the might of Soviet armour. While London, Paris and New York gained something from the war, no matter how hard the struggle, a civil war was fought for the best part of two years in Poland as the Poles struggled in vain for their liberties.

In this struggle Poland had no friends. Abandoned by its new found ally the USA in the naïvety of the American belief that together with Uncle Joe the two main powers could usher in a new world order, and with Britain powerless to challenge the Soviet tide, the struggle was bound to fail. The 'iron curtain' when it closed would divide west from east through Berlin with Warsaw on the wrong side.

As Poles came to terms with the new order and reviewed their losses and gains they came to accept, as Joseph had predicted a few months before, that it was better to have a communist Poland than no Poland at all. Arguably, the peoples that occupied Polish territory would be divided now not by race but by the ideological beliefs of its population and their degree of cravenness towards an occupying power.

Those on the other side of the curtain had the choice of returning to Poland, perhaps, to meet a fate worse than exile, or to make their lives elsewhere and hope that one day they would be reunited with their motherland. As the world-war ended, these decisions were for the future. For the present each citizen had to pick up the strands of life again in the hope of a better life.

For Sophie, largely oblivious to the new power struggle, it was a happy time. Through the Red Cross she was able to establish that Adam was alive and to write and receive a letter from him. While she had never doubted his survival, the knowledge that he was well and in good hands lifted the black cloud which descended and dismayed her whenever she thought about him. She received a letter from Mary with the surprising news that she was in Germany and working on a farm there. And her younger daughters had come through here in Poland itself without physical harm.

In all these things she rejoiced. But the source of her happiness was not in these things, no matter how glad they made her but in *her* Ludvig. As this tremulous and frightening peace came to them, Ludvig became irremediably ill from the wasting disease of his cancer. He took to his bed and from this unlikely vantage point and, with her help, attempted to make his peace with the world.

Now she was needed as never before and there was no competition for his affections. Whatever they were these women, or whatever they were now, they were no longer to be seen or heard. Which of them, she told herself, would want him now, this disease-ridden and skeletal man, constantly racked with pain and who could hardly reach the lavatory unaided, let alone bed them. From the local doctor they had some help with the provision of pain-killers and sedatives, but after some time they lost their effectiveness.

Sophie fed and washed him and found the time to hold his hand and wipe his brow. In his lucid moments he spoke to her not only about things unknown to her, things that had happened to him, but of his love for her. Ludvig was able to convey that whatever the circumstances his love for her had always been deeper, far deeper, than anything he had experienced with any other living being.

Sophie did not need to hear these protestations of love. She knew that he had always loved her in his own way and to his own capacity for love. While there had been many moments of heartache she had always felt sure that he would return to her – that he belonged here on this farm with her. She did not need him to do more than this: she would always be grateful that he was the father of her children, and that it was *his* energies and talents that had secured them all this home- this farm – which she treasured and fought for as she did for her children.

Sophie did not need to be loved as she loved him: it was always enough to know that his desire for intimacy with her remained, and in his own way, as a potent force in his life. As she looked down at him now, she thought how absurd men could be: for Ludvig not to know – what he was agonising about now and seeking to establish – that it was always enough for her to be needed by him, and that she forgave him everything.

They spent many happy hours together between bouts of agonising pain. They looked through their photo albums and reminisced about the precious moments in their life together: the birth and childhood of their children, family holidays and parties, his career and the moments of his advancement: and they discussed the good times and the bad, the moments of laughter and sadness. And as time passed they were able to kiss each other tenderly as two very good friends, and smile and laugh about the ludicrous and transitory nature of life.

At this time, Rosa reaching the age of fourteen, and before her time, had left school. She had not done badly there, but no one thought of her as an intellectual or destined for preferment in this world. She was a sturdy, pleasant girl, who quietly blended into her surroundings and kept herself to herself. Rosa felt content enough, knowing she was a competent person in a wide range of practical things; and with many of these skills needed on the farm, she had her place.

Rosa remained watchful and secretive but there was enough hope and love in her life to avoid these traits slipping into deviousness. On social occasions, however, she said very little, preferring to listen and observe; and it was only her few very close friends who knew the strength of her inner convictions and the deep passions she brought to her life.

Rosa busied herself about the farm as her mother devoted herself to her father. She loved her father deeply and without question but she could not bring herself to spend time with him. There was the issue for her of his concentration camp confinement and the horrible things he must have endured. He might need to talk about the camp but she did not want to listen. And then she hated sickness, and he was very sick indeed: far better she thought to get about the domestic tasks and to leave her mother to tend to his needs. Rosa heard her mother singing as she went about the house and she wondered about it: but it was a relief to her to see them both so happy despite his pain and she thought that this happiness proved her reticence in things of the heart to be right.

Ludvig heard his daughter moving about the place and coaxed her to give him a few minutes from time to time. He asked her to read to him and, removing herself from him to the safety of a high-backed chair, she did so: haltingly and grudgingly at first, but with growing confidence and even pleasure. Later, when he was gone, she would remember these moments. They began to bridge the gaps between them which, even if not entirely closed, was enough for them both.

As Ludvig grew more ill, Sophie sent for her youngest daughter Lucie, and she stayed with them until his death. Lucie could make nothing of it. Two years younger than Rosa she was a very bright girl indeed and a promising future was seen for her. She forgave none of her family, whom she saw as abandoning her, and despised herself for needing them. She spent as little time with her father as she could without making a fuss and helped Rosa about the farm. Grooming the horses she thought: "Animals are more reliable than humans," and she told the animals so.

Lucie was twelve years of age at this time. She stood out from her family in an important respect: she was beautiful. Her beauty was understated, so that if you had no interest you might not notice it at all. Her hair was very fine and of a precious colour, neither black nor fair, but indeterminate – a kind of grey, soft and gleaming, the greyness of youth. Her skin was opalescent, her eyes blue-grey and her long eyelashes, without mascara, quite black. Lucie was both *withdrawn* and *bold* and it was only when you gained her confidence that you became aware *that she was truly remarkable – and capable of almost anything*.

It seemed to Lucie that a lesson of her life was not to rely on other people too much. Not that life with Herman and Mary was bad: they looked after her, she knew that, and looked out for her. Although she did not like Herman, she did admire the skill with which he conducted his life: the way he looked ahead and his good judgement and shrewdness. Thanks to Herman they all lived very well and she could look forward to a privileged position of some kind when – one day, she too would exercise influence and even power.

But deep down Lucie despised all these adults: they had all screwed up in her life time: politicians, generals, the church and the intelligentsia: you name it they had fouled up. At least the Germans had tried to do something: a lot of it wrong, of course, but at least they had tried. Now it was up to people like her to sort it out. Hopefully, these adults would not mess it up again before people like her were old enough to take it all over. At least Herman, for all his faults, knew how the world worked. He would be able to point her in the right direction, but in the end it would be up to her.

Herman continued to keep his head down. It was difficult to know how things would work out and which political faction would come out on top. He kept his membership of the communist party a discrete secret since you never knew how people might take it, and the Soviet authorities themselves were notoriously hard on anyone not kowtowing to the official line, and the fashion could change at any time. Far better he thought to be a highly professional public servant going about his duties in a conscientious way and making nothing of it. He thought he had the gift for it and his talents would be required whoever came out on top, which he expected to be Soviet approved functionaries.

Around him the Soviet Union exacted a terrible price for the ruthless war waged against it. Whole factories were stripped down and sent east with hundreds of thousands of men and women to work in them when reassembled or elsewhere in the forced labour camps: not just prisoners of war or political undesirables but others with tenuous links to politics or war.

But not Herman. He remained untouched. In these matters many claimed virtue and credit for helping you. Did he escape because of his own foresight? Was it chance? Could it have been the anti-fascist credentials of Ludvig? There would be an irony in that. *Was it the Jew-boy?* Surely not.

The finger of fate had pointed to others very close to him. His neighbour Philip Strauss had an Austrian father, although he had worked for twenty years as a specialist producer of clay bricks in premises he owned in Katowice. Philip had no interest in politics and had played no part in the war. However, he was skilful and persistent and a man of good taste and so might be suspected. His neighbours coveted his possessions and denounced him to the authorities as a German sympathiser – after all times were difficult and one had to do one's best.

The authorities arrested Philip. He pleaded that the output of his small factory could best be put to use in rebuilding Soviet towns if he remained in charge of it here in Katowice. The authorities would have none of it: they had quotas to fill and they needed him. They packed him off to a camp in the Soviet Union.

There was an unfortunate consequence. Philip had a young and beautiful daughter of 15 years of age, well-liked at her school and by the protesting neighbours. She too was arrested and despatched on a train to goodness knew where. "Oh dear," the neighbours said, "what a pity. But she will be all right. Quite an adventure for a young girl, we expect."

Being a practical person and with his eye on other things, Herman set out to help his brother-in-law to secure an income for his family after his death. He helped Ludvig to obtain an official pension in reward for his police duties over many years and which would be paid out to his widow. It was a difficult mission which he performed with great delicacy. Then by making difficult enquiries, and at no little expense to himself, he obtained for Ludvig a lump sum by way of compensation for wrongful internment in Sachsenhausen. It was not a fortune but it cleared the family debts and meant that they were able to pay for the medical treatment Ludvig needed in those last days.

There was a terrible irony in this: Herman, perhaps, an instrument of Ludvig's incarceration, had now become the conduit of its recognition as a wrong. But no one, even Ludvig, thought it to be ironic: they regarded it as a great deed of Herman's, and one for which he should be given unqualified praise and recognition.

As Ludvig's illness reached its final stage they received a letter from Adam addressed to his father. Sophie regarded any letter from the family as common property. On this occasion she opened and read it, and after thinking about it for a while, tore the letter up, without mentioning it to anyone.

The letter had taken a long time to reach them. In it Adam said that he had learned from a neighbour that Ludvig was up to his old tricks again with women in the town, and that enough was enough. He despised his father for his womanising, he did not understand how he could make his mother suffer more from his tricks, and vowed that he had broken off all contact with him for fear that if they met again he would kill him with his own two hands.

Three days later Ludvig died. He was given a solemn Catholic funeral. It was attended by many people: his family and friends, his neighbours, former police colleagues, and some business customers in the town. Although the funeral was widely publicised by word of mouth, none of the despised women of his fancy and dalliance attended. Those who laid him to rest knew him well and grieved for his passing.

There had been many moments over the past few years when Sophie had found herself alone and this was just such a time. Absent from the funeral had been her son and elder daughter, scattered by the winds of war quite outside her reach. As she mourned Ludvig, she grieved also for these absent children, feeling their loss keenly now that the war had ended. But there was no comfort in it, and for the thousandth time she picked herself up and went on: the good Lord would cause something to happen and she would see them again.

Mary heard about her father's death far too late to do anything about attending the funeral, even assuming that there was something which could be done to make a journey home. She received a card and when she read it she walked out into the orchard among the trees breathing in the familiar smells and taking deep breaths. She crossed her arms as if in pain, and surprised at what was happening to her body, fell down onto the wet grass where Georg found her some time later insensible to this world.

And when later Georg established what had happened, he blamed himself: that he had been so selfish over these past months, so wrapped up in his own affairs that he neglected entirely Mary's needs for her family. He made her a promise that as soon as it was possible to travel he would take her back to her mother. But neither of them had any inkling of when that might be possible.

They found themselves living in the British Occupied Zone and while life was economically difficult they felt secure. They had made a commitment to each other to stay together and, if possible, to marry. After some months Georg made contact with Magda's parents and they told him what had happened to their daughter and how she had met her death. They had assumed that all was well between him and their daughter, and expressed their amazement that he had not known of the death, and pressed him for information as to why their daughter was on the train at that time and her ultimate destination.

He decided to say nothing, not wanting to cause them any more suffering. But being determined people they did not leave it at that. Some days later Georg had a visit from the police who, in a rare instance of cross-sector cooperation, interviewed him about her death. Of course, it was an absurdity. Georg was not the pilot of the British plane that had shot up the train. He produced the note that Magda had left him. The policemen joked about the curious reports they had to follow up and went away.

"What a people you Germans are," exclaimed an indignant Mary. "You arrange for the death of millions of citizens of other countries without a murmur of protest from any of you, carefully recording their disappearance from this world, and now you want to bring a British pilot to account for shooting up a train."

Herman protested: "No, no, be fair. Her parents wanted to know all the facts and those two were doing their duty," as they should, he thought.

On the strength of this information they obtained a copy of the death certificate and got married in a Registrar's Office in the nearest town. Their farming hosts were their witnesses and no one else but a few farm-labourers wished them well and toasted their health. They did not feel sorry for themselves for the times favoured the brave and cash rich. Georg had already secured the freehold of a neighbouring farm, where the menfolk had been decimated in the war, and a week after their marriage they moved in: and three months later Mary became pregnant.

The knowledge of these happenings had to be communicated to Mary's Polish relatives by postcard, for in the brave new world that followed the ending of the war you could travel for some distance north to south, but not very far from west to east.

Joseph had not succeeded in travelling very far west and found himself moving back east to Katowice. With the assistance of his Soviet mentor it had been easy enough for him to join the Soviet-supported Polish army but it had proved far more difficult for him to find an appropriate role in it. It was immediately obvious to his superiors that he was not a fighting man, and even when he was toughened up by a vigorous training course, they thought that it would be unlikely that he would frighten the enemy.

His knowledge of foreign languages was thought useful in intelligence matters and first he was used to monitor political news and military bulletins reported in Poland and to translate them in three languages: Polish, Russian and German. Then as he did this with complete reliability, accuracy and political correctness, he was thought a likely man to manage censor services, first of the mail and then increasingly of newsprint: books, pamphlets and later of broadcasts.

At first this was a very humble task and the results almost entirely useless. Based at the main post office in Katowice, and in charge of a team of Polish enthusiasts for the new-order, he oversaw the mail from military personnel. His task was to ensure that no information of military value was passed through the post. Any news which revealed location of troops, the type and the use of weapons, or the morale of the fighting forces was deleted or the letters destroyed. All this he thought entirely reasonable and it was only to be expected that Soviet officers stationed there, under the flimsiest of subterfuges, would be the ultimate authorities.

Little by little, however, as a seamless process, the information catchment area grew to the monitoring of Polish life in general, and of 'anti-
Soviet forces' in particular. Little by little his usefulness was recognised.
Poland's male and educated population had been decimated by the
war, and the restriction of Polish education by their Nazi conquerors
to basic skills had reduced the stock of able helpers to the new
authorities.

It was not that there was no enthusiasm for the Soviet masters: Poles
on the whole, although not communist, were grateful to the Soviet Union
for throwing out the Germans, and some, and an increasing number,
came to see communism as a unifying force, as a necessary protection
in the uncertainties of the postwar world.

Joseph was grateful for the recognition of his usefulness to the new
Poland. In this he knew that his Jewishness was seen as an asset and
not a disadvantage. The Soviet authorities and their puppet Polish administration discouraged anti-semitism, although many Poles retained
their anti-Jewish prejudices. He thought it brave and honourable of the
new regime. *But it was better than this for Jews.* The communist authorities saw the Jews as outside the old political order and owing nothing
to the corrupt old regime, perhaps, even with scores to settle of their
own: they could be trusted to play their full part in the new society that
was being built.

So whatever his reservations, and there were many, Joseph became
an enthusiastic supporter of the new regime, and began his climb within
the Department of Public Security as an intelligent and worthwhile
public servant, and loyal party member.

This new role and purpose in life did not make Joseph a happy man:
he had never felt more alone. Living close-by to the neighbourhood in
which he was brought up he had no family or friends. With the sole
exception of his sister, safe and secure in Moscow, everybody he had
known had been slaughtered without mercy during the war years.

Casting his net wider he tried to re-establish his Jewish network: but
with very few exceptions these Jews had decided that postwar Poland
with its racial prejudices and bitter memories was not for them. They used
the envelope of opportunity created in other countries, guilt-ridden by
their inability to help save Europe's Jews from the German savagery, to
make a new beginning in friendlier climes.

This young man no longer appeared in society as an orthodox Jew.
The beard, ringlets and black cap were no more. Now he dressed neatly
in his uniform or in a smart civilian suit and did his best to merge into

the background. In a sense he was becoming the background: part of the hidden presence that was to govern and direct a new Poland.

Those Jews who remained in P. were left to carry the burden of their own survival, unable to rejoice in a victory which so many dear to them, better than them, could not share. *"Why, me? Why should I survive and not them?"* they said to themselves, without an answer other than the whims of fate. And sometimes left alone, and cut off entirely from distant cousins and acquaintances on the wrong side of an iron curtain without chinks, they decided that this survival, this life, was not worth a candle and quit it all together.

Joseph had the consolation of his sister Rebecca. They could write to each other, and then if Joseph's career prospered, it would be possible for them to meet in Moscow or Warsaw. He threw himself into his work because this was the way that he could keep these hopes alive and bring forward the time that they could meet. In this way of thinking, he failed to recognise the talents and resourcefulness of his sister. Rebecca was a very talented musician living and working in a country which above all others appreciated musical genius, and an early meeting might result from her musical talents rather than his political contribution.

When she was to play, and always when she *contemplated* a work to be played, Rebecca thought of her parents. Once she knew that they were dead, and probably how they had died, she vowed to keep them alive in her life. She imagined them walking hand in hand to their personal disaster, to their death, and the image of them being together even at this terrible moment was a small consolation.

With a musical instrument in her hand she felt their presence. She saw her father smile at her encouragingly, and the familiar way he dropped his head a little as he urged her to start again. She heard his voice. "Repeat. Play it again." She knew she could play it better, and that she should, not only for herself or the audience, but for him.

In this way Rebecca was able to keep her father alive and they shared precious moments. Every composition of value, she thought, had been written for him and, as her world was music, she and he would live forever. What they shared and continued to enjoy could never be exhausted and her love for her father would be an everlasting joy.

In his loneliness Joseph began to visit Sophie whenever a reasonable excuse could be made. After Ludvig's death, she found their conversations comforting. Joseph listened to her and she could speak to him. On one occasion they visited Ludvig's grave and on the way back she told him about Peter and what they had to do to bury him. She explained that although they had pleaded Peter's case to be buried in consecrated land with a proper burial service the fact of his suicide had made that impossible.

Joseph listened quietly to her story. "More likely," he said, a little bitterly, "that you couldn't raise the right sum of money." They arranged a time when they could go to Peter's grave. She saw that he was very moved to see how well cared-for it was, with it's cut grass and fresh flowers. Joseph had a prayer book with him, a Mourners Kadesh, and with her permission and standing side by side, he chanted in Hebrew a Jewish prayer for the dead, his voice ringing-out over empty and sodden fields.

CHAPTER 28

NOTHING MUCH WAS made of Adam's escapade in H. and it was soon forgotten in the greater scheme of things. He busied himself in the Division's kitchen in the humble tasks of food preparation, assuming nothing and saying very little: and he was left alone. In a few days time the Division moved on but he didn't. Felix, occupying himself with the task of getting back home, observed his friend from a distance, vaguely aware that all was not well. When nothing seemed to change, he sought help for him, but in the flux of battle it was the dead and dying that received attention while the living did the best they could.

Eventually it was realised, ahead of a victory when all could stop and rejoice, that Adam needed help: and he was shifted back to a nursing home near Cologne, where the physically ill and mutilated, and those like him who had ground to a halt, could recover in peace until they could face the world. There he could join the multitude of the damaged, lost and misplaced.

The establishment was makeshift: no more than a large country house adapted for the exigencies of the war: a rambling building on three floors with a variety of rooms large and small, and staffed by a miscellany of nurses professional and voluntary from a number of countries, and a handful of hard-pressed doctors. Feeling a fraud, Adam contrived to be allocated space in a small room tucked away at the back of the house which he shared with a British soldier, who seemed physically unharmed, but who slept all day. There for the time being at least he could hide away unnoticed and nothing would be expected of him.

For some weeks he lived in a dream-like state. He slept a lot and ate at the appointed times. Each day he exercised by walking in the grounds and then, as he felt more real, further afield, becoming a familiar figure in the nearest small villages. After a while he began to talk more freely to the staff and, as his confidence grew, to the other inmates. They, like him, were all in a stage of recuperation. There was a steady ebb and flow of patients, and he could trace the improvements which led to their release, and monitor his own progress.

When he cared once more about it, other inmates brought him up to date on the happenings in the outside world. He learnt without surprise of the tightening of the Soviet grip on Poland and the imposition of the puppet provisional government at Lublin: of the proposed boundaries of the new Poland which gave to Russia what it had demanded from the days of the Tsar and which only Hitler had played with conceding in the past. He learned that Poland was now to be extended to the west with the acquisition of large tracts of eastern Germany. And he thought about the consequences of the huge movements of population these changes would require.

When he exclaimed to his informant that these were not the changes that they had all been fighting for and that Churchill had promised the Poles something much better, he was given an astounding piece of news: there had been a General Election in Britain and Churchill had been defeated. "No good putting your faith in him mate, he's finished," said his respondent with relish.

That he couldn't understand. What sort of country was it that would calmly vote out such a national hero when the peace settlement of a war he was so instrumental in winning was yet to be concluded? What did they want? How could they wish to have a country fit for heroes and, at the same time, the greatest hero of all thrown on the dust heap of history?

But as he thought about it, and discussed it with the others, he came to another opinion and warmed to it. *A genuinely free and democratic nation did not need heroes. Heroes were the problem. It was politicians who considered themselves above the law and who wished to act out their fantasies upon the world stage that caused all the difficulties.*

You couldn't imagine Hitler and Stalin calling genuinely free elections in their countries and being voted out, could you? And the thought that the Soviets would hold free elections in Poland when the citizens of each and every town stared down the muzzle of a Russian tank was absurd. But nevertheless it was truly astonishing. What did these British have to be so confident about that they could do such a thing and rejoice in it?

After some weeks he was able to write to Eva, and through the Red Cross to contact his mother, and it was seen by his carers at the nursing home as a marked stage in his recovery. He had received very little medical care as such. All that had happened was that he had returned to normalcy. The terrible pressures of deceit and the danger of discovery had passed and would soon be repressed and forgotten.

As the past began to recede, he was able to think of the future and once he had achieved that step he was saved. For while Adam had felt fraudulent at the home when he compared himself to the physically injured and impaired, he had been seriously ill. Those who had cared for him had made little of their worries. They knew his mental state was precarious, but little could be done: nature had to take its own course.

On the sitting-room wall in Hammersmith, Harry had continued to plot the progress of Allied forces across Germany on his wall-chart. When the lines came to a halt and peace was declared without any news of Adam, they began to worry. At Eva's factory most of the other girls had heard something about their loved ones – husbands, brothers and boy friends – and while not all of the news was good, at least they knew their fate.

And then one night this irreligious girl experienced what she came to describe as a spiritual experience. She dreamt that she was awake. There at the foot of her bed was an ancient Asian figure, turbaned and richly-dressed in rare silks. This was a majestic figure but – in her dream – she was not scared or awed by it. He spoke to her kindly and told her that he had been sent to look after her. She was not to worry about Adam. He was safe and would be returned to her. And then he blessed her. She felt strangely moved by this message, and a great sense of peace suffused her, banishing all her fears. She wanted to thank him but before she could do so he was gone.

There she was sitting on her bed in her familiar room at peace with herself and trembling with the experience. It was so strange to her that she said nothing to anyone about it. But being an impulsive girl and, longing for Adam to return, she could wait no longer, messenger or no messenger. On a bright sunny morning, in time taken off from work, and accompanied by her father, she travelled in his cab to the Spy Centre and demanded to know Adam's whereabouts.

The receptionist made a call. They were sorry but there was no one there who could help her. Eva made a further demand and further calls were made. The receptionist remained sorry but as she was not family no information could be given her. They refused to leave and sat there ready to defy any effort to remove them.

The receptionist shrugged his shoulders as if to say that it was their prerogative. They sat there for another hour. A further call was made. And then at last a senior American officer appeared. He had come from his home to see them. He introduced himself as responsible for Adam; he shook Harry's hand warmly; kissed Eva on both cheeks, and told them that Adam was safe and well, and would be back with them shortly.

He would answer no other questions. He said to them that they should be proud of Adam, as he and the entire American people were proud. They said that, of course, they were proud too. He shook hands with them again and they were out in the street.

"OK, my girl you're old enough," said her father, "now we drink to the health of this hero of ours." They found the nearest pub and drank themselves silly. And once they had told the publican why they were drinking, and for whom, the beer was free.

One Sunday morning there was a knock on the door of a respectable Hammersmith terraced house and, when it was answered, Adam was on the doorstep: unannounced and godlike, bronzed and uniformed, heroic and very real. After all those nights and anxious moments, he was sitting in Eva's kitchen, smiling and disparaging himself, while granny fussed over him with undrinkable tea and home-made fruit-cake.

Not that Eva had ever doubted that he would return. She was not surprised. There had been no more visitations in the middle of the night but she had been left with the warmth and certainty of what had been shown and revealed to her.

Eva threw her arms around him and hugged and kissed him at short intervals until at last he said enough. They asked him innumerable questions, which he found ways of not answering; and they called him a hero, which he denied. Well, they chorused, you are our hero, so there. And when they repeated it several times he began to think that they might be right.

They thought he looked tired from his journey but when after several days he looked the same they realised that he had been suffering and all was not yet right. And when he told them that he had spent a short time in a nursing home to recover from mental exhaustion, but that he was all right now, they quietened down and stopped asking questions and waited for him to tell them what he chose to speak about; and bit by bit he told them something of what had happened to him.

All over Britain, and one supposed wherever this terrible war had wreaked its damage, these scenes were repeated over many months as the victims of it, those who had stayed at home as well as those that didn't, counted the cost.

In this very same street there were families where fathers and sons and, sometimes mothers and daughters, did not return: and others where there was nothing to return to at all: families where the passage and trials of time, and hardships endured, had been too much, and pre-war bonds had been broken.

Every successful reunion was greeted with bunting, balloons and flags: astonished children, fresh from hugging the happy returnees, were astonished to see their parents hugging and kissing the neighbours, and on occasions absolute strangers. A spirit of anarchical joy gripped the most unlikely people; complete abstainers got drunk at improvised street parties, and adults who should have known better perched precariously on lampposts waving union jacks.

And then as the pride of the nation limped its way home from foreign climes previously only imagined, the joy subsided, the flags were put away and the day-to-day grind of surviving in war-ravaged Britain took over. Elsewhere on the battlefields and killing grounds of Europe, the suffering and tasks of recovery were much greater, but for the moment the British had no appetite for the suffering of other people: Britain had done its bit and now it was a time for British people to look after themselves.

Adam found himself a hero and after a little while he began to accept that he was one. Everyone made kind remarks to him. While he continued to wear his uniform, strangers would stop him in the street and shake his hand, thanking him and all his fellow Poles for their courage and all they had done. And then at a grand ceremony at a swanky London hotel he was given one of the highest awards that the American Government could award a non-American: the Silver Star. The local newspaper reported it and for a time the neighbours, recognising him from his photograph in the paper, treated him as a celebrity.

When Adam looked in the mirror he didn't see a hero. He was not at all sure what the image told him. He knew now that of the forty-four agents parachuted into Germany over half had not returned. Perhaps, those people, many of whom had been his drinking and card playing friends and companions, were the real heroes: and if one was going to be truly rigorous, perhaps all those prisoners beaten, shot and degraded: all those people for whom there was no street party at all.

And then he was not recognised at all. He was a civilian. No longer on the payroll of the US Government he had to find his own way until he had made some decisions about his future. He rented a room in a street near to Eva's and found himself a job as an assistant in a food store in Muswell Hill in north London. He had his own ration book and an open invitation to stay in Britain without any pressure to make an immediate decision to remain.

He was twenty-two years old. He had spent six years under the most intense pressure, during which he had served in three armies, and had witnessed great cruelty and endured great risks. It seemed to him that he had never had a childhood or adolescence and now he was being asked to be an adult. What he needed now was a period of time when he asked nothing of himself and nothing was asked of him. But life is not, of course, like that. It is not often that you are given the luxury of what you need: too often life grips you by the throat, lifts you up and dumps you down in a place not of your own choosing

He began to drift into a life in Britain: he had a job and workmates, and a steady girl friend and a social life with and through her; but the central dilemma of his life was unaddressed. Did he return to Poland? At bad moments in France and in Germany, he longed to be home. How absurd it had seemed were he to die so young in a foreign field not of his choosing. At times the waves of nostalgia, of longing, were over-whelming: he was a Polish farm-boy away from the soil he needed to sustain him, which gave him his identity, and from which he had been torn against his will.

Could he return? The simple answer was that he could if he chose, and both the British and Polish Governments would permit it. But would he be safe on return? Would the new regime treat him as a political undesirable given that he had been a German soldier and an American spy: lure him back and dispose of him. Questions like these were dis-cussed by the large Polish community in London at formal and informal meetings across the city. Adam was not political but in the Polish cafés and clubs politics could not be ignored.

The short answer to his question on the wisdom of returning was that he would be crazy to risk it. There was no end to the number of Poles who reminded him of malignant Soviet actions and intentions: the deliberate destruction of the Polish Home Army at Warsaw, the luring back to Moscow of the leaders of the Polish Provisional Government and their arrest, trial and execution.

But Mikolajczyk, the Prime Minister of the Polish Government in waiting in London had returned. If he could, why not Adam? "A fool, thank God the only one. For the moment it is a convenient fig-leaf for the Soviets, but when they no longer need him, they will dispose of him. You'll see," was the response from the realists.

He supposed it to be true but it did not lessen the longing. Perhaps, there was a way round it. Should he join the Communist Party? Membership would show his good faith, that he was not anti-Soviet, and that he recognised the reality of a Soviet domination of Poland. He rang the British Communist Party and asked whether he could join. They asked him questions and then rejected him. "If you stay in Britain and can prove it, contact us again," was their advice.

Adam dreamt about the opportunities back home: the land and properties he had always admired were available for a song. With all that he had learnt, and all that he had seen, he could soon become a very important person in P. – perhaps, *the* person.

The Spy School had wound up and his major was to return home. Out of the blue came an invitation to a posh farewell drinks party at his rented accommodation in Chester Square: one of the most prestigious addresses in London.

The major's Georgian house was large and beautifully furnished, the marble entrance way and hall led into an imposing lounge. Adam costed what he supposed to be genuine antiques and oil paintings and the value came to well over six figures. The major was embarrassed by this splendour and hastened to explain that it was home for a great many American officers and much the cheapest way of accommodating them all.

At the end of the evening the major and his wife – a homely and motherly woman in her forties who had corresponded with Adam and sent him $5 bills – asked him to stay, and then they shyly made him an offer which they urged him to accept. The major made a long speech. He reminded Adam that he was of Polish descent and cared deeply about the fate of Poland. And then he said: "I'm sorry to say Adam that there is no future for Poland. The 'iron curtain', as Churchill has described it, has come down, and Poland will become communist, a satellite state of the Soviet Empire."

As for the old-world, for a country like Britain, the future was bleak: exhausted and economically bankrupt as a result of its struggles, for which all credit must be given it, Britain would remain impoverished. The major said, "Britain has become the victim of socialism, and anti-free enterprise notions and practices which will prevent its recovery."

Then the major said something Adam could hardly believe. He looked very self- conscious as if he was not wholly in control of the words he was saying – but out they came.

"Adam the place for you with your energy and drive is in America. As you know we have lost our son in the Pacific war. Molly and I would like to give you the opportunity to join us, to live in our home under our patronage, care and protection. You should get yourself a college education and make something of yourself – and we can help you do it. We leave in ten days and if you want you can be on that plane with us. Take your time: it's a big decision: but say yes." He put his arm round Adam's shoulders and Molly kissed him on the cheek.

Adam was overwhelmed by the incredible generosity of the offer. Whether the major and Mollie would be proved right by events in Poland and Britain he did not know and could not guess, but their sheer goodwill and generosity of spirit was unbelievable.

Outside in the streets he knew that the major was right about Britain's problems: Britain was in a desperate state with half its housing destroyed or unusable and its economy destroyed. The British may have voted for a land fit for heroes but their chances of achieving one were minimal. People like him would have no chance. No doubt it was going to be a fairer society: but what did equal shares in a bankrupt society amount to in the end?

He talked it through with Eva. She did not want to go to America but, showing a wisdom beyond her years, said that the decision was up to him and, if that was what he decided, she would go as well. Her father was incandescent with anger. "You want to take my daughter to America," Harry exploded, "you're out of your mind."

Harry reminded him in forceful terms that it was a supine Roosevelt with his naïve view of a postwar world with a peace guaranteed by the two great powers that had sold Poland down the river. "You'll see," he said emphatically, "when the war memorials to the dead go up in Britain and Poland the years will be 1939–1945, and in Russia and America it will be 1941–1945, and why?" and then answering his own question: "Because it was Britain that came to the assistance of Poland while the Russians and Americans were swanning it back home. They only got themselves into it when the Japanese and German's attacked them."

Adam said hastily that he did not know anything about politics and that anyway he hadn't decided yet. But then he added unwisely: "You're not being fair. We couldn't have won this war without America – and they were helping Britain long before they came into the war. They're a very generous people. Britain is not so very clever. In Britain you prefer to have no heroes. Churchill was a real hero wasn't he? And he made Poles promises that were relied on. *And what did you do?* Vote him out in the middle of peace talks that would settle the future of *my* country."

Harry was stung. "Generous are they? You know what we say, 'over paid, over sexed and over here'. That describes them. Oh, yes, and big headed as well. All this boasting about winning the war and how everything is marvellous there and hopeless in Britain. If it is so bloody marvellous there, why is there so much poverty, and why so much prejudice about black people? They should sort out their own problems before criticising us. And as for Churchill, of course, we are all very grateful to him. *But what we want is a land without heroes.* No more ideologues, no more politicians with their dreams and fantasies of power: and no more wars for the right to rob your neighbours. *What we need in Britain – and in Europe too – is a really boring time and a land without heroes.*"

Hostilities having ended Eva came off the sidelines and led him away.

"Very, clever Adam, I must say that you handled that well," she said sarcastically.

"Oh, well I can't please everybody," was the response.

It was the custom of the Kitsons to invite their friends to tea on Saturday afternoons and Adam and Eva remained within the golden circle of their friendship. At one of these gatherings Timothy took a chance to talk to him. He led Adam into the garden by the arm and told him how much he admired what he had achieved in Germany and said that he was a real hero.

"Do you really think so?" responded Adam.

"Yes, I do. All our agents were brave, of course, but there is a vital difference between what you did and, say, an agent dropping into France. In France there was an organised resistance waiting to help, but in Germany you were among a hostile population. That made your work particularly heroic."

Adam paused, hesitating, and trying to find the right words in English.

"During this war, Mr Kitson, I did a number of terrible things, and I didn't do some things that I might have done – that I should have done. I am not a good person. *Perhaps, I am not the person you think I am.*"

"I'm sure you are," came the warm reply, "you are much too critical of yourself. How old were you when this all began? Sixteen? Well there you are, you were confronted with all these awful situations with no experience of the world; wanting to look after your family and to keep them safe and not knowing how to do it. You did remarkably well. Don't punish yourself."

Adam told him about the major's offer and how tempted he was to take it up.

"It is very generous of the major, Adam, the Americans are a very generous people and there must be wonderful chances there for you. But if you are tired of our little and overcrowded island you could go to Australia, Canada and other places in the British Empire. You would get the same chances there. At this moment you are a very fortunate boy, the whole world has opened up for people like you. But what about Poland? You must be missing your family and you can return, can't you?"

Adam explained just how dangerous it would be for him.

"Yes, I see, I didn't realise just how difficult it would be *for you*."

He became thoughtful.

"You remember, Adam, that you told me about Miss Zbucki. She seemed a very fine person. What do you think she would say to you if she was here?"

"Miss Zbucki?" Adam considered for a moment.

"*She would say that I shouldn't give up on Poland, that I should continue to love my fellow Poles whoever they are now – and love Poland.*"

"Would she expect you to endanger your life by going back?"

"No, she wouldn't."

"Well then, perhaps Miss Zbucki has the answer for you."

As he led Adam back towards the house he said: "I admire you, Adam, because you discovered in the cruellest of all circumstances that solidarity, although essential to survival, was not enough: that life presents one with moral choices. You had the courage to choose – yes, yes, I am sure you did – and you can be proud of yourself. I'm certainly proud of you." He squeezed his arm affectionately.

Adam said over Sunday lunch that he had a decision to tell them about. He had told the major that he was going to stay in Britain. He would remain a Pole. He would always be a Pole. One day Poland would be free. He would pray for it and while there was little he could do now, if there was anything he could do later, he would do it. He raised his glass:

"Long live Poland."

They cheered and drank his health, and then his mother's health, and then the health of all his relatives and friends, and then the health of his country once again.

"Long live Poland," they all said, and then they sang three choruses of 'he's a jolly good fellow'."

In the kitchen where he helped Harry to wash up Adam said: "*I've been meaning to ask you Harry. Do you play cards?*"

EPILOGUE

CHARACTERS

Katya and Alfred Diels
Katya and Alfred Diels sold their delicatessen shop in Auschwitz in 1945 and moved to Bonn where they opened a similar establishment. They prospered.

Rebecca Finkelstein
Rebecca Finkelstein, the girl rescued by Jan at Auschwitz and moved on to a German farm, did not ultimately survive. The farmer was obliged because of his jealous and fearful wife to let her go. He did his best to be helpful, procuring her some new identity papers and buying her a rail-ticket through to the Swiss border. She was arrested on the train by the Gestapo and sent back to Auschwitz where she was killed.

Fredrich Von Hempel
Fredrich Von Hempel, the SS officer, fought bravely in retreat across Russia, Poland and eastern Germany. He was awarded the Iron Cross First Class. He surrendered to British troops in northern Germany. After the war he became the Marketing Director of a leading German engineering firm in Dusseldorf. While on a family holiday in 1946 he climbed to the top of Ulm Cathedral and threw himself to his death.

Julia Von Hempel
Julia Von Hempel, his wife, was killed at her home in Hamburg in 1944 by an Allied air raid.

Heinrich Hildenfeldt
Heinrich Hildenfeldt, Paula's SS admirer, was killed in battle by Soviet troops in 1944.

Karl Hoffman
Karl Hoffman, Adam's factory manager in Germany in 1941 was sent to manage a factory in Krakow. He retreated from there in 1944, ahead of its Soviet occupation, to western Germany. He and his large family all survived the war.

Jacob and Judith Lieberman
Jacob and Judith Lieberman, the two Jewish children discovered by Adam and Erik in France in 1943, ran to a relative's house once the arresting party had moved away. They were hidden on a remote French farm, owned by a gentile, until the liberation of France in 1945. They survived.

Wilhelm Muller
Wilhelm Muller, Ludvig's fellow prisoner at Sachsenhausen, made his way back to Vienna. Upon the Soviet occupation of the city he was arrested and shot as a political undesirable.

Hannah Rubenstein
Hannah Rubenstein, Adam's forced-labour fellow worker in L. in 1941, survived the war and returned home to West Berlin. She was the only survivor of her immediate family.

Elizabeth Schwartz
Elizabeth Schwartz, the housekeeper in H., welcomed the return of her husband from Italy in 1946. He had deserted from the German army in 1944 and lived rough for nearly two years.

Karl Smitt
Karl Smitt the German soldier attacked by Adam and his fellow forced-labourers in Krakow died of a blood clot to his head caused by kicking. In retaliation SS soldiers selected three Polish pedestrians at random and shot them in the same street as the attack.

Hilda Strauss
Hilda Strauss was sent to a camp in the Russian Gulag where she was forced to provide sexual services for the guards. After frantic efforts to

recover her by the family the Red Cross established her whereabouts. At first the Soviet authorities denied that she was in the camp maintaining that there were no Poles held in camps in the Soviet Union. After two years she was returned to her home a physical and mental wreck.

Philip Strauss

Philip Srauss was sent to a brick factory in the Gulag in Siberia where he worked as a labourer. He was given a brick quota which if fulfilled earned him a daily ration of half a loaf of bread. After a year his female guard took mercy on him and enabled him to escape. It took him a further three years to walk back to Poland. He was frequently detained but successfully maintained the pretence of being a derelict with mental problems. Ultimately he was shipped across the Czech border and made his way back home.

Elizabeth West

Elizabeth West, the young British spy captured by Adam in France, was tortured by the Gestapo and, in the end, made a full confession implicating others. She was executed by firing squad.

Miss Zbucki

There is no definite information about the fate of Miss Zbucki. Her many friends remain optimistic about her.

Errata
Page 206 line 23
"mother" should read "grandmother"
and line 34
grandchild should have inverted commas